Blinded

BOOKS BY TEYLA BRANTON

Unbounded Series
The Change
The Cure
The Escape
The Reckoning
The Takeover

Unbounded Novellas
Ava's Revenge
Mortal Brother
Lethal Engagement
Set Ablaze

Colony Six Series
Insight (prequel)
Sketches
Visions
Travels

Imprints Series
First Touch (prequel)
Touch of Rain
On The Hunt
Upstaged
Under Fire
Blinded
Street Smart
Hidden Intent

Other
Times Nine

UNDER THE NAME RACHEL BRANTON

Lily's House Series
House Without Lies
Tell Me No Lies
Hearts Never Lie
Your Eyes Don't Lie
Broken Lies
No Secrets or Lies
Cowboys Can't Lie

Noble Hearts
Royal Quest
Royal Dance

Finding Home Series
Take Me Home
All That I Love
Then I Found You

Other
How Far

Picture Books
I Don't Want To Eat
Bugs
I Don't Want to Have
Hot Toes

Blinded

TEYLA BRANTON

WHITE
STAR
PRESS

This is a work of fiction, and the views expressed herein are the sole responsibility of the author. Likewise, certain characters, places, and incidents are the product of the author's imagination, and any resemblance to actual persons, living or dead, or actual events or locales, is entirely coincidental.

Blinded (Imprints Book 5)

Published by White Star Press
P.O. Box 353
American Fork, Utah 84003

Printed in the United States of America
ISBN: 978-1-939203-98-4
Year of first printing: 2018

To my husband, without whose support I'd probably be a lot crazier than I am.

Chapter 1

The antique music box inside the battered dish cupboard was lovely, but the imprints on it were even better. Someone had loved and cared for this treasure long before it had ended up in the attic at this May estate sale. Long enough ago that when I touched it I experienced only a warm, soothing satisfaction instead of any vivid emotions the owner might have once experienced. The imprints hadn't been left by the former owner of the house, a widow who had died a few weeks ago at the ripe old age of ninety-two, but were most likely from her mother as a child.

The dish cupboard that had protected the music box wasn't worth the price the estate sale agents were asking, but the music box, with a separate price tag of two hundred and ten dollars, was a good value. I could resell the little wood box in my antiques shop for over five hundred after I fixed the music assembly—if I could bear to part with it. The lid of the box featured intricate roses inlaid with mother-of-pearl, and several of my customers collected similar boxes.

"Nice," Paige Duncan said, studying it. In her navy suit

and with her perfectly ironed, shoulder-length blond hair, the detective looked incongruous in the dirty attic where we sorted through treasures and junk alike. Someone had made a half-hearted attempt at cleaning the attic, but it was still dusty.

I placed the music box in the blue reusable grocery bag I'd brought to carry any small treasures I might uncover. Down on the main floor, Paige's partner, Shannon Martin, who was also my boyfriend, was guarding a mirror and a rolltop desk for me. He wasn't in uniform, but he was carrying a gun, and he had his badge, just in case, so I knew my future inventory was perfectly secure. That was more than I could claim when I went hunting on my own. Estate or "tag" sale attendees could be rather ruthless at times. I'd once had a set of antique balance scales, complete with weights, torn right from my hands by a woman with spiked heels and equally spiked blond hair.

Since we'd left Shannon talking with the employee of In Loving Memory, who was in charge of this particular estate sale, I hoped he'd charmed important information from her. His doing so was far more likely than me finding an imprint to confirm a possible series of geriatric murders.

"Anything?" Paige asked, her eyes briefly straying to where the only other occupant of the attic was examining a rolled-up rug in the corner.

I shook my head. We were here investigating In Loving Memory, and since Friday was my usual day for garage and estate sales, I was happy to play the part. The Portland Police Bureau didn't pay me huge consultant fees, and the double duty would help keep my store, Autumn's Antiques, afloat. My ability to read emotions imprinted on certain objects was the reason they wanted me on the job, but estate sales were my business, and I'd report anything that seemed out of the ordinary.

So far I'd come up with nothing in either imprints or suspicious activity.

Yet several competitors had noted In Loving Memory's sudden wealth of clients and reported their suspicions that the deaths of those new clients might not have been accidental: an air tube dislodged while a night nurse was in the kitchen, a fall down the stairs, a drowning in a hot tub, another fall—this time on an icy walk. There was no proof that these incidents were any different from the many similar instances that claimed the lives of the elderly each year. That this company had tripled their net worth in the past two years, and had been planning to conduct auctions for many of the owners before their deaths, could simply be a matter of coincidence.

However, when several of the adult children of the deceased estate owners claimed that family heirlooms had gone missing before and during the sales, the police had finally decided to investigate.

I glanced at the guy in the corner with the rug. He was a grungy man, probably in his fifties, with weeks-old scruff on his face, wearing worn jeans and a black and gray patterned button-down shirt over a black T-shirt. Could the rug have any real value? And if so, how could he possibly pay for it?

These estate sales, where nearly the entire contents of a deceased person's house were offered to the public for sale, attracted a varied clientele and contained as much overpriced junk as they did treasures. Attending them was a little like voyeurism; no place was off limits and everything not previously snapped up by the heirs was for sale, to be pawed over and examined by strangers.

For me, the glimpse into these strangers' lives was true a hundred times over. Not only could I sense emotions left on beloved objects or on things frequently used, but I often experienced the stronger imprinted memories as though I'd lived them myself. In emotional crises, people imprinted on almost everything, regardless of an object's emotional or monetary value.

My gift—or curse as sometimes it turned out to be—was called psychometry. Which was the fancy, scientific way of saying I somehow used areas of my brain that other people couldn't, a talent inherited from my birth father.

I refused to answer to the title psychic.

Paige, the grungy man, and I were joined in the attic by two older ladies and a clean-cut young man with an engaging smile who was likely a grandson. One of the women looked agile, perhaps in her late sixties or early seventies, her dark hair, flecked heavily with gray, swept up in an elaborate twist at the back of her head. Her aqua suit reeked of money, but her casual attitude made her appear at home in the dusty attic. By contrast, the other white-haired woman, at least in her mid-seventies, looked frail and pale in her peach dress, and I wondered how she'd climbed the steep, narrow flight of stairs.

I let my bare hand glide over the slat-back of a child's rocking chair made of oak and maple. It was from the early eighteen hundreds, the rockers underneath added much later, and the rush seat had been destroyed, perhaps eaten by mice. At a hundred dollars, the chair was a steal. I winced, though, as a negative imprint grabbed at me.

"You will sit in this chair, Beatrice, until you behave. Heaven knows I have enough pain in this horrid life without you adding to it with your sneaking and trickery."

My face stung as Momma's hand struck, the action tumbling her long, black hair forward over her shoulders. Hurt filled every corner of my body. Momma didn't want me. I knew she didn't. Not like the boys. I was too distracted, too undisciplined. I hadn't meant to spill the flour when I was making the bread. I should have stopped myself from writing in it, though.

When Daddy got home I'd be in big trouble. He'd probably make me stand in the corner while everyone ate dinner. I might not get to eat at all, unless Tom snuck me up a bit of bread later. If he didn't get whipped for cutting lessons again.

"Are you buying that?" a svelte voice said practically in my ear.

The voice gave me power to snatch my hand from the chair, to remember that I wasn't Beatrice, but Autumn Rain, owner of an antiques shop, twin to Tawnia Winn, and part-time consultant for the Portland police.

I turned to see the spry old lady on my left, her eyes fixed greedily on the little chair.

Greedily? No, eagerly. I liked to give everyone the benefit of the doubt, especially someone whose relatives might be reselling this chair at another estate sale in the very near future, though the older woman looked healthy enough at the moment.

"It's all yours," I said. "Great price."

I shouldn't be so picky about negative imprints because I could probably make six hundred or more from it, even after replacing the seat. But I wouldn't be able to bear having it in my store, not with that imprint—now over eighty years old—still retaining so much potency. I suspected that unless someone bought and loved that little chair, the imprint would remain strong for another eighty years.

My ability to read imprints wasn't always an advantage.

With the many bargains I had to pass up, it certainly hadn't made me rich.

"Thank you, dear." The woman glanced once at my bare feet before nodding to the young man to take the chair. He came forward with a slight stoop to his shoulders.

"Finished?" Paige asked me in an undertone. She grimaced slightly, showing her white teeth, perfectly straight except for a slight sideways tilt of a canine. It made her look a trifle like a movie star I'd seen in some old show.

"I just want to look over there." I indicated the corner with the rug, even though I really didn't expect to find anything in the attic. If someone had pushed the old man who had lived here down the main stairs where he'd been found dead, anything they'd touched or imprinted on should be closer to the crime scene. Then again, that same person could have been responsible for tagging all these items, so an imprint could be anywhere, and I'd already checked all the other rooms.

The attic was now becoming quite full of shoppers. The grungy man was gone, leaving the rug behind, but five other customers, one with a child in tow, had trekked up the narrow attic staircase.

"Why don't you wait for me downstairs?" I told Paige. "You can help Shannon get my desk out to his truck." Since we were undercover as bargain hunters, he'd brought his own vehicle instead of his unmarked white police Mustang.

Paige scanned the faces around us, probably searching for potential danger. The old women were examining the dish cabinet, only to be beaten out by a forty-something man wearing a bad toupee. I was glad for them because it wasn't worth the asking price.

"All right," Paige said. "Hurry, though. We still have one more sale to check out today."

"Just don't scratch the desk."

"Yeah, yeah." She stepped around a young couple holding hands and headed with relief toward the stairs. Though she was only in her mid-twenties, there was a reason she'd made detective so early—one that didn't take into account her family's long history with law enforcement. Paige got her hands dirty if she had to, and she was a crack shot with her Glock 19, but she was serious and conservative by nature. Slumming through other people's belongings was a tad beneath her, even if the items had a price tag she couldn't afford on her detective's salary.

I grinned at her retreating figure. Good thing she was dating a doctor, going on six months now. He'd even passed Shannon's approval, though we had yet to go on a double date.

I wiped dusty hands on my jeans and padded my way to the rug in the corner. I never wore shoes if I could help it—due as much to my hippie, flower-child upbringing as to an old injury to my back. With bare feet, I felt closer to the earth, connected, though most people didn't understand my feelings. Not even my twin, and she had been driven to jobs in three different states before finally finding me. I believed in fate only to a point. I knew Tawnia and I were invisibly connected in the same way I'd been connected to my adoptive parents. We belonged together.

I touched other tagged items on my way to the rug, testing for accusatory imprints. A dresser (trace of resentment), a trunk full of disintegrating clothes (sorrow), a lamp (nothing), a broken end table (faint burst of surprise followed swiftly by anger), and a doll covered in black marker (blissful preoccupation). No sign of a murder or a plot to swindle victims' families. Shannon had to be wrong on whatever his gut was telling him.

A smile touched my lips as I anticipated telling him exactly how wrong. In fact, I was looking forward to it far more than I should. It had been a rather boring winter and spring these past five months since he and I had helped bring down a drug-smuggling and child-trafficking ring in Salem. Shannon had been forced to take two weeks off to recover from the gunshot wound in his thigh, and then his captain had sent him off to a training program for several weeks, probably to make sure he actually healed the rest of the way before getting shot again. When he'd returned, Shannon had been lent to Vice and had gone undercover for two months to help catch members of the Portland branch of the same drug ring we'd busted open in Salem. I hadn't been invited along.

Shannon's new work schedule had put a serious damper on our romantic intentions. I'd seen him only twice during his time undercover. Once when he'd come to my shop at closing time, dressed in a disguise, and we'd stolen kisses before he had to slink away. And another time he'd been waiting for me in my old rusty Toyota hatchback, and we'd laughed when once again it wouldn't start.

I'd missed him, but maybe taking our relationship slow was the right thing to do. I still felt guilty about dumping my last boyfriend, Jake. Though he had remained my good friend, and we helped each other out in our connected shops, I knew Jake had been hurt when Shannon had come between us.

This week I'd seen Shannon every night except the two I dedicated to working out in my taekwondo black belt class. After our rocky start, I was beginning to think Shannon might just be *the one*. Which was good because I was thirty-four, and the birth of my niece nearly nine months earlier had me thinking of the future.

I reached the rolled-up rug and set my shopping bag containing the music box on a crate marked *flannel*. Gingerly, I brushed the surface. I'd learned to be careful. Strong imprints could trap me in a recurring loop from which I couldn't break free. I didn't want to pass out here without Paige or Shannon to guard my back.

The rug sported a detailed, elegant pattern that modeled an older style, but though I didn't know as much about rugs as I did other antiques, I was certain this one was fairly new. It wasn't worn or dirty, and it didn't smell of the dust that plagued the rest of the attic. Even more interesting, my fingers tingled when I brushed the rug, hinting at strong imprints somewhere close. Not covering the entire rug, but focused, perhaps where someone had touched or lain, or cleaned a spot. People didn't feel much passion at foot level, so these imprints might be important. Maybe even what we were looking for.

"There's nothing else of value here," announced the old woman who'd taken the child's rocking chair. "We'd better hurry and check out the rest of the house, or maybe that other estate sale across town." Her voice was authoritative, and shoppers gravitated to the stairway quickly in obvious hopes of beating the woman and her frail companion, who inched her way slowly across the attic. The man who'd decided on the dish cupboard enlisted another man to help him ease it down the steep stairs.

Ignoring them all, I unrolled the rug, trying to pinpoint the imprints. The rug was about my height in width, but much longer, likely used in a wide hallway. The price tag of three thousand dollars seemed ludicrous, unless it was a name brand

I didn't recognize—entirely possible since I dealt with old and not new furnishings. The back had a thin spongy layer that would make it skid resistant when placed on a wood floor or tile. Unlike the top of the rug, the off-white sponge showed a little bit of dirt.

The tingling became stronger.

All at once I found the imprint and . . . *I was squatting in a dark hallway, lifting the corner of the rug. Just a tug and it would be over. My muscles bunched in preparation.*

The imprint vanished as strong hands closed over my mouth and eyes, yanking me from the rug. My head twisted back as someone pulled me tightly against his chest.

A man's chest. A man that wasn't Shannon.

My martial arts training kicked in, and I began to struggle. The man behind me gasped as I elbowed his stomach, but the barrel of a gun jabbing into my side gave me pause.

"Don't move," a whispered voice growled. A second man.

Instinctively, I tried to look in his direction, but the man holding me kept my head still. The second man shoved a wad of cloth into my mouth, following it with a strip of tape plastered across my face. I could barely breathe. Another piece of cloth cinched tightly over my eyes and around my head.

Guess I'd found what I was looking for. There must be something forensics could find on the rug that would incriminate someone—and perhaps that person had stashed the rug here, hoping it would be overlooked. But how did that person know about my ability, or that I was working for the cops? With my jeans, my bare feet, and my short-cropped brown hair, dyed auburn on top, I didn't look official by any means. Paige did, and even Shannon might be pegged, but I looked like a legit bargain hunter

"What now?" asked one of the men.

"Here." A hand pushed me face first into the rug. The edges curled around my body, and I mentally berated myself for not fighting back. I might have survived a bullet, but if they got me out of here and someplace alone, I'd be in worse trouble. Besides, since being locked in a root cellar at a commune during one of my other cases, I'd become claustrophobic. Just thinking about being closed in brought on the panic.

As the rug squeezed tighter around me, the imprint began again. My arm or maybe my cheek was touching the place where it had been left.

I crouched in a dark hallway, lifting the edge of the rug. Just a tug and it would be over. My muscles tightened, ready to pull.

Footsteps in the darkness. A glimpse of pale feet. Waiting for the right moment. Waiting

Now. I pulled hard. A hoarse cry pierced the quiet night, followed by a loud crash. One more thud and then nothing.

All finished. Wait. My finger was bleeding on the rug. I needed to get out of the house before someone saw me.

Some part of me knew I was Autumn and that I was rolled in a rug. That part knew I had to struggle and fight so Shannon and Paige could find me. But I was caught in the imprint, the memory that wasn't mine. Caught reliving again and again a murder in the dark.

They say your greatest strength can be your greatest weakness, but I never really understood that until I began to read imprints. Psychometry might be the name for my ability, but right now psycho might be a better one. I was trapped more surely by the imprint than the rug.

I pulled the rug again. The same crash and the same helpless scream.

I'd give a lot at this moment to be as blind as the rest of the world.

I never saw anything new when I experienced imprints for a second or additional time. Never. Sometimes I might forget something after seeing it only once, but the imprint itself didn't change. What I saw came through the eyes of the person actually imprinting on an object, filtered through their experiences and intelligence. That meant imprints could often be misleading.

Not this one. Intent to harm was present. Determination. The act. What I couldn't know, because the person hadn't been thinking about it, was his motive or identity. It was so dark in the imprint that I couldn't see anything besides the rug and a pale flash of feet down the hall, perhaps at the top of a staircase. I might be witnessing the homeowner's cause of death.

I yanked the rug again. My victim fell.

No, it wasn't me. I was Autumn—not whoever had left this imprint. That person was only worried about their job. About the blood.

Nausea threatened to choke me.

Why hadn't the murderer destroyed the rug? Or if he worked for In Loving Memory, why hadn't they discounted it and placed it in a prominent location so it would sell fast? The police obviously hadn't considered the rug as evidence at the time of the owner's death, but now that complaints had been filed, the murderer should be covering his tracks. It didn't make sense to overprice the rug and hide it in the attic.

More important, why abduct me? Because I could feel that I was being carried down the stairs. Across a room.

I pulled the rug again.

My panic grew. *Please, Shannon,* I thought. *Find me.*

The tips of my toes jabbed into the stomach of one of the men, the rug not quite large enough to hide all of me. Would someone notice, or were the men wearing bulky enough clothing to hide what little of me emerged?

The moving stopped. "What a great choice," a woman said. "I hope you realize, though, that this is a cash-only sale."

I tried to scream, but I was too busy waiting for the flash of pale feet. Wait. Maybe I could use the imprint to my advantage.

Now! I lurched with the movement in the imprint, pulling the rug not only in my mind but also jerking my whole body.

My feet slammed against hard muscles, and then I was falling head first. Still firmly trapped inside the heavy rug.

"Oh, my," the woman said to one of my captors. "Are you okay?"

"Just tripped," the man grunted.

Again I waited in the dark. Waited for the pale feet.

A tear skidded down my cheek. My breath was hot.

My stomach heaved. I was probably going to suffocate. I jerked again with the pull of the rug, but this time my abductors were prepared.

"Thank you so much," the woman trilled. "We hope you'll attend one of our events again in the future. We have a sign-up sheet here if you'd like to be notified of other estate sales. No? All right. If you change your mind, please visit our website."

Then we were moving again. I gasped for breath, willing myself to be calm so I wouldn't suffocate. A little hard to do when reliving the thoughts of a murderer plotting to kill someone.

I heard a door open and felt the sensation of being dropped. My body seemed to be level, so the vehicle was probably a van.

"Hurry," said a man's voice.

"Shouldn't we check her?"

"She'll be okay. You felt the way she was moving."

I saw the pale feet and jerked the rug again.

This time the action was less real, disembodied. Further away. I didn't feel the roughness of the rug on my fingers. I did hear the crash and the scream. My head tumbled through black space as I fought to retain consciousness.

Chapter 2

*T*he crash wasn't inside my head or in the imprint. Because this time it ended with the squeal of brakes and another crash. More screaming. Then I heard a loud *boom!* Something heavy fell on top of me. My lungs tried to suck in air, but there seemed to be none available.

My panic exploded into dark nothingness.

Blissful nothingness.

"Autumn? Autumn?" Shannon's worried voice came at me with annoying repetition.

Why didn't he leave me alone? I really needed to sleep. I'd have to remind him that sneaking over to my apartment in the middle of the night when he was under cover was jeopardizing his mission. He'd listen to that. He was a stickler for rules.

Wait a minute. He wasn't undercover anymore, except at the estate sales, which didn't really count as undercover. And it wasn't my soft mattress under me but hard tarmac. I could smell something burning.

I forced my eyes open to see Shannon's rugged face close to mine. Even in their worry, his eyes were the most beautiful I'd ever seen in a man. Something in the green-blue color or in the heavy frame of brown, slightly curly lashes made them stand out. Those eyes alone could make criminals confess, especially female criminals. Before we began dating, I'd purposefully avoided looking into his eyes as much as possible, but now there was no reason not to drown in them.

Except I couldn't quite focus. Or breathe, for that matter.

"She's still having problems." Shannon glanced upward at someone who stood nearby, casting a shadow over us.

"The ambulance is here." It was Paige, her voice tight with exhilaration. I knew that meant she'd gotten to use her gun. That was the only thing besides talking about her new boyfriend that cut through her usual calm composure. "They can take her to the hospital."

That got me awake. "No ambulance. I'm fine." My damaged bank account certainly couldn't afford any more medical treatments.

Ignoring me, Shannon waved someone over before moving to my other side, every movement of his compact form undeniably graceful. His hair was that color between brown and blond, just beginning to show some of the lighter streaks the sun painted liberally in his hair during the summer. He'd recently had it cut after finishing his undercover work, so the ends were sadly missing the curl he normally sported. I loved those curls. I wanted to rub my hands through them. It was just as well the curls were missing, though, since my hands wouldn't obey me.

The next second, a paramedic arrived and something plastic was shoved over my face. I breathed in, relieved to feel my lungs expanding with oxygen.

Shannon pulled my head onto his lap. "Is that better?"

The pain in my chest was diminishing, and this close I could definitely see him better. The sun prematurely crinkled the skin around his eyes, giving him a healthy, wholesome glow. Since he hadn't been working overtime the past few days, he was clean-shaven. His eyes watched me intently, demanding an answer.

I nodded and struggled to sit, though I left the oxygen mask on, just in case. I felt as weak as I had after a serious bout of the flu. When I was finally sitting upright, I briefly pulled the oxygen mask away from my face to speak.

"I'm fine. Just a little winded." I looked around, noticing for the first time a gray van burning some distance away.

"They're gone. They had backup waiting. A sedan. Jumped into it when they saw us pursuing. They hit the van with something big as they drove away. Paige got the license plate number, but it's probably bogus."

This time I pulled the mask to the side of my face, holding it there so I could speak and still benefit from the oxygen. "You let them get away?"

He gave me a flat look. "Hmm, let's see. It was either that or let you burn to death in the van."

"Oh, in that case, good choice."

The hint of a smile quirked one side of his mouth. "Fortunately, that rug had you well-protected from the fire, though it almost smothered you before I got you out."

"Where is it?"

"The rug?" he shrugged. "Still in the van. I loosened it just enough to pull you free. Paige was covering us so we couldn't grab the entire thing with you in it. Why, was it important?"

I shuddered, remembering the horror. "I'd just discovered a very strong imprint about a murder when they jumped me.

And there might be some blood on it. The rug might have been used in the death of the homeowner."

Shannon nodded at Paige, who took off toward the fire-fighters on the scene, presumably to enlist their help in preserving the evidence.

"I doubt there's going to be anything left," Shannon said. "It's clear those men didn't want to leave evidence."

Me included, apparently. "I didn't even get a look at them before they jumped me. Did you see them?"

He shook his head. "Only the basics. Dark dress shirts, slacks. Brown hair. Average height. Looked like half the men we've seen at these things. What I don't understand is how they're connected to our case. If someone's been murdering old people to sell their estates, that's one thing, but these guys felt different. Experienced. Prepared. Not many people would dare to do this much damage in broad daylight."

"Organized crime?"

Shannon set a hand on my arm, as though driven to touch me. "That's what it seems, but it has to be related to our estate investigation, or why would they take you right after you discovered the rug?"

"How would they even know I could read imprints?"

"Well, you said there was blood. Maybe they thought you knew more than you do. Or maybe you were just in the way."

I could tell he wasn't satisfied with the explanation, and neither was I. In Loving Memory might be dirty, but the company didn't seem prosperous enough to afford muscle that blew up their own vehicle in the middle of a police chase.

I was still feeling winded and light-headed, but I took one more deep breath of the oxygen and pulled off the mask, handing it to the paramedic hovering nearby.

"Will we be transporting?" the man asked.

I shook my head, narrowing my eyes at Shannon. He breathed a heavy sigh. "No," he said. "But thanks." He waited until the man left before adding, "Are you sure you're okay?"

There was tenderness in the words, and I leaned into him. "Yeah, pretty sure."

"If I hadn't caught a glimpse of your bare feet when they dropped that rug as they left the house . . ." He left the statement unfinished, which was fine with me. "Anyway, I didn't make it to the curb in time to stop them from leaving, but I made sure they didn't get far."

A lump formed in my chest, an emotion too big to examine. I kept my face impassive. "The important thing is my antique desk and mirror. When you chased after me, were they damaged?" The bulge of my wallet in my back pocket informed me that the store's mortgage money that I'd planned to borrow to pay for the items was miraculously intact.

Shannon gave a warm chuckle that made me feel marginally better. "I hadn't loaded them yet, so they're still with the lady in charge, who, by the way, is one of the company partners. But besides that tidbit, I didn't get a scrap of useful information from her. If she knows anything, she hides it well."

"What does your gut say?"

He hesitated. "Never mind my gut. Do you have your sister's drawing? You look like you need a recharge."

He was talking about Tawnia's hand-drawn copy of the first picture someone had taken of her and me together less than two years ago. Tawnia had made it especially for me, smoothing each line while thinking about us and our relationship and the miracle we both felt at finding each other after being raised in separate adoptive homes. The small drawing held positive imprints, which gave me strength, and I normally carried it with me to counteract any strong negative imprints I might run into.

I shook my head. "She's making me a new one. Remember that imprint on that steering wheel you had me read last week after that hit and run? Well, I touched the drawing after to get rid of those feelings, and I left an imprint of my reaction."

It was one of the rare times it had happened, me detecting my own imprint, even though I'd used the drawing to regain my strength many times before. Imprints were fickle that way; everything depended on a person's state of mind. Reliving the experience of an angry driver killing someone with a car had affected me differently than other imprints I'd read. Of course, that experience was now a part of me like all the other negative imprints, each stealing a tiny piece of my well-being. A small price to pay if it meant protecting people.

"I don't have my watch today," Shannon said. The watch in question had been a gift from his grandfather years ago and held several strong imprints imbued with love. "We'll have to get you some protein on the way back to the estate sale. I sent officers there, but I want to question anyone they find myself."

"Guess our cover's blown."

"Yep. Or mine and Paige's at least."

Paige sauntered over. "So, are we going back to question everyone?"

"I'm ready." I tried to stand, but my knees wouldn't hold my weight, and my chest was hurting again. I was going to be angry if I'd broken another rib. But I suspected the real weakness was from that repeat imprint. I needed time and a lot of protein to recover.

"I'll have someone drive you home," Shannon said, helping

me to the curb. "You need to rest. And until we get a handle on what happened here, we'll have a police detail watching your place."

I was about to protest—something I sometimes did just to keep him in his place—but another wave of dizziness prevented me.

"At least put on your rings for now," Paige said, as Shannon sprinted off to talk to the uniformed officers now canvassing the scene.

"Right." I dug in my pants pocket for the antique rings I normally wore every day. They buzzed with mildly pleasant imprints, which had many times softened the shock of a sudden negative imprint I stumbled on accidentally—usually while shopping or running errands. I'd taken them off before the estate sale so they wouldn't interfere with any new emotions I might detect, but I needed them now.

Except the buzzing from the rings was strangely muted. Maybe even missing altogether.

"Is something wrong?" Paige said, noting my frown.

"I've had these rings a long time. I think maybe the imprints are losing potency—and they were never strong to begin with."

"Which was why you could wear them. It was bound to happen." Paige's hand went to the V of her navy suit. "Well, I'd let you touch my new necklace, but then you'd probably experience what I did after Matthew gave it to me last night."

I shook my head. "No way do I want to see you lip-locking with Matthew—however cute he may be." I felt a stab of jealousy as I spoke. She'd been able to pursue her relationship these past months while Shannon and I'd been in limbo.

Paige laughed. "His parents are coming to town, and we're all going to dinner."

"Must be really serious."

She held up a hand to reveal crossed fingers. "I hope so. They may totally hate me, though."

The idea wasn't as ludicrous as it might sound. Paige often came across as too serious, especially when talking police business. It was all she'd ever known. Her father and brother were police detectives, and her grandfather was a retired detective. Following in their footsteps, her life's main goal had always been to serve on the force. The first time I'd met her, I'd thought her eagerness a little vulture-like. Now it was endearing.

"If they hate you, I'll send them some really bad herbal tea." I held up my hands as she began to protest. "I know, as a punishment it's not much, but it's all I got. You're better with a gun than I'll ever be. Seriously, Paige, if they have a problem, it's their loss, and Matthew will still be crazy about you."

That elicited a smile. "At least *my* family likes *him.*"

Which was saying a lot. Her father had begun a thorough background check on Matthew within hours of discovering his name, beating Shannon to it by a matter of minutes. At least we could be sure there were no secret financial woes, convictions, or vindictive ex-wives cluttering up Matthew's past.

Shannon was coming back with Peirce Elvey in tow, my favorite of the officers Shannon and Paige worked with. He was a short man with flaming red hair and a penchant for telling jokes. He didn't treat me with the half-believing, half-patronizing attitude that marked most of the other officers' interactions with me, so I liked him an awful lot.

"Hey, Autumn, I hear you were in that explosion. How many of me do you see? Because I always wanted a twin. Triplets would be even better." Peirce's expressive grin wrinkled the many freckles on his nose.

"Sorry, only one. Does Detective Martin have you on babysitting duty?" I rolled my eyes at Shannon, but there was no real bite in the words. Probably because I was having trouble focusing. Good thing I already had heterochromia—which meant my right eye was hazel and my left blue—or the blast might have given me enough of a knock to cause the condition.

"Looks like I am. You don't spit up like my son, do you?"

"No, you're confusing me with my niece. But if it will make you feel better, I might be able to come up with some baby talk." I actually still felt a bit nauseated after my stint wrapped in the rug, and I wasn't all that sure I'd keep down whatever was left of my breakfast.

I lifted a hand to Shannon. "Okay, I'll go with your babysitter, but to my shop, not home. And before you can protest, Tawnia's watching the store for me today, so it's not like I'll really have to work. And I won't be alone." That should alleviate all his worries. My sister was good at taking care of people—as long as you didn't expect her to cook anything remotely healthy—or even edible for that matter.

Shannon helped me up, nodding subtly at Peirce as he walked me to the squad car. Instead of annoying me, his concern made me feel warm inside. Uh-oh. I'd fallen big time.

"You coming by tonight?" I asked Shannon.

"Yeah. But I'll call you in a bit after we talk to witnesses at the house. Are you sure you don't want to go to the hospital?"

"Why, so some young intern can shine a light in my eyes, take several X-rays, and then send me home with a painkiller and tell me to rest? You know I don't like taking pills, and I probably wouldn't fill the prescription anyway."

His brow furrowed. "You have a headache?"

I did, though I didn't know exactly when it had started.

But the pain was natural, given what I'd been through. What worried me more was the continued dizziness. Maybe both symptoms could be explained by a busted ear drum. I'd have to ask Tawnia.

"I'm fine," I insisted. "I'll just take a nap in my back room. I might not be ready for dancing tonight, but I'm definitely up for dinner—if it's not pasta again." Shannon loved pasta, but I hadn't found an organic variety that pleased me. Shannon, on the other hand, would probably be as happy as my sister with those microwavable noodles in a cup. Ugh.

"You're always up for dinner. Oh, that reminds me." Shannon fished in his pocket and pulled out a couple bills, pushing them at Peirce. "Get her some protein, would you? She'll tell you where."

"I hope that's coming out of your police budget," I said. "We're on the job, remember?" I never turned down food. Ever.

Shannon just winked at me.

Without another word, I slid into the back seat of the police vehicle. Pierce's rookie partner, Mac Delaney, was already behind the wheel, and he nodded at me politely. I could feel Shannon's eyes on us as we drove off. Though I couldn't read people the way I could objects, I didn't need an imprint to tell me what he was feeling. It was complicated working with someone you cared about. When his boss got wind of our relationship, my consulting would probably be limited to reading imprints down at the police station. No more undercover investigating, at least not with Shannon and Paige. After the day I'd had, I couldn't bring myself to feel sad about that. In fact, I had to stop from calling the captain myself.

I laid my head back against the seat and listened to Peirce's running dialogue about life at the precinct. I must have laughed a dozen times, but afterwards, I couldn't remember anything he said.

I kept thinking about the rug, the men, the explosion. And about my antique rings.

Not only was something not adding up, but it was completely wrong. I felt weird, something that couldn't be explained by dizziness or my headache.

"Don't you like some restaurant around here?" Peirce asked.

I looked up to see that we'd entered the street where my antiques shop was located. "Yeah, Smokey's. It's across the street from my shop. But you know what? I'll send my sister over. I need to lie down."

Delaney pulled over in front of my shop, nestled between Jake's Herb Shoppe and a music store that specialized in jazz. Peirce jumped out to open my door, and I didn't protest as he helped me from the car. My legs felt better now, almost normal, but my head still spun. Maybe I would have Tawnia take me to the doctor after all.

"Gotta check it out inside first," Peirce said. "Just in case. Detective Martin's orders."

I let him go into Autumn's Antiques first, the buzzing of the electronic bell I'd installed making my head ache even more. Inside, no one was at the counter. Through the interior adjoining double doors leading into the Herb Shoppe, I could see my shared employee, Thera Brinker working at the counter with Jake, but Tawnia wasn't with them. Or anywhere nearby. I couldn't feel the connection I normally felt when she was around, as if a string connected from my chest to her, one that thickened to a rope as we grew closer.

I'd always felt that kind of connection with my adoptive parents, Winter and Summer Rain, and when Tawnia had first shown up in Portland, experiencing it with her had confused me until we uncovered her identity. Before that discovery, I'd hoped I was feeling Winter. That he was still alive. He hadn't been, but finding Tawnia had dampened my loss, and the appearance of my strange ability on the day of Winter's funeral had given me a new direction in life.

"She's not here," I said.

Fear bit at me. Where had my sister gone? My phone was still in the pocket of my jeans, and I hadn't felt it vibrate, but I'd been distracted. With my chosen sideline of reading imprints, I always worried Tawnia would get involved and be hurt. It had happened before, so I was more careful than ever not to involve her. But we were identical twins, and though I kept my hair short and wore much different clothing, people who didn't know me well might still mistake her for me.

Friday mornings were my slowest part of the week, but she wouldn't have left the shop without letting me know. She worked part-time as an artist for an advertising firm, and that's one reason why she'd volunteered to cover for me. She could work on her projects in my back room while saving me from having to pay someone to be in the shop. In return, I babysat my niece whenever Tawnia had to go into the office or run errands.

A heavy feeling lay over me. What if those men who'd taken me from the estate sale didn't have anything to do with that rug? What if it was personal? I'd ruffled a few feathers in the past year. Someone might want to take out their frustration on my family.

With a glance at my worried face, Peirce headed toward my back room. "Stay here. I'll check it out."

He'd gone only a few steps when my sister appeared in the

doorway behind the counter, her long brown hair smooth and shiny. My niece, Destiny Emma Winn, was fast asleep in her arms.

I still couldn't feel my normal connection with her. There was something wrong—something terribly wrong. The very air in the shop felt different.

"Ah, I thought I heard you." Tawnia smiled, happy to see me. "How'd it go? Find anything worth buying? Wait, you probably didn't since you're back early. But that's a good thing because I was just about to call you." She hesitated, her eyes traveling over my face. "Are you okay? You look sick. And your clothes are sooty."

Unlike my twin, who was good at playacting, I'd never been able to hide my emotions. They were always right on my face in plain view. Of course, she'd be able to see my worry.

"They ran into a little trouble," Peirce began, "but Autumn's okay, and I'm just here until they figure out what happened."

"What *did* happen?"

Peirce opened his mouth, but I shook my head, silencing him. "A couple of guys tried to steal some evidence," I told my sister. "Shannon and Paige gave chase."

Tawnia's lips pursed. "Yeah, right, and I'm sure that's the whole story. You know I'm going to get the rest out of you eventually, but right now you'd better come sit down. You look awful."

First *sick* and now *awful,* words she commonly used around me. My sister needed to learn some new adjectives.

I stumbled with another bout of dizziness, and Peirce and Tawnia rushed to my side.

"Detective Martin says I'm to get her some protein." Peirce's arm went around me. "But she insisted on coming here first.

She said you'd take care of it since Smokey's is just across the street." He waved the money Shannon had given him.

Tawnia blinked at the cash but didn't take it. "Must have been some imprint if she needs that much food."

"Is everything okay?" Our friend Jake came through the doors linking our stores. His eyes, soft and liquid like creamy dark chocolate, showed a gentleness that some might find ludicrous given his muscled chest and the short, finger-width locs that framed his face. He was solid and familiar to me in times of trouble, and I nearly burst into tears at seeing him.

"Give me your keys, Jake," I said.

He blinked once but pulled them from his pocket without asking any questions. I held out my hand, and he placed them on my palm. One touch verified what I'd already suspected. Tears stung my eyes, and I gritted my teeth in an effort to keep them away.

"No imprint," I whispered. "I can't read the imprints."

Silence filled the room, though we could still hear Thera helping customers in Jake's store.

"Maybe there aren't any imprints on the keys," Tawnia said.

I knew there were. Both Jake and I knew. Mostly they were about his feelings for me. Or his former feelings. Though five months had passed since I'd last touched them, there was no way the strong imprints had faded that fast, and I knew of no way but time and repeated imprinting that could fade or remove imprints.

Shifting the baby to one arm, Tawnia put her other arm around me in a hug, leading me to the narrow back room that ran the width of my shop.

"Sit," she told me before laying the sleeping baby in an antique crib I kept in the corner. My niece—I called her by her first name, Destiny, while her parents used her middle name, Emma—was here at least three times a week, so she'd needed somewhere to sleep. I was the only person Destiny was happy with besides her parents.

I sank into my ratty easy chair, whose indeterminate color I'd long forgotten, pulling out the footrest.

Tawnia placed her hand on my forehead. "You don't feel hot. Look, let's try this again."

Jake already had my parents' small book of poetry in his hands. I kept it here for emergencies, the comforting imprints on it strong enough to soothe any horrifying image.

I couldn't help the gasp of loss as I ran my fingers over the book. I felt nothing. Nothing but dizziness and the headache. No emotions or experiences that weren't mine. No imprints from my parents. No stories at my fingertips. There'd also been no buzzing of imprints as I'd walked by my antiques on the way to the back room, no connection with my sister, even when she'd put her arm around me.

I was blind.

More than a dozen times over the past twenty months I'd wished my ability hadn't evolved, that I hadn't developed that part of my brain, but the actual reality was terrible. I'd lost one of my senses—one that I understood now was every bit as important to me as any of the others.

I shook my head, returning the poetry book to Jake and struggling not to give in to tears. How had this happened? Something in the blast? Had I been deprived of air too long?

"It's stress." Tawnia knelt down by the chair, taking my cold hand in hers. "You read too many imprints, is all. You just need to eat—I've got a chicken salad in the fridge. It'll be okay."

"I'm not hungry."

Jake and Tawnia exchanged stares, and I could tell this news disturbed them more than my not being able to feel imprints.

I wanted to scream and cry and stomp around, touching everything, but I was too exhausted to get up from the chair. Maybe Tawnia was right. Maybe I simply needed rest. *Yes, that's it.* I wasn't going to let emotion control me. Firmly, I pushed my panic into a manageable pile in the center of my chest where it sat like a cold chunk of rock.

"I'll order something from Smokey's." That would make me feel better, if any food could.

"Uh, about that," Jake said, shooting another glance at Tawnia. "Didn't you tell her?"

Tawnia paled, and her grip on my hand tightened. "Oh, no. She looked so . . . I got distracted."

"What is it?" Peirce asked.

Tawnia glanced at the officer and then back at me, her eyes huge. "You have to be able to read imprints, Autumn, especially today."

That jerked me from my stupor. "Why?"

"Because Nicholas Russo was here looking for you. He wants you to read an imprint."

"He seemed quite insistent," Jake added.

The connection clicked into place. Nic Russo. The organized crime boss I owed a favor. I swallowed hard, unable to speak.

This was not good at all.

Chapter 3

Nicholas Russo was the charismatic leader of an organized crime family based in New Jersey. The group had once been run by his uncle, but because of his uncle's deteriorating health and the death of his male cousin—or supposed death since Tawnia's neighbor Dennis Briggs, AKA Damian Franco, was still very much alive—Russo had essentially ascended to the throne and taken over. He was charming, intelligent, attractive, and utterly ruthless. Exactly what their organization required.

"He's waiting for you at Smokey's," Tawnia added, coming to her feet. "Like I said when you got here, I was going to call you. He arrived when I was feeding the baby, and Jake talked to him." Her eyes narrowed. "Did you really promise a mob boss that you'd read an imprint for him?"

It had been my part of the bargain for his promise to let Dennis remain dead to his crime family, but I'd never told Tawnia. Half of me hoped good old Nic would forget my promise. After all, with the birth of his fourth child, his first son, he'd profited by his cousin Dennis's refusal to rejoin his loving family every bit as much as Dennis profited by getting out of the unsavory business. As far as I knew, Dennis's ailing father still didn't know his son was alive—a good thing if even a small portion of what I knew about the man was true.

"That was kind of dumb," Jake added. "Promising anything to a mob boss is dumb."

"I said I would have to be sure it wouldn't lead to anyone dying," I offered in my defense. "I'll just tell him I can't do it."

This was the only good side to losing my ability, though the rock in my chest said otherwise. That hard lump was growing again, threatening to explode once more into full-fledged panic. Reading imprints had become a part of who I was—a large part. How would I feel hunting for antiques when I would never catch a glimpse into an object's past? How would it feel never to solve another crime or reunite another missing person with loved ones?

"Uh, Autumn, you just don't say no to a guy like Nicholas Russo." This from Peirce, who fingered the gun at his waist.

He had a point, and an angry Nic Russo wouldn't be a good thing for me, my friends, or my family. My anxiety ramped up a notch.

I needed to call Cody Beckett. My biological father and I weren't close, but I'd seen the crusty old artist several times since our first meeting five months ago, and he'd been forthcoming about his past, our heritage, and his ability—our shared ability. Maybe this had happened once to him. Maybe he knew how to get it back.

"I think we should call Detective Martin," Peirce added.

"No." Just because I was in love with the man—or thought I was—didn't mean I was going to let him take control of my life. "I'll find out what Russo wants first. Then if I need to, I'll call Shannon."

Peirce's normally good-natured face remained solemn. "Russo might have some connection with that business this morning."

"Probably. But he wasn't part of trying to abduct me, or he wouldn't have come here."

Tawnia gasped. "Someone tried to abduct you?"

I nearly screamed in frustration. "I was fine. Shannon and Paige were there, remember? Anyway, Russo may have some answers."

Jake scowled. "You can't go see him alone." Sometimes he and Shannon were uncannily alike, co-captains of the Autumn-needs-to-be-more-careful club, which was irritating, but I supposed it was also the reason I loved them both.

"He won't hurt me. Not as long as he needs me."

"What if you can't give him what he wants?" Tawnia glanced toward the crib, where Destiny was moving, probably awakened by the tension in the room. Grabbing the side of the crib, the baby pulled herself sleepily to her feet and waved at us with a chubby hand, her face stretching into a captivating smile. Tawnia rushed over and swept the baby into her arms.

I knew what my sister was thinking, that Russo wasn't above using my family to get what he wanted. But we had something on him too—the fact of his cousin's survival. If I had to, I would use that information to stall him long enough to talk to Cody about getting back my ability. But since I'd never really betray Dennis or his young family, I wasn't sure a threat to expose Russo's lie to his uncle would buy me much more than a day or two.

It took way more effort than I imagined to pull myself to

my feet. My easy chair always seemed to capture a person in it, and today I wouldn't have made it out at all if Jake hadn't offered a hand. I smiled and pulled away as quickly as I could without offending him. No way did I want him to suspect I might still have feelings for him. Which I did, but not the right feelings. I'd loved him for years—I still loved him—and if Shannon hadn't come along, Jake and I would be a couple. But with Shannon in my life, the world held new colors and emotions. The right kind.

The minute I was on my feet, Destiny pushed against her mother in a valiant effort to reach me. That baby loved me almost as much as her mother, and because she hadn't seen me for more than five minutes that morning, she was anxious to play.

Tawnia tried to hold her back, but she was as helpless to deny Destiny anything as I was. I took the baby, cuddling her close, breathing in the baby smell of her—this time spit up mixed with baby lotion. The aroma shouldn't be pleasant but was actually the greatest comfort I could imagine. The heavy feeling in my chest lightened.

"Hi, sweetie, how are you? I missed you, too." I kissed her cheek, and she reciprocated, opening her mouth wide pushing it against my skin. Okay, so we needed to work on the closing and puckering, but I felt happier anyway. Even the pounding in my head lessened. Only the dizziness continued with the same intensity. I'd have to remember to ask Tawnia about breaking an eardrum. The blast could have been responsible, and maybe it was affecting the imprints.

I did seem to hear fine, though.

I snuggled Destiny for a few more minutes before giving her back to her mother. Ever since her birth, my own biological clock was ticking. I wondered how Shannon felt about kids.

Strange that I didn't know, when I knew Jake was hoping for a half dozen.

"I can't let you go alone," Peirce said.

"You can come," I told him. "But don't call Shannon yet."

I headed to the bathroom to clean up a little before my meeting with Russo. What I really needed to feel completely ready was a long, hot shower, a new dress that cost more money than I had in savings, and a couple of guns. I had my concealed carry permit, but I never carried unless Shannon and I were heading to the range. The gun Shannon had given me—the second now—was locked in a small safe installed under my counter. With Destiny growing older, the rule was that the gun was on me or in the safe. So far, except for our weekly range trip, it was always in the safe. My weapons of choice were my hands and feet, though I had to admit they wouldn't be much against Russo's goons.

I washed my face, reapplied a touch of makeup, and ran damp fingers through my dark brown hair, fluffing the red, dyed part on top. Then I took a wet rag and rubbed at a dirty spot near the buttons on my fitted blouse. My efforts were wasted; I still looked like I'd been rolled in a rug and almost burned to death. I did feel calmer, though. Maybe now I could read an imprint. My eyes darted around the small bathroom, but I could see nothing I knew held an imprint. Except my antique rings, which still had not even the slightest buzzing.

Great.

The lump in my chest exploded into panic, and I clutched at the sink in an effort not to curl into a miserable ball on the floor. I squeezed my eyes shut until the panic subsided, and until my dizziness lessened enough to see my reflection in the mirror once again.

"You can do this," I whispered.

Sitting on the closed toilet seat, I washed my feet in the tiled floor basin I'd recently installed between the toilet and the new pedestal supporting my sink. The basin wasn't much over a foot wide, and only a couple inches above ground level, but the attached sprayer did the job and made my employee Thera happy. She was always worried I'd contract something walking around without shoes, though I'd reminded her numerous times that there were normally more germs on a doorknob than on a sidewalk.

Tawnia waited for me in the back room outside the bathroom door, but, thankfully, the men had withdrawn into my shop. "Feeling better?"

"Do I look better?"

"Sure," my sister lied.

I was normally the transparent one, but this time I could see right through her.

"Look," she rushed on, "I don't think you should go."

"I have to go. Don't worry. Peirce will be there."

She nodded, and I could tell it took great effort for her not to continue her protest. Instead, she hugged Destiny tightly.

That was when I spied the drawing on my worktable next to several other drawings Tawnia had been working on. I picked it up. "You drew this today?"

"Yeah. Kind of funny, isn't it? It just came to me."

It was a drawing of the two old women from the estate sale with the young man carrying the rocking chair. Like me, my sister had an unusual ability. Hers was to draw people and things she'd never seen but that actually existed. Usually, her drawings linked to my cases. Knowing she would be here drawing this morning, I'd been half afraid that she might have drawn the burning van and become frantic with worry as she had in other past cases. Instead, it was the two harmless old ladies she'd somehow focused on.

Maybe her talent was off a bit as well. Then again, the ladies benefitted from my rejection of the chair, which represented a loss of hundreds to me. Maybe I'd been more upset about that than I'd thought, and Tawnia's ability picked up on my emotion.

Tawnia studied my face. "Did you see them?"

I wanted to say no, but withholding information from her was not the same thing as an outright lie she'd see right through. "Yeah. They beat me out of that little rocking chair. Well, I let them have it. The imprints—"

"Hmm. So you could read imprints earlier today."

"I read a lot of them." I stifled a shudder at the memory of the repeated one on the rug.

"When exactly did they stop?"

"I'm not sure. There was this one that was kind of bad, and then a loud noise." No way was I going to bring up exactly what those men had tried to do to the van and me inside of it. "Made me dizzy. Weak. But I didn't have your picture, and it was only when I put back on my rings—" I held them up. "They don't buzz, and I couldn't feel you here when I came into the store."

Tawnia's brow furrowed. "I felt you."

This was an important admission, something she'd never shared with me before. My sister wasn't big on owning up to any special ability. She claimed it was her connection with me that inspired her drawings. But our biological grandmother had drawn scenes that had happened across town, scenes she'd never witnessed. They'd locked her in a sanitarium for it and she'd died there. Her son's greatest regret was not getting his mother out, but Cody had only been a teenager at the time.

"It's like the other times when you've read too many imprints," Tawnia said in a voice that was meant to soothe. "You'll see. You'll rest and eat and pretty soon you'll be reading more imprints than ever." A coaxing smile slid over her face. "Think of it. People throughout the entire world, even in countries that don't yet have running water, will line up and pay you money—or sticks or carvings or whatever they have—just to see you touch something. Then you can pay for Emma's college and her wedding to a rich prince who adores her and who will give me an island somewhere for my very own so that I can draw without interruptions. The prince will buy all my paintings at exorbitant prices, and we'll both be rich and famous. Everything's going to be okay."

Normally my sister's silly imaginative stories made me laugh, but now I only wanted to remind her that though I'd passed out, thrown up, and otherwise become incapacitated after reading imprints, I'd never stopped feeling them altogether.

"Thanks," I said instead. "Just save room for me on that island."

She winked. "You can have half of it."

It was time to go.

I didn't take my gun. On the way out of the shop, I touched four items I knew held positive imprints, pretending to adjust their positions on their shelves. Nothing but dizziness. It was as if a part of me was missing. An arm, a leg. An eye. Leaving a gaping hole in its place.

"Look," I told Tawnia as she accompanied me to the door,

"I might have broken an eardrum from that loud noise this morning. Do you know what symptoms I'd have?"

"Well, pain in that ear for starters. Maybe it'd leak fluid. I'll have to look it up on the Internet to be sure. Why, does your ear hurt?"

"No. But I'm a bit dizzy."

Tawnia looked hopeful. "Maybe that's why you can't read imprints."

I knew before I returned that she'd have a list of symptoms, a dozen cures, and an appointment with her doctor for me. At least she'd be busy and not worrying quite as much while I was in the viper's lair.

Jake, trailing behind us with Peirce, showed no sign of stopping at my shop door. "You've got customers," I reminded him. Friday was a big day for his store, and Thera couldn't handle all the customers alone. Randa, our other part-time employee who was also Jake's sister, was still in high school and wouldn't get here until after two.

"I called Jazzy," he said. "She's coming right in."

"Are you sure about that?"

Jazzy Storm was one of the girls Shannon and I'd freed during the child trafficking case we'd solved in Salem. The fifteen-year-old runaway hadn't wanted to go back to her deadbeat parents, and Paige had set her up with an attorney who'd agreed to help her become emancipated, but who had ended up fostering the girl instead. Jazzy was too far behind to attend regular school yet, so she helped out in our stores a couple times a week—more to keep her off the streets than for her usefulness. She had many bad habits, which her guardian suspected she'd get rid of right about the time she stopped using her made-up name. The attorney secretly paid her wage to encourage us to employ her long term so she'd have more stability. I'd convinced Jake to agree to the arrangement, and after five long months, she was finally becoming a bit helpful. We still made sure to keep a close eye on our cash registers and our inventory when she was around.

"Thera knows the score," he said. "And we're not going to be long. I mean, you can't do anything for Russo right now."

I shrugged, annoyed at the implication. For a long time, even before we broke up, Jake had hinted that he wanted me to pull back from any situation that might be dangerous, and I suspected he hoped my condition was permanent.

No. That was uncharitable. Jake might wish a lot of things, but he wouldn't want me to be miserable.

Then again, reading imprints had changed me from a trusting, friendly person to someone more jaded, more careful. Where once I'd embraced everyone without reserve the way my hippie parents had, now I didn't offer my hand for fear of touching a piece of jewelry. I reserved judgment until imprints had verified my first impressions. I avoided places people commonly left imprints—like libraries and secondhand stores—unless I was wearing gloves.

Imprints complicated things. But at the same time, they opened up an entirely new world where I understood people and experienced them as I never had before. A world where my efforts helped people and changed lives for the better.

Could I adjust to a "normal" life again? Maybe the choice wouldn't be mine.

I offered Tawnia what I hoped was a confident smile and strode outside into the bright sunlight. However, it felt more like slinking out. My eyes roved the street, looking for danger, but besides Peirce's partner lounging against his squad car, all I saw was the sleek black sedan parked across the street, a bit down from Smokey's. If I hadn't been so out of things earlier, I would have noticed it before.

Nicholas Russo was slumming. The man owned a host of fancy restaurants and other businesses, and was up to his ears in exporting, importing, and real estate, both in New Jersey and on the West Coast. He was certainly accustomed to better than what Smokey's could offer—at least in the way of ambience. Smokey's food, in my opinion, compared favorably to any fare five times the cost, and Russo would probably recognize that. I hoped Smokey's didn't become his new favorite hangout whenever he was in town—or, worse, that he would decide to buy the place.

The sidewalk felt warm and rough on my bare feet, and though the sensation wasn't the connection with the universe that I craved, the heat and familiarity of the sensation was comforting.

"Delaney's going to keep watch out here." Peirce thumbed at his partner. "Just in case."

I opened the door to the restaurant with a bit of rag I casually palmed from my pocket before remembering it wasn't necessary. It seemed I'd finally learned to protect myself from random imprints when I no longer needed to make the effort. Neither Jake nor Peirce commented, though Peirce rushed to hold the door for me. Maybe they hadn't noticed.

Inside Smokey's, Russo had appropriated two well-lit tables near the back, pushed together to form a larger dining area. One of Russo's men, a massive guy in dress pants and a blazer, sat with him. I recognized the man's bald head instantly from our last encounter. Charlie was his name. Two other men, dressed similarly, sat at the long snack bar along the wall opposite the kitchen area. Though they were enjoying coffee, they were obviously alert.

Bodyguards, I guessed. Russo never went anywhere without a few.

The place smelled heavenly, as always, and despite my claim that I wasn't hungry, my stomach growled. At least part of my body was working normally. Maybe eating something high in protein would help me recover. Some good fat couldn't hurt, either. Smokey's was mostly organic, from their brownies to their famous pot pies, and their proteins and fats were healthy.

Kristy, a rounded brunette waitress I knew fairly well from my biweekly visits, greeted us as we came in. "Hi, Jake. Hi, Autumn." To me, she added, "You look hungry." Which I supposed was her way of saying I looked as lousy as I felt. Her soft brown eyes scanned Peirce in his uniform. "You want a table for three? Or are you taking it with you?"

"Not today. I'm here to see him." I indicated Russo with a flick of my chin.

Her smile faltered. "Oh, lucky you. I'm just hoping he's a good tipper."

Apparently, Russo hadn't gone out of his way to be nice.

"So are you actually eating with him?" Kristy asked. "Or do you just want a drink?"

"I'd like a pot pie. Beef. And my usual turkey club. But double the meat." I grinned at her. "Put it on his tab."

She laughed. "Coming right up. Your usual to drink?"

Strawberry smoothie, she meant. It was my latest habit. "Sure. Thanks."

Kristy looked at Jake and Peirce. "Anything for you?"

They shook their heads, both looking as if they were heading to a funeral—my funeral and maybe their own. Peirce found his voice. "No, thanks, ma'am. Just some water, please." Not a trace of his usual levity. Jake nodded agreement.

I sighed. "Thanks, Kristy."

Russo had spotted us, and he set down his fork, lifting an imperious left hand. I remembered now that he was left-handed and missing half a middle finger next to his thick wedding band. As I crossed the cool tile toward him, I could see he hadn't changed in the intervening ten months since our last, nearly fatal, encounter. He had black hair with no trace of gray, and his well-defined features weren't overly prominent. He didn't look Italian, and he didn't have an accent when he spoke English, but he wore a dark suit that was most likely Italian and cost as much as I made in two years. Possibly more. He wasn't fat, but he had serious bulk, and an air of power and charisma that made him compelling. He invited trust, but trusting him would be a huge mistake.

Still, he *had* stayed away from his cousin and his little family. He would expect me now to uphold my end of the bargain, so I'd have to tell him the truth—or bluff. I wasn't sure which would help me stay alive. Too bad we couldn't have cut and dyed the top of Tawnia's hair and had her talk to Russo. She'd have convincingly rattled off a few fake imprints and we'd be finished. Of course that option was off the table—no way was my sister getting anywhere near this creep.

Russo stood as we arrived at the table. I hadn't felt underdressed before in my jeans and blue blouse and bare feet, but I did now. "Autumn Rain," he said, swallowing my hand in his two larger ones. I noticed he was careful not to let his ring touch my skin. "It's a pleasure to see you again." His eyes narrowed as they flicked over Peirce's uniform, but he didn't acknowledge either of my companions, which irked me.

"You remember my friend Jake Ryan, don't you?" I said, placing a steadying hand on Jake, who looked ready to burst. I'd seen Jake lovingly escort old women through his store, explaining the benefit of one herb or another. I'd seen him spoon-feed baby kittens who'd lost their mother. But he could also appear intimidating, as he did now, with his locs framing his strong face and his muscles flexing beneath his snug white T-shirt. His jaw already showed signs of new beard growth since his last shave, making his dark skin even darker in those spots. This was the Jake that some of my more romantic customers sighed over when they thought I wasn't watching.

"Yes," Russo said in a bored tone that told me I was wasting time. "We talked a few minutes ago in your store."

"And this is Officer Peirce Elvey. He's a friend of mine and happened to be driving me home today when I learned of your visit." I didn't mention my sister. I couldn't remember if he knew I had a sister, but I wasn't going to bring her to his attention.

"How fortunate," Russo said dryly. "Will you join me?" He indicated the chair across from him.

"Sure. I already gave my order to the waitress." I sat down, flashing a smile I knew was forced in the direction of his companion. "Hello, Charlie."

The bodyguard startled slightly at his name. His head dipped in a sharp nod, his eyes going to his boss, obviously at a loss to know how to react to my remembering him.

Russo didn't immediately bring up the reason for his visit, and I wasn't about to do his work for him. Sitting down caused another dizzy spell, and I gripped the edges of my seat until the faces around me stopped moving.

"Are you all right, Miss Rain?" Russo asked.

I nodded. "Just a bit of a headache." That much was true. Seated next to me, Jake slipped me a packet of herbs, which I knew was an herbal headache remedy he must have taken from his store while I was in the bathroom. Smiling my thanks, I opened the package and dumped it into the glass of water already on the table in front of me. Not sure how much good it would do when most herbal remedies were steeped in hot water to extract their healing properties.

"They have a surprisingly good pot pie here," Russo went on, picking up his fork. "I hope you ordered one."

"I did."

In fact, Kristy was coming over with it now. "Had a few in the oven in preparation for the lunch crowd," she said. "I'll bring your sandwich in a bit. I had them put extra strawberries in your smoothie."

"Thanks."

She nodded, and with a nervous look at Russo added, "Is everything all right, sir? Can I get you anything else?"

"No. This will suffice."

She dipped her head and skittered away.

I concentrated on my food for a few minutes, stopping only to respond politely to comments Russo made about the restaurant, the city, and the weather. I even remembered to ask about his ten-month-old son, who had finally started crawling. Since Destiny had mastered that months ago, I couldn't help feeling proud of her.

"His three sisters dote on him," Russo said, with a note of disapproval. "He only needs to open his mouth and they all come running."

I hoped his wife was all right. During our last encounter,

I'd learned his wedding ring contained an imprint of him hitting a woman, but he was married for a second time, and I didn't know if the imprint was of the woman he was married to now.

"They all live with you?" I ventured. "Your daughters?"

He tilted his head back, regarding me with one arched brow. "Yes. My first wife is gone. We had two daughters together. The other daughter and my son are from my second marriage."

Gone? I wondered if she'd met an untimely accident. Maybe I didn't want to know.

"Looks like the second time was the charm," I said. "I mean, you got your son." I'd finished my pot pie, my smoothie, and half the club already. If Russo was surprised at the amount of food I ingested, he didn't mention it. Only an occasional smile at the edges of Jake's mouth showed that he'd noticed, but he was well-accustomed to my eating habits.

My headache was feeling slightly better, and I wanted to see if I could read an imprint, but my stomach clenched at the idea. I told myself that was because of what I might accidentally find, not because I might have lost my gift forever.

"So," Russo said, when I paused between club halves. "I bet you're wondering why I'm here."

"You want me to read an imprint." I was pleased to find my words sounded remarkably calm, given that I'd been dreading this day for the past ten months. Now my dread had multiplied because seeing Russo again made me sure he'd never believe me if I told him the truth about losing my ability. If I didn't stall or figure out some other way to resolve his request, whatever it turned out to be, he'd make me pay.

Russo pushed his plate forward and tented his hands on the table. "I hope you'll be able to help me. It shouldn't take long."

"You remember the stipulation?"

"Yes." His mouth pursed momentarily. "I can assure you no one will be harmed from the knowledge you give me. I am doing business with some longtime acquaintances, and I want to be sure they don't plan to double-cross me. I also want to know if they have secret intentions that will affect my company negatively. If I find that to be the case, I will simply refuse to do business with them."

Relief washed over me, and Russo didn't miss the change in my expression. He laughed, "Really, Miss Rain, I'm not in the habit of knocking people off—if I can help it."

It was the "if I can help it" part that bothered me. I had to tread very carefully here, because all too easily I could be the one knocked off. Or I could find myself in a lush prison, faking imprint-reading for the rest of my short life. Worse, one of my friends or Tawnia might play a part in his revenge.

Chapter 4

I glanced at Peirce, who was eyeing the two men at the counter, and then shifted my gaze to Jake, whose face showed no expression. Only in the clenching of his jaw could I see that he was worried about what would happen when I told Russo I couldn't help him.

I had no intention of doing that. In fact, as I ate, an idea formed in my head. If I could learn enough about the object Russo wanted read and exactly what he expected to be on it, I might be able to give him what he wanted to know without actually reading an imprint. I was sure Shannon and Paige would help me track down the particulars. Even if it turned out that I was wrong, Russo couldn't hold me accountable for an imprint that was, after all, a momentary impression of a single person's experience, filtered only through their eyes. They may or may not know the entire truth, but a slight portion. I wasn't sure how I could make Russo understand that, though, without reading a few of his own objects, and I couldn't do that if my talent didn't reassert itself. The only object I remembered reading of his from our last encounter was his wedding ring.

"Well?" Russo said.

By the sudden pressure of Jake's hand on my knee under the table, I assumed Russo had repeated himself.

"What is it exactly that you want me to read?" I asked.

"A document. A rather lengthy one, and the pens they were written with." He smiled. "My future business partners may think I'm a little eccentric, but I insisted we handwrite a portion of the contract we intend to sign, more particularly what each person expects to obtain from the arrangement."

I had to admit, obtaining a relevant imprint that way was a lot more likely to work than sneaking into their offices and stealing a few personal objects. The contract had to be important, and by writing out certain details, the authors would have considered their words carefully. Unless they completely controlled their feelings and thoughts, which they had no reason to do, their anxiety and intentions should be clearly imprinted on the documents and the pens they'd used.

"When were these made?"

Russo smiled. "Aren't you supposed to tell me?"

I gave an impatient shrug. "Was it last year? Five months ago? You said they were longtime acquaintances. I'm trying to get an idea of how long this has all been in the works. If it's been too long, whatever I discover may be outdated. And our agreement was only *one* reading." I smiled, though my eyes challenged his. "I wouldn't want you to waste it."

A spark of anger in his eyes warned me that I was treading dangerous waters. He'd told me once that if it hadn't been for my apparent involvement with a police detective, he would simply force me to work for him. That was even before Shannon and I were an "us," so I had to give Russo some credit for being observant.

"The agreement was begun last week," Russo said finally. "That's when we signed the initial intent, and also when I let them know about the handwritten part. We finished the actual signing a few days ago. Before this, any involvement between me and this company occurred only when it was absolutely necessary. Frankly, I don't trust them, and I know they don't trust me."

"If they aren't on the level, you intend to make them pay?" I was pushing, but I had to be sure.

"Yes. However, it will simply be with breaking off the contract. There are several clauses that give me a way out depending on what you find. They have a lot to lose if I pull out. If it makes a difference, I believe your involvement will save lives on both sides."

Was he sincere? I didn't know, but I'd have to find out before I told him anything. I couldn't have a blood bath on my conscience. I already had enough baggage with all the negative memories I'd read over the past months. I tried to relegate them to a deep corner of my mind, but they would always be a part of me, and I had to live with that.

"Do you have the contract here?" I asked.

"It's secured at my hotel. I hope you will go with me to a conference room I have arranged there." Russo hesitated before adding, "Your friends may accompany you."

I wasn't surprised he didn't have the document on him, and I certainly hadn't expected that he'd allow me to take it home and study the pages. I guessed a blindfold was somewhere in his plans, thus the reason for the private conference room.

I swallowed, my throat feeling abruptly dry. "Okay, I'll help you."

At my side, Jake stiffened.

"First," I continued without looking at Jake, "there's

another small matter I will need resolved to my satisfaction." I picked up my water glass and drained the last of the ice that had melted since I'd finished the rest of the liquid. I didn't blame Kristy for not refilling it; every time she came over, Russo ignored her and Charlie glared.

As I set down my glass, Russo looked at Charlie, who jumped to his feet and called out in the now-crowded restaurant. "Waitress! We need water here."

Okay, I guess I'd get more water.

Kristy hurried over and refilled everything in sight. Jake and Peirce reached for their water at the same moment I did. I let my hand slip down the cool glass instead of lifting it.

"What is this other matter?" Russo asked.

"Does anyone know you planned to come see me?"

His brow furrowed. "Just a few people in my organization."

"Are you sure?"

"Yes, of course. Why?" He sounded offended.

I tried not to clench my hands, now folded on my lap. "Because a few hours ago, someone tried to abduct me, and when that failed, they tried to kill me by blowing up the van I was inside of."

Next to me, there was a swift intake of breath. Jake's. I spared a glance to see that his eyes had widened and his anger was closer to the surface. I hoped he wouldn't share these details with Tawnia.

I refocused on Russo, who stared at me as if I'd begun speaking a language he didn't understand. I continued, "If doing this job for you entails that sort of danger, I don't want any part of it. Either you have a leak, or someone in your organization doesn't want me near your contract. Before I risk giving you what you need, I have to be assured of my safety."

I'd meant this only as a stalling tactic, but Peirce was nodding as if it made sense. That got me thinking maybe I hadn't been targeted for stumbling on the rug and its evidence. Maybe the case of the geriatric murders and the attempted kidnapping weren't connected.

Except by me.

I gripped the edge of the table. Dread crawled across my shoulders and down my spine, and another bout of dizziness followed on its heels. Jake touched my elbow, and I appreciated his effort, but what I really wanted was Shannon. I felt safe with him, and I guess when it came right down to it, a girl wanted to feel safe with the man she loved. She wanted to know he had her back. Jake would do anything for me—I knew that—but in the middle of a firefight with organized crime, he didn't have what it takes.

At one time that hadn't make a difference, but with my talent ruling my life, I found danger more often than I cared to admit. Or it found me.

Maybe that would change again if my talent didn't return. I couldn't help but wonder if losing the ability would affect how Shannon felt about me. I'd become the person I was now in large part because of the experiences my ability had thrown my way. Would I become yet another person without it?

"How fortunate you didn't come to harm," Russo said, arching a thick, dark brow. "What did these people look like?"

"I can't identify them, but there were two men. Could be anyone." *Even yours,* was my implication.

Russo frowned and exchanged a glance with Charlie, who waited expectantly. That Russo didn't immediately proclaim that his organization was in no way responsible in this morning's events worried me. It might mean he was having problems, or suspected someone, and I could think of nothing less safe than getting in the way of a power struggle between two organized crime factions. At last, Russo gave a slight nod, and Charlie rose and headed for the door. The two men at the counter stared after him but didn't follow.

"I will get back to you about this," Russo said, relaxing in his chair. "It will be resolved to your satisfaction, and then you will help."

It wasn't a question, but I treated it as such. "Sure." I decided to take a drink of water after all. Two gulps went down easily, but I nearly choked on the third when Russo pulled out his phone.

"What number can I reach you at?"

I froze, not exactly sure I wanted a crime boss to have my cell phone number.

"Why do you need that?" Jake growled beside me. Next to him, Peirce's eyes grew wide.

Russo gave a shake of his head. "How else am I supposed to contact her? I almost missed her today, and I doubt you want me hanging out in your herb shop waiting. Even if I had the time to spare." Waste, he meant.

If Russo wanted my phone number, I had no doubt he could find other means to obtain it. So to Jake's obvious disapproval, I rattled off my number. Then Russo gave me his.

"This is my direct line," he said. "Please contact me if you discover any more about these people."

Yeah, right, I thought with a mental roll of my eyes. *You'll be the first one I call.* Not with every bit of his charisma working overtime. What was next? Would he want to become Facebook friends? Not that I was ever on the computer long enough to check out the page Tawnia had put up for me.

Russo signaled for his check, and I felt a stab of satisfaction that he was paying instead of me. But we weren't finished yet.

I scooted to the edge of my seat. "Before I go, I'd like to know exactly who I'm dealing with—besides you, of course. Who is the other party to this contract?"

Russo's blue eyes narrowed. "Why is that necessary? I would prefer if you didn't come into the reading with preconceived notions."

"Whatever I learn isn't going to change an imprint. And if your business partners have a connection with this morning's incident, the more I know, the better I can defend myself."

He met my stare, the muscles along his jaw tightening across his broad face. I lifted my chin slightly to remind him I wasn't one of his lackeys to be cowed into obedience.

"Okay," he said finally. "I'll give you a name. In fact, I can even show you a picture." Pulling out his phone again, he swiped at the screen.

I felt an urge to take it from him and skim through his pictures. Did he have one of his baby son? His daughters? A part of me also wanted to see if my talent had returned, but it was probably better not to experiment reading imprints around him. Who knew what dark secrets his phone might hold?

He extended the phone to me, but kept it far enough away that I couldn't easily touch it. Smart man. I rested my hands in my lap and focused on the woman in the picture.

No, it can't be. Surely my eyes were playing tricks. I blinked to clear my vision.

"Name's JoAnna Hamilton," Russo said. "She's the head of Innovation Software."

My mouth felt dry again. It looked like a surveillance photo, and the subject didn't appear to be aware she was being watched. Her gray-flecked hair was pulled up in an elegant twist. She wore tasteful jewelry, tall high heels, and an expensive suit.

Not only did I recognize the woman, but I'd talked with her. She'd been in the attic with me at the estate sale, the one who'd purchased the rocker.

She was also in Tawnia's drawing.

Any remaining thought that my abduction hadn't been planned vanished. Exactly like my ability to read imprints.

Chapter 5

I should have known the old woman didn't belong at that estate sale. Who rummaged through other people's stuff dressed in a tailored suit that likely had a brand name I couldn't even afford to say? She had seemed at home, and that confidence should have alerted me to something wrong even more than the suit. Normal old ladies were retired by her age, and they didn't act like they owned everything and everyone around them. They didn't speak with such authority that strangers followed their mere suggestion.

What was she doing at that sale?

Probably following me after learning about Russo's intentions regarding their contract. But Shannon usually noticed those kinds of things, and he hadn't mentioned anyone following us. Then again, in the past he'd tried to protect me by not mentioning that we were being followed, and if they were professionals, even he might not have noticed. We weren't expecting a case with mob connections.

"I take it you know JoAnna?" Russo's voice shook me from my thoughts.

"I met her this morning at an estate sale—just before I was abducted." No use trying to hide it since my face would have already verified his assumption.

Russo's face darkened. "I see."

"I'll be in touch." I stood abruptly.

He arose also, inclining his head as though giving permission. This time he didn't offer his hand, and I was glad.

I left the restaurant flanked by Jake and Peirce, feeling Russo's eyes and those of his goons following me. We waited for a break in traffic and crossed the street, where Officer Delaney joined us.

"You gave him your phone number?" Jake said as we entered my shop. "Did you really have to do that?"

I was surprised he'd waited so long to bring up the subject. "What else could I have done? Besides, maybe I'll need a favor from him someday."

"No way. Not worth it."

I couldn't imagine it ever happening, either, but in my line of work, it might not be all that bad to have a mobster on speed dial.

My line of work. I reached out to touch one of the toy horses on display. I knew it contained an imprint of a little girl receiving the horse from her grandmother, followed by fading imprints of the grandmother playing with it as a child and receiving the toy from her own grandmother. After those, there were only feelings of satisfaction that I imagined must have come from the original owner. Together, the imprints told a story of love, of family, of continuity.

At this moment, however, it was simply a nice antique horse.

I choked back a sob, biting my lip hard so the tears wouldn't fall. My head pounded and I fought another bout of dizziness.

"What's this I'm hearing?" Tawnia emerged from behind one of the new shelves I'd installed last month to hold crockery, a dust rag in hand. Destiny was in a front-facing carrier strapped to her chest, and the baby held one of my antique toy soldiers. "You gave that monster your phone number?"

Withdrawing from the toy horse, I shoved my hand in my pocket before she could see I was shaking. Or maybe my hand wasn't shaking. Maybe that was the dizziness.

"He'll need to reach me. I can always change it." I smiled at the baby. "Hi, sweetie, did you miss me?" Destiny held out her arms, begging for me to rescue her. I loved that baby.

Tawnia ignored her daughter's efforts to escape the carrier. "Look, I made an appointment at my doctor's for you. He didn't have any openings, but the nurse will look at your ears."

"I can't afford it."

"You're going anyway. I'll pay." Her eyes narrowed as she dared me to contradict her.

Before I could respond, a tinkling of the electronic bell above my doorway signaled a customer. No, not a customer, but Shannon and Paige.

My stomach flip-flopped to see Shannon. He strode purposefully across the room with sure, compact movements. Funny how just seeing him could still do that to me.

I glanced at Peirce, but he shook his head.

"I called him," Tawnia said.

"I was coming anyway." Shannon slipped an arm around me. "No one there saw anything useful."

Jake didn't seem outwardly bothered by Shannon's show of affection, though I wished he would return to his own store. But maybe he figured he wasn't needed there since Tawnia was in my shop cleaning instead of helping at his register as she often did during rushes.

"How are you feeling?" Shannon added.

"That depends on whether or not you brought my antiques." Saying it helped keep me from weeping at the loss of my ability. Why had I never realized how much was hidden from the ordinary person? They had no clue—*I'd* had no clue. Until it was gone.

Paige laughed. "I told you she'd say that, didn't I?" She brought out my blue grocery bag from behind her back, obviously empty. "Well, someone had taken the music box from your bag, so that's gone, but even though a woman tried to get someone to sell them to her, we got the two larger pieces. They're in the truck, and we actually got them at a discount after what happened."

"My partner might have implied that they were evidence." Shannon shook his head.

If I had anything close to a best friend after my sister Tawnia and Jake, Paige was it. "Thanks," I said, taking the bag. The loss of the music box hurt, but right now it would only serve as a reminder that I couldn't read imprints.

"So what did Russo want?" Shannon asked, telling me that Tawnia had filled him in on that score.

I detailed the lunch and our conversation, with Jake and Peirce inserting comments every so often. I didn't mention to Shannon that I couldn't read imprints, and no one else did either, though Tawnia kept nodding her head significantly at him each time I looked her way.

"I find it very interesting that this JoAnna Hamilton was at the estate sale," Paige said, whipping out her phone. "I'll get someone working on that angle right away. We need to talk to her as soon as possible."

"She has to be responsible," Tawnia agreed. "I bet she's heard about Autumn and knows she'll be exposed when Autumn reads the contract."

Shannon frowned. "It could just as well be someone in Russo's organization. They'd be much more likely to know about Autumn's ability, and those people always have a lot to hide. If Russo had everyone involved in the contract handwrite a portion of it—including his own people—maybe it's not the competition he's actually testing."

"But Hamilton obviously followed Autumn," Paige countered. "That can't be a coincidence."

My sister's anxiety was growing with each point of discussion. Finally, she interrupted. "That's all fine and good, but you know what? Autumn has to go see the nurse about her ears. Her appointment is in fifteen minutes. And someone will need to take her."

"My ears are fine." I was still dizzy and nauseated, and my headache had returned in force, but I could hear well enough.

Tawnia glared. "She might find something."

"I think you should go," Shannon said. "I'll take you." He glanced at Paige, who nodded in agreement.

"I'll head over to the next estate sale while you drive her there," Paige said. "Peirce and Delaney can drop me off at the station for my car. We can meet up after."

"I'll get the department to pay since you were hurt on the job." Shannon's gaze shifted back to my sister. "Can you text me the address of the doctor's office?"

I knew they weren't going to let up, and besides, I did want to know if there might be a physical reason for my inability to read imprints. A reason besides being wrapped up in a rug with a horrifying memory—and nearly burning to death.

I handed Destiny the blue grocery bag, and she grinned as if I'd given her the most fascinating toy of the century. She loved magazines, too, but we had to be vigilant about her ripping off and swallowing tiny pieces.

"Jake?" came a soft voice from the other side of the room.

We all looked toward the adjoining doors of the Herb Shoppe to see Jazzy Storm waving at Jake. The teenager still had the blue hair she'd sported when we first met, but the attorney she now lived with had nixed the nose ring and bought her clothes that covered a bit more of her body. "A customer has a question about a new line of herbs. Thera sent me to get you. We're kind of busy."

"Sure, thanks." With a worried look at me, Jake hurried off.

"Well, let's go." Shannon's hand pressed against the small of my back.

We were nearly to the door when Jazzy, who was still hovering near the doorway, came scooting over, her face drawn. "Uh, Autumn, before you go, could I talk to you for a minute?"

I glanced toward the Herb Shoppe and saw that while they were busy, the line at the register wasn't as long as she'd implied. "Sure."

"She has to go to the doctor right now," Tawnia put in.

I shrugged. "I have at least a minute."

"I promise it won't take long." Jazzy glanced at my sister and then at the police officers. "But could I talk to you alone?"

What had the girl done now? The last time she'd pulled me aside, she'd been caught shoplifting CDs from the shop next door, and the owner had given her two days to pay for the music before he pressed charges.

"Let's go outside," I said, ignoring the others, who were exchanging pointed glances. To Shannon, I added, "I'll meet you at the truck."

"I guess we might as well unload your stuff then." Shannon held up a hand to prevent Tawnia's protest. "It'll only take a few minutes. I promise, I'll get her to your doctor's on time." He motioned to his partner and the other officers.

Outside, the sun felt bright and clean and full after the emptiness of my suddenly imprint-free shop. The heat spread from my bare feet to my entire body. I waited until we put a few yards of sidewalk behind us.

"Okay, what's up?"

"I know what you're thinking," Jazzy said, "but it's not me. It's Claire."

This took me by surprise and my step faltered. "What's going on?" Claire Philpot, the attorney who fostered Jazzy, was a poised, wealthy, accomplished woman, who seemed very much in control of her life.

"She's sad." Jazzy scrunched a brow that was in desperate need of plucking, though it was hard to tell under the thick layer of makeup. "I mean, she tries not to show it and all, but I can tell. It's something about her husband. I hear her crying sometimes. And I overheard her defending herself and her husband on at least two phone calls."

Claire's husband had also been an attorney, but he'd died years ago of a heart attack. He'd been posthumously accused of misusing a client's funds. Claire maintained his innocence, but the details of what really happened had never been uncovered. Paige told me once that Claire had looked into the matter at the time of her husband's death, but she'd found no evidence to exonerate him.

"I think it involves a lawsuit." Jazzy looked up at me, her blue eyes earnest. "Can you help her?"

"Maybe she doesn't want my help. I am, after all, a little . . . uh, strange. If she wants my help, she knows where I work. I do owe her a favor." Claire had helped me out on the same case that had introduced me to Russo. I actually owed her two favors now, the second for taking in Jazzy, though I wouldn't admit as much to the girl.

"She won't ask for help," Jazzy protested. "She thinks she can do everything alone, and she doesn't like to air her business."

"Exactly my point." I rubbed the pounding in my right temple. Behind us, Shannon and Peirce entered my shop, hefting the rolltop desk, while Paige and Delaney carried the mirror.

I stopped walking, not wanting to add any more steps that I'd have to retrace to Shannon's truck later. "Claire's a bright woman and a great attorney. If she really needs me, she'll make the decision to ask for help."

Jazzy's words rushed on. "I think if you talked to her, she'd ask a lot sooner. I've told her tons about you and what you do. At first she didn't believe, but she already liked you from the other times you've met, and you have a way of getting people to talk to you. You know, like I talked to you about my mother and my grandfather . . . the drinking . . . and what they did to me. Why I ran away."

"Okay, I'll make it a point to talk to Claire." Not that I could help with my ability gone, but it wasn't like the tough, self-centered Jazzy to be so concerned—and that meant something probably was going on with her benefactor.

The tenseness in Jazzy's face relaxed. "Thanks so much." She glanced behind us at the door to the Herb Shoppe. "Well, I'd better get back inside. See you later."

A slow whistle drew my attention. "Want a ride?" Shannon and his blue truck had pulled up in the street next to the car parked between us at the curb. Traffic diverted around him, some honking their horns.

I waved him forward to an empty parking space. "That was fast," I said, opening the door and climbing inside.

"Your sister is kind of insistent."

"She doesn't like being late for anything. I don't see what the big deal is since they'll make us wait fifteen minutes once we get there anyway."

Shannon laughed. "It's because of people like you that they schedule patients early."

"The old chicken or the egg argument. Which came first? Who cares? Anyway, I don't even want to go to the doctor. Or the nurse." There was a note in my voice that said I was lying, but Shannon didn't call me on it. Neither did he pull out into traffic.

He took my hand in his warm one, the slight roughness of his skin sending a shiver of awareness through my veins. "What's going on?"

"What do you mean?"

"I mean what's going on with you? There's something, isn't there?"

Once, I would have scoffed and told him to mind his own business, but I couldn't exactly do that now that we were dating. Except I didn't want Shannon to know about the imprints just yet. I didn't want him to exclude me from the job or to coddle me. Keeping it from him was silly, given that Peirce Elvey would likely mention it at some point, but I would do it anyway. For now. At the same time, his knowing there was something wrong, despite all the time we'd been separated in the past five months, meant that our relationship was as strong as ever.

I moved into his arms. "Nothing this won't solve." I wasn't good at prevarication, but I was good at distraction. I kissed him, and he lost no time in kissing me back. Even the fact that I'd been blinded, that I wasn't all there, didn't seem to matter for that moment. His arms tightened around me and our kiss deepened. It was the kind of kiss women dream about. The kind that reaches to the tips of your fingers and toes. That sends fire licking down your skin and makes you understand why people get married and stay married. That feeling didn't come along with just anyone.

A banging on the half-open truck window startled both of us. We looked over to see Tawnia, with Destiny still hanging in her carrier. "You've got only seven minutes now. Can't you do that later?"

Chuckling, Shannon put the truck into gear. I waved at Destiny as we drove away.

We were late enough to the appointment that we only had to wait five minutes before the nurse saw us. "So what happened?" she asked. To her credit, she barely glanced at my bare feet.

"I was near some gunshots without earplugs," I said. That much was true, and she didn't need to know the rest. If I told her about the explosion, she'd likely send me to the hospital to check for a concussion, since the doctor was booked. No way could I afford that.

"Do your ears feel full? Is there a ringing sound?"

"No. Well, maybe a little ringing. Mostly I'm dizzy and nauseated. Less now than before. I ate something so maybe that helped."

"What about a headache?"

I nodded.

"But you hear just fine?"

"Yes."

"Any other symptoms?"

"No." I couldn't exactly tell her that I could no longer read imprints.

She typed a few details on a small computer and then began examining my ears. "Does this hurt?" she asked several times. Each time I said no.

Eventually, she sat down and looked at me. "I can't find anything wrong with your ears, or indication of another problem. I'm not sure why you have a headache or the nausea. It may be that you need rest, but it could be totally unrelated to the noise. My recommendation is that you see your doctor. Maybe even an ear, nose, and throat specialist, especially if your ear begins to feel full or congested. When there's no sign of ear damage or infection, sometimes that can indicate something more serious. Without further examination and tests, which I'm not qualified to do, I can only tell you that your eardrums are not broken and there appears to be no reason for the symptoms you're experiencing. However, it may be that your body is reacting to some trauma, and in a couple of days it'll clear up on its own." She repeated her recommendation to make an appointment with the doctor on my way out, and also gave us a list of warning signs that should send me to the emergency room.

I didn't make an appointment.

"That was a waste of time," I said as we headed for the truck.

"Well, you do have symptoms." Shannon opened the door for me.

"I was in an explosion, so a headache is natural. Like everyone keeps saying, I probably just need to rest." I had no idea about the nausea, which had come back in full force after leaving the examination room. As Shannon shut the door, I laid my head against the seat. I didn't typically take over-the-counter headache medicines, preferring more natural means, but I was probably going to cave in. My sister would be proud.

Shannon drove me back to my shop, and I didn't protest. Though I wanted to go with him to the second estate sale, I was far more interested in learning more about JoAnna Hamilton. I knew Paige wouldn't be able to pass along any information about her soon, so that left the Internet. Besides, if I went with Shannon, I might lose my lunch. In fact, if I moved too much at all, I might lose it.

"Peirce is going to be outside your shop," he said as he pulled up to the curb. "With Russo and that Hamilton lady mixed up in this, we can't risk someone taking a second stab at you."

"Aw, don't make him stay out there. It's hot out."

"It's only May. He'll be fine."

"You're going to cost me my one friend on the force."

"I thought you and Paige were tight."

I rolled my eyes. "You know what I mean."

He caught my hand. "I'll come back when I'm off work. We have a dinner date, remember?"

"Call me first. I'd better see how I feel." There were two of him now.

He snorted. "Take something for that headache, would you? Do you need me to walk you in?"

"No. Definitely not." To prove it to him, I jumped out of the truck. I held my posture straight until he drove away.

It was then I noticed the police car parked across the wide street outside Smokey's, and several cars down from that sat a black BMW that sported a few noticeable dings. I'd seen the car before, and I was pretty sure I recognized the scrawny blond figure hunched over the wheel: Ace, a former police officer turned private detective, a man Russo had hired in the past. I was glad Shannon hadn't seen him because the two men didn't get along. Ace, whose last name I'd never learned, hadn't been around much since almost dying in our last encounter with Russo. I'd even wondered if he'd left the business. Apparently not.

And apparently Russo wasn't the trusting sort.

I wondered if the old lady had a representative out there somewhere as well, and what that person might be willing to do to follow orders.

Sighing, I walked into my store. Limped, really, though it wasn't my leg or foot that hurt so much as my entire body. Inside Autumn's Antiques, I still felt no buzzing of imprints. Only a ringing in my ears that I couldn't completely attribute to the electronic bell above my door.

"Good, you're back," Tawnia said. "How'd it go?" Destiny must be napping again in her crib because she was nowhere in sight as my sister rang up a solitary customer at the counter.

Before replying, I waited until the customer left with an antique lamp I'd found at an estate sale last week. "Ears check out fine."

"What did she say to do?"

"Rest."

Tawnia grimaced. "Sorry. No change with the imprints?"

I shrugged.

"You should go see Cody. I mean, since he can also read imprints. Maybe this has happened to him before."

"I was thinking about calling him." Our biological father lived nearly an hour away in Hayesville, so a phone call would be faster than a visit. "But I want to look up something on the Internet first."

Tawnia nodded. "It's about that old woman, isn't it? Well, I already pulled up everything I could find on her. I left the tabs open." She gestured to the computer. "I'm sorry to say that I need to take off now. Randa's here, helping Jake, and she and Thera can keep an eye on things here. You could even go home to rest. In fact, if you go right now, I'll give you a lift. Better yet, why don't you come home with me? I only have to stop at work for a few minutes to check in with my creative director. After, I'll make you a nice dinner."

Nice for Tawnia meant something frozen and plonked in the microwave. "Thanks, but I've got a date later with Shannon." I didn't plan on going anywhere near her house until after this case was solved. I didn't think she'd be in danger on this busy street, but I wouldn't chance anyone following me to her quiet subdivision and possibly mistaking her for me.

"You sure you're okay?"

"Yes. You go on home."

With a hug and a flurry of gathering up her laptop and baby things, Tawnia left the store with Destiny. I felt nothing as she left, and I desperately missed the disconnecting feeling that I normally experienced. Of the invisible cord between us stretching thin. A cord that appeared to no longer exist.

Before I could round the counter and look at the information Tawnia had uncovered on the computer, my door rang, and I turned, expecting to see a customer, or maybe even Claire Philpot here to pick up Jazzy. Instead, Kolonda Lewis stood in the doorway in all her elegant beauty.

I'd thought the day couldn't get worse, but I was wrong. I stood for a minute staring at my old rival, my face feeling tight and my tongue fat.

"Hi, Autumn," she said. "Is now a good time? I was in the neighborhood, and I thought I'd stop by. I have to admit I've been curious ever since you called."

That's right, she was here because I'd asked her to come, a call I should have made ten months ago. But I really didn't want to talk to her now.

Chapter 6

Kolonda Lewis was a college teacher who had been raised with all the privileges her wealthy widowed father could provide, and his legacy still supported her in her chosen profession. Ebony hair fell around her face in gentle waves, and her skin was the color of rich dark caramel, her eyes large and brown. As usual, she wore a clingy dress that advertised a healthy bank account and a figure most women envied.

Now was most certainly *not* a good time. I'd been rolled in a rug, caught in a bombing, and I had agreed to read imprints for a mobster. Not to mention that I'd lost my ability. I looked worse than Kolonda looked good.

Kolonda's gaze wandered the length of me, but she didn't comment on my appearance. Instead her eyes shifted to the double doors leading into Jake's shop, and I knew she was more curious about what he'd been up to the past ten months than whatever I might say. Lucky for her both things were connected.

I'd called her because I wanted Jake to be happy. I called her because he hadn't. Maybe he thought my feelings for Shannon were a passing thing, and I suppose he could be right, but I doubted it. Not when the world stopped rotating every time Shannon kissed me.

I'd never had trouble finding dates, and I'd had a few crushes before, but Jake had been the first one to fall for me. He was my first real boyfriend and still one of my best friends. It was hard to give him up even though I'd found someone else, but I knew that for either of us to go on with our lives, he had to let me go. That meant I couldn't allow him to have hope. He needed to move on.

He'd loved Kolonda once, and I knew he still harbored special memories of the time they'd had together. Years ago, she'd ended their relationship by her father's command because he said Jake wasn't good enough, and she'd loved and respected her father when he was alive the way most children didn't these days. Her heart had been broken, though, and she'd regretted her decision all these years.

Of course, things might have changed in the ten months since we'd last met. For all I knew, she might be engaged and head over heels in love with some new teacher at her school.

I glanced around to make sure we were alone. "It's about Jake. I wanted you to know . . . well, I'm dating someone else now. Jake and I aren't together."

"Oh." She caught her bottom lip in her teeth, white against the darkness of her skin.

I could have told her on the phone, but I'd meant to chat her up first, maybe touch something of hers to verify that she still had feelings for Jake. With my ability MIA, that was out of the question now.

Kolonda glanced again to the adjoining doors. There was

something more in her delicate face now: hope. I hadn't been wrong. I should have called months ago.

It was still hard to let go. Right now I had Shannon, but in a very real way I still had Jake, watching me from the sidelines, ready to step in and mend any possible broken heart. Always ready to catch me if I fell.

Okay, maybe I called Kolonda as much for me as for him. Until this moment, I thought I was being unselfish, but now I knew the truth. I didn't even have to learn it from an imprint. If Jake didn't go on without me, I wasn't sure I could let him go entirely.

"It's his busy time now," I said, "but he's free tonight. Isn't there some college lecture or concert you can invite him to?"

She reached out and touched my arm. "Thank you for calling me. I really appreciate it."

"You're welcome." I hoped she could look beyond our last encounter when she'd clung to Jake but he'd chosen me instead. Strangely, that same day had marked the beginning of my relationship with Shannon.

It was also the day I'd made my questionable deal with Russo.

I turned from Kolonda, not wanting to share the emotion I couldn't hide. I'd done the right thing, and now I had to get back to work and find out who was trying to kill me—or at the very least kidnap me. It made sense that JoAsnna Hamilton had a hand in my abduction this morning, given her proximity and Russo's request, but that didn't mean it was true.

I went behind the counter and sank onto a stool, my muscles protesting at the effort. I'd sustained bruises, that was for sure, but I wouldn't know how bad they were until I had time to examine myself thoroughly. I pressed a key to bring the sleeping computer to life.

"Uh." Kolonda still hesitated in front of my counter. "What if he . . . what if he says no?"

She was fearful after the last time, which I could well understand. Jake wasn't one to wear his emotions out in the open, and it had taken us a long time to go from friendship to something more. I thought for a moment. "You still own those apartments, don't you? The ones you asked his help with the last time? Isn't there something you could ask his opinion on?" Jake had once worked construction and he'd have contacts who could help. He loved to play the hero. Come to think of it, maybe that's why he was still holding onto hope about me.

"I do have mold growing in one of the bathrooms. I hired a guy who said he'd have to demolish the whole room, but that seems rather severe."

"There you go then. Ask him about that, and see what happens. You'll know if the spark is still there."

I clicked a tab on the computer. Only when I was sure she was leaving did I let my eyes follow her a bit wistfully before I settled down to work.

JoAnna Hamilton, recently turned seventy-six, was harked as a self-made billionaire who built up a software business out of nothing. Deeper examination revealed that in her early years Hamilton had received support from a nameless donor—probably her father, who'd apparently abandoned the family when JoAnna was a baby. Of JoAnna's half brother, Ralph Shatlock, ten years her junior, there was little information, except that he'd taught science at two eastern universities and had received several grants to research nanotechnology. All mention of him dropped off the Internet about three years ago, but I couldn't find an obituary, so maybe he'd opted for a private company or early retirement.

Maybe he worked for his sister.

Hamilton's company, Innovation Software, had a half-dozen subsidiaries, the most prominent being HealthTech, which made software for medical schools, doctors, and pharmacies. Another subsidiary, VisionGames, created a line of surprisingly successful video games. While the companies had raked in the cash in previous years, rumor now had it that Innovation Software had fallen on bad times, barely repulsing a hostile takeover last year when their stock had plummeted. I wondered if Russo had anything to do with either their downfall or their survival. The bottom line was that, even at a reduced price, the company was worth millions.

In her personal life, JoAnna had been less successful, plagued by a series of quick marriages and equally quick divorces. Unfortunately for her former spouses, her prenuptial agreements held up in court and her fortune remained safe. No children emerged from her unions, and her heir apparent was Winston Drewmore, the grandson of her cousin Marribel Hamilton, all of whom lived together in a twenty thousand-square-foot lakefront mansion with an indoor pool and tennis court. A picture of the house in Lake Oswego filled a sizeable corner of the screen.

No mention of organized crime, Nicholas Russo, or In Loving Memory. I hoped Paige had better luck at finding something useful. Of course, being a police detective, she had a lot more information at her fingertips than I did.

I had no idea how much time I'd spent staring at the computer screen, but my headache was considerably worse, making it difficult to concentrate. *I have to do something,* I thought. I couldn't just sit around waiting for my talent to kick in—if it ever did.

Shannon wouldn't want me to go anywhere. He'd want me buttoned up safe inside my store, protected from any further attack, and with Peirce playing watchdog, I wasn't likely to make it far without him calling reinforcements. I loved Shannon, but I wouldn't live my life in fear.

Well, maybe I would cave into fear just for today.

Swallowing the sudden lump in my throat, I rifled through the drawer under the counter, coming up with a long-expired bottle of pain pills. Downing two without water, I reached for my phone, pressing the icon of Cody Beckett's face.

He answered after only two rings, which told me he'd taken to carrying his new phone around as he worked on the oversized statues he carved in one of his fields. Some of his projects took more than a year to complete and went for a steep enough price to keep his agent happy.

Tawnia had suggested the phone, after trying a week to contact him so she could take Bret and the baby to Hayesville to meet him. I suspected Tawnia and I were Cody's only contacts.

"Hi," he said, sounding out of breath. "What's up?"

"Did I get you at a bad time?"

"Nope, just working. But I need to get down and find a drink anyhow. And it's probably lunch time." Rustling came from his end, crackling almost like static.

"Hours past lunch, actually." I imagined him climbing down the tall stacks of straw that helped him reach his latest carving—a boat bursting from a huge log. He was at the point of adding color to the carving, or so Tawnia told me, but I couldn't remember exactly what she'd said about his process.

"So what's up?"

"I have a problem." No use pretending I'd called for any other reason. Though I'd forgiven him for what he'd done to my biological mother, we didn't have anything near a normal father-daughter relationship, and probably never would, despite Tawnia's determination to invite him to every family gathering. My father was Winter, the man who'd adopted me. Cody understood that, and we were both fine with letting each other live life any way we saw fit. That meant not a lot of forced talk or meetings, connecting only when the mood hit, as it sometimes did, often late at night.

"What is it?"

I could hear nothing but silence on the other end now—no rustling or uneven breathing. "Did you ever lose your ability to read imprints?"

He didn't answer right away. My heart began pounding as loudly as my head.

"How'd it happen?" he said finally.

"I'm not sure. I got stuck in an imprint loop, and then there was an explosion nearby. Not a big deal."

He chuckled without mirth. "Is that the version you told your sister?"

"Okay, it was horrible. I kept waiting to see these feet, and I pulled this rug so the person would tumble down some stairs. I think it was a man's imprints, and that he murdered someone. I—I couldn't breathe." I was having a hard time breathing now, my panic rising at the memory.

"What about the explosion?"

There was nothing else to do but tell him the entire unvarnished story, so I did—the rug, the kidnapping, nearly smothering to death. "The police were following and shooting at them," I finished, "and they crashed and tried to dispose of the evidence by exploding the van. But I'm not sure if *evidence* refers to the van and the rug. Or also me inside the rug."

"But you're okay? Other than the imprints, I mean?"

"I'm fine."

He sighed. "No imprints." For the first time, envy laced his words. "Do you know how long I've wanted to get rid of this curse?"

No, but I could guess. "I thought I wanted that, too, but it's not like I thought. It's like . . ." How to explain?

"Like having an arm cut off. Like being blind. Like knowing something important is missing."

"So it *has* happened to you."

He hesitated. "When I took drugs, yes. But it was only temporary. That's why I did drugs so much when I was younger. I used to think anything was worth getting rid of it—until I learned it wasn't."

This was something new, something I hadn't known about him. Not the drugs, but the reason he'd used them after his mother had died in a sanitarium and left him an orphan. He'd tried to escape who he was. With no guidance or purpose in life, it wasn't hard to see how he'd spiraled downward. But he'd pulled himself out after the incident with my mother and claimed he'd been clean ever since. I believed him.

"How fast did it come back?" I asked.

"Right away. A few hours after I was sensible again."

Not a lot of help. "I'm sensible."

"Yeah, but to get rolled up in that rug, forced to repeat that imprint."

"I've been caught in a repeat before. I usually just pass out."

"Then maybe it's the combination of the imprint with the explosion. It's upset your system. Or put it to rights."

"Permanently?"

"I don't know." He felt sorry for me, I could tell by his tone, but the envy hadn't quite left, either. Maybe I *was* better off and I'd eventually come to terms with my loss and be happy for it. He'd experienced imprints for a lifetime longer than I had and could know better.

"What am I going to do?" I took a deep breath, letting it out slowly to push my panic back into a manageable lump in my chest.

"Well, there's this guy," Cody began. "Easton Godfrey. Lives up by you in Beaverton. When I get back to the house, I'll text you his number."

For some reason that struck me as amusing. "You're texting now? Really?"

"How else am I going to keep in contact with your sister without spending all my time yappin' on this phone? She's rather persistent. Anyway, you have to be really careful with this Godfrey. He ain't nice, and he doesn't care who he hurts, but he might be able to find you some answers. You can tell him I sent you, but don't give him any personal information, including your name, unless you want him hounding you for the rest of your life like he does me. Appears on my doorstep at least twice a year. Have to run him off with the shotgun."

"Who is he? How can he help?" Unless the man shared my talent, I failed to see how he could be of use.

"Didn't I say? Easton's one of them scientists." He spat the word like a curse.

A scientist. Since my ability had a scientific name, it followed that someone might be studying it. Had they found others like me? Could this man figure out what was wrong with me before Russo decided I was holding out on him and take revenge on my friends and family?

"Believe me," Cody went on, "he'll be more than happy to

give you a few tests. In fact, if he could, he'd lock you up in a room, plaster you with electrodes, and never let you go. Then I'd have to rescue you before he zaps you with too much electricity or whatever to make you tell him about Tawnia and the baby. He'd love to have a baby who might have our ability. You know, to train her from small. Don't worry, though. I got my gun and I could take him, even if that meant going back to jail, which is almost worse than anything."

I shook my head, stifling a groan. Even if I didn't know Cody was our biological father, his stories would alert me to his relationship with my twin. Their creative side didn't seem to know when to quit. But where Tawnia's exaggerations were usually amusing and had no basis in reality, Cody had already once come to my rescue with a gun in hand, so I didn't find his story in the least amusing. "I won't tell him anything about Destiny or Tawnia. I'll be careful."

If this man could help me, I'd be able to get rid of Russo. Maybe I could stop feeling like a vital chunk of me was missing.

"You wait a couple days before you call him," Cody said. "Your ability might come back on its own. If it doesn't, then you decide if you want to go see Easton. It ain't an exaggeration when I say he's dangerous. Oh, and you'd better tell that detective of yours where you're going so Easton will have to let you go."

A shiver went through me. "I get it already. Text me the number, and I'll think about it."

"Good." He paused before adding. "I'll be finished next week. Tell your sister, okay? She wanted to see the boat before my buyer picks it up."

"I'll mention it. But when you see her, don't tell her about the scientist. That's between us."

"Deal."

I said goodbye, hung up, and texted Tawnia about the boat, knowing that with everything going on, I'd probably forget about it later. If I weren't so embroiled in my own troubles, I'd want to check out Cody's boat carving myself. Last I'd seen, it was only partially finished and rose nearly two stories high. Tawnia texted right back, and I felt a distinct relief knowing that at least we still had the texting connection. *Go, modern technology.*

To my relief, the headache was easing. Tawnia would laugh herself silly if she knew I'd taken a non-herbal remedy.

I could do nothing more for the moment about my lost ability, and I refused to stay at the store and wallow in fear. JoAnna Hamilton was a good place to continue my investigation, not only because Russo thought her a person of interest, but because I didn't for a minute trust Russo's explanation of what he wanted me to do with his contract or what he planned to do with the information. Once, I would have trusted my gut, let myself get caught up in his charisma, but imprints had conditioned me to become a skeptic. People were rarely what they seemed at first glance.

Easing myself off the stool, I made my way to the door. I thought about letting Jake know I was leaving, but he'd probably want to go with me, and I didn't want his chivalry getting in the way of his reunion with Kolonda. Besides, with any luck, I'd be back before closing and he'd never know I'd been gone. If I didn't return in time, Thera would come over after the rush eased at the Herb Shoppe and close up for me. My work as a consultant for the Portland Police Bureau had conditioned the widow to be ready to pitch in at a moment's notice.

I would lock my outside door, though, and turn over the

sign alerting my customers to enter through Jake's, a courtesy we offered each other during slow times. It cut down on shop-lifting—not that I had much of a problem with that these days.

As I glanced behind me at my antiques shop, feeling a renewed loss at the absence of the buzzing that signaled imprints, I spied Jake and Kolonda through our connecting doors near his display of dry packaged herbs. They made a striking couple with their matching bronze skin and black hair, his muscles emphasizing her petiteness. He was smiling.

With a sigh, I strode out the door, ready to face JoAnna Hamilton.

Chapter 7

*T*oo late I remembered my watchers outside. If I managed to find Ms. Hamilton's house, I couldn't exactly bring the police to her doorstep and expect her to talk to me. But after what happened that morning, neither was I stupid enough to go alone.

I needed to remember to buy a wig with longer hair like Tawnia. Then maybe I could go around incognito. But that thought got me worrying about my sister. What if the people who jumped me this morning thought she was me and followed her when she left my shop? I shook off the thought as paranoia. We looked different enough, and she had all the baby equipment to further obscure any resemblance.

I ducked into the jazz music shop next door, fairly certain I hadn't been spotted by the officers since the doors were so close. Or if they had glimpsed me, they'd think I went back inside my own store. The owner of the jazz shop, a long-haired, baby-faced kid barely out of college, looked up from a group of equally young customers. "Hey, Autumn."

"Hey, Stu." That was usually the extent of our conversations, except for a notable time four months ago when he'd wept on my shoulder after his girlfriend had dumped him.

"I need to go out the back," I said. "That okay?"

"Sure, help yourself."

Unlike me, he had a door into an alley that let out on the opposite side of the block. I'd have to walk back around to my side of the block to enact my plan, but at least Peirce and Delaney wouldn't be watching for me that way.

The day was warm, but not overly so, and the walk did more to assert my sense of self than anything else that day. As I rounded the corner and crossed the street, now only a half block down from my shop but on the opposite side of the road, I threw a colorful silk scarf over my head. A gift from a local shaman, it was purple, mauve, and green. Beautiful and bright enough to hide me in plain sight in case Peirce glanced up the street instead of over at my shop.

I reached the BMW with the dings, opened the passenger door, and slipped inside.

Ace didn't show surprise that I'd climbed in his car, and his customary man-with-a-secret smile on his tanned, narrow face didn't falter. "Hello, Autumn. What's up?"

"You tell me. You're the one parked on my street. Who are you working for?"

"Just making sure nothing happens to you before you complete your business with my client."

"Russo."

Ace shrugged his scrawny shoulders. The former police officer turned private detective was still good at keeping his mouth shut. Maybe that was why Russo kept hiring him.

"Well, you're doing no good here, not with my buddies in blue hanging around." I gestured to the police car ahead of us, separated by several other parked cars.

Ace laughed. "Peirce and Delaney? That's not protection."

"I've seen Peirce shoot," I retorted, not bothering to hide my annoyance. "And I've never had to send someone into a burning building to rescue him. How are you feeling these days anyway? We were worried there for a while that you wouldn't make it." After we'd saved Ace from the warehouse, Shannon had said he was too ornery to die, and he'd been correct.

"That was different." But Ace had the decency to look away. "Anyway, I do what I'm told. It pays the bills. Especially the hospital bills."

I let the matter drop. "Russo thinks JoAnna Hamilton might have plans to double cross him. What do you think?"

"I don't know a thing about the woman, and until this week I hadn't talked to Russo in ten months." Bitterness laced his voice, though I could see no sign of it in his face.

I contemplated him for several long seconds. Was he telling the truth? I didn't know him well enough to say.

"Well, maybe we should pay Ms. Hamilton a visit." It was sad involving him in my plan, but any backup was better than none, and he at least could pose as a civilian in his T-shirt and jeans. I didn't know if he carried a weapon, since he'd never answered the question the last time I'd asked, but he had to know what he was doing, freelancing for a mob boss.

Ace shrugged. "If what you say is true, Russo will already be looking into her."

"So? You know I can find things no one else can." Or I could have before today.

His eyes narrowed, and the smile cranked down a notch. "Maybe if that weren't true, you wouldn't get into so much trouble."

"Maybe if you didn't work for a mobster, you wouldn't have almost died." I held up a hand as he opened his mouth. "I know, I know. You've got to pay the bills." I put on my safety belt. "Well, let's go."

"I can't go anywhere, I'm working."

"You have to follow me, right? There's no reason we can't go together."

He rolled his eyes. "Fine. Where to?"

"JoAnna Hamilton's."

He started the engine and pulled into traffic, doing a U-turn so we didn't have to pass the police car. He seemed slow about it though, and I followed the path of his eyes to a white van parked three stores up from my shop. The side windows were partially darkened, but two men were inside, and one glimpse at them told me they weren't casual shoppers.

Were those more of Russo's men? Or maybe JoAnna Hamilton's people? Or maybe they worked for In Loving Memory, the estate sales people, who could still be responsible for my abduction. Had they spotted me? I tucked my head as they looked our way and watched the side mirror as we passed. They didn't pull out behind us, though I could see Ace still checking them out in his mirror. We turned the corner and the tenseness in his body relaxed.

"Who were they?" I asked.

He smiled at me. "Who?"

"Those men in the white van."

He laughed. "You need a new job. I didn't see any men in a

white van, and if you did, it was probably an annoyed husband talking with his son while his wife went into some store."

Suddenly I wondered if I had seen what I'd expected instead of what was actually there. I wanted to grab his steering wheel to see if he'd imprinted on it, to see if he was telling the truth. As if that would do any good now. I fought down the gaping loss inside me and stared straight ahead.

"Then again," he drawled, "if you ever get bored working with the police, you can work for me."

"No thanks." Even if I could stand Ace, I would never do that to Shannon. A woman officer Shannon once dated had accepted a similar offer from Ace and had been shot and killed doing a job. Working privately might bring me more income than my consultant's wage, but working with Ace on a regular basis was never going to happen.

Lake Oswego was about twenty minutes south of Portland. If I'd been driving and I didn't get lost—which I typically did—I could have done it in fifteen. By contrast, Ace was so methodical in his driving that I wondered how he'd ever put the dings in his BMW. At least the ride was comfortable and dependable, which reminded me that my rusty red Toyota hatchback was still at my mechanic's for a long-overdue new muffler.

Many exclusive houses dotted Lake Oswego, and none of them were alike, except in their uniqueness. No tract housing here, especially right on the lake. But what surprised me was that despite his claim not to know much about what was going on, Ace knew exactly where JoAnna Hamilton lived. Without asking for directions, he steered the car up the drive to the house and into a circular rotunda, which featured a large water fountain. The steeply gabled house, covered with rock in different shades of gray, seemed to go on and on. The homeowner association fees alone were probably more than the mortgage I paid on Autumn's Antiques, though admittedly I'd owned my store before housing boomed and then crashed.

I'd been to nice houses before—Kolonda's, for example, and the attorney who fostered Jazzy—but this was in another league entirely. Newness and luxury oozed from every bend and corner: copper accents, slate roof, elaborate flowerbeds, decorative windows. And I hadn't yet set eyes on the pool, tennis court, or dockside barbeque the Internet had talked about. The only thought my dazed brain could come up with was to wonder why the old woman had wanted a secondhand antique rocking chair.

"You sure about this?" Ace pointed his ever-present smile in my direction.

"Of course. You have a gun?"

"Won't need one."

I seemed to recall him saying something similar the last time—and that hadn't worked out so well for either of us. I took out my department-issued phone and turned on the GPS feature I normally kept off so I didn't feel the department was keeping tabs on me, and updated my location. If I went missing, Shannon and the others would know where I'd been. Comforting thought.

I pushed open the car door, fighting brief vertigo. The spell was shorter than it had been earlier but still a reminder of my danger that morning. Someone was playing a deadly game. I couldn't forget that.

I strode up the cobbled walk, not turning to see if Ace followed, but secretly relieved that I could hear him behind me. The doorbell sounded like someone playing chimes, which at this place wasn't in the least pretentious. Above our heads in the entryway, two security cameras angled downward, and I wondered how many more cameras might be scattered over the estate and who watched the feed.

A line of black ants marched across the porch, and I studied them, experiencing a strange satisfaction at their presence in the face of such luxury. One ant deviated from the rest, angling over to my foot, where it turned again, circumventing the obstacle.

I gave the house's occupants several minutes before lifting my hand to ring again. No sooner had the chimes stopped than one of the double doors swung open to reveal a woman I recognized from the estate sale that morning, the frailer one, still in her peach dress.

She tilted her head, the white hair staying firmly in its bun. "May I help you?"

"I'm here to see JoAnna Hamilton," I said.

Her eyes wandered down my jeans, as though contemplating the dirty streaks left after the explosion and fire. Her gaze hesitated several long seconds on my bare feet. Coming to my face again, she gave a little gasp. "Don't I know you?"

"We met this morning at the estate sale."

"Oh, yes, the rocker. JoAnna is really excited about it. I'm afraid she won't be interested in selling." Her blue eyes wandered from me to the ants, and an eager smile came to her lips.

"That's okay. Can I talk to her?"

"What?" The woman looked back at me, her eyes blank.

"Ms. Hamilton," I reminded her.

"That's me." She blinked. "Oh, you must mean JoAnna. I'm Marribel, her cousin. Please come in." She looked past me to Ace, including him in her invitation. I wondered why she would so easily trust two strangers, but maybe crime wasn't common out here. Of course, she had the security cameras and whoever might be watching. I hadn't really planned on going inside, or exposing myself any more than necessary, but now that I was here, the idea of this old lady or her cousin trying to hurt me—or ordering me taken—seemed ludicrous. Besides, I had Ace with me. Not quite as good as Shannon, but good enough.

I'd never been inside such a place. The entryway was impossibly wide and the curving staircase long and gracious, like something from the old south. The paint, the wallpaper, the marble floor, the railings, the molding, and the carpet on the stairs—everything gleamed with newness. I bet there were hundreds of places no one had yet left imprints. The paintings, statues, and carvings were perfect, and among the newer pieces, I spied more than a few antiques that were unusual enough to have been handpicked. They were mostly higher-end pieces than what I carried in my shop, but that didn't stop me from appreciating them. Studying the collection, I knew I had at least one painting and a statue that would interest JoAnna Hamilton. Maybe even a certain rolltop desk.

Smiling, I followed Marribel Hamilton under an archway into a sitting room decorated with expensive new furniture. Off-whites and beiges, with the occasional splash of color. Tasteful, but no antiques here. Even the abstract paintings looked new, and I didn't recognize any of the artists, but I wasn't really into the modern wave of abstract paintings. I only recognized them because of Tawnia's familiarity with the art world.

When invited, I sat on a beige leather sofa that was so comfortable I found myself wanting to lie down and have a nap. Instead, I settled back, the sofa cuddling around my body, and gave a little internal sigh. Maybe it was time to rethink the Victorian couch at my apartment. The woodwork on the piece was wonderful and I'd reupholstered it myself using extra padding, but it couldn't begin to match this for comfort.

"I'll be right back," Marribel said. By the way she moved, I judged she would likely be a lot longer than she hoped.

"So what are you going to give as your excuse for being here?" Ace asked.

His words brought me back to the edge of the sofa. It said a lot about my state of mind that I hadn't actually thought this all the way through.

"I mean, you can't just accuse her of trying to kill you this morning."

"No, but I can ask her if she saw anything. And why she happened to be there exactly when I was."

"And I would reply that I was trying to see what kind of person you are." The new voice was imperious, and I jerked my head to the other side of the room, opposite the way we'd entered. JoAnna Hamilton stood there, measuring me with hard gray eyes—and obviously finding me lacking. She'd changed from her aqua suit of that morning to a long, youthful, summery dress that some might have thought would look ridiculous on a woman of her age, but instead brought out her femininity. Her bare arms were tan and supple, the muscles defined, and I guessed somewhere in this house she had a gym and a personal trainer to go with it. No wonder I'd first thought she was younger than her seventy-six years. Her hair was still twisted up in an elaborate knot on the back of her head, but tendrils had escaped to soften her aging face with such perfect preciseness that it had to be orchestrated rather than happenstance. The thick yellow gold necklace and matching bracelet screamed money in the way silver or white gold simply couldn't.

I had the feeling she was one of those people who could destroy another human being without a moment's regret. Maybe coming here had been a mistake.

I stood up quickly, which was another mistake because my dizziness kicked in again. "JoAnna Hamilton?" I asked unnecessarily.

"Yes, as you very well know." She strode further into the room. "And you are Autumn Rain, adopted daughter of Winter and Summer Rain, both deceased. You are a consultant for the Portland Police Bureau, and you use your gift of psychometry to help them solve cases, especially to find missing people."

So much for thinking our encounter that morning at the estate sale was anything but purposeful. At least she hadn't mentioned Tawnia or Destiny.

Her eyes flicked over Ace, who hadn't bothered to stand, but she didn't go into his background, which told me she either didn't know him or considered him extraneous. His eyes narrowed slightly, but his secretive smile didn't change.

"Please have a seat." Without offering a handshake to go with her strange greeting, JoAnna Hamilton sat across from us in a leather chair and crossed her ankles, her dress falling aside enough to reveal flat sandals on her brown feet.

I resumed my perch on the edge of the sofa. "You knew I'd be at the estate sale this morning."

She inclined her head. "I wanted to see for myself if what I'd learned of you was true."

"Because of the contract?"

Her gray eyes glittered. "Yes."

"And what did you decide?"

"That I cannot allow you to touch that contract."

"You plan on double-crossing Russo?" I glanced at Ace as I spoke, but he showed no reaction.

Ms. Hamilton shook her head. "If you've done your research, you'll understand that I need this deal for my company, and I intend to abide by the contract. That's all Russo needs to know. My word shouldn't be dismissed lightly."

"Then why not allow the reading?"

"Tell me, Ms. Rain. Would you like someone taking a peek into your life?" She gave me a derisive smile. "Maybe you wouldn't care, but I have lived a lot longer than you have, and some secrets are meant to be kept."

I felt exactly the same way, especially about those closest to me. I didn't want to know their secrets.

"So to keep me from reading the contract, you cleared everyone out of that attic and had your goons roll me in that rug?"

"What are you talking about?" Her fingers dug into the armrests of her chair. "Why on earth would I do anything like that? I hadn't even made you an offer—how could I make one before Russo actually contacted you? But now that you are here, I don't think you'll turn me down."

That made even less sense. "You were going to bribe me not to touch the contract? You think I actually have a choice?"

She lifted her narrow shoulders in a half shrug that said my welfare wasn't her concern. "You could simply pretend, couldn't you?"

"It's not that easy."

She studied me, arching one brow. "No, I suppose for some it wouldn't be. Still I must present my offer to you. A lot depends on it. Approaching you was the only solution my brother and I could agree on."

"Your brother?"

"Ralph Shatlock. He's a scientist."

My intuition was kicking in major time. "What does he have to do with this contract?"

"You don't know?"

I stifled my exasperation. "I may need to do this reading for Nicholas Russo, but I am not in his confidence." I didn't hide the distaste in my voice. I glanced at Ace to see if he'd volunteer anything.

"Don't look at me," he said. "I'm just paid to watch."

Hamilton's mouth pursed, increasing the wrinkles around her lips, despite the Botox injections I suspected she paid for on a regular basis. Whoever said the rich aged at the same rate as the poor didn't know what they were talking about. Money didn't eliminate the years of effort when you scraped and built a company from the bottom up, but it did buy the latest products and procedures to erase some of the results.

"My brother," Ms. Hamilton said, "is an expert on nanotechnology. His team is working on a series of 3D printers that use a mix of hardware and software to copy pretty much anything that has ever existed or can be imagined—a fork, a book, a vase, and even human organs. Layer upon layer, the printer, using raw materials or even cells from a patient's body, builds whatever you need. In the case of organs, the composition is scanned from the original organ still inside the patient's body or scanning other similar healthy organs from a relative as a base. The flaws are fixed, the DNA matched perfectly. That means no rejection. Such technology, as you must realize, is earth-shattering. We're not the only ones developing these printers, but we hope our partnership with Nicholas Russo will help us be the first to get them into the population on a large scale."

I'd heard of people who talked about using nanotechnology to help an organ repair itself, but to "print" an entire new one? That sounded like science fiction.

Next to me, Ace was nodding. "Saw a documentary on TV. They printed a real metal wrench with moveable parts. Quite amazing."

Hamilton didn't look impressed. "That's one of my competitors—not the most advanced, though. They have funds but not the vision."

"Your brother is head of your research department?" I asked doubtfully. Since discovering my ability, I had learned to be less skeptical about a lot of odd things, but printing organs was over the top.

She smiled. "You still don't believe." There was a gleam in her eyes I didn't trust. With a graceful movement, she came to her feet. "Come with me." She left the room without waiting to see if we would follow. I scrambled after her.

She led us through a spacious hallway to a staircase going downward. Not as wide as the curving one in her entryway, but large enough to support four adults abreast. I glanced at Ace, feeling a tremor of anxiety, but his grin was eager.

We descended into a large family room and proceeded down a long hallway to a large metal door that seemed out of place in this residential setting. Hamilton punched in a code on a pad by the door. "A work of the finest engineering, this lab—the whole basement, actually—given that we're so close to the water. Haven't had one problem with seepage. This isn't our main facility, of course, but it is unknown to my competitors, so my brother does a lot of his work here these days. Work he does alone or with only a couple of assistants. He's not here now, or you could meet him, but I can show you something I think will impress you."

The lab consisted of an impossibly large space filled with tables, machinery, and computers. There was too much to take in all at once, so I focused where Hamilton was pointing. "This is a printer," she said of the large, rectangular machine that stood as tall as my waist. "Probably the fastest in existence. Of course, while we hope to see every home in the world equipped with one of these—a smaller, less expensive version, of course—the real money will be in nanofactories where anything a person desires will be created at almost zero cost from base materials, or even recycled materials. Need a new vacuum? Throw in the old one, click on a design, and out it comes. It's the future."

She went on, but I didn't hear. I was staring at the two identical music boxes on a table next to the 3D printer. One of them had been in my blue shopping bag that morning when I set it down to check the rug for imprints. Now here it was—how could she claim not to have something to do with my abduction?

JoAnna Hamilton saw my stare and picked them both up. "Which is the real one? Can you guess? There wasn't time to reproduce the music assembly, but since the real one is broken anyway, you wouldn't be able to tell by that. Go ahead, examine them." She replaced the boxes on the table.

I ran my finger over the mother-of-pearl roses and the maple exterior, hefting each in turn. Which was the real antique? Without my ability to read the imprints I knew were on the original, I really couldn't tell.

"Where did you get them?" I asked.

She laughed. "When you disappeared so suddenly, I went

back to the attic and took one out of a shopping bag I found there. I noticed you'd been carrying a similar bag, and I thought it might make a good gift for you when we finally had our chat. I had my brother scan and print a copy so you could see for yourself exactly what's at stake with this contract."

That meant she'd expected me to investigate her all along and had specifically prepared this demonstration. However, how she'd known about me in the first place was still a mystery. It had to be from someone inside Russo's organization.

"You may keep it," she said, tapping one of the music boxes.

I made no move to take it. "A bribe?"

"Of course not. Pay me for it if you wish, though it's not necessary. I would simply ask you to consider rejecting Russo's request to read his contract."

"I can't do that," I said slowly. "I have a family." I held her gray eyes for a long minute, and in the end, she was the one who looked away.

She placed one of the music boxes in my hands, and my fingers curled around it only to prevent it from falling. "Very well. Then perhaps you'll consider telling him only what is connected to the contract. Nothing else."

"I don't know that I can lie to Russo."

She sighed. "If you don't, people will die."

What was that supposed to mean?

Ace snorted. "Even if you and Russo don't develop this stuff, others will. Lives will still be saved. Hunger ended everywhere, etcetera, etcetera. Why do you think you are the only ones who can do it right? Why should you be the ones to profit?"

Anger flashed in Hamilton's eyes. "I'm not talking about nanotechnology or these printers. You know absolutely nothing. And how dare you talk to me like that in my own house!"

The ice in her voice would have cowed most intelligent men, but Ace stood there, another stupid grin plastered on his narrow face.

Time to leave while we still might get out in one piece. "Shut up." I pushed Ace toward the door. To Ms. Hamilton, I added, "Don't listen to him. He's not really with me." Perhaps finally becoming aware of his vulnerability, Ace moved across the room and out the door before us. I started to follow.

"Will you consider my offer?" Hamilton asked, the ice in her voice gone.

I paused in mid-step, glancing at Ace's retreating back to make sure he couldn't hear. "What offer is that exactly?"

"I will pay you a hundred thousand dollars to keep quiet about anything you find on that contract."

"Anything that doesn't have to do with a double cross, you mean?"

She inclined her head. There was a tenseness in her face, an all too human plea I couldn't ignore.

"I'm not even sure why you're worried," I said. "Most people don't believe I can read imprints."

She gestured to the room around us. "I've seen the extraordinary. With a brother like mine, life is never common. Besides, if you weren't on the level, Russo wouldn't be using you."

Using me. That's what people like Russo did best. I sighed. "Look, you don't have to pay me. I don't use my ability that way. Financial gain isn't my first priority, or believe me, I could make a lot more money than as a consultant for the police. If whatever you have to hide has nothing to do with your business with Russo, I'll do my best not to tell him. Personal lives should remain personal."

"What if it does have something to do with Russo but not with his business?"

It was an odd question. Was she nursing a personal crush for the man? No, she was far too old. Perhaps she had another business deal with one of his competitors. Or perhaps she had stiffed him in the past. "One thing I made clear to Russo was that the information I passed on couldn't lead to any deaths. I meant it."

She studied me, as though searching my depths to see if I told the truth. Finally, she relaxed. "I used to be like you. A very long time ago."

I don't think so, I thought. But I said nothing as I preceded her out of the room, up the stairs, through the sitting room, and into the entryway where Ace was opening the door.

I followed him onto the front porch and down the stairs, absently stepping over the line of ants. JoAnna Hamilton followed us. "I'll be in touch," she said.

Her eye caught on the ants. Lifting up her dress slightly, she stepped on them, crushing them into black smears.

Chapter 8

On the way back to my store, I pondered again how Ace had claimed to know nothing about JoAnna Hamilton or Russo's business and yet had driven straight to her house. I wasn't sure if that meant anything. He could have been watching her for Russo, or maybe as a private detective, he simply kept up on people his clients were interested in.

One thing for sure: Hamilton had a secret she wanted kept from Russo, and it was entirely possible she'd had me kidnapped that morning to scare me into keeping quiet once Russo made his request. Maybe she'd planned to make me disappear until Shannon and Paige stopped her men. In fact, unless employees from In Loving Memory had been trying to keep the rug away from discovery, there wasn't another soul I could think of who might have an interest in me.

Wait. What about Russo and Hamilton's competitors? Maybe they'd heard about the contract and my future reading and thought taking me would prevent the business deal.

Not likely.

What was I overlooking? Though my gut said Hamilton wasn't responsible for the rug incident, she was still my main suspect—and Shannon was going to flip when he heard I'd gone to see her.

Of course, what he didn't know couldn't hurt me. I grinned.

"What's so funny?" Ace asked.

My grin vanished. "Nothing. What was that attitude back at Hamilton's anyway? You've got a chip on your shoulder the size of Vermont."

"Just telling it like it is. These people aren't even real. They pay to get whatever they want. The only people who walk away from them unscathed are those who have the same kind of power."

"You going to tell your employer about this visit?"

"If it's relevant."

It certainly was. If Russo suspected Hamilton was paying me to withhold information, I'd be in big trouble.

"I'm going to give Russo what he wants," I told Ace. "What I promised."

"How are you going to do that?" Following directions I'd given him earlier, Ace pulled over to the side of the road opposite the little alley that would lead back through the music shop to my side of the block.

"What do you mean?" I froze, my hand on the door.

"You didn't touch a single thing except that music box." He pointed at the box I'd almost forgotten in my lap. "Why's that, Autumn Rain? Whenever I used to see you in the police department, and that time we worked together, you were always touching everything. But not today."

I knew my face betrayed me, but braving the insinuation, I lifted a hand. "No gloves. Do you know how tiring it is to always experience imprints? Of course not. You have no idea."

The words were the truth at least, which might help me look sincere.

"This is different. You're on a case." His voice was less sure now.

"JoAnna Hamilton knows what I can do. Unlike you, I'm not going to offend the woman in her own home. Besides, I almost died today, trapped in a rug with the ugliest imprint I've seen in months. That took a lot out of me." I shook my head. "Look, I'm finished here. Thanks for the ride. Next time I'll ask the cops instead."

I pushed the door open and escaped. The heat on the sidewalk wasn't as noticeable as before, and I checked my phone for the time. Almost six, and that meant nearly time to close up. If I hurried, I could let whoever might be manning Autumn's Antiques go home or back to Jake's store. Since we'd drifted apart, Jake had begun staying open an hour later, probably so we didn't have that awkward moment when we both headed home at the same time. With my unreliable car, leaving before Jake often meant walking home, instead of on the back of his motorbike, but I didn't mind. Of course, tonight I'd have a police escort.

My phone showed a text from Cody Beckett containing a phone number for Easton Godfrey, the scientist he'd told me about. As soon as I could find a snatch of time, I'd call and see if he had any ideas about fixing what was wrong with me.

I had to bang on the back door of the music shop for Stu to let me in so I could go through his shop to get to my store, but when I finally stepped onto the sidewalk, the police car was gone. I hoped that meant Shannon had pulled them off detail and not that they'd discovered my subterfuge. I paused to stare up the street, but the white van I'd seen with Ace was also gone. Maybe he'd been right about it after all.

The outside door to my shop was unlocked and Thera was at the counter helping a customer who was buying more of Jake's herbs than my antiques, but our connected computers were set up to sort out what funds belonged where. If Jake became involved with Kolonda, I wondered if we would be able to continue the system. I hoped so. It really helped on the days I went antique hunting, or when I went out with Shannon and Paige to work a case. Sharing our two main employees, both part-timers, also made sense since our rushes tended to come at different times.

Thera smiled at me as I entered. She was a large woman with stately white hair and a kind face, and as usual, she wore bulky blue beads around her neck that she claimed were calming. "You have a visitor in the back." She reached for the music box. "That's beautiful."

"Thanks, Thera. I can close up, so unless Jake needs your help over there, you can head out."

She set the music box on the counter. "Jake's gone already, and he's left only Randa, so I'll stay in case she needs help. And before you ask, yes, I'm still planning on being here in the morning. Randa is, too, though I heard her saying something about leaving early for a date."

Saturdays were my busiest day, so both our employees usually came in. Sometimes Tawnia as well, especially if I had an appointment. I also had a martial arts lesson Saturday mornings, but that was before the store opened.

"Oh, good. I'm glad you'll both be here. I asked Tawnia to work too because I think I'll be on a case with the police."

I paused before asking. "How are your grandchildren? Are you going to see them this weekend?"

"Yep, on Sunday. They're growing like weeds. Just like your little niece."

I groaned. "I can't believe she's almost walking. Tawnia walked at nine months, but I was ten and a half." Summer had carried me everywhere, Winter had told me. I'd eaten with them, slept with them, and grabbed things from their hands as they worked. I could imagine them both, toting me around the Herb Shoppe, letting me play with empty boxes and picking me up the second I let out a peep. They had waited years for a baby, and to them everything I did was amazing.

Warmth filled me as I remembered my adoptive parents. I'd been very lucky. Tawnia had landed with good people too, but they'd been uptight and more than a little pushy. She was driven toward perfection and success from an early age. With Destiny, she was trying to strike a balance between my upbringing and hers. On the other hand, I was simply spoiling my niece rotten.

Picking up the music box, I headed with it for the back. I'd have to fix the music assembly before trying to sell it. Tawnia wasn't waiting for me in the back room, and some part of me knew she wouldn't be, or she'd have mentioned the possibility of returning. Instead, Shannon sat at the long worktable where I cleaned and repaired my antiques. His fingers drummed on the scarred wood, his eyes fixed on his phone lying flat on the surface. So much for hoping Peirce and his partner had simply been called away. Shannon must have come to take over.

"Hi," I said, forcing a cheerfulness I didn't feel.

Shannon arched a brow, regarding me silently. He stopped drumming the table and set aside his phone.

With a longing peek at my easy chair, I set down the music box and pulled myself up on the end of the table near him, tucking my feet under me. "What?"

"What's the point of assigning officers to watch you if you don't stay put?"

I shrugged. "I had a quick errand. I didn't want to bother them. Wait, does Peirce know I ditched him? Because I really don't want to make him hate me."

"No, he doesn't. I only found out myself after I let them go and came inside. They did see you outside briefly, but they didn't realize you'd gone next door. You shouldn't have left."

I rolled my eyes. "You would have ditched them too."

He pushed back his chair and came to his feet, reaching for me, his hand sending sparks of electricity rippling over my skin. He pulled me to the edge of the table until my legs dangled, wrapping his arms around me, his mouth coming down over mine. He didn't need to say a word because I knew he was reliving that morning and how he'd found me in the rug. I knew he worried about a time when he would arrive too late. But we both knew I wouldn't quit. Not now. Just as he wouldn't.

"I missed you," I said when we came up for air.

He laughed. "We've been together almost every day this week."

"I meant before. You were gone too long." We hadn't talked about being apart yet, and I needed to say it.

"I told them no more undercover. Not now. Maybe not ever."

"Good."

Then we were kissing again, and the time we'd spent apart drained away as though it had never stood between us. I was dizzy, but now I couldn't say it was because of this morning's blast. Whatever, I let it take me.

Of course it couldn't last. Shannon was a detective, and he knew me well enough to understand that I hadn't simply dashed to the grocery store. He knew I'd be working the case.

"So what did you do?" he asked when he finally pulled away.

"I was about to ask you the same thing. Did you find anything at the other estate sale?"

"You mean besides a lot of other people's junk?" Shannon paused. "Not really."

"Something strange happen?"

"I guess you could call it that. The son of the deceased showed up at the sale, claiming that some of his dad's personal belongings hadn't been transferred to him, or more particularly a watch and some coins. Then a customer came up and started haggling with one of the employees over a bust of George Washington that was priced at nine hundred dollars. The son claimed his father had only paid two hundred the year before so why not give it to the man for less? The employee sold it, but Paige took the buyer's information in case there's a problem later."

I chewed on the corner of my lower lip. "Overpriced? Hmm, the rug seemed expensive, too." I didn't know if that meant anything, but it was a connection of sorts. "Where'd the customer find the bust, do you know?"

"A closet, I think. Is that important?" His eyes were locked on my mouth. I stopped chewing my lip, heat rushing through me.

"Maybe not." I reached for him again.

He put his arms around me but didn't lean in for a kiss. "Now you. Where did you go?"

"I went to see JoAnna Hamilton."

The confession took a few seconds to register. Then he dropped his arms and exploded. "You did what?"

"Shh. Keep it down. I might have customers out there." I hadn't heard the jangling of the bells over the door, but a customer might have wandered over from Jake's. "Don't worry. I wasn't alone. Ace was outside, and I got him to come along."

His eyes were stormy now, his hands like vises. "That's supposed to make me feel better?"

"I guess not." Given, I meant, what happened to Ace's last partner. "I did have my GPS signal on."

"I know."

So that's what he'd been doing on his phone, following my return to the shop. I didn't know if that comforted or annoyed me.

"Hamilton's just an old woman," I told him, "though not as old-looking as her age would have you think. She's well-preserved. Anyway, she's hiding something from Russo, something she's afraid I'll read on their contract."

"So she decided to do something about it by kidnapping you?"

"Maybe not. At least she didn't make a move while I was at her house. She only asked me not to reveal anything personal to Russo. Offered me a hundred thousand dollars, in fact."

He thought about that for a moment. "That still doesn't mean she's harmless. You had Ace with you, and she wouldn't be able to explain if you'd disappeared with him there."

"I thought you didn't like Ace."

"I don't. But he was a good cop—once. I'd still rather you not trust him."

I knew why so I didn't push. "Anyway, the contract is about

nanotechnology and 3D printers." I reached for the music box where I'd placed it close to the wall. "She made an exact copy of this. I couldn't tell them apart. She thinks that soon they'll be able to print organs using nanotechnology and cells from the patient's own body."

He gave a short whistle. "I've read about that research, but I thought it was only in the beginning stages. Maybe after our guys finish the background on her, I'll go check it out myself. But do you really think she had nothing to do with this morning?"

I hesitated. "She's the only person I can think of who seems to have a reason to get me out of the way, but I didn't feel in any danger there. Maybe she's changed her mind."

"Maybe?"

"Well, if she didn't do it, her competition could be behind what happened, though it seems unlikely. How would they know about me unless they have a plant in Russo's operation? And stopping me wouldn't necessarily stop the contract from going through. Besides, wouldn't they wait to see if I possibly discovered something that would destroy the deal?" I sighed. "For that matter, we don't even know how Hamilton found out Russo wanted me to read their contract."

Shannon frowned, his finger tracing the bare skin of my arm. His touch alternately sent flames and goose bumps rippling over my flesh—heaven after so long apart. "The In Loving Memory people might be responsible. I mean, if they have been offing old people and stealing from their estates, it would seem natural for them to cover it up."

"The rug did have an imprint. But again, how would they know I could read it?" I chewed on my lip some more. "How did the owner of the house at this morning's sale die, anyway? Was she the one who fell down the stairs?"

Releasing me, Shannon pulled out his cell phone and checked his notes. "Yep. That's it. But there was no rug in the hallway at the top of the stairs when the police were called in. At least none that I see in the crime photos or in the write-up."

I met his gaze solemnly. "I believe she was murdered."

"The rug is pretty much a loss. We put a rush on it, but forensics hasn't found anything useful."

"According to the imprint, that rug was lying at the top of some stairs less than a month ago."

"That would match the time she died." Shannon sighed. "There's nothing we can do but keep checking the estate sales In Loving Memory conducts, though I don't know how well it'll work after blowing our cover today."

"They probably won't remember me. I was in the rug, remember? And I didn't go back and drill anyone."

He nodded, his brow creasing. "I suppose."

"What's wrong?"

"I don't really want you to go to any more sales. If you're right, they could be planning another murder right now. And who's to say they'll stop at old people?"

The thought was sobering. A background check had shown nothing out of the ordinary with the owners or employees, so all we had to go on were a few complaints from heirs of the deceased and a sudden increase of business—both of which could be explained away. Except for me and the now-destroyed rug. But without my ability, I wouldn't be able to find another piece of evidence, even if I went to more of their estate sales.

"You need to stop worrying about all of this right now." He put away his phone and slid his arm around me. "You should rest." There was a plea in his voice I couldn't ignore.

I snuggled against him. "Okay." For now, I meant.

"I'm going to talk to the business owners tomorrow morning," Shannon said. "If you come with me, you might be able to discover something." His suggestion showed me I wasn't fooling him at all. He knew I wouldn't be spending the day in bed, and if I was with him, he could keep an eye on me. Maybe that wasn't all bad.

"If I go, it'll blow my cover."

"It might save a life."

Not without my ability. "Look, there's something I need to tell—"

The jangling of my bells ran over my words, signaling a visitor to my shop. I jumped down from the table, glad to have my confession about my missing talent delayed. The sudden movement sent the world around me shifting. For an instant, I thought I felt the thin invisible cord connecting me with my twin, but it was gone almost as soon as I noticed it. Probably wishful thinking.

"You okay?" Shannon was at my side, his hands steadying me.

"Yeah. Just tired."

"Why don't you close up, and I'll give you a ride home?"

"What about our date?" I wasn't letting him go that soon, not when I'd just gotten him back.

He laughed. "We'll watch a movie."

Usually, I'd opt for dinner and dancing, but tonight I'd rather sleep. A movie was a good compromise. I picked up the music box. Maybe I'd have a chance to look at the music assembly at home later.

We emerged into the store to find Claire Philpot striding powerfully up to my counter. The fifty-something attorney had her dark, shoulder-length hair down today, unlike the other times I'd met her, and it made her softer, more attractive. She wore a short-sleeved burgundy pantsuit with matching flirty high heels and slightly dangling earrings. Her light brown eyes were accentuated by subtle makeup, applied by an expert hand, turning ordinary features into something more. She looked exactly what she was—a confident, successful woman, who enjoyed the good life.

Except today nearly imperceptible lines of worry along her forehead made me aware of an inner anxiety, and her eyes were slightly reddened, as though she hadn't slept well or had spent part of the night crying.

"Hello," I said, unsure how to address her. Paige always called her Claire, and I thought of her as such, but I really didn't know her all that well. "Did you come to pick up Jazzy?"

"No, my assistant picked up Jessica an hour ago. That's not why I'm here."

Jessica. That's right, her ward's real name was Jessica Sandstrom. I'd almost forgotten. My own father, Douglas Rayne—already called Winter by his friends because of the early onset of white hair—had legally changed his name to Winter Rain after falling in love with my mother, Summer. Because of his example, I called Jessica by the name she'd chosen, but it appeared Claire didn't believe in placating the child. I hoped it wasn't too long before the girl grew up enough to use her legal name, or at least picked something that better suited her.

"Okay," I said. When Claire didn't continue, I added, "Is there something I can do for you?" Jazzy had been right, apparently; the situation must be serious for Claire to come to me of her own accord.

"It's about the company my husband worked for, McGregor and Clancy. They've brought a lawsuit against me—or rather my husband's estate. They claim he embezzled funds before he died, and now they suddenly want the money back. However, I went over my husband's accounts very carefully before I switched everything to my name, and there was no indication that the law firm is correct. There were no incoming funds near the day in question, no odd transfers. They don't believe me, of course. In the lawsuit, I'm named as an accomplice."

Shannon snorted. "They can't prove anything, if there's nothing to prove. So give them the information about his accounts and let them try."

"It's not that simple." Claire brought a hand to my counter as though steadying herself. "This sort of allegation could damage my career and set me back years. My husband, when he died, was getting ready to leave that firm precisely because he didn't like the way they played out their cases in the papers. It helped draw public support and win cases, but he didn't feel justice was always accomplished that way. He felt terrible when guilty people sometimes got off and innocent people were damaged by the publicity. Either way, it wasn't good law—not in his opinion or in mine. That's why he was going to leave."

"Do you think pinning this loss of funds on your husband was retaliation for his plan to quit?" I asked, settling myself on the stool across the counter from her. Apparently, this was going to take a while.

"As far as I know, Bridger never got the chance to tell them he was leaving. His heart attack was unexpected." Grief edged her voice, and I knew she still mourned him. This was the other side of love, one half without the other. I wondered if the half left behind ever mended. It hadn't with my father. He'd mourned Summer—and stayed faithful to her—every remaining day of his life.

I glanced at Shannon. He could be that for me, if the loss I'd felt when he was undercover was any indication. As though sensing my thoughts, he stepped closer until our jean-clad legs touched, sending heat licking up my skin, despite the material separating us.

"That's not all," Claire said, her voice taking on a puzzled note. "There was something in his accounts I couldn't explain, but it wasn't related to the company."

Ah-hah, I thought. *This is why she's really here.* "What do you mean?"

"A ticket purchased to Japan during a time I know my husband didn't go abroad. I mean, one of his clients at McGregor and Clancy had a company there, and he'd been over to visit with them, but not at that time. Also, a sizeable amount of money was transferred from his accounts three different times to accounts I don't recognize."

I found that interesting. "So money was actually missing, not appearing without explanation."

"Exactly. I remember seeing the three transfers when I was joining the accounts, but it didn't seem relevant. I mean, all his other funds were there, and those transfers really weren't much if you counted the overall total. He worked a lot of years and did consulting on the side. If he wanted to make some purchases, well, more power to him."

Obviously, she wasn't worried about a secret love nest somewhere. That told me a lot about their relationship and why she still grieved his death so deeply.

"How much is not much?" I leaned over the counter, placing my linked hands on the hard surface.

"Eight hundred thousand dollars total."

I wanted to whistle but refrained. It'd take me more than

twenty years to even earn that kind of money, much less save it in an account.

Shannon scrubbed a hand through his hair. "When were these withdrawals made?"

"All within six months before his death. I tried tracing the accounts where the funds were transferred, but all they would tell me is that they've been closed." Claire shifted her weight, her eyes capturing mine. "I'd like you to take a look at some of his things. I need to know if Bridger *was* into something questionable. Maybe that money *is* somehow connected to this lawsuit. I can't go into this case blind. If it goes to trial, I'm going to have to play their game in the media, and anything that throws a suspicious light on my husband won't help me in the end." She paused before asking, "Will you do it?"

"I'd like to try." For the first time since losing my ability that morning, I was angry about it instead of sad and lost. Why had it vanished now when so many people needed me? Why not three weeks ago when all I had going on was a screwdriver Paige had discovered in connection with a non-violent robbery at an insurance office?

The furrow in Claire's forehead relaxed. "Thank you. I really appreciate it." She reached over the counter and touched my hands, her gold bracelet falling onto my skin.

I stiffened, worried about a possible imprint, before remembering that I wouldn't be able to read it. "It's not a problem," I said, my mouth feeling stuffed with cotton. "Besides, I owe you one for what you're doing for Jazzy—Jessica."

A smile touched her lips. "No. I owe you for that. She's exactly what I've needed. I don't see my two kids much now that they're grown and raising their own families. I always regretted not having another child, and now Jessica is that for me."

Her eyes were bright with unshed tears that showed her sincerity, though I knew for a fact that life with Jazzy these past five months hadn't been all peaches and cream. "I only wish Bridger were here to help her. He was good with teenagers."

"So are you, apparently."

Claire patted my hands before finally withdrawing hers. "Her tutor thinks she'll be able to go back to regular class if he works with her the rest of this month and then throughout the summer. It's mostly getting her up to speed with reading and grammar. Math, too, but she's almost there with that." She laughed. "Maybe with luck, we'll get rid of the blue hair."

"Don't hold your breath." I grinned, but I was having trouble focusing. There seemed to be two of her now.

Shannon drew out his phone. "If you don't mind, I'd like to look into your husband's old employers. What did you say the firm was called?"

"McGregor and Clancy."

"Would you mind giving us the other particulars? My partner has a way of finding information that no one else can, and since you two are acquaintances, you can be sure she'll be discreet."

"I was going to talk to Paige anyway—after Autumn checked out my husband's belongings. I was hoping something there would give Paige enough to go on."

"Why don't you email the information to her as soon as possible?" Shannon asked. "She can at least begin tracing the banks."

I rubbed my aching temples. I knew Shannon was involving the police department as much from his feeling of duty toward Jazzy as for the suspicious circumstances and Claire's connection with Paige. I was glad he felt responsibility toward Jazzy because I'd vowed to make sure that none of the girls we'd saved got lost in the system.

"Autumn?" Shannon's hand was on my back. "You okay?"

I nodded carefully because my headache was quickly becoming a raging inferno behind my eyes.

Claire frowned. "Jessica called and told me something about you having to go to the doctor. I probably shouldn't have come to see you today."

"That's okay. It's just a headache."

Claire pulled out a card. "You have my contact information, but here it is again just in case. Call me when you'd like to, uh, see Bridger's things. Next week is fine. Or whenever you feel better."

I took the card, plastering on my face what I hoped was an encouraging smile. I knew what it had taken her to ask me for help. Her need to know had overcome her desire for privacy, and though I'd never tell another soul about the personal, irrelevant imprints I would also find at her house, the way I saw and felt about her would probably change because of what I would experience there.

"We need to get you home." Shannon helped me from the stool as Claire exited the door.

I locked the day's meager proceeds in the safe Shannon had installed under the counter for my new pistol, this time a Kahr .380. It lay on a black velvet surface, the metal barrel shining brightly in contrast to the black of the grip. Aware of Shannon watching, I picked up the holster lying next to the Kahr, clipped it on the waistband of my jeans near my back, slipped the gun inside, and pulled my fitted blouse over it. Not as good a concealment as with a heavier shirt, but I'd put a jacket over it.

I was *not* wearing the gun because I was afraid.

"You should have taken that to Hamilton's." Shannon was smiling at me, and I knew he was pleased. Maybe he felt his shooting lessons weren't wasted. Since I wasn't shooting any better than I had the first time we'd gone—I'd hit the paper man in the heart so many times that I'd shredded the paper—I wasn't sure how he could take credit, but I did feel slightly more comfortable carrying the gun these days, which wasn't saying much.

"Maybe next time." I didn't point out that with all the dizziness, I was probably more of a danger to myself with the gun than to anyone else.

As we walked to the outside door, I glanced at Jake's place through the now-closed double glass doors that connected our shops. Still a lot of customers there. I wondered if Jake was with Kolonda and if he was having a good time.

Shannon frowned at my gaze, misinterpreting my thoughts. "You want to say goodbye to him?"

I shook my head. "He's out on a date—I think."

Shannon stepped closer, leaning over slightly until our lips were only inches apart. "Are you okay with that?" I knew that wasn't what he was really asking.

"Of course." I felt his nearness acutely, and I couldn't help bringing up a hand to cup his neck, pulling him toward me until our lips met. He deepened the kiss, sending a shot of adrenaline to my body. I felt completely alive this close to him. Almost, I could forget my loss.

Almost.

Reluctantly I broke away to turn on the alarm and motion detectors.

Though it was after six, it was still light outside, signaling the coming of summer. Shannon led me to his blue truck, helping me carefully inside before climbing in himself. I wondered if I looked fragile to him. I did rather feel that way.

"What was Ace doing here anyway?" he asked, bringing the engine to life.

"Keeping an eye on me, I think."

"For Russo?"

I fingered the mother-of-pearl on the music box. "Who else?"

"After what happened last time, Ace told me he'd never work for the man again. Apparently Russo doesn't pay failures, and Ace almost getting killed was a big failure. I'd think Russo would have to be paying him a lot to get him to change his mind."

I snorted. "Or maybe Ace got some money up front this time. I would insist on it if I were him."

"Well, if I know one thing about Ace, it's that he'll do anything for money. The grapevine has it that he hasn't been getting many paying jobs these days, so I'm not surprised he's back to working for Russo." A pause and then, "Did Ace ask you to go in business with him?" The words were so casual, I wouldn't have understood their significance if I hadn't known what Shannon had already lost.

"Yeah, but I said no, of course."

Shannon swore, a short, explosive sound. "That guy needs a new profession."

We stopped for Chinese takeout from a semi-organic restaurant I frequented that didn't mind making my food a bit differently. Minutes later, as we walked from his truck to my apartment building, a man in worn jeans and a black T-shirt caught my eye, emerging suddenly from the shadows cast by the trees lining the sidewalk. His back was toward me now as he headed away, but I had the strange sense that he'd been watching us.

Silly. Though understandable after what I'd been through that day.

I clutched the music box in my hands and squinted after him. His hair reached his collar and I could see a healthy amount of facial hair that told me he was either growing a beard or he hadn't shaved in a while. He was on the tall side but had only a medium build, nothing really to call my attention— except perhaps the purpose with which he walked.

What had he been doing lurking around the parking lot? And why did he seem familiar? Maybe if I could glimpse his face.

"Autumn?" Shannon opened the door to my building. He had a set of keys like all my friends and half my neighbors. I was forever shutting myself out and forgetting where I'd put them.

I glanced behind me as the man disappeared, seeming to bleed into the distance. "Coming."

Shannon strode inside the lobby, but as he neared the door to my bottom floor apartment, he pulled out his 9 mil, holding up his other hand to warn me to stop.

I froze.

Chapter 9

Time seemed to slow as my senses kicked into alert. Flesh tingling with readiness, I moved carefully, peeking around the corner to see what had alarmed Shannon. The outside door to my apartment was slightly ajar. It stuck that way sometimes when I was in a hurry, and I only caught it when I locked up.

Except I was sure I'd locked the door this morning, and since Shannon had picked me up for the estate sale, he'd watched me do it.

Shannon motioned me back as he pushed open the door and edged into my apartment. I went after him. I didn't have a death wish or anything, but he was alone and this was my apartment. If he needed backup, well, I wasn't Paige, but I'd do what I could.

It was almost a letdown when Shannon searched the kitchen, bath, and two bedrooms, only to come up empty. There was no sign anyone had been inside. I *had* shut and locked the door, hadn't I? Maybe one of my neighbors had returned something, or maybe Jake had stopped by for the extra helmet to his bike or whatever else he'd left here over the years we'd been friends.

With Shannon gone undercover, Jake and I'd spent more time together, mostly watching movies with a few friends. Once we'd gone out dancing.

That's it, I decided. *Jake stopped by. Probably wanted the helmet to take Kolonda for a spin on his bike.*

Or maybe the man in the worn jeans had somehow made it past my locks. But what motive could he possibly have? I groaned at my irrationality. The man hadn't been in my apartment, he hadn't been watching me, and I definitely wasn't about to reveal my paranoia by telling Shannon about him.

Weariness settled over me as I unwrapped my clenched fingers from around the wood of the music box and set it on the coffee table. With a nod at Shannon, I forced myself to the bathroom for a quick hot shower and a rubdown with a homemade comfrey and arnica liniment to help ease my sore muscles and prevent more bruising. After dressing in a pair of army green sweats and an orange T-shirt, I joined Shannon on my Victorian couch, where he'd dug into his boxes of takeout. I sat next to him, wishing I could pull Summer's afghan over me so I could feel her imprints, but I had enough imprint-carrying antiques stuffed into my tiny apartment to know that my talent hadn't yet resurfaced.

Shannon frowned as he handed over a box of takeout. "I saw you lock the door this morning. You pulled it shut. I remember that."

I was already so far beyond the fact of the open door that his comment took a moment to register. "Jake must have stopped by for something. You know how that door is." Not broken exactly, just a little stiff.

"I guess." He took a bite of sesame chicken.

He'd bought noodles for himself and rice to go with my

meal, but I wasn't really hungry. That added to my worry. My sister and I were both infamous for our huge appetites, and eating always helped me recover. Tonight I'd asked for extra beef, because protein revitalized me better than anything else, so I was determined to see if it helped. I forced the first mouthful down.

Gradually, the dizziness that had been my semi-constant companion since that morning lessened and my eyelids began to feel heavy. The next thing I knew, someone was carrying me to bed. Though I knew it must be Shannon, I was taken back in time to after Summer's death when Winter and I would watch television so late that he'd have to carry me. At age eleven, I'd already gained most of my height, but he hadn't seemed to mind. Those had been good times, even though we both mourned Summer.

Laying me on the bed, Shannon smoothed my short hair and kissed my forehead. "Sleep," he murmured. I wanted to cling to him, but my limbs wouldn't obey. Darkness called to me, enticing as any warm embrace. I felt comfortable and safe. I knew Shannon wouldn't be leaving, that he'd stay with his gun handy to protect me.

Wait. Isn't there something I need to tell him?

Drifting. I heard voices from far away and figured Shannon was watching television. Or maybe he'd called Paige so he wouldn't have to stake out my apartment alone.

Had someone other than Jake been in my apartment that day?

Dreams filled my head. Dreams of Shannon. Of the passion in his kisses. His arms holding me. In the dream, I wasn't blind or missing anything. Shannon's grip tightened.

Abruptly, it was hard to breathe. Not because of his nearness, but because of how snug his arms felt. Because of how they widened and thinned until they became a rug rolled around my body, smothering me and cutting off everything.

I waited for the feet and then yanked the rug.

Crash. Tilting inside the rug. Hitting something hard. Unable to breathe. My chest constricting.

The feet . . . pulling the rug.

JoAnna's feet crushing the ants.

Shannon's arms squeezing tighter.

A scream ripped from my throat. I sat up in bed, my heart pounding. The room was completely dark, except for thin moonlight streaming through the bedroom window. My shelves, stuffed with antique toys, books, and music boxes made familiar comforting shadows in the darkness, but still my heart throbbed.

Footsteps reverberated through the apartment. The door to my room flew open. "Autumn?"

I relaxed as I heard Shannon's voice.

The room flooded with light, and through squinting eyes, I saw him checking all the corners. Finding nothing, he hurried to my side. I was about to tell him it was a dream when more footsteps stilled my tongue.

I blinked at the newcomer. "Cody?"

White hair askew, Cody rubbed sleep from his eyes, his weathered face showing in that instant every one of his sixty-six years. "What happened?"

"Just a dream. What are you doing here?"

Shannon put his arms around me, bringing back memories of suffocation. I tried not to pull away.

Cody shrugged. "I came a couple hours ago. Thought you might need me." Uncertainty had crept into his words. For the first time, I noticed he wore gray pajama pants, the end of a belt sticking out awkwardly from under a dingy white T-shirt. A belt with flannel pants? He didn't look like a man who owned a hundred acres or invested in real estate, and whose massive art sculptures sold as fast as he could create them. Apparently, he came prepared to stay at least this night because his customary jeans were missing.

"He keeps saying that," Shannon said. "I told him I'd keep you safe."

"No, I meant with the imprints." Cody shifted uneasily.

Shannon cocked a brow. "What's he talking about?"

"Did your ability come back then?" Cody asked. "I guess I should have called before coming."

"No," I said softly, "it didn't."

I turned in the bed, and Shannon's arm fell away. My teeth closed over my bottom lip in an effort to keep my voice steady. "Look, I've been meaning to tell you—it seems after what happened this morning . . . I—I can't read imprints."

Shannon stared at me for a full thirty seconds before erupting. "And only now you decide to tell me this? If you can't read imprints, why on earth did you go see JoAnna Hamilton?"

I bristled at the lack of sympathy in his voice. Jake and Tawnia had at least felt sorry for me and had tried to understand my loss. I bit down on my hurt. "I was going to tell you earlier when Claire Philpot came to the shop. But reading imprints is not my only asset, and I need to find out why Russo's contract is so important. That's why I went to see Hamilton." My icy tone told him what I did was none of his business. I knew he'd remember it from our early days.

"You should let the police do that. You should let *me* do that."

I glared at him. "Are we back to that again? I was with the police when I was abducted this morning, remember? Look, I'm tired and disoriented, and I need to sleep. Maybe you should leave." It wasn't like Shannon to try to limit what I did. I mean, not since we'd fallen in love. What was his problem?

He scowled. "I'm not going anywhere until I know who's out to get you. With Russo and Hamilton involved and billions of dollars at stake with this nanotechnology, there's too much going on."

"Well, then do your watching somewhere else. I need to sleep."

"See that you do." Shannon jumped up and stalked from the room.

I didn't really want him to leave. I wanted him to take me in his arms and apologize. I wanted him to say he loved me despite the loss of my ability. I wanted him to tell me it would be okay. My eyes followed him out the door, only to land on Cody, who'd pasted a sardonic grin on his face.

"I'd say it's love," he said.

"Shut up."

"He's just worried about you. If he didn't care, he wouldn't be."

"Are you kidding? He's always acted this way." Even way back in the beginning when he'd fought his attraction to the barefoot weirdo who claimed to read imprints. "He's been a lot better lately. I thought he trusted me more."

"He has a right to be worried. You almost burned to death. That kind of thing changes a man."

"Is that why you're here?"

"I thought you might need me."

This from the man who hadn't known I existed until five months ago. Did he think that coming to my rescue now was fulfilling his biological duty? No matter how he tried, he couldn't take Winter's place.

Cody sighed and limped over to the foot of my bed,

plopping himself down without an invitation. The injury wasn't one left over from the gunshot wound he'd received during my last case, and I wondered what had happened.

"I figured I can go with you," he said. This close, I could more clearly see his eyes, one blue and one hazel. Like mine and Tawnia's. "I can touch whatever you want and tell you what the imprint is."

"That's the stupidest—" I broke off.

Actually, it was a good idea, provided Russo and anyone else would go for it. But if Russo found out about Cody, his freedom would be in jeopardy. Did he know that? Of course he did. He'd lived a long time, dealt too often with imprints not to understand the implications.

A lump formed in my throat because though I'd forgiven him for the past, I didn't know that I would take the same risk for him if our situations were reversed.

"What happened to your leg?" I asked, buying time.

He looked ruefully down at it. "Fell off a stack when I was finishing up a couple days ago. Doesn't hurt much now."

"Did you go to the doctor?"

"Did you?" he asked.

I couldn't help my grin. "A nurse."

He snorted. "I'm fine." He leaned forward and heaved himself to his feet, but not before I saw the bulge of a pistol in a holster. That explained the belt at least.

My eyes strayed to the closet where I'd placed my Kahr on the top shelf.

"Anyway, let me know if you want me to read something," Cody said. "I was free this weekend anyway."

"I think Tawnia was going to drive down sometime to see your sculpture."

He shrugged. "Maybe on Sunday." Without another word, he limped toward the door. "Hope you don't mind. I crashed out in your other room."

Winter's room. I didn't know how I felt about my biological father sleeping in the bed of the man who'd been the best father any child could ever have, but I knew Winter wouldn't mind. In fact, if Winter had still been alive, he would have welcomed Cody with a friendly hug and let him stay as long as he liked.

"Uh, Cody?"

He paused and half turned. "Yeah." His voice was gruff, a tone I recognized. He expected rejection.

"Thanks for coming."

"Well, this way you don't have to go see Easton. I can be your eyes until your ability comes back." He nodded and shut the door behind him.

It wouldn't be the same, of course, because hearing about something was nowhere near experiencing it for yourself, but it could get me through this pinch. Despite my unhappiness at the whole situation, I felt marginally better.

Even so, I still planned to go see Easton Godfrey. I wanted to learn whatever he knew about my ability, and if there were others like Cody and me. And Tawnia, of course. Her talent might be different, but she was still apparently using more of her brain than most people. I'd often wondered what it would be like to have been gifted with a musical ability, or perhaps some athletic talent, but tonight I just wanted my own "thing" back.

The sleep had done me good, but the clock only read ten in the evening, which explained my grogginess. I must have fallen asleep at dinner and slept maybe a couple hours. I wondered how much of the Chinese food I'd actually eaten because I was hungry again.

Pulling myself from the bed, I slowly walked to the door, my body aching worse than before my shower. Had Shannon left? I hoped so, though if he had, I knew he wouldn't go far. He was hard to get rid of even before we started dating. Determined, some might say. I'd called him annoying, usually to his face. Why he'd tolerated it, I had no idea.

I barely made it to the door when I heard angry male voices. I couldn't hear what they were saying as they were trying—unsuccessfully—to keep it down, but I recognized the voices. One of them was Shannon's. He hadn't left. My tensioned eased.

The bedrooms, kitchen, and bathroom in my apartment all opened directly onto the living room with no hallway, so I'd be seen the minute I emerged. I paused, wondering if I should go back to bed and forget the pair of them. But with my recent nightmare still clinging to my mind, I didn't want to turn out the lights. Not yet.

I eased the door open.

"I just said you can't think like that," Cody was saying, his voice low and angry. "I *know* she's wished a hundred times that she couldn't read imprints. So have I. But what you gotta understand is that we're like a seeing man living with a bunch of blind people. Sure, this man feels weird and out of place, and everybody makes fun of him because he's different and he wishes he was like them. But then suddenly—boom!—one day the guy can't see anymore, and he understands how much he depended on his sight. It's an entire sense lost. He can adjust—just as Autumn will if she has to—but it ain't fun and it's a whole lot scary."

Shannon paced a few steps. "I'm just saying that she

shouldn't put herself at risk! Whoever was behind this morning's attack thought nothing of paying three thousand cash for a rug they destroyed ten minutes later—not to mention the van they torched. That means they're serious. It was a dumb thing going to see Hamilton. She could have been taken again."

"I don't like it either, but it's her life. You can whine and complain or shut up and help her. Besides, she didn't go in alone. You said she had that detective with her. It worked out okay, so move on. Or maybe you'd rather lock her in a jail cell till you solve your crime."

I appreciated Cody's defense, but I didn't like him mucking about in my love life. I'd better make him go to Tawnia's so Shannon didn't kill him.

Whatever Shannon was about to retort was interrupted by a knock on my door; my bell was busted and I hadn't gotten it fixed yet. I bet the neighbors were here to complain about the noise. They were mostly older folks who went to bed early, and despite having a soft spot for me after watching me grow up and lose both my parents, they needed their sleep.

Shannon glared at Cody as if he were responsible for whoever was at the door. Cody started to limp past him to open it, but Shannon beat him to the door. I decided I'd better make an appearance or my neighbors might think something had happened to me. They'd never met Cody and hadn't seen much of Shannon around lately.

Shannon yanked at the door, seemingly carelessly, but I noticed his hand near his Glock. There was a moment's hesitation that told me he was surprised at my visitor, and then, "May I help you?"

"Yes," said a cultured voice I recognized only too well. "I need to see Autumn Rain immediately."

I emerged from my room, but the newcomer was obscured by Shannon and Cody. I could see her companion, however, a man I recognized from earlier, though instead of casual clothing he'd sported at the estate sale, tonight he wore a gray suit.

"Who are you?" Cody growled.

"JoAnna Hamilton, and this is my cousin, Winston Drewmore. Well, actually he's my cousin's grandson, but we don't bother with all the removed stuff. It's imperative that we see Ms. Rain tonight."

"What is the nature of your visit?" Shannon asked.

"Who are you?"

I waited for Shannon to pull his cop card, but instead he said, "I'm her boyfriend."

"I see. Well, your romance is none of my concern, and it certainly doesn't make you privy to my business. Now, if you'll please get Ms. Rain."

Next to her, Winston put a hand on her arm, his eyes going to me. JoAnna Hamilton craned her neck to see around Shannon, then pushed her way past him. "There you are, Ms. Rain."

"Please, come in," I said with a hint of irony that she ignored. "Have a seat." I indicated my Victorian couch.

She came forward, wearing yet another outfit, this time a purple linen skirt and matching suit coat. Her hair was freshly pinned up on her head, with no straying hair. Her eyes traveled the length of the room, pausing occasionally on some of the antiques I couldn't bear to part with. Despite the clutter, every-thing I owned in my entire apartment wouldn't adequately furnish even three of JoAnna Hamilton's large rooms.

Hamilton nodded at Winston, and he led the way around the couch, the back of which faced the door in an effort to divide the room into a sort of entry/living room arrangement. It mostly succeeded.

Drewmore's head skimmed my antique chandelier that was too big and hung too low for the room, but that I kept there anyway because I loved it so much. He cast me an apologetic grin, which I acknowledged with a nod. Hamilton sat on one end of the couch, but Drewmore remained standing near her side.

I walked toward them, only to be joined by both Shannon and Cody. "We can make her leave," Cody said under his breath, though his voice carried throughout the room anyway. "You need more sleep." He eyed me uncertainly, his voice holding a question unrelated to his comment, and I shook my head almost imperceptibly.

No. My gift hadn't returned or I'd feel the buzzing from the strong imprints around me. Sleep, it appeared, wasn't the cure. Or at least not just a few hours.

My stomach rumbled, reminding me of why I'd left my room, but there wasn't a trace of the takeout on the coffee table. I'd give Shannon points for cleanliness and good food practices if my stomach weren't so empty.

"Why would she want to make me go away?" Hamilton asked with crisp derision. "I was gracious to her when she came to see me this afternoon."

"It's after ten," Cody pointed out.

Hamilton's mouth pursed. "Who are you anyway?"

How to explain Cody? "He's my . . . uh . . . my—"

"Bodyguard," Cody stated with a scowl. "I make sure nothing happens to her."

Her eyes dropped to his injured leg. "I see."

The insinuation—if Cody couldn't prevent himself from

being hurt, how could he help me?—wasn't lost on anyone in the room, but I was relieved that Cody didn't take offense. Folding his arms across his chest, he waited until I sat in Winter's favorite chair and then positioned himself behind it. The chair was almost as old as the one in my antiques shop, and nearly as comfortable. Summer's afghan perched on one arm, but I carefully avoided it, worried that the stress I was feeling would be enough to make me leave a negative imprint. That would make a difference once my ability returned.

If it returned.

I swallowed hard and brought my bare feet up under me. No need to stand on ceremony in my own house. My visitors could see very plainly how I lived.

Shannon crossed the room and stood in front of the fireplace, farther away from me, but closer to Drewmore, which indicated that Shannon thought he was the only threat—if there was one. My bet was on Hamilton.

"What brings you here, Ms. Hamilton?" I asked.

"It's my brother, Ralph Shatlock."

The nanotech genius. Why was I not surprised?

"What about him?" I said, my gaze going to the coffee table where the music box she'd given me sat between an antique bowl and some figurines.

"My brother didn't show up for our meeting tonight," Hamilton said, "and I can't reach him on his cell phone. I believe he's been taken by someone, and I want to hire you to help find him."

Chapter 10

*O*kay, so I was surprised. Not only that she would ask me for help, but that Shatlock had gone missing in the first place.

No one spoke for several seconds, and then Shannon said, "Is there anything besides his absence at the meeting that makes you think he might be missing?"

"Maybe he met a pretty woman," Cody added.

Hamilton gave him a quailing look, which Cody met with a feisty grin.

"What they mean," I said hurriedly, "is that maybe your brother is so intent on his work that he forgot. I know an artist, and she sometimes forgets everything when she's working on a project." No need to tell Hamilton the artist was my sister.

Hamilton nodded, indicating that her brother had also done this, but her presence still suggested that something made today different. I had the feeling it was big. JoAnna Hamilton wasn't one to come begging—or even demanding—help so late on a near stranger's doorstep, especially a stranger with a talent that was questionable at best. That she had come to me meant she was desperate and didn't expect much help from the police.

"The lab at my house was broken into this evening. Some of our software was stolen and everything else was smashed. We'll be set back months—years if we can't find software backups. I had a meeting with Russo, so I wasn't home."

"That's a good thing," Drewmore said, looking down on her. "Or they might have taken you too."

The concern in his voice made me study him more thoroughly. Winston Drewmore appeared to be in his late twenties. He had brown hair, tanned skin, blue eyes, and a build that showed he regularly worked out, perhaps with a trainer. He was nice-looking, but there was nothing in his looks to set him apart from a crowd, except a slight forward hunching of his shoulders. I couldn't help thinking he should be out on a date or something, and leave the real work to the big boys.

Hamilton harrumphed, as if daring anyone to be stupid enough to kidnap her. I wondered if it had been the same arrogance that had prompted her to show Ace and me the lab this afternoon.

"What time was this?" Shannon's hands flexed at his sides with impatience. He wanted details so he could decide if there had been a real crime.

"I met with Russo at seven." Hamilton's back was very straight, and though her voice was modulated, I had the feeling that inside she was screaming, but whether it was for love of her brother or worry about her business, I couldn't say. "My brother was supposed to be at the meeting, but he never showed. I'd talked to him earlier, before I went to my office to get some projections I needed for the meeting, and he said he'd be there. He was heading to my house to get his plans and other information from the lab."

"These were to bring to the meeting?" Shannon asked.

She nodded. "Diagrams, plans, research, back up programs—that sort of thing. Russo insisted on these as part of our arrangement. He wants to keep a set to make sure we can replicate our trials if anything were to happen to Ralph."

A sinking feeling grew in my stomach that had nothing to do with lack of food. "But your brother didn't show up."

Hamilton hesitated before saying, "It's only fair to tell you that we weren't about to give that information to Russo anyway, not until we knew he was satisfied with whatever Ms. Rain might find on the contract." Her eyes flitted to me, making me feel somehow responsible. "And even then we'd make sure it was coded so Russo couldn't access it without our help."

Drewmore shook his head. "Ralph should have given Russo's coded backup to me. I would have kept it safe." His voice held a determination that raised him in my estimation. His gaze turned toward me, meeting my stare. "I'm really sorry to involve you in this, Ms. Rain, but as I told JoAnna, we need to find Ralph and learn where that information is. Everything at the lab, all our latest work, is missing or destroyed—including our backups. Without those, we stand to lose everything. Worse, with a bit more development, those plans can eventually create printers that will replicate virtually anything, including weapons and munitions. Given the correct building materials and programming, that could put dangerous weapons into the hands of terrorists, and on our own soil."

That explained Russo's involvement. I doubted he was

interested in creating a new heart for an ailing man, or a new lung for a child with severe asthma. He wanted even higher stake items. Did Hamilton and Drewmore have any idea who they were getting into bed with?

Dismay must have shown in my face because Drewmore nodded. "I see you understand the implication."

"I'm thinking of Russo," I said. "You can't let him control this."

He nodded. "That's certainly not our intention. I know it seems rather dangerous what we're doing, but we retained control. It's listed in the contract. Russo only participates in the proceeds."

"Not if you give that mobster the plans!" Cody shot.

Drewmore flashed him a rueful smile. "As JoAnna said, the information would be coded. The backup program we intended to give him for safekeeping would erase itself if he attempted to access it, which in itself would violate our contract. He's only supposed to hold it in the event of sabotage or . . . or something like what happened tonight. We thought it was a good idea because we could access the information if it ever became necessary."

My appraisal of Winston Drewmore improved further. Not only did he seem older now, but for the first time I realized he wasn't JoAnna Hamilton's heir solely because of blood but because he was a business man in his own right. He'd been groomed well.

"It's all very high tech," Hamilton added with a glimmer of excitement in her voice. "It's the same type of program we put on our computers in the lab. Any unauthorized access would cause vital parts to be erased. We make sure to protect ourselves."

"You kept no other backups off-site?" Shannon looked incredulous.

"We do keep parts of our information off-site and in use at our bigger lab, but the most important things we keep close. Besides the backup Ralph made for Russo, I have an automatic backup system in the lab. Password protected, fire safe, and impenetrable by strangers. Well, unless you take a sledge hammer to it apparently. That machine was completely destroyed and the software is now useless. I had another backup on a portable hard drive in my safe, but the safe was open when I got home—that's why I believe my brother was there at some point. He's the only other person besides me who knows the combination."

Shannon paced a few feet away. "What about your security cameras?"

"The recordings are destroyed and there's no sign of a break-in. Whoever did this either waited for my brother or they knew my codes to get in." Hamilton narrowed her eyes at Shannon. "What are you anyway, a cop?"

When he didn't immediately reply, she muttered a curse. "You are a cop, aren't you?"

"A detective, to be exact. Homicide Detail with the Portland Police Bureau. We also investigate assaults, kidnappings, and missing persons. And you should be at the police station reporting this right now."

"I can't risk Russo finding out about this. He has eyes everywhere."

"So you came to me instead?" I asked.

She shrugged. "I trust you, young lady. You don't like Russo any more than I do."

"Are you sure he wasn't the person who ordered the

break-in?" I felt compelled to say. "Maybe he decided he doesn't need you." Remorse flooded me as I thought about how I'd brought Ace into her house. Had he somehow managed to disable her alarm and glimpse her code? Or maybe he'd put in a code of his own? He'd been alone only for a short time, but you never knew with guys like him. Maybe Russo suspected Hamilton had no intention of allowing him to access the nanotechnology.

Ms. Hamilton frowned. "At this point, I can't be sure of anything. It's possible Russo is responsible."

"I think it was our competition," Drewmore put in. "This deal with Russo will push us to first in this race. We'll have more than enough funds to develop our products, and money is always the main concern."

I noticed Cody had slipped over to the couch and sat beside JoAnna Hamilton, far enough away that she didn't give him notice, but his hand rested on the seat beside him, his fingers stretching for JoAnna Hamilton's purse. It's what I would have done, if my gift hadn't deserted me. After a moment of touching the purse, he nodded slightly, and I understood that everything JoAnna had told us tonight was the truth as she knew it, or that at least there was nothing imprinted on the purse to refute her testimony. Too bad he couldn't test Drewmore in a similar way, but the man wasn't carrying anything Cody could touch.

"So what would you like me to do?" I asked.

"Go to the lab and see if you can find anything about what happened," Hamilton said without hesitation. "I'll pay you, of course. Your going rate." She seemed to suddenly notice Cody's hand near her purse, and she scooped it up and placed it in her lap.

"You need to report this," Shannon said.

She shook her head. "Not yet."

"What if I promise to keep it under wraps?"

Hamilton thought about it and then finally nodded. "Okay. If you're sure you can do that, but only after Autumn takes a look at the lab. I know how long the police will take to process the scene. We may miss a window of opportunity." She stood, as if expecting immediate compliance.

Cody scowled and Shannon sighed. I met his eyes and gave him a nod, indicating that I wanted to do this. If Cody went with us, he could find the information every bit as easily as I could have if I hadn't gone blind.

Shannon took out his phone. "I'll get my partner and a couple others to meet us there."

"No police cars," Drewmore stated. "They may be watching."

"Do you think there might be a ransom?" I asked.

JoAnna Hamilton shook her head. "There's not enough money in the world to reimburse them for the knowledge in my brother's head. If someone has taken him and he refuses to cooperate, they'll kill him."

Silence fell over the room, and even though it wasn't my problem, not directly, I felt eager to help Hamilton's brother. I suppose it's why I was in the business.

I arose and the vertigo was back. Shannon grabbed my elbow. "You okay?" he mouthed. Still seated across from me on the couch, Cody's scowl deepened.

I nodded. "I need to get changed. So does Cody." I wondered what Hamilton and Drewmore would make of my supposed bodyguard's worn jeans and whatever else he chose to wear. He certainly didn't look like a bodyguard, but I needed him too much to make him stay at the apartment.

Ten minutes later, we were in Shannon's truck, following Drewmore's car through Portland, heading toward Lake Oswego. I lay back, resting my head on the seat. Next to me, Cody stared out the window into the darkness, wearing paint-splattered jeans and a blue shirt, his white hair only marginally tamed. On my other side, Shannon drove in silence. I had a bad feeling about this, though that might be my empty stomach growling.

Shannon bent over and fished for something inside a mini cooler he must have taken from my kitchen. "I thought you might want this. I brought a fork. I know how you hate chopsticks." He plunked a box of takeout in my hands and immediately I perked up.

"Thanks." I ate as unobtrusively as possible, seeing that I was squeezed between the two men. There was little worse than smelling food you weren't going to eat.

"I think you have an admirer," Cody said into the silence.

I turned to him, fork poised in the air. "What?"

"Young Drewmore. He couldn't take his eyes off you."

"You're seeing things." I looked at Shannon for confirmation. He kept his eyes on the road, a hint of a smile touching one side of his mouth. I rolled my eyes. "I imagine that would go over well with Hamilton, and don't forget that he has very big reasons to please her."

"She's not his mother," Cody said.

Shannon glanced over at us. "No, but she holds the purse strings and, even more important, his career."

"Maybe he's part of this," I said. "Maybe he paid someone to steal the copies of the research. With those, he could write his own ticket with Hamilton's competition or go off on his own entirely."

Cody nodded. "That might explain why there was no sign of a break-in, but wouldn't he have taken them in a less conspicuous way?"

"Not if he didn't want to make himself a suspect." Shannon signaled and turned into Hamilton's drive. "But he seems rather young and ineffectual to do something like that."

"Oh, come on, he's not all that young," I said. "I'm impressed with him. He could have done it."

Shannon laughed. "So that's how to impress you—to show you're capable of a crime?"

"That's right." I was glad we were back to joking, the tension between us gone.

"I need to touch something of his," Cody said. "So we'll know."

I frowned. "That might be harder than you think. You're lucky to have found an imprint on Hamilton's purse. She probably has a dozen of them." Imprints were funny sometimes. If a person didn't really care about an item and nothing traumatic happened while they were holding or using it, they wouldn't leave an imprint. Clothes were notoriously bad for imprints, especially those often washed, as they lost bits of themselves with each cleaning. Something about the material didn't preserve them, with the exception of quilts and similar items that weren't often washed, like Summer's afghan.

The sudden thought that I might never experience my mother's imprints again made me mourn her all over. For a few seconds, I focused on keeping my breathing steady.

"Uh-oh, look who's here." Shannon brought the truck to a halt behind Drewmore's white sedan. Standing in the light from the row of lampposts in front of the mansion was Nicholas Russo.

Chapter 11

Russo was flanked by his bodyguard Charlie and the same two men he'd been with at Smokey's. He wore a black suit and stood with his hands behind his back, his wide shoulders squared and his broad face unsmiling. Drewmore and Hamilton walked in his direction, Hamilton with her head held high.

"I gotta hear this." Cody sprang from the truck, and we hurried after him.

"What are you doing here?" Hamilton's high voice carried as we made our way toward them.

Russo's dark eyes flicked to us and then back to Hamilton. "I've had Ms. Rain watched. As her particular talents are of use to me, I wanted to make sure to protect my interests. I thought to discuss this with you privately, but it seems you have brought Ms. Rain and her friends here after your visit to her apartment. May I ask why?"

For a brief instant, JoAnna Hamilton curled in on herself, the picture of dejection, but almost as quickly, her back straightened and she met Russo's gaze with determination.

"This is a family matter, Russo. It has nothing whatsoever to do with you."

Russo's jaw tightened, though the rest of his face remained calm. The look unsettled me, made me feel anxious.

"You still have that squirrel watching me?" I bit down my anxiety enough to ask. "What do you think I'm going to do, skip town? I told you I'd read the contract. You don't have to force me."

Russo's gaze shifted to me. "I assure you, my actions are solely for your welfare. I am sorry for any problems this has given you, but after what happened this morning, I need to make sure no one interferes with my business, and unfortunately for the time being, you are part of that business."

I'd suspected as much from the moment I'd seen Ace outside my store, but I had my own point to make. "I assure you that I don't need your protection. If I see Ace again, I'm going to call the police and put a restraining order on the man—even if I have to make something up."

Russo studied me, his head slightly tilted. "If you're referring to the private detective I hired last year to look into my cousin's disappearance, be aware that he is no longer in my employ and hasn't been since our last encounter. I don't reward mediocrity, and he proved a disappointment. If he was watching you, it wasn't by my command."

Russo hadn't employed Ace? Then why had he been outside my shop? I met Shannon's gaze and he nodded, pulling out his phone. I knew he'd get someone tracking Ace down.

"Ace is the man who was with me earlier," I told Hamilton, watching her reaction carefully. Could *she* have hired him to watch me? After all, he'd known exactly where she lived. Maybe that's why she'd let him into her lab.

She looked aghast. "You brought that man here, believing he was hired by Russo?"

"I made sure Ace knew I'd fulfill my promise regarding the contract," I said. "I believed that was the only information he'd take back to Russo. Ace doesn't usually exert himself for much more than the basics. Besides, I needed backup. For all I knew, you were the one who tried to kill me this morning."

Her chin lifted. "I most certainly did not. And if I'd known this man, Ace, had his own agenda besides being your backup, which apparently he does, I most certainly wouldn't have allowed him into my lab. The only reason I took you there was to make a point, to show you how important our technology is so that you would understand why I—" She didn't have to finish. I understood exactly what she couldn't say with Russo hovering nearby. She wanted me to understand why she was making a deal with the devil, and why she didn't want me to tell him her secrets.

"Well, whoever he's working for, he can't have learned much," Shannon said. "Ace was an officer once, and he has a good record." Knowing his dislike of Ace, I appreciated how much it cost him to say that.

Hamilton scowled, apparently not comforted, and I really couldn't blame her. With her brother missing and Russo showing up on her doorstep uninvited. What was she hiding from him anyway? It had to be serious, if she'd allowed me into her lab—and if it would cost lives, as she'd claimed.

During this exchange, Russo watched us with clear interest, and I realized he hadn't known Ace and I had come to Hamilton's earlier. He waited for silence before clearing his throat and adding, "If it means anything, Ace did come to me a few days ago when I arrived, hinting that despite a very occupied schedule, he was available to me, but I told him I'd brought enough of my own men."

We all looked up as Paige entered the driveway in a red Mazda, followed by an unmarked white Mustang that I knew belonged to the precinct. It looked a lot like the one Shannon normally drove, except for the dent in the bumper. Paige wore brown slacks and a dressy, fitted, pink blouse swirled with varying tones of brown, an outfit that told me she'd been on a date with her boyfriend when Shannon called her.

Russo stared at Hamilton. "More visitors, it looks like. Are you going to tell me what's happened?"

JoAnna Hamilton sighed and nodded at Winston Drewmore, giving him permission to explain.

"We have hired Ms. Rain," he told Russo, "to help us find JoAnna's brother. We believe the reason Ralph didn't show up to the meeting tonight wasn't because he was working but because someone prevented him from coming. At the time we were with you, someone broke into the lab on these premises. All the hardware and software has been removed or destroyed, and our backups are missing—possibly they're with Ralph."

Russo's nostrils flared. "And when were you going to tell me all this?"

"When we determined it necessary," Hamilton said, a touch of imperiousness entering her voice. "It's possible Ralph disappeared to avoid capture and that he managed to secure the data."

She hadn't mentioned any of those thoughts to me, and I suspected she was trying to placate Russo. After all, her safe had been opened. But I supposed Ralph Shatlock could have taken the hard drive from there and run for it.

"We'd better hope you're right." Russo's gaze went to me. "Well, let's get on with it. Maybe you can tell us what happened."

"There is a matter of payment," Cody said. "Autumn's standard fee is five hundred dollars an hour."

I barely stopped myself from gaping. The truth was, I'd never charged anything to use my talent, even when I'd been specifically sought out to find someone. Instead, I encouraged people to purchase something at my store. That way we all won. Only the police paid me, and they had a limit of fifty bucks a day.

"That won't be a problem," Drewmore said. "Now, if you'll just come with me."

He led the way to the front door, through the house, and down the stairs. Inside the lab, the destruction was immediately apparent. Machines had been smashed, pieces of glass, metal, and plastic scattered over the floor. Wooden tables were cracked in half as though by some deranged giant, filing cabinets caved in and overturned, and stray papers lay everywhere. The music box Shatlock had "printed" was also destroyed, splintered into a hundred little pieces.

Violence marked this deed, signaling that whoever had been here meant business. I could see why Hamilton worried about her brother.

Behind me, I heard gasps and murmurs of amazement. Drewmore didn't show any reaction, though maybe he'd already been inured to the sight.

Russo shook his head. "This was personal. Who hates you this badly, JoAnna?"

"Competitors, of course."

"Who are these competitors?" Paige asked. When no one

answered, she added, "Please don't touch anything until we're finished."

She motioned to the two plainclothes officers I recognized vaguely from the precinct to begin their examination of the room. One man was lean and had graying brown hair, while the other had black hair, a barrel chest, and a narrow chin. I remembered this last officer had once asked me to read his wife's wedding ring to confirm her affair. I'd refused and recommended marital counseling. As far as I knew, they'd worked things out and were still together.

Hamilton bristled. "I hired Ms. Rain to examine this lab. She will touch what she wants."

"I'll be careful," I told Paige, and she nodded. Motioning to Cody, I followed the officers farther into the room.

Drewmore came with us. "Is there anything I can help with?" he asked, tapping me lightly on the shoulder.

"We need something they might have touched," I said. "But most of this damage looks like it was done with a sledgehammer or something very heavy."

"What about the filing cabinets?" Cody hobbled in that direction, and I followed. We lost precious minutes while the officers checked for fingerprints, and then, squatting down, Cody picked up the scattered drawers and pushed them over to me one by one as I sat on my heels. I watched him carefully for signs of an imprint, but he didn't react, so I shook my head after touching each drawer and pretending to read it.

"Could everyone step back?" Cody growled after a few minutes, his hand poised over the handle on a drawer. I wondered if his skin tingled like mine did when approaching a strong imprint.

"Please," I said. "I need to be alone."

Shannon ushered everyone back, but they were still watching. Cody shifted his weight until his back was toward them. Taking a deep breath, he let his hand fall. I waited several seconds, knowing that was a lifetime in a terrible imprint. Cody emitted a tiny grunt. I closed my hand over his, ready to pull him away from the handle, hoping I could do it without attracting notice.

My world tilted, and there it was, an imprint that seared me until I existed only in the memory that wasn't mine.

Anger, burning hot anger. He was supposed to be here. Did someone warn him? The information we'd found on the computer was useful, but the flashing warnings announcing that the data had been destroyed because of unlawful access meant that any information the computer still held wouldn't be enough. We needed complete data—or the scientist himself. I yanked out the drawer, spilling it to the ground.

The imprint ended and began again, but Cody and I both pulled away from the drawer. I let out an involuntary gasp as I fell back, head reeling, onto the cool cement floor that had been painted with a rubbery gray layer of enamel.

Shannon was at my side in an instant, looking between me and Cody. "You felt that," Cody said in a low growl.

I nodded. Somehow I had. I swiveled my weight around, reaching for the drawer again but stopping short of touching the handle. Not even the slightest tingle. Did that mean Cody had somehow facilitated the reading? Instead of being discouraged, I felt a surge of hope. Cody or no, I *had* felt something. Maybe I wouldn't always be blind.

"What did you see?" Hamilton poised over me in her purple skirt. Behind her, Russo watched us both with hooded eyes. He still didn't trust Hamilton, maybe even less now, but I bet he'd go through with the deal in an effort to get his hands on the software and diagrams.

Unless we never found Ralph Shatlock alive.

Everyone waited. Even Paige and the officers paused in their examination of the room.

"They were definitely looking for the data on nanotechnology," I said to JoAnna Hamilton, not looking at Cody. "I think their original plan was to take your brother, but he wasn't in the lab when they got here like they thought he'd be." I shifted position, readying myself to come to my feet. I didn't like everyone looming over me.

"They can't have missed him by much." Drewmore extended a hand to help me, but Shannon stepped in and helped me up himself. If we'd been alone I would have teased him about it.

JoAnna frowned and began pacing.

"What is it, JoAnna?" Russo's voice was casual but bordered on command.

She stopped pacing and sighed. "I was sure they'd taken him. The time stamp on my safe upstairs says it was accessed *after* the door down here was opened. If Ralph was the one who opened the safe, that means he was still in the house when they got here."

Shannon's expression darkened. He hated when people intentionally hid important information.

"Maybe he's still here hiding." Drewmore started for the door, and we all followed, separating as we spread throughout the house. I followed Cody. Hamilton followed me, but she was called by Shannon to open a locked door, leaving us alone.

"Look, the safe," Cody said when we found it at last in an upstairs sitting room. He reached out one hand to the door and the other to the combination dial. "There's an imprint . . . I see him opening it. He knows the combination. Must be Shatlock. He's hurrying. Fear. There's another man in the hallway waiting. A lookout. I can't see his face. That's all."

Before Cody removed his hand, I set mine on his once again, but this time I couldn't feel the imprint or see the men he described. A lump formed in my throat.

"Give it time," Cody said brusquely, without meeting my gaze.

An hour later, with the house thoroughly searched, the only thing we found out of place was a set of footprints in one of the back flowerbeds. These we supposed might have belonged to the man in the hallway from the safe imprint, or one of the people who'd wrecked the lab, or perhaps the gardener.

While Paige and the two officers finished up in the basement lab, the rest of us sat down at the rectangular table in Hamilton's large kitchen, where a pair of dainty white ladies' gloves were the only centerpiece. Hamilton put the gloves away while Drewmore made a pot of coffee and offered me a cup, which I refused.

"Got any protein?" I asked.

He reached in the fridge and pulled out a wedge of cheese. "Will this do? Or we might have a pork chop left over from dinner."

"This is fine." I sat nibbling on my cheese while everyone discussed who might be responsible for the break-in and what we should do next. Everyone but Shannon, who stood up to pace by the window, staring out at the dark lake, and Cody, who edged around the room, touching things. Occasionally, he met my gaze and shook his head.

A shuffle at the door drew our attention, and we all looked to see Maribel Hamilton coming into the kitchen from a door that I'd learned during the search led to the garage. Her peach dress was askew, as if she'd dressed hastily and misaligned the buttons. "Oh, I didn't know we had visitors," she said, her hands clutching a large black purse to her bosom. After wandering in confusion over the group, her eyes settled on Drewmore. "Has something happened, dear?"

An odd expression I couldn't decipher appeared on Drewmore's face. "I called you, Grandma. Remember? We agreed you were staying at your friend's tonight after the bridge party. I was going to pick you up in the morning."

Maribel frowned. "I decided I didn't want to stay there. Her bed is too hard. I made her drive me home. Besides, I remembered your voice sounded odd, and I had to make sure you were okay."

"Of course he's safe," JoAnna Hamilton snapped. "I'd never let anything happen to him. You know that."

"Yes, JoAnna." Maribel smiled, but her eyes didn't quite meet her cousin's.

Drewmore stood and went around the table, placing a hand on his grandmother's shoulder, a gentle smile of real affection on his face. "Why don't you go upstairs and get ready for bed? I'll come up and see you in a minute."

Maribel looked up into his eyes and nodded. "All right." Still clutching her purse, she slipped by the table and disappeared through the far kitchen doorway.

"Sorry about that," Hamilton said to no one in particular as Drewmore reclaimed his seat.

"So, who exactly is your competition?" Shannon asked as though the interruption hadn't occurred. "Obviously, they'll be suspects."

Hamilton exchanged a glance with Drewmore before she

spoke. "Our two main competitors are Print Perfect and Tarragon Inc. Both have created 3D printers and have brought a watered-down version to market. However, Print Perfect is struggling with funds and Tarragon has run into problems with some of the models they released in Japan. That means we are poised to be the leader in the field, but they can't know how close we are, not unless someone's told them, and who would do that? Aside from our family, only a couple of our engineers have the whole picture, and when they aren't here working with Ralph, they practically live at our other facility which has been under guard since we had some problems a few years ago. We have a profit-sharing program in place for those particular men that will make them rich. It's hard to imagine them betraying us. Even if they did, they don't have access to complete copies of our information. That is—or was—available only here."

Drewmore glanced at Cody, who was fingering a decorative ceramic bowl on the counter. "Tarragon has connections in Japan, and some important investors, but I don't see how they or Print Perfect can be responsible. They don't have the manpower or connections, I wouldn't think."

Something Hamilton had said bothered me, but I couldn't quite pinpoint it. It had to do with Tarragon, something that clicked with another tidbit of information I'd picked up that day, if only I could remember what.

"We'll check them out," Shannon said, pivoting on his foot. "But maybe it's not either of them. Maybe this is payback for something else." His gaze rested on Russo at the foot of the table. Sitting next to him, bald Charlie stiffened.

Russo carefully set down his cup. "If you're implying that the payback is pointed at me, yes, several of my competitors could be responsible for such a thing." He glanced at Charlie and then at his other two bodyguards at the end of the table. "However, none of my men would have passed information about the contract to my competitors, so it's unlikely they would have knowledge of my impending deal with JoAnna, much less know her lab codes."

If his men were all loyal, how did JoAnna Hamilton learn about me and my role with the contract before I did? I needed to ask, but not with Russo hanging around. "What about Ace?" I asked instead. "Maybe he went to them."

Shannon shook his head. "He's obviously got an agenda, but he's mostly small time. He's been a cop. He knows the score."

I wondered how Ace had started working for Russo in the first place. I looked at the mob boss, but he answered before I could voice the thought. "Charlie called him off the Internet the first time we used him. He was good at finding things so we used him on a case-by-case basis, up until the last fiasco. Frankly, I don't much like the man, and not just because he's an ex-cop. But then, I don't like most people. I find them incompetent." His lips turned up in a hint of a smile. "Present company excepted, of course."

Nobody returned his smile.

"At any rate," he continued, "Ace was never told anything important about my affairs, and I doubt he could learn anything vital in one visit here with Ms. Rain, even if he was allowed to see the lab. He was likely trying to ingratiate himself with me."

I thought he underestimated Ace, which was almost as bad as overestimating him as Russo had done in our case with the Japanese mobster Joben Saito, when he'd sent Ace into Saito's lair without backup. That blunder had almost cost Russo's cousin his life, and mine—and Ace's and Shannon's as well. I clamped my jaw tight so I wouldn't say anything.

Wait, I had it now, the thing that had been bugging me when Hamilton had been speaking earlier. She'd mentioned Japan. Hadn't something else about Japan come up that day? I couldn't remember. Maybe it was only my thoughts about the old case.

Shannon studied me, his eyes somehow communicating desire, though I doubted anyone except me would be able to tell. "We still need to find out for sure what Ace was doing watching Autumn's store." Though his gaze didn't move from my face, my reaction from his stare traveled down my body, saturating every inch with yearning. No wonder I'd avoided those eyes before we started dating.

"I'd think finding out who tried to kidnap Ms. Rain would be higher on the list," Russo said dryly. "It can't be a coincidence. Maybe it was an attempt to stop our business deal, and if we find the perpetrator, we might find who tossed JoAnna's lab."

Shannon spared him a glance. "Well, we're also working another case, so what happened to Autumn could be related to that, but you're right, it is a lead, and without anything more indicating where Ms. Hamilton's brother has gone, we'll examine every aspect carefully to see if what happened to her is connected."

Something had to be connected. Right now all we had was a series of events that didn't make sense: old people dying, missing heirlooms, the awful imprint on the rug, my abduction, Ace's odd behavior, JoAnna Hamilton's secret, the ruined lab, the missing brother, the man in the hallway. And sitting above it all, the 3D printing technology, and nanites that might eventually create weapons or a child's lung. Technology I didn't want either Russo or his enemies to have.

"What about the Saitos?" I asked. "Could they be involved?"

Russo shook his head and Charlie actually smiled. "Still in prison and all their funds confiscated. No, I'd have heard if he'd regrouped enough to pull off something like this."

I was glad. Among other things, Saito had tried to kill a child for revenge, and he deserved to rot in prison for the rest of his life. Even with all the many evils Russo had committed, a part of me didn't believe he was capable of such a thing. He'd at least wait until the child was grown before enacting his revenge. Not much comfort, when I thought of it that way.

Which reminded me of Russo's first wife. What exactly had happened to her? Maybe I'd ask Paige to contact the police in New Jersey to see if they knew anything. For some reason, it suddenly seemed very important, but Russo wouldn't thank me for bringing it up.

"So, Mr. Russo, how about giving us the names of people you think could pull off this break-in and have a reason to do so?" Paige said from the doorway, where she'd apparently been standing long enough to hear the end of our conversation. I could tell from her expression that she and the other officers had found no new leads in the basement lab. "Nanotechnology aside, it's entirely possible that damaging you, and not Mrs. Hamilton, was the motivation."

Russo's eyes narrowed. "Actually, there are half a dozen competitors that come to mind, but I will have to get back to you on their names. I need to do my own review first."

"That will waste time," Shannon said with poorly concealed impatience.

Russo stood, his bulk towering several inches over Shannon. "Nevertheless, I will do it. So unless you have reason to detain me, I think I'll leave so I can get to work." When Shannon didn't respond, Russo flicked a hand at his men, and they arose, following him to the door. "I'll be in touch, JoAnna. Please call if you hear from your brother."

"See them to the door, Winston," Hamilton responded.

Drewmore stood and opened the door leading into the garage, the same one his grandmother had entered before. Russo didn't seem to mind the back exit, and I wondered if using them was a habit with him.

Paige glared at Russo's back until he was out of sight. "He'll never give us any names."

"No," I said. "He's going to find out if any of his enemies did this so that if they have the backups, he can negotiate and keep any stolen nanotechnology for himself."

"I don't believe any of his competitors would have the knowledge necessary to have done this or to understand the importance of our research," Drewmore said. "We've kept negotiations very low key."

"Well someone knew." Shannon met his gaze without blinking. "And if the men who destroyed the lab did catch up with Shatlock before he got away, Russo might have the means to track them down. He might try to recover Shatlock for his own purposes."

"He could get Ralph killed!" JoAnna Hamilton shoved back from the table and came to her feet, her face pale.

I thought it was decent of her to worry more about her brother's life than the information he held. By the tight look on her cousin Drewmore's face, I couldn't say the same for him.

"Well, he might not give you a name, but I know at least

one man he's been at odds with for ten years." Hamilton's eyes gleamed.

"JoAnna, are you sure?" Drewmore said, edging closer to her. "If Russo finds out . . ."

"We have to protect Ralph."

Drewmore nodded and she continued, "The name's Frank O'Donald. We don't know exactly what happened between them, and I'm sure the conflict isn't new, but it definitely escalated when Russo took over running his uncle's business. If he's involved, it'll be what Russo needs to start an all-out war."

She exchanged a glance with Drewmore, and I knew there was more they weren't saying, but I couldn't force them to elaborate.

"Thank you," Paige said. "We'll put some feelers out and see if they have a presence in town. I heard about them when I worked vice, but the only thing I really remember is that they're big into drugs and they're located somewhere on the East Coast."

Hamilton nodded. "That's probably right. I'm not sure."

"So you don't know this Frank O'Donald?" Shannon asked, obviously picking up on the same undercurrents I was sensing.

"Russo mentioned him a few times, but we've never met." Hamilton met his stare without flinching, but it didn't mean she was telling the truth.

"Well, there's nothing more we can do here." Shannon walked over to where I sat at the table. "But we'll have people working on it all night. Now that Russo knows and there's no need to keep it under wraps, we'll be able to utilize more personnel."

"Then you'll let us know?" Hamilton pushed in the chair where she'd been seated.

"Of course. But call us if you hear from your brother."

"All right."

Hamilton walked Shannon and Paige to the door, this time the front entrance, trailed by the other two officers and Cody, who was still fingering things in a way that made me nervous. Drewmore and I brought up the rear.

"Thanks for coming," Drewmore said to me. "I could see that wasn't easy for you. All the violence left behind, things most of us never realize are there. It must be a challenge having such a gift."

"It can be." I still wasn't sure what had happened when I'd touched Cody in the lab, but I hadn't lost the hope it had given me.

Drewmore gave me a smile that had something a little more in it, something that made me take notice. He had none of Shannon's rugged good looks or his compact grace, and certainly not his eyes. He also didn't have Jake's broad shoulders and eye-catching locs, but his face was pleasant, his lips full, and his gray eyes were warm like granite left in the sun instead of cool like Hamilton's. He was younger than I was by at least five or maybe six years, though I often passed for younger, and his face lacked the arrogance of other wealthy young businessmen I'd met. Under other circumstances, I might have been interested in him. He *was* interested in me—or pretending to be, which I suspected was more likely. I wondered if he had an object he wanted me to read.

"Well, I'm sorry to have played a part in your coming here," he said. "Maybe when it's all over, I can make it up to you. Dinner, perhaps."

It didn't seem to bother him that I had a boyfriend; maybe

as Hamilton's heir, he didn't feel the same rules applied to him. Or he really wanted that object read.

"We'll see," I said. "I just hope we find your cousin."

"He's a smart guy. And paranoid to the point that he should probably see a doctor about it. If he got out before those men found him, I think he'll stay safe." His glance fell past my stained jeans to my bare feet, and his smile faltered. I nearly laughed aloud. Could he picture me as his date at one of his high-society business events? I very much doubted it. It took a certain kind of man to put up with my eccentricities. I'd once had doubts about Shannon in that respect—in fact, I still had some of those doubts.

Winston gestured for me to go through the front door where the others conversed outside at the bottom of the porch steps. I started forward, but then stopped. "Uh, Mr. Drewmore, any idea where he might go? Shatlock, I mean."

"Please, call me Winston. And I hope you don't mind if I call you Autumn."

I nodded. "Sure." Whatever made him more open toward me. "So, is there someplace he might go?"

"JoAnna would know better than me, but I really don't think there's any certain place. Ralph lived at the lab."

"He wasn't there this afternoon."

Winston grinned. "It's Friday. He always goes to the movies on Friday afternoons. Usually a double feature. Sometimes I play hooky and go with him."

I didn't want to like Winston because I knew he and Hamilton were hiding something—maybe the secret she didn't want me to read on the contract—but I found that I did like him. I wished I could read a few of his imprints so I could understand what kind of a man he really was. Strange. I hadn't always depended on imprints to tell me who should be my friends.

"Last I heard, Ralph planned to go straight to the meeting after the films. He was supposed to have the backup ready beforehand. I assumed he had everything with him, but I guess he didn't if he came back here."

"If they'd been watching him, wouldn't the theater have been a better place to try to take him?"

He shrugged. "They must not have known about the theater. He's only been going the past six months since he moved the most sensitive things away from the main lab. As I said, he's a little paranoid, and he wanted to guarantee more security."

"That seems to indicate he doesn't trust someone."

"Yeah, but he's always been like that. Look, here's my card, in case you think of anything else you want to ask me."

"Thanks." Pocketing the card, I went out the door and onto the porch. There was no sign of the ants under the lights, and I wondered if they'd been sprayed with poison and washed away.

JoAnna Hamilton watched me walk toward them, her eyes granite and her face unwelcoming and stiff, quite a change from a few minutes earlier when she'd expressed worry about her brother. Her eyes shifted to me and then to Winston.

Oh, so I'm not good enough for him, am I? I thought. I guess being good enough to help her find her brother was one thing, but that was as far as her trust extended. Good thing I wasn't interested anyway.

"I'll send you a check for your services tonight," she said. "And I would appreciate your continued work on the case. You can bill me for the hours."

"All right." Most people who sought me out simply wanted

a one-time reading, and it was my own obsession about finding whoever was missing that made me continue searching. I was never paid for the end result, which was probably why I still had trouble making the mortgage on my shop.

Shannon reached for my hand, which was a little gummy from the cheese. I was too tired to care. "Let's get you home," he said.

I curled gratefully into his arm, letting him make our farewells. Winston put his own arm around Hamilton, as though protecting her or comforting her, or maybe both. I wondered again about her secret, though a part of me was glad not to know it.

Cody preceded us to the truck, his shoulders hunched and his limp even more pronounced. I felt a fleeting guilt at having dragged him from his bed with my problems.

Paige waved the other officers to their car. "Go ahead and start processing. Get whoever else is available to help. I'll be in bright and early." Under her breath, she added, "Guess I'll have to cancel waterskiing with Matthew tomorrow afternoon." She didn't sound all that upset, and I knew it was because she thrived on the job.

I perked up. "You're letting him see you in a swim suit? Now I know it's serious." She had a smashing figure, so it wasn't actually the suit but the fact that her hair would be wet that was significant. I'd never seen her without her thick blond hair ironed perfectly straight.

"Matthew's seen me in a suit before." She rolled her eyes. "So are we going to see the owners of In Loving Memory in the morning? Or are we going to pass the case on to someone else?"

"Oh, we're going." Shannon's voice was grim, and I knew he was thinking of me rolled up in that rug.

"Good." Paige motioned to me and Cody. "Come on, guys. You're with me. I'll drive you home."

I looked at Shannon. "You're not coming back with us?"

"I promised JoAnna Hamilton I'd meet her at the precinct to start the paperwork on her brother. With the break-in, we can't assume he got away. They could have found him later. But I'll swing by your place after I'm finished. Paige can stay with you until then."

"No one needs to stay," Cody growled. "I can take care of Autumn. Heck, she could probably whip anybody who tried anything—and do it with one hand tied behind her back."

That made me laugh. He looked like someone might blow him over with a slightest breath, and my head was once again pounding so hard I felt I might explode. I was glad Paige was coming back to my apartment. She was great with a gun, and around her I didn't have to pretend to be tough like I did with Shannon. I hated showing weakness around him. Though I'd never really stopped to examine why, I thought it might be related to how Jake had begun protesting every time I wanted to use my ability. Shannon hadn't been that way so far, but given his reaction at my earlier visit with Hamilton, how would he feel about me being in danger if things progressed between us? It was a conversation I'd make sure we'd have later.

He'd put anyone who'd been abducted on official watch, I thought, and it was true, but I knew my treatment was special.

Maybe that was okay.

Shannon gave me a too-brief kiss on my lips, ending before I had the chance to enjoy his touch. It was just as well. I was dead on my feet and my dizziness wasn't from his closeness.

I fell asleep on the way back to my apartment, and Paige had to wake me to go inside. Most of the apartments in my building and those around it were dark, and though the moon was shining, the middle-of-the-night stillness felt sinister. Rubbing the sleep from my eyes, I looked around carefully, but nothing was out of place. No lurking figures, no strangers walking by.

This time my apartment door was securely shut. Even so, Paige entered first, hand on her holstered weapon, and a part of me thought she was disappointed when she didn't have to draw her gun.

As we waited for Paige to check the rest of the apartment, the music box caught my eye, reminding me of the smashed one at the lab, the copy. Or at least what JoAnna Hamilton told me was the copy. I picked up the small box, the smoothness feeling cold against my skin. I wished the music assembly worked, so I could wind it up and see what song it played.

"Well, goodnight," Cody nodded in my direction before heading to Winter's room.

I clutched the music box more tightly and watched him go, my world turning around me, oddly distorted as though I was peering into the wrong end of a pair of binoculars. I'd long ago packed or given away Winter's things, and my sister often slept there when her husband was out of town, but it was different having my biological father sleep there.

Stop obsessing, I told myself. The man had come to help and he needed a bed. I owed it to him. The bed, not my heart.

"I'll take the couch," Paige said, after checking my bedroom.

I nodded, wondering how much she'd sleep.

Leaving my bedroom dark, I set the music box on one of my shelves. I had two other antique music boxes with in-laid pearl designs—a heart and a kissing couple—and a half dozen others with various designs. Maybe I'd keep this one, too. It held the last pleasant imprint I'd experienced.

I sloughed off my jeans, not bothering to find my sweats, and slipped between the sheets. Before I drifted off to sleep, I thought of the man walking away from my apartment earlier. My apartment was filled with antiques, some worthless and some more expensive than I should keep here without an alarm, but nothing had been touched.

If someone had broken into my apartment earlier and left the door open, what had they been looking for?

Chapter 12

Sweat ran down my temples, the back of my neck, and down my sides. Everywhere. My muscles strained, and I felt invigorated.

"Harder!" Steve shouted, tossing his brown hair from his eyes.

I kicked at the red rectangular pad in his hands, snapping my foot at the last second to increase the power. Today I wasn't wearing the rubber-soled socks I'd begun wearing to practice to blot out any stray imprints. While in the normal world there weren't usually many important imprints at foot level, at a place where kicks were vital, that didn't always hold true. I'd gotten tired of feeling frustration or anger left on the pads by others. Today I couldn't feel them.

"Yeah! That's what I'm talking about! Again!"

I lashed out once more, sending his lean frame backward, fueled by his rare praise.

He nodded and lowered the pad. "You're ready."

Ready, he meant, to test for the rank of second dan, or second-degree black belt. I felt ready. Though most of my earlier ranks had been earned as a teen, if you counted the time put into practice, not to mention real life experience, I'd crammed double the learning into this past year than I'd put in through all my years as a youth. Unfortunately, black belt testing was still months away. But my instructor, a fourth dan, had begun to include increasingly difficult sparring matches and move combinations, mostly, I thought, to keep me from getting killed.

I bowed. "Yes, sir! I'm ready." Which was good because during the night, my question had changed from *what* had they been looking for at my apartment to *who* had they been looking for, and since I was the only one living there, I needed to be ready to defend myself. So I'd dragged myself out of bed in the wee hours of Saturday morning to endure the two hours of intense workout at my weekly semi-private taekwondo lessons.

Steve returned my bow, and we both laughed, walking off the mat together. Near the edge, I stumbled, falling hard on my knee. "You okay?" Steve asked.

I nodded, jumping to my feet before he could offer me a hand. "I don't know what happened." Except I did. It was the dizziness again, though I'd felt strong and surprisingly rested when Shannon and Paige had dropped me off here this morning.

As we left the mat, we were joined by Andrea Mathews, a fellow student who shared my private lesson with me. We'd once had a third member, a greasy-haired man with a vindictive streak, but he'd begun teaching at another studio, and we'd all been glad to see him go.

Andrea pulled out the elastic that held her thick golden hair, shaking her head and running her fingers through her hair to cool off. Her face was beautiful and feminine, an asset that masked her strength and ability to crush her opponents.

She waited until Steve took his leave and then said, "I loved how you pushed him back like that. For a minute I thought you'd knock him on his butt."

"I wish." I led the way to the showers. I still couldn't best Steven in a fair bout, but with surprise in my favor, and maybe a handful of keys, a real life battle with someone on his level wouldn't be as hopeless as it might have once been.

As we passed the window where observers could watch our training, I couldn't help glancing at Cody, who wore the paint-splattered jeans and blue shirt of the night before. Both looked a decade old. He watched me with an expression I'd never seen before, but as soon as he caught my gaze, he dipped his white head in acknowledgment and turned away.

"Who's that old guy anyway?" Andrea asked. "Do you know him? He was staring at you the entire time."

"Just a friend helping out with a case I'm consulting on." She knew about me meeting my biological father, but I didn't want to talk about it today.

She laughed. "I like that—the consultant using a consultant." She held the locker room door open for me. "You heading to your shop?" She knew I opened at nine and that usually I was in a huge hurry to shower so I could help Thera or Jake or whoever opened for me.

"Not today. My sister and my employees are covering for me. I have an interview I'm going to with the police. We're working two cases that might be related."

"I wish I could consult for that detective." She gave a longing sigh. "You're so lucky to be dating him."

"Don't you mean he's lucky to be dating me?"

She slammed open her locker, the door bouncing off the neighboring one. "Isn't that what I said? Anyway, you're amazing together, don't you think?"

I did think that, or wanted to, but all at once there was a part of me that felt, well, dead inside—despite how well I'd slept after leaving Hamilton's. It wasn't about Shannon, though, but the thought that without my ability, I could be changing into someone different from the person he might be falling in love with.

I was still thinking about this as I left the studio dressed in a gray, floor-length knit skirt that was snug at the waist and hips, angling wider toward my feet, and a dressy red blouse with buttons, my handbag slung over one shoulder. Cody followed me a half pace behind. Shannon and Paige waited for us outside, having already replaced the officer they'd left to protect me when they dropped us off. At some point during my two-hour workout, Shannon and Paige had changed to their usual detective attire—dark slacks and a dress shirt for him, a navy skirt and dress shirt for her.

Shannon's eyes, tracing over my freshly washed hair, were a caress. "Good workout?"

"Yeah." The electricity arcing between us was so strong, it was a wonder no one else could see it. The heat shoved my worry to the back of my mind. Ability or no ability, we'd work things out.

"We have news," Paige said as soon as we were inside Shannon's unmarked police Mustang, with Cody and me in the back. "That little trouble JoAnna Hamilton mentioned her company had a few years ago was none other than the death of two prominent scientists who worked for her."

I blinked, leaning forward. "That sounds serious. Why wouldn't she give us more details for something like that?"

"Perhaps because the deaths were presumed an accident," Paige shifted slightly in her seat as though to gauge Cody's reaction as well. "The two men were boating and apparently hit a reef or something. Broke up the boat pretty bad. They drowned, and most of their belongings were never found. Left behind wives and a couple kids each."

"How sad," I said.

"The interesting part," Shannon added as he deftly passed the car ahead of us, "is that three days later there was a breach at their facility. The police came to investigate the alarm and arrested a couple teens. The teens swore they were paid to break in, but there wasn't any proof, and since nothing was taken, the investigation was dropped."

I sat back in my seat, exchanging a look with Cody. "That must have been when the company started employing live guards. But how does that relate to what's going on now?"

"No apparent connection," Shannon said, "but it shows a pattern. It's remotely possible the incident was a first attempt from a competitor and last night was a second."

"We have a call out to the investigating officer," Paige added. "Sometimes they remember things that aren't in the written report. That might give us a lead."

Shannon's eyes met mine briefly in the mirror. "There's more. Get this, the main lab back then was located in New York, and Hamilton had an apartment there for ten years. But they moved their entire company here two years ago, presumably to build on some family land they have just over the Oregon border in Washington, right in the backyard of both her two main competitors."

"Why's that important?" Cody asked. "Things cost less here—real estate, employees, and such, which is why the other companies were here in the first place, I'll bet."

"Well," Shannon said, "it seems a little unusual to me that

Hamilton was so vague about that mobster Frank O'Donald she claims Russo is at odds with. I mean, if she lived in New York long enough to meet Russo in neighboring New Jersey, she would have at least heard of Frank O'Donald and known that he operated in New York."

I snorted. "Not everyone keeps an eye out for organized crime bosses. Aren't you grasping at straws? We don't even know where Hamilton met Russo. He has enough businesses here and in Washington that they could have met here."

"It's a coincidence I don't like," Shannon insisted.

He had a point. I made a mental note to ask Hamilton where she'd met Russo, or maybe I'd ask Winston since I liked him better. "I'm not sure why it matters if she knows this O'Donald guy, but if she does and she's hiding it, there's probably a reason, which I doubt we'll like."

Shannon signaled and pulled over. "Here we are."

The sign on the bottom floor of an office building read *In Loving Memory.*

"They agreed to meet us this morning," Paige said, opening her door. "But just so you know, they weren't very happy about it, especially when Shannon and I blew our cover yesterday and scared away some of their customers."

"Tough," Cody growled.

My feelings exactly.

In an outer reception area, we were met by the brown-haired woman who'd been running the auction we'd attended yesterday morning. She was older than I was, I thought, though her face looked younger than her hands and other exposed skin. I wondered if that meant plastic surgery. She wore a short black skirt and a blue shirt, both of which would have been appealing on her nice figure if they hadn't been so tight.

"Detective," she greeted Shannon with a smile. "I hope there wasn't a problem finding our place." She held on to Shannon's hand a little too long for my comfort, and her smile was excessively bright.

"Not at all, Ms. Frampion. You know my companion, Detective Reed, and these are Autumn Rain and Cory Beckett. They are consulting on the case. Everyone, this is Keeley Frampion, part owner of In Loving Memory."

Ms. Frampion nodded at us, her eyes running over me without expression, and then over Cody, her face showing a slight distaste that made me angry. I knew Cody didn't look like much, but he was a talented artist who donated more to charity every year than most generous people did in a lifetime. "Come right this way. The other two owners are waiting in our boardroom."

We followed her tight black skirt down the hall to a medium-sized room that felt crowded to me with the rectangular table filling up most of the space in the middle. Like the outer reception area, it didn't look poor or dingy, but neither did it look upper class—exactly what you'd expect from a company running estate sales. More wealthy accommodations would hint at taking advantage of clients, while dire need might indicate that they didn't make enough money to survive, much less help their clients. It felt practiced, faked, and I would have loved to place my hands over everything to verify this assumption through imprints.

"These are my co-owners, Vernon Waite and Boyd Nye," Frampion said. "Well, Vernon is also my brother-in-law. Gentlemen, these are Detective Martin and his colleagues." She left it to Shannon to finish the introductions, obviously not remembering our names.

Waite, a rounded, brown-haired man of average height, offered his hand first, his smile ready and insincere. His hand was so clammy, I wished I hadn't taken it. Cody didn't, and I knew that was because Waite wasn't wearing a ring on his right hand. Cody wasn't a people-lover, and he wouldn't extend himself with these strangers if there wasn't something to learn through an imprint.

The other man, Nye, was dark and hairy, and too lean for his tall frame, causing his large nose, eyes, and other features to jut unbecomingly. His expression was suspicious, and he wasted no time on a smile. He wore a ring, and Cody took his hand, though his expression showed no hint of what he might have discovered. I, of course, felt nothing but dizziness, which caused me to grip the top of a chair.

"Please have a seat," Waite invited.

I sat next to Cody, who reached out and fingered a remote on the table. I set my hand briefly on his, wondering if I could repeat what had happened in the lab, but I experienced nothing except more dizziness. Waite stared at me, one brow arched, and I casually withdrew my hand. Let him think what he would.

"As you know, we've had several complaints about missing items," Shannon said. "You have assured us cooperation by agreeing to send over lists of full inventories, but we need to ask a few more questions." He started with their clients, wanting to verify how many they'd known previously and if the company helped them liquidate belongings before death.

"We do help some people ease their retirement in that manner," Waite said. "Many of the older generation were hit hard by the economic downturn. But we keep full records for anything we sell, and those are provided to the heirs upon request. We can't be responsible, of course, for any sales their relatives may have made to other companies."

"At least three heirs have filled out complaints claiming that items went missing after the death of their parents," Paige said.

Frampion shook her head. "Impossible. You have to understand that they're grieving. They're likely recalling an earlier time when they saw it and have mixed up the dates. We keep very strict records." Waite smiled at her, and she beamed like a child given praise. Nye stared out the window looking bored.

I wanted Shannon to ask about the rug. The imprint proved it had recently been in the main part of the house. Why had it been tagged with such a high cost but moved to the attic where it would seem like junk? I gave an involuntary shiver at the memory of the imprint.

Shannon and Paige were talking about the company's overall increase in clients now, and Cody stood up to pace the room.

"We have increased our pre-need marketing ventures," Waite explained. "Naturally, those clients leave instructions with their heirs to liquidate their assets through us since we already have a working relationship and a familiarity with their situation. Others, we loan money now when they need it, and they agree to let us conduct the estate sale and collect our payment after they pass on. That's been a big attraction recently. Of course the heirs can opt out by paying back the loan, if they prefer." By pre-need, he meant pre-death, and I wondered if making a deal with In Loving Memory was tantamount to signing your own death certificate.

"So," I said in the lull that followed Waite's pronouncement, "what happens to the stuff that doesn't sell?"

"We have one of the highest sell-out rates." Frampion's eyes barely skimmed me. "One of us tries to be personally on-site much of the time to guarantee that everything runs smoothly. We discount only after the first day, or to smooth over any upset." She colored as though remembering that such an upset had occurred yesterday, and I guess that was our cue to thank her for discounting my items.

Not in my lifetime. "So what happens to the items you don't sell?" I asked, because she really hadn't answered my question.

Frampion glanced at Waite and then at Nye. When neither spoke, she said, "We do what all estate sale companies do. If the heirs don't wish to keep the items, we donate them to charity."

"We'll need a list of those items for all the estate sales this past year," Shannon said, with a nod in my direction.

"I'm afraid that won't be possible." Waite drew his gaze away from Cody, who was touching the frame of a print on the wall. "Once the heirs sign off on them, they're donated in bulk to charity."

Paige blinked. "No itemization?"

"That's right. At that point, we no longer care what happens to the items. If we feel they may sell at another estate sale, we may buy a few items ourselves and feature them at another sale, and those things we do itemize, but for the most part that doesn't happen. From what I understand, the charity we use distributes to many different outlets, and they also don't keep itemized records, except in how many pounds of items. Mostly it's clothes and shoes that are left."

"So there's no way to track the items after they're donated," Shannon said.

Now we were getting somewhere. If a murder weapon was purposely overpriced and later sent to charity, even if the police began to suspect foul play, they wouldn't be able to track the item, unlike objects sold and itemized at the estate sale itself. Anything else would be lost in a trail of charitable outlets.

Waite glanced at his watch. "I'm afraid we have to close this interview. We need to do the rounds at our estate sales in a few minutes. We hire excellent employees, but we must keep track of them. If you have any more questions, please let us know."

"Better yet, let our attorney know," Nye said, speaking for the first time since the introductions. His jaw worked and his nostrils flared. "I'm not sure who has been feeding you information, but my father started this business, and I've worked very hard all my life to make it what it is today. I trust my partners and the business model we've created. The ideas we have may seem odd to some, but they are working—and working well. I suspect this investigation is nothing more than sour grapes from our competitors. Now if you'll excuse me, I have a client I need to see." He unfolded his tall frame and stalked from the room.

"Uh," Waite said, standing. "You'll have to excuse him. He's rather sensitive about the business. It was failing up until a few years ago, and he's given most of his time to turning it around. He's afraid this investigation will be bad for business."

Shannon came to his feet. "I can't pretend it won't impact your business, but clearing your company of wrongdoing is a good thing. The increase in, uh, your business is dramatic enough that it is disconcerting."

Frampion smiled up at Shannon from her seated position. "I assure you, detective, it's due to hard work and not to anything nefarious. We both joined the company two years ago exactly because we saw the business was on the upswing." She stood, placing a hand on Shannon's arm. "Let me get those files for you. I believe I left them in the lobby. We'll give them to you on your way out."

That quickly we were out of the building and on the street.

"Well?" I said, eyeing Cody. "Did you pick up anything on Nye? From his ring?"

Shannon and Paige paused in mid-step, looking at him. Paige knew about Cody, of course. I'd confided in her after the last case when I'd learned he shared my ability.

Cody shook his head. "I mean, there was an imprint, but all I picked up was his feelings about his son. He died recently, or at least it feels that way to him. I think he's clean. Can't say for the others."

I scowled, not wanting it to be true. The gaunt man looked like someone who would hurt others for his own gain. Or maybe to protect the legacy of a company handed down by his father.

"What about the rest?" Shannon asked.

"The furnishings, the pictures, the remote—everything came from estate sales as far as I could tell. But there was nothing involving murder, or robbery for that matter."

"Did you pick up anything, Autumn?" Paige looked at me expectantly.

Shannon hadn't told her about my inability to read imprints? I fought to hide my surprise, unsure what to make of that. I became aware of Paige and Shannon watching me, Paige expectantly, and Shannon with a hint of an apologetic smile. That he hadn't confided in her was nothing to apologize about. It told me he'd kept my confidence, placing me above his own partner.

"I felt nothing important," I said truthfully. I didn't mind

Paige knowing, but it felt good not to have someone treating me like I was broken.

Because I *was* broken. I felt it with every breath I took.

"Then we're back to square one." Paige started across the street where we'd left the Mustang.

"Not exactly," I said, keeping pace with her and Shannon. "I know the rug was used in a murder. After what they told us, I think they purposefully overpriced it so it would end up in a charity shop somewhere. No way to trace. No evidence to get rid of."

Paige sighed. "I'm guessing the same thing. But our evidence was destroyed in that fire, and the men who took you are nowhere to be found, so we don't know who hired them. Meanwhile, how do we find objects that might have been used in other murders? Even if we knew what to look for, we wouldn't know where. The police didn't find any suspicious objects at the scenes."

We'd reached the car, and I opened the rear door on the passenger side. "I'm not surprised they didn't find anything. They were probably placed in an attic with a bunch of junk."

Paige opened her own door. "To be honest, I don't think they really looked too far, since the deaths appeared accidental. At least we have the MO now, and we can thoroughly investigate any future deaths and also any overpriced items at their estate sales. That is, *if* they don't change the way they've been operating."

"Of course they'll shake things up." Shannon started around the car where Cody had already climbed in the rear seat. "They know we're onto them. They also know we don't have any real proof, so all they have to do is lie low for a while. But we're all overlooking something here. We don't have to wait until they kill again because we do know the whereabouts of at least one more overpriced object."

Paige snapped her fingers. "The George Washington bust! I'd forgotten about that. It was stuffed in a closet and probably wouldn't have sold at all if the owner's son hadn't shown up to complain about missing items and verified that it was purchased for much cheaper." She sat in her seat and took out her phone. "I'll call the buyer now. We need to get to it before that threesome in there"—she tipped her head toward the building—"remember its existence and make it disappear."

I knew her unspoken fear was the same as mine: maybe they already had.

Chapter 13

"So if we find an imprint on the bust, you'll test it for other evidence?" I asked from the back seat.

"We'll send it to forensics regardless," Shannon said. "If the bust is what bashed in the head of its owner, instead of a slip on wet tile as he entered the hot tub, there may be enough evidence even if there's no imprint. But an imprint would certainly help identify a suspect at this point."

Paige shot me an apologetic look from the front seat. "I'm sorry you have to experience another potentially nasty imprint. You could always let Cody do it instead. You don't both have to try."

She was always asking me to read things, so her sudden attack of conscience felt odd to me. I stole a look at Cody next to me, who'd suddenly become more alert.

"That's okay," I said, my throat tightening. I needed to tell Paige about losing my ability, and I would the first moment we found a little privacy. I didn't want to become emotional in front of everyone.

She mistook my subdued tone. "Are you sure you're up to it after yesterday?"

I was prevented from making a response when the person she'd called answered. We listened as she briefly explained the police interest in the bust.

"No," she said after a pause. "He doesn't have to be home. We'll pick it up and deliver it later." A note of exasperation entered her voice. "May I remind you that this is a murder investigation? No, please do not touch the bust or move it anywhere." Pause. "Yes, we'll guarantee a reimbursement if anything happens to it. We'll be there within a half hour." She hung up, shaking her head. "As if I can really guarantee that. Do you really think they're going to want it back if it was the murder weapon?"

"Probably sell it on eBay for ten times more," Cody muttered.

I laughed, surprised he even knew what eBay was. My sister had done her best to update him with technology; he even had a computer now so she could email him baby pictures.

"Where to?" Shannon asked.

"Let me plug it into the GPS." Paige started punching buttons on the dash.

I intermittently held my breath and hyperventilated on our journey, half expecting someone to beat us to the evidence. But when we arrived at our destination fifteen minutes later, Paige and Shannon went to the door of the house and returned with the bust in Shannon's gloved hands. He hesitated for a moment before shaking his head, indicating for Paige to open the trunk. "We need to get this fingerprinted first."

I nodded and Paige stared at me where I lounged against the car, my long skirt fluttering slightly every now and then with a stray breeze. "What, no protest?" she asked. "You could probably convince him."

Shannon snorted. "Get in the car." As he placed the bust in the trunk, his eyes met mine with a question.

I nodded. Yes, I needed to tell her soon.

At the station Paige was inundated with information about Frank O'Donald and Hamilton's two main competitors, Tarragon Inc. and Print Perfect. She excused herself with a gleam of excitement in her eyes. When Shannon finally brought the bust to me and Cody in the small interrogation room where we waited, she hadn't yet joined us.

"There was blood evidence on the bust up in this area"— he indicated the forehead—"so don't touch there, and a lot of prints, which they've already taken. The man was found drowned in his hot tub, though, so they'll need to do more tests for traces of chemicals, but they've cleared it for you to touch down here. Normally we'd record this part, but I know Cody would rather remain anonymous."

I jumped up to stand at Cody's elbow as he reached out to the bust with one knuckle. I fought the urge to place my hand over his. The past two times hadn't given any result, and I had no reason to believe this would be different. His face paled as he made contact. He shut his eyes grimacing. His entire arm shook.

I waited ten seconds, the longest seconds I'd ever spent. Cody groaned. Unless he passed out, we had no way of knowing if he was stuck in a repeating loop or just experiencing a really nasty imprint. He groaned again, and with a glance at Shannon, I grabbed Cody's hand.

And saw.

Waiting in gruesome anticipation. The choking smell of

chlorine in an enclosed space. A man approaching, wearing a swimsuit, a towel over one shoulder. So old. This will be easy. The old man easing into the hot tub. Now. Down on the back of his head. Not too hard, but hard enough. White head slipping almost gracefully beneath the water.

The vision vanished and I became aware of Shannon holding my hand. I knew instantly that I'd failed to remove Cody's hand and that Shannon had saved both of us from a repeating loop.

"Thanks," I said.

"You saw it?" Cody asked, his voice gruff and his face pale.

"An old man was hit with the bust as he went into the hot tub." I felt so dizzy I could barely stand, but I reached out for the bust before Shannon could stop me.

Nothing.

Nothing but dizziness and an urge to vomit. I collapsed onto the nearest chair. "It was exactly the same feeling as on the rug. But I don't think I saw the whole imprint. Did you see hands?"

Cody shook his head, looking as beat as I felt. "Has to be one of the owners."

"I can't really see Ms. Frampion hitting someone over the head," Shannon said dryly.

"But can you see her hiring someone?" Paige asked, walking into the room. I wondered how long she'd been at the door without me seeing her. Since she didn't ask about the bust imprint, I gathered she'd heard enough.

"Not really." Shannon paced to the end of the table and back again. "Unless it was a real lowlife, it would have cost a lot. But that Waite is greasy. He could have done it in a heartbeat."

"The other man, Nye, or whatever, is just as scary in his

own way," I added. "Reminds me of that Frankenstein-looking guy on that old show . . . Herman Munster, I think he was called."

Cody shook his head. "Naw. It was none of them. If they're responsible, they hired someone. You said those guys who took you were professionals. They must be the ones doing the killing."

"Even if they pulled together the funds," Shannon said, "where did small-timers like In Loving Memory find guys like that to hire?"

Cody rubbed his chin. "You got a point. Last I checked, killers ain't listed in the phone book."

I thought Shannon's definition of small-timers might need to be adjusted, what with two likely murders and who knew how many more, but I wouldn't argue the fact right now. "What happened to me might not be related. Not with Russo and his ilk roaming around. Who knows how many people are out to get him?"

Shannon scowled. "Well, we'd better figure something out before there's another murder victim or abduction attempt."

Paige nodded. "Look, I found something that might be a possible lead."

We all gazed at her expectantly. My empty stomach growled into the lull, and I hoped no one heard.

"One of our detectives called to set up a meeting with Tarragon Incorporated—that's one of the companies JoAnna Hamilton listed as possible suspects. At first the detective was referred to Tarragon's attorneys at McGregor and Clancy, but eventually he got through to Mr. Tarragon himself."

"Ah-hah," I said, feeling more energetic. "So Tarragon must be hiding something if they won't talk to us directly."

Paige smiled. "Possibly. But that's not exactly what I was getting at. Shannon told me about Claire Philpot's visit to your shop yesterday, and she emailed me the information about the money taken from her husband's account. The thing is, her husband worked for none other than McGregor and Clancy. With all the law firms around, it seemed an odd coincidence, tying in with our case this way, so I called her. Not only did her husband work for the firm, but one of his clients while he was alive was Tarragon Inc."

My jaw dropped. "You've got to be kidding."

"Nope."

"Great, just great," I said. Another connection to our case, and none of us believed in coincidence.

"I think we'd better rush tracing those bank withdrawals Claire said her husband made," Shannon said. "We need to know where that money was going."

My hope at the possible lead dimmed. "You think he might have been paying someone off? Maybe something involving Tarragon?" There were many possibilities, including the sudden death of JoAnna Hamilton's scientists. I thought of Claire and how she was still so much in love with her dead husband. Would knowing he'd been guilty set her free or destroy her?

Paige paled. "I didn't even think that far. The timing works. If Bridger was into something, maybe his heart attack was a good thing. Claire's a strong woman, but I don't know if she can survive knowing he did something like this."

I knew what she meant. Claire would fight to the death for what she believed, but what if there was no longer something to believe in?

"While you trace down the banks," Shannon said to Paige, "I'd better talk to Claire again. We need to know exactly what

McGregor and Clancy claim her husband did. Whatever it is, it could be connected."

I nodded. "Cody and I'll go with you."

"No." Shannon's voice was firm. "You two go eat lunch. You both need to recover before you read any more imprints. I'll let you know when we need you."

We were being dismissed, but for once I didn't care. My stomach was complaining and I felt terrible, as though I'd been reading imprints all morning. What was wrong with me? I'd felt fine upon waking and my workout hadn't been more strenuous than normal. I was beginning to feel a bit desperate.

"I could eat," Cody said.

An understatement, I knew. It was from Cody that my sister and I had both inherited our love of food and the ability to pack it in. He wasn't as slender as I was these days, being larger boned, but he didn't have much extra weight on his solid frame. I believed reading imprints used more calories than we realized.

Before we left, Shannon pulled me aside in the bullpen where all the officers' desks were neatly packed in together. "Look, I know you need to pick up your car at the mechanic's before noon, and I'm going to have Peirce drop you off there and you can drive it to wherever you're going to eat. He's actually off duty and coming in only as a favor to me because Captain Piante won't authorize any more surveillance. Since we discovered the bust, he believes you were simply in the wrong place at the wrong time, that the rug was the real target. I'm not sure he's wrong, but regardless, I don't like it, so keep Cody with you and your cell phone handy. We'll meet up as soon as I get a handle on how McGregor and Clancy figure into this. If Paige finishes first, I'll send her to stay with you."

Despite Shannon's worry, the captain's conclusion allevi-ated some of my own concerns. He'd only been captain for two months, replacing the former female captain, but the man hadn't risen to his current position by perpetuating a lot of mistakes.

"I'll be fine," I told Shannon, glad he didn't ask if I was carrying my pistol in my purse. I didn't want him to know he'd won that battle. I might not feel as worried as before, but if anything did happen, I felt more prepared. "It's broad daylight, and we'll just grab a bite and go to my store."

I really should be at Autumn's Antiques if I wasn't on police business, though a nap was looking more and more appealing at the moment. Maybe I could sack out for a few minutes in my easy chair. In fact, my sister would probably insist on it.

"Just keep your eyes open." Shannon's voice was intense.

"I will. You need to trust me. I'm not going to do anything I can't handle."

"I do trust you." He hesitated a heartbeat before adding, "But that doesn't mean I'll ever stop wanting to protect you."

I smiled. "Right back at you."

His voice took on a lighter note. "Guess that's my cue to say I'm sorry about last night. About how I reacted to you going to see Hamilton. You did a good job with her."

"Thanks."

Cody motioned to me across the room, angling his chin in another direction. Following his gaze, I couldn't help but stiffen.

"I see you found Ace," I said to Shannon.

Shannon whipped around. "Actually, he's probably here trying to get information for one of his so-called cases, but it's about time I asked him a few questions. Wait. Where are you—?"

I was already striding toward Ace, who was dressed in his usual worn jeans and T-shirt. "Who are you really working for?" I demanded. "I know it's not Russo. Why were you outside my store?"

Ace's eyes gleamed, their color so nondescript that I couldn't pinpoint the hue. "Relax," he said, grinning. "I never said I was working for Russo. Truth is, I'm actually on another case. Did you know that guy next door to you, the music guy, has been married before? Yep, he's cut out on child support."

"Baloney," I said. "Stu doesn't have any children or an ex-wife."

"I can check out your story," Shannon said, catching up to us.

"All right, all right." Ace held up his hands, his grin still bright. He looked small and thin compared to Shannon, and he hunched in on himself as though trying to appear less threatening. "I was here yesterday morning on another case when I heard what happened. I decided to do a little investigating on my own with the hope of snagging Russo as a client again. Unfortunately, that didn't pan out."

Shannon shook his head. "You went to see Russo days ago. We talked to him, and we know he told you to get lost." There was no mistaking Shannon's own desire to tell the private detective to do the same thing.

Ace straightened, and I saw the men were actually the same height, though Shannon was much broader. "Yeah, what of it? I thought if I had something to sell, he'd change his mind. Anyway, I've got other work lined up now. I don't need him."

"But you do need the precinct, apparently." Shannon gave

him a smile that held no friendship. "In fact, I think you probably hang around more these days than when you worked for us." That was stretching it a bit, since Shannon had been away so much these past months, and he couldn't have kept tabs on Ace.

Ace laughed companionably, as though they really were friends. "At least I get paid more now."

I doubted that, unless his starving artist look was meant to attract clients.

"We'll have to do lunch sometime," Ace said. "Right now I'd better get back to work." He turned and sauntered away.

Shannon's teeth clenched and his hands fisted at his sides.

"Yep," I said, keeping my face deadpan. "I definitely dislike him more than I used to dislike you."

Shannon blinked, his eyes going to my face. "You never disliked me."

"I did too. You were annoying, rude, and arrogant. And did I mention annoying?"

"Ha. I'm the one who thought you were annoying, not to mention out to fleece everyone."

I took a step closer. "Oh? And I bet you thought me unattractive. Totally not your type."

"That's right. Barefooted hippie."

I took another step, watching the amusement in his fascinating eyes turn to something else. I could see the pulse on his neck, beating fast. "Know-it-all pig."

"Deceiver."

A throat cleared. "Uh, I hate to interrupt this mating dance, but I'm dying of starvation here. I ate breakfast before six, you know. Can you two do your very strange wooing on your own time?" Cody settled against the front of the empty desk closest to us, a sardonic grin on his weathered face. "Not that I don't enjoy a good show, but the fireworks between you two are hot enough to burn down the police station."

I did feel rather warm. Stepping back, I glanced around the room, but the few officers present were suddenly extremely busy, their gazes averted. I stifled a laugh.

Shannon grinned. "Thanks," he said to me in an undertone. "I'm always afraid I'm going to start something with Ace. I almost went for him."

"I know."

"Come on." Cody tugged on my arm. "Our ride's here."

Shannon's eyes were still on me as we left, eyes that made me want to melt into him. "Annoying," I said under my breath.

"Who, me?" Cody asked.

"No. Him." Annoying, compelling, and all mine.

Maybe.

Cody laughed. "That didn't work all the other times I bet you said that about him. You're hooked. Face it."

"I was thinking steak," I said, ignoring him. "I know a place, Stan's Grill. Meat with no hormones. Not even too expensive."

"Lead on."

Peirce drove us to my mechanic's in his own minivan, which I knew he'd bought last year after the birth of his second child. As I exited, he pressed a small roll of money into my hand. "That was from Shannon yesterday. I forgot to give it back to him."

I pocketed it. "Thanks." The only thing better than a good meal was a free one that was also delicious. After the fiasco yesterday, it was the least the department owed me, though I suspected the money was Shannon's. Hopefully someone would reimburse him.

Peirce didn't pull away from the curb. "Uh, Autumn?"

"Yes?"

"You okay now?"

I knew he was asking about the imprints, but I purposefully misunderstood. "I feel a lot better."

"If you want me to stay with you, I can. I was going to my wife's parents, but she'd understand, and they don't like me much, though I think they're finally warming up a bit."

"We're good," I said. "But thank you."

Cody waved at him. "Go and make nice with your in-laws. You're stuck with them so you might as well make the best of it. Don't you worry. I'll take good care of Autumn." He spoke confidently, and with the bright sunlight streaming into Peirce's eyes, I was sure he couldn't see Cody's age and exhaustion. Peirce shouldn't worry. Cody was a tough old bird when he needed to be, and he'd already proven he'd take a bullet for me. I suspected his presence was the only reason Shannon had let me leave the station.

Peirce drove off, and within minutes, I'd given the mechanic my debit card and we were chugging away in my rusty Toyota, which ran almost quietly compared to the din it had made before replacing the muffler.

"Why don't you buy something better than this rust bucket?" Cody said.

"Shh. You'll hurt her feelings."

He rolled his eyes.

"Besides, I've seen what you drive." His gold Honda hatchback was every bit as bad, and he didn't have the excuse of being poor like I did.

I turned a corner and the black sedan following two cars behind did the same. My stomach lurched.

As I drove, I kept checking my mirrors. I'd been in exactly

one car chase, and though I'd gotten away, that didn't make me an expert. After several more turns, I decided the black sedan was definitely following us. My heart started thumping hard, but at Stan's Grill, I doubled back in the parking lot, passing the sedan, and recognized one of Russo's men in the front seat.

So, he's keeping an eye on me. Oddly enough their presence made me feel safer. How much my life had changed in the past two days.

I took out my phone and texted Shannon: *No need for police escort when I have Russo's men following me. Ha ha. Arrived at restaurant. All is well.*

By eleven fifteen, Cody had consumed two steaks—and had made good headway on the rice and fries that came with them. He ate with relish, as though he hadn't eaten food this good in a long time. Probably not since Christmas dinner at Tawnia's, most of which I'd had to cook, since my sister was about as handy in the kitchen as I was in a shoe store. I felt a little sliver of guilt that I hadn't made more effort to see Cody. He'd more than paid his dues, but I knew he still beat himself up about his past regularly. Maybe it was time I made more of an effort. Besides Tawnia and her little family, he was the only relative I had.

That might change. I might start my own family.

With Shannon.

I shivered slightly, remembering his eyes and the way I felt whenever he was near.

Maybe it was good I could no longer read imprints. Maybe not doing so would keep me more focused on family. Of course, without my ability, I might also miss some dangers I could otherwise protect them from. Imprints could come in handy, especially with teenagers.

"Are you going to eat that?" Cody pointed his fork at my second steak.

"What a silly question." I pulled the plate closer. It was really good, and if another plan hadn't been formulating in my mind, and if I had more cash, I might order another. I hadn't felt dizzy once since I began eating.

I threw down Shannon's cash and everything I had in my wallet on the table before Cody could get out the wad he usually carried in some pocket. The man didn't own a debit card, and I suspected he would store his money in his mattress, or some similar place, if his various rental properties hadn't required the use of a bank.

"This is on the department." I looked at the bills and added, feeling rather foolish, "Though I guess you can leave a tip."

He did, and the waitress gathered up our bills with a smile, so I knew it was a good one. I grabbed my handbag and headed for the door. I started to open the door with the napkin from the table, before I remembered that I didn't need it anymore. Dropping the napkin into my purse, I pushed the door open and went outside. Behind me the door started shutting, but Cody pushed it open again.

I blinked in the sunlight, feeling momentarily disoriented. Maybe I should go home and sleep. No, I had to get to my store. If I wasn't helping Shannon and Paige catch bad guys, I should be there, though the truth was, my store didn't need me today, not with Tawnia covering for me. Now that I thought about it, there was something else I could do.

Cody bumped into me, cursing under his breath. "Should have known."

"What?" I asked as we continued down the walk.

"Imprint on the door. Forgot my napkin."

"Sorry."

"For what? I'm old enough to know better."

True, but I knew from personal experience that it was easier to protect myself in the winter when I had an excuse to wear gloves.

In the car, I pulled out my phone, bringing up Cody's text from yesterday with Easton Godfrey's number. It was time to talk to the scientist who studied psychometry.

Cody leaned over far enough to glimpse the name. He might be in his sixties, but he had the long-distance vision of an eagle. "Oh, no. What are you doing? You ain't calling him, are you?"

"Of course I'm calling him. I need to know what happened to me, and if I'll ever get it back."

"Can't you let it go? If it's gone, maybe it's meant to be. And at least you won't have to touch a doorknob and witness some idiot husband berating his wife because he's angry about money. You could live a perfectly fine life without those experiences."

"Okay, so those kinds of imprints are awful." I fumbled in my bag and came up with the book of poetry that had belonged to my parents, shoving it at him. "But this . . . Cody, I can't let them go."

His hands touched the book, his face softening. He'd be seeing my parents at their wedding, feeling the love in their hearts. But just as quickly, his face hardened once more. "You did without imprints for thirty-something years. Don't you think you can again?" There was an undercurrent of pleading in his gruff voice. "And don't give me that business about being blind. I know that's what it feels like, but it'll pass. Once, part of my tongue stayed numb after my hack of a dentist worked on me, but I stopped noticing after a year or so. I adjusted. You will too."

"Cody," I said softly.

He nodded once. "Okay, let's call him." Then he added with a scowl, "Maybe we'll get lucky, and he won't answer."

"You don't have to come with me."

"Yes, I do. I abandoned you once. I ain't doing it again."

Technically he hadn't abandoned me or Tawnia because he hadn't known we existed, but it was all the same to him. He was worse than I was about guilt. I'd told him I forgave him, and Tawnia had echoed the sentiment twenty times over, but Cody still had something to prove. To us, to himself. Maybe he didn't really know. I understood that because every time I saw Jake, I felt bad for not being there for him in the same way that he was for me. Maybe it wouldn't matter if I didn't care about him so much.

Which reminded me of Jake's date with Kolonda, and I stifled an urge to text him to ask if it had gone well. He needed space right now to find a future without me.

Godfrey's answering machine picked up on the third ring, but he'd left his cell phone number on the message in case of emergencies—guess he didn't want to lose out on any weirdos— so I dialed that instead. He answered almost immediately. I could hear voices and noise around him, and I wondered if he was at a family gathering or perhaps in a crowded restaurant. I gave him my first name and explained that I knew Cody.

"You share his gift?" he asked, eagerness lacing his voice. Gradually, the noise from his end of the phone disappeared, and I knew he'd gone somewhere more private. "Are you related?"

"I do share his gift, but I'd rather not say how I know Cody. Anyway, the reason I'm calling is because I can't do it anymore. Yesterday, my ability vanished. I was trapped in a repeating loop with an awful memory, and I was also in a car crash that ended in an explosion." Not wanting to explain further, I left out the gunfire and my connection with the police. "Do you think you can help? I use my ability for work, so it's kind of important."

"I'm almost sure I can help you. Can you meet me at my office? I'm on my way there now."

"Sure. Give me the address."

I hung up feeling more positive. For all of Cody's dislike of the man, at least he wasn't involved in our case, and that meant no real possibility of serious danger. Maybe with his help, I'd be myself before morning.

Chapter 14

Easton Godfrey's office in Beaverton was only ten minutes away from the restaurant, and I drove there in silence. As we pulled up in front of a rectangular, one-story building, Cody mumbled, "It says something that he's willing to drop everything to see you on a Saturday."

"Um, that he's nice? Helpful?" I turned off the engine and put the keys in my purse. The black sedan was still following us, but the driver parked out on the road.

Cody rolled his eyes. "Desperate, more like. He's afraid to let you get away. There ain't a lot of people like us. He only knows two others besides me."

"Two is a lot more than I know of, so that makes him someone I need to talk to."

"It's not just psychometry he studies. It's the whole gamut of psychic abilities. Most people he studies have only a hint of talent, though. They get things right only part of the time and only if they're in a certain mood."

"You mean fakes?" Given a certain amount of tries, anyone could get a certain number of guesses correct.

"Not fakes. Just that they aren't as strong as you and me."

I reached for my door handle. "You mean their brains didn't develop quite as much." I wasn't psychic, and I hated that designation. It made it seem as if at any minute I'd start reading people's minds, levitating, or growing antennae.

Cody rolled his eyes. "Whatever."

The building was set back on the large lot to make room for two rows of parking in front. There was no sign except one in the window proclaiming they were open. Only one other car sat in the lot, an old cream-colored sedan which I assumed belonged to the scientist. The nearest building lay to the right beyond an empty expanse of tarmac, where a few stacks of rusting iron made a good privacy barrier. On the left side was a narrow road and beyond that another similar building that seemed to sell plumbing supplies to contractors during the week.

The growing heat already made me feel sticky, though the air smelled remarkably clean. A bird winging its way across a palette of blue sky and puffy white clouds calmed me—until I saw Cody checking his pockets for an extra magazine for his pistol. I hurried ahead.

Cody trod heavily behind me as we approached. There were no flowerbeds, trees, or other greenery in sight except a wilted plant in a pot near the glass door. White aluminum blinds covered two large windows on either side of the door.

A man opened the door before we reached it, dressed in a white lab coat. "Hello. Are you Autumn? I'm Easton Godfrey. It's great to meet you." He had thick black hair sprinkled slightly with silver, and large brown eyes. I judged him somewhere in his fifties, perhaps a decade younger than Cody. His height was average, his skin great, but he was only borderline good looking, in part because the right side of his mouth twisted unnaturally when he smiled, as though some of the muscles there had grown the wrong way. He thrust out a hand, gripping mine in a limp manner that repulsed me.

I held his hand tighter, shaking it firmly. "Thanks for meeting with me on such short notice, Mr. Godfrey."

He looked at our hands as I let go, his brow furrowing, perhaps in surprise. I hoped I hadn't squeezed too hard. My height was average for a woman and I was on the thin side, but with my martial arts training, I was stronger than I looked.

"Please, call me Easton," he said.

"Okay." Since he hadn't pushed for my last name, I'd go with whatever he preferred.

His eyes went past me and his voice became more wary. "Hello, Cody. Nice to see you again."

"Not for me. I told her not to come."

"Well, uh, yes. Come in anyway, would you?" Easton held the door open and ushered us inside. Was it my imagination that he glanced around the parking lot? Was he looking for possible witnesses?

Inside was a narrow room with a waiting bench and a small desk. "I test a lot of indigents and college students," Easton said, seeing my stare. "Pay them for tests, too, if they show any ability. We run on a grant, though. Not much money for furnishings. Please come this way."

He led us down a hallway decorated with several framed diplomas and into what looked like a doctor's small examination room, complete with a sink in the left corner. A table in the middle of the room held a laptop and a monitor, their backs together with the monitor facing the door. One chair sat on the far side and two chairs on the side closest to us. Against the back wall rose two tall bookshelves full of books and several dozen shoe boxes. Easton indicated that we should sit in front of the monitor.

"We're not here for testing," Cody said, scowling at the monitor.

"I'll have to do a few tests if I'm going to help your daughter."

Cody flushed. "What makes you think she's my daughter?"

"On the phone Autumn declined to say that you were related, but I can tell that you are—mostly because of your eyes. Heterochromia can be caused by trauma, but when two or more members of a family have different colors of eyes, it's obviously inherited. Am I wrong? Isn't she your daughter? Her hair's dark, but she does look a bit like you did when you were younger."

That shut Cody up because he wasn't accustomed to announcing our relationship. Neither was I.

When it became clear that neither Cody nor I were going to confirm his assumption, Easton Godfrey skirted around the table and sat, powering up the laptop. "Anyone want water?" he asked. "Please help yourself at the sink while I pull up the program I need."

"I'll have some." Cody returned with a paper cup of water for each of us.

"Okay," Easton said to me. "I'm going to show you a series of pictures, and I want you to tell me if you know what each is—without seeing it, of course."

"There's no way I'll know." I wondered if Tawnia could. Or if she'd be able to draw it, though the images she drew usually had to do with my cases, a sort of symbiotic twin thing.

Easton gave me an easy smile. "This is just to relax you, to get your mind going. But you'd be surprised how many people have crossover abilities."

"I don't," Cody said.

"Well, people are different." Easton's words were mild, but there was steel in his eyes.

"I've lost my ability," I reminded him. "So even if I did have any crossover, I don't think we'd be able to test it."

"Actually, sometimes a cessation of one ability magnifies another one."

I could tell he meant to conduct his tests before he told me anything useful, so I might as well get them over with. I'd even try my best.

He showed me a few pictures on the monitor facing us to give me an idea of what I would be trying to guess. "Let's begin then," he said. "I'll look at the picture on my side for ten seconds and then I'll ask you to guess."

After each guess, he showed me the actual picture, but I got them all wrong, or at least enough that he quit trying. For some reason, he didn't have herbs or antiques in his picture collection, and I guessed items I was more familiar with. I mean, whoever thought of choosing an aardvark? That wasn't something I thought of on a daily basis. Now, chamomile and music boxes were more my speed. I'd have to be psychic to guess his pictures—which I suppose was the point.

Next, he brought out a box from a shelf against the wall and gave me wrapped objects to identify. I got them wrong too. My dizziness surfaced momentarily, however, as I held them to my forehead, according to his rather theatrical request.

Finally, he drew out a pack of cards, spreading them in a fan, and asked me to predict what card he would pull out next.

I utterly failed again, getting only the eight of spades right and the two on the two of hearts.

Yep, no precog ability here, I thought. I wanted to say "I told you so," but he looked dejected enough.

"It could be that what happened to you yesterday did affect every ability," he said with a frown.

I shook my head. "Look, the only thing I've ever been able to do is read imprints on objects. And only certain ones."

"Imprints?"

"That's what I call the emotions and scenes I experience, since they seem to be imprinted on the objects."

"Imprints." He appeared to be tasting the word. "I like that. We normally refer to them as signatures, but imprints is much more apt. I think I'll start using the term in my tests—if you don't mind."

"That's fine." I didn't hide the impatience in my voice. This whole hour had been wasted, and I was already wishing I hadn't come. As for Cody's fear of the man, well, maybe he'd softened with age. Even if Easton tried to detain me, short of pulling a gun, I doubt he'd have success.

"What happens to you now when you touch something you know has an imprint?" Easton asked.

"Nothing. Except for a couple times." I explained how I'd experienced the imprints when touching Cody.

"Are you sure you were *only* touching Cody?"

I hesitated. "Well, no. I might have been touching the object, too, but I was definitely touching Cody."

He typed something on his laptop, staring at his screen momentarily before saying, "Okay, so you feel nothing. What about a headache or dizziness? Or maybe goose bumps, nausea, or hives?"

"I did have a whopper of a headache all day yesterday. Only a bit today. And I've been dizzy."

He pounced on that. "Dizzy? When? How long? Tell me everything you can remember."

"She was in an explosion," Cody groused. "For crying out loud, of course she's going to be dizzy."

"Maybe." Coming to his feet, Easton took down another box from the shelf behind him. "Here are some items I've collected. Some, I know have signatures—imprints—on them. Some don't. They aren't all the same, but Cody might recognize a few of these from the tests we did with him years ago."

Ah, so Cody had agreed to be tested at one point. I'd figured as much, but it was nice having it confirmed.

Easton dumped out ten objects on the table. "Before we test you, Autumn, I'm going to have Cody verify that there are imprints. Cody? Without telling Autumn which ones have imprints and which do not, please examine the objects."

Cody grimaced. "You had a couple of really nasty ones, if I remember correctly. I ain't going to touch them. Don't worry. I'll still be able to tell which ones." He held out his fingers over the objects, and I knew he was testing for tingling. He nodded. "Okay four of these have strong imprints. Two have fainter ones and six have none at all."

"Fascinating," Easton breathed. "I thought only four of them had imprints. The other people I tested must not have been strong enough to read the additional signatures. Either that or I suppose they could have imprinted their own feelings. But you didn't even touch the objects, and you could still tell they had something—you've been keeping secrets from me, Cody."

"What of it?" Cody thrust his chest forward and grinned.

"Anyway, I couldn't always feel the tingle before I touched them. It came later."

"The others can't do that?" I asked.

"No. And they could only feel those four stronger imprints with their receptive hand."

"Receptive hand?" I asked.

"That's the hand you're most in tune with. For most people, their receptive hand is not their dominate hand. So if you're right-handed, that would mean your left."

I stifled a laugh. "Uh, isn't it kind of weird to say most people when you only know four people who do what we do?"

Easton's nostrils flared, and I knew I'd offended him. "Not only were my subjects tested thoroughly, I have, of course, studied psychometry in detail. There are eight others documented in the world, and I am the foremost authority in the US on the subject."

Probably because no one else wanted the job. This time I managed to keep the words inside.

"Anyway, Cody's the only one I've found who can use either hand equally well. He also can use his arms and his face."

I nodded. "I've never noticed any difference whatever I use."

"What about your feet? Can you feel imprints through them?"

"Of course. I can feel them with any skin. Didn't I already say that?"

Easton grinned, looking more and more excited. "That's wonderful. Cody, you can't feel them through your feet, can you?"

Cody shook his head. "You know I can't. You tested that. I seem to remember something about a little electric shock when I didn't succeed."

Easton waved a hand as though to dismiss the words. "That was then. Hmm, maybe it's because Autumn goes around barefooted and that makes her more connected to everything. Either that, or she's a lot stronger than you are. We sometimes see that in successive generations. Something to do with better nutrition."

An unease slithered across my shoulders. I hadn't noticed him looking at my feet, and the long skirt covered all but my toes. Not something to call attention. His powers of observation were stronger than I'd expected.

"Or maybe her genes have mutated," Easton added pensively. "There are some tests we could do to see. But we'd need to do them in a medical lab with a colleague of mine."

Great, now I was a mutant. Anyway, none of this was helping, and I certainly wasn't interested in visiting a medical lab to have needles jabbed into me. "So have any of your subjects ever lost their ability?" I asked. "Or any of those you've read about?"

"Yes. Bear with me a bit longer, if you will."

I sighed, wondering if all scientists were so methodical.

"Okay, I want you to do what Cody did," Easton directed. "Hold your hands above the objects. See if you can feel any vibrations or tingling."

I passed over them slowly: book, shot glass, bracelet, toy, bell, photograph of a family, basketball trophy, handwoven basket, vase, stapler. From experience, I suspected the toy, the photograph, the bracelet, and the trophy would have some type of imprint. The other possibilities would be the vase and the shot glass.

I felt nothing. I shook my head. "Sorry."

"But normally you'd feel tingling?"

"Yes."

"Would it affect your energy level? Make you tired?"

"Not unless I touch them."

"Okay, so touch them. One at a time. Slowly. Tell us if you feel anything."

I touched them all, one at a time, but there was no change, except my dizziness returned strongly enough to nauseate me. I had to stop several times to regain equilibrium.

"This is useless," I muttered, rubbing my temple where it had started pounding. I stood to leave.

"Quite the contrary." Easton looked up at me, hand pausing over his laptop keys.

"What do you mean?"

"Every time you touched an object that has an imprint, you experienced dizziness. Isn't that right, Cody?"

I looked at Cody, and he nodded, a deep furrow of consternation between his eyes.

"And that headache?" Easton went on. "Well, that came after you touched the stapler. I can tell you now it was used in a homicide."

I sank back down in my seat. Slowly, I retouched all of the items, easily identifying those with the strongest imprints by my bouts of dizziness. "I thought I was just light-headed. But I don't think I was always touching something every time I felt dizzy the past two days."

"Well, there would have been some residual disorientation because of the explosion." Easton sat back, a smile on his face. "And even when you touched things with imprints, the dizziness may not have kicked in until after several strong imprints left a buildup. Basically, I believe you are still experiencing imprints, but that the trauma of being caught in a nasty repeating loop caused your brain to overload. To protect itself, it has stopped allowing the imprints through to your conscious mind. I would also hazard a guess that you are a bit claustrophobic, which exacerbated the problem when you were trapped in the car during the crash. Thus adding to your brain trauma."

He was spot on about the claustrophobia, even if he didn't realize I'd been wrapped in a rug during that repeating imprint.

"I always wondered what could happen if I went too far," I said. "I mean, I've passed out before, but I wondered if—" If experiencing the imprint of someone dying would kill me too. I'd experienced a woman losing consciousness before she died, but I'd passed out when she did in the imprint and let go of the object before her heart stopped—thankfully.

Easton smiled widely, the right side of his mouth quirking even more oddly than normal. "Think of your condition as running with a severely injured leg, or like a computer programmer whose tendons are so overused they cease working and need an operation to return to normal."

"If that's true, how do I fix it?"

"Oh, that's the easy part." He paused, apparently enjoying his own expertise. "Don't read signatures—I mean, imprints. You'll need to wear gloves to protect yourself, and something on your feet. No imprints at all."

Gloves? Why did that seem familiar? "It's that easy? For how long?"

He shrugged. "A day, a week, a month, a year. I really don't know. This is unexplored territory."

"You could be wrong."

"Yes. But I'm not." He said it with confidence rather than arrogance.

"Once I had tendon pain and the doctor made me stop

working on my sculptures for six months," Cody said. "Then I had to limit my work after that for a year, and do arm exercises to make sure it didn't happen again." He frowned. "Worst six months of my life. Fortunately, I was able to cheat a bit."

This was all good news, but the thought of remaining blind for six months made me feel panicky. I breathed slowly, trying to calm my thumping heart.

"I don't think it'll be too long," Easton put in. "You're accustomed to reading a lot of imprints, and that has likely built your endurance. The fact that you experienced two events since the loss of your ability indicates that your brain felt well enough to let something through. As I said, I think it was the combination of the repeated loop and the claustrophobia that caused the loss in the first place. The explosion couldn't have helped, either. Your brain needs time to rest before it can interpret more imprints."

"What about good imprints?"

He arched a brow. "Good imprints?"

"Positive ones, I mean. Negative imprints—the bad ones—they make me feel awful. I always need a lot of protein to recover after experiencing them. But the positive imprints, the ones with good emotions and memories, they have a strengthening effect."

Easton blinked. "Really?" he asked, his fingers typing at an incredible rate, though he never looked down at them. "I've never heard of that."

"It's true. I've noticed the same thing." Cody stood to get himself another glass of water.

"You never told me."

"You never asked. Besides, I'd had enough of your needles and prodding." The two glared at each other.

"Well?" I asked. In my bag on the table, my phone vibrated, loud enough for everyone to hear, but I ignored it.

Easton shifted his gaze to me. "Anyway, you should read no imprints. None at all. Good or bad. You'd still be using the same mental muscle, so to speak. You should even take off your rings, if they have even a hint of an imprint. Let your brain completely reset. I'd bet it doesn't want to open up enough to see what kind of imprint is trying to get in, positive or negative. Once you start reading them again, you can test yourself to see if the good ones actually strengthen you or if it's only an illusion."

"So I should recover fully?" I pulled off my antique rings, dropping them into my bag.

"Absolutely. The human brain is a miraculous thing. I mean, look at what you two can do." Easton paused and then tumbled on, "Now if you'll give me a little more information, I'd like to set up another meeting. We can discuss those other tests I mentioned."

"She'll be in touch." Cody pulled me to my feet. "But don't get any ideas. She's not a lab rat."

Hands leaving his keyboard, Easton leapt to his feet, rounding the table like a spider pouncing on its prey. "It's for science. For humanity. What we're becoming."

Cody snorted.

One of Easton's hands had landed on my bag, but I pulled it out from under him. "How much do you pay?" I recovered enough to ask, though it was more to poke at Cody than for any real interest.

"Don't answer that," Cody growled, pushing me out the door with one hand, the other snatching up his cup of water. Together we hurried down the hall.

Easton came after us. "I have just a few more questions."

"Another time," Cody said over his shoulder. "We're on a schedule."

"You will at least let me know what happens, right?" Easton sounded so anxious I felt sorry for him. "When your ability returns."

"So you can write a paper about it?" Cody sneered.

"Yeah, so what? It'll help others."

Cody yanked open the front door.

"I'll call you," I told Easton. "I promise."

"Okay, good."

"Thanks again for seeing me."

"Make sure to use the gloves," he called as I stumbled out into the bright daylight. "And some shoes!"

Cody paused behind me, and I turned to see him dumping the water from his paper cup over the wilted plant by the door. I kept my smile hidden until I was in the car. Just when he was at his most grouchy, he went and did something like that.

"What?" Cody said when he joined me.

"Nothing."

He looked up at the building where Easton stood in the doorway. "You can tell what kind of a man he is by his plants. If a man doesn't take care of his plants, you know he doesn't give a hoot about anyone else."

"No, it just means he's forgetful, or has too much else on his mind." I happened to like plants, and I tended the herbs by the window in my kitchen faithfully, but my sister had already killed three of the comfrey starts I'd given her, and I knew she'd sacrifice anything for me.

"Not with him, it doesn't. You think this is the end, but it isn't. It never is with him." He paused before adding, "We should have changed license plates before coming. He'll find you somehow. Look at him all smug in that stupid white coat—like he's a real doctor or something."

"I called his phone, so he has my number."

"Yeah, but you can change yours."

"And he really is a doctor. At least twice over. Maybe three times. One was in psychology. Didn't you see the framed diplomas?"

He snorted. "Probably printed them off the Internet. We'd better make sure he doesn't follow us."

I shoved in the key and started the engine. "What happened between you two anyway?"

"Nothing. I made sure of that, but not before he stuck one too many needles into me. And he was always popping up when I least expected it. Still does. It creeps me out. He's one of the main reasons I have a shotgun by my front door. That's all I got to say." He folded his arms over his chest and stared out the window. Apparently, the subject was closed.

"Put on your belt," I reminded him. According to Shannon, I drove too fast and too erratically. He was wrong, of course, but I believed in seat belts for a lot of reasons.

Winter hadn't been wearing his seat belt on the day of the bridge collapse when we'd ended up in the Willamette. I unbuckled mine and swam free; he was found in the river pinned under debris a week later. Identifying his body hadn't been fun.

"So where to now? The store?" Cody asked.

I thought for a moment as I headed out of the parking lot. As I turned, I spied the black sedan pulling away from the curb by the road. A chill shot down my spine. I'd forgotten all about Russo's men, but there they were waiting for us.

"To my store," I said. "I have gloves and some moccasins there." It would be better to go to my apartment so I could rest, but I kept my most comfortable shoes at the store for emergencies. "Then we'll talk to Shannon and Paige and see what's going on with the case. We have too many suspects. We need to narrow things down."

My biggest concerns involved the two nanotech companies and Frank O'Donald, Russo's enemy. I didn't know enough about them to get a feel for who might be involved—and especially who might have tried to grab me. While I was pretty sure the folks at In Loving Memory were hiding something, I didn't think they were behind my abduction. They hadn't even known about me, so unless there was a connection between the murdered retirees and the nanotech companies or organized crime, they weren't high on my list of kidnapping suspects.

It also worried me that I'd heard nothing about JoAnna Hamilton's brother. Why hadn't he contacted the police? Who was the man Cody had seen waiting in the hallway in the safe imprint at Hamilton's? If that man hadn't been caught by whoever demolished the lab, he should have important information for us.

"Uh, can you slow down?" Cody asked. "This isn't a race."

I looked over to see him gripping the armrest on the door.

He was wrong. It was a race. A race to prevent another early death of a retiree. Or to prevent another boating accident, van bombing, or lab break-in.

I was feeling disoriented again—and that's when I began to suspect that I'd left an imprint on my own steering wheel, probably on the way over to see Easton Godfrey, and though my brain wasn't letting it come through to my consciousness, I must be experiencing it on some level. I should be grateful it wasn't a strong imprint, or I might have crashed the car. I'd have to replace the steering wheel cover—again.

"Give me those napkins in the glove compartment," I told Cody. I always kept the extra napkins from takeout there in case I ever needed them to mop up strange spills, check the oil, or protect myself from imprints. I had quite a collection of napkins now, some dating back over a year.

Using the napkins on the wheel, I made it to the shop. As I got out, I saw Cody leaning over to put his hands on the steering wheel, and I gave him a hard look.

"Don't even think about it." I didn't want him reading my imprint until I knew what it contained.

Maybe I should have asked Easton if he'd heard of a way to remove imprints. Like me, Cody had never managed to get rid of any. He typically threw things out and repurchased. You could do that when you owned several rental houses and had clientele that would pay big money for your amazing art sculptures.

It was almost two o'clock, and my store was still busy. Good for me. Jake's little sister, Randa, sat at my counter ringing people up, while Tawnia packaged their purchases. Behind them in a playpen, Destiny tore apart a magazine someone had given her. Thera was helping someone else over by the dressers, and I saw that my new rolltop desk had already sold. I loved a fast turnover, but I felt a little disappointment; I'd looked forward to examining the beautiful desk more closely.

"Shannon called," Tawnia said, looking up at me as I went around the counter. "He says you're not answering your phone. He's worried."

Right. Someone had called me at Easton's. I pulled out the phone to find a missed call and two texts—all from Shannon.

The first said he and Paige had Hamilton's major competitors coming to the precinct and asked if I'd like to watch the interviews. The next just said: "Are you okay?"

I texted Shannon back to let him know I was fine. I suspected he'd come looking for me soon, if I didn't give him that much. I would if our situations were reversed, especially if someone had wrapped him in a rug and tried to blow him up.

"Are you good to stay later?" I asked my sister. Tawnia had her long hair pulled up today, revealing her cheekbones. The waiting customers looked from her to me, and I knew they noticed our resemblance. That happened more and more these days, now that she'd lost the weight from her pregnancy. She still had ten pounds on me, and I figured she'd better keep it if she wanted to have enough milk for Destiny.

"Sure. As long as Emma's happy." She glanced over at Cody, who was standing uncertainly next to the customer at the counter. "I mean, I'd thought about driving down to see Cody's sculpture later, but I'll wait until he goes back home."

Cody grunted as I texted Shannon again, letting him know I would meet him at the precinct.

Little Destiny had abandoned the magazine and was standing in the playpen, gripping the sides and bouncing her body up and down in excitement.

"Look who's happy to see you," Tawnia said.

I swooped up the baby, smothering her little face with kisses. She laughed and grabbed my dangling silver earrings that I'd forgotten I'd put on when I changed after my workout. My heart filled with her presence and my anxiety eased. I took her with me to the cupboards under the counter to search for my moccasins and gloves, letting her grab the edge of the drawer as I slipped the soft leather over my feet. Most shoes gave me a terrible backache, one of the reasons I didn't wear them, but these didn't do more than chafe the backs of my heels a little. The worn, washed-out color complemented my gray skirt, which was completely unplanned. Next went on the gloves, a thin pair made of tan cotton that fit me like a second skin. They looked ridiculous this time of year, as if I was about to go out into the garden with a trowel.

Tawnia was talking to Cody and wrapping the last customer's purchases as I straightened. She frowned, her eyes wandering over my hands and down to my feet. "I'm not even going to ask, though I'll expect a full report later."

"Good. I need to get down to the police station. You shouldn't have to stay here more than another hour or so. Things should be calm enough by then."

Cody tried to say hello to the baby, but she buried her head in my shoulder.

"We'll be able to handle it." Randa turned from the cash register. Jake's little sister wore her hair braided in tiny cornrows to the crown of her head, and from there her hair swung in frizzy waves to halfway past her back. I'd always envied that hair. "So did you know that Jake went out with Kolonda last night?" She looked at me as if expecting me to leap onto the counter and proclaim my rights to Jake.

I nodded. "How does he seem today?"

She frowned and her next words came more reluctantly. "Happy. But after the last time she dropped him—I don't want him hurt again."

Like I'd also hurt him, was the implication.

"A lot of time has passed since they were together," I said. "And her father's dead. He was the one who made her choose between her family and Jake when she was in college."

I wanted to go into Jake's shop to see for myself if he was happy. I'd know by looking into his eyes, but right now wasn't a good time. I was too emotional with the loss of my gift, and the last thing I wanted was to hint that I needed him. If I'd known romance would have messed up our friendship this way, I would have never let him give me that first kiss.

Destiny reached up and yanked on my earring. "Sorry, sweetie, I have to go," I told her, "but I promise to spend a lot of time with you really soon. Okay?"

In answer, she reached for my other earring. I laughed and looked at Tawnia. "Do you want her, or should I put her in the playpen?"

"Give her to me. I'll have to settle her down first. Get her interested in some toys." She reached for the baby, her voice lowering as another customer approached the counter. "But before you leave, I have something to show you. Sketches I did earlier during a break."

We left Randa and Cody with the customer and headed to my back room. On the worktable lay one of my sister's numerous sketch books.

"I was trying to work up a new ad for a customer who sells a line of rugged outdoor clothing, you know, hiking stuff and the like, but instead this came out." Tawnia flipped the page and pushed the book over to me.

Immediately I recognized Easton Godfrey at the table in his room, typing on his laptop. Tawnia had the room perfect, down to the sink in the corner and the shelves along the back.

"It's not detailed because I knew right away it wasn't something I could use for my work, but I also knew I'd have to get it out before I could draw something of value." She laughed. "I mean something of value for work. Does it help you at all?"

"I don't know about help, but we did talk to this man today." By the look of the drawing and the way the boxes were still on the shelf, it had taken place before Cody and I had arrived.

"A suspect?"

I hesitated. Easton might not be a suspect, but I didn't want Tawnia or Destiny anywhere near him. Though Cody tended to bluster, there was real dislike in his manner toward Easton, and I wasn't about to trust the man. At the same time, she was my sister, and I'd eventually tell her everything. Or most of it. "Not exactly. He's just someone I thought might know something, but it's too early to tell if his information is good." If the glove and shoe thing worked, I might be even more interested in learning what else Easton knew about my ability.

"Well, okay." She turned the page as Destiny tried to pull her hair from her clips. "Then I drew this."

I pulled the sketchbook closer when I saw the two men in the drawing, the older one with a friendly hand on the shoulder of the other, as though introducing him to someone we couldn't see. The older man was a stranger, but I knew the younger one: Winston Drewmore. He looked happy and relaxed. The older man stood slightly above average height, shorter than Winston by a few inches, lean with no bulk. Hair more gray than anything else. Could be any boardroom executive with a penchant for healthy food or a love of running. Nothing impressive or memorable about him except he didn't seem to have the weight challenges people sometimes did as they aged. "About what time did you do this?"

"Let's see, I'd just given Emma a little lunch and was nursing her to sleep. Twelve thirty? One? I don't know exactly. But right after I did the first one."

That would put it near the time I arrived at Easton's office.

I studied the drawing, especially the older man, wishing it were a little more detailed. "Can I take this with me? The younger man here is part of our case, and I'd like to know who the other guy is." It could be one of the company's scientists, but the bold confidence in the man's face indicated that he was someone accustomed to giving orders.

"Sure, take the whole book. I hope it helps."

"Thanks, and I owe you one for today."

Tawnia shrugged. "After all the times you watch the baby when I have to go into work? I'm the one who owes you."

"I don't so much as watch her," I said, "as we hang out and play together." I gave Destiny another kiss and a tickle before going to find Cody.

In my shop, Cody was off browsing my antiques, but Jake was waiting for me by the counter. My heart skipped a little, glad to see his friendly face.

"Hey, Jake," I said, moving away from the counter where Randa was helping a customer, her eyes darting to me in encouragement. "How'd it go last night? I heard you had a date with Kolonda." Head-on was the best way to confront the situation. I needed to let him know I was excited for him.

He grinned, his face all at once becoming more vibrant. I loved his smile—I always had. "Not exactly a date," he said, "at least not in the beginning. She has a mold problem. But after I checked out her rental, we caught a play at the college. It was fun."

"I'm glad." Our initial impetus had taken us halfway across the shop where we now stood near the double doors between our stores. I swallowed and forced myself to continue. "I think she likes you."

His dark eyes were warm and inviting. "I like her, too. She's a wonderful woman."

That was good, exactly what I wanted. "So maybe you'll get back together?"

For a moment he said nothing, shifting his weight in an unconscious way that made his muscles move attractively beneath his white polo. Then he shook his head slowly. "No. I don't think so."

Why not? I didn't ask the question, but it was there in my eyes, and after all these years, Jake knew me well enough to see it. "It's just not going to work out."

How do you respond to that? Part of me wondered if he was offering me a chance to change my mind, a chance to think about him differently at some distant point in the future, a chance for me to understand that I still had a choice—but another part of me was abruptly so tired at holding our friendship together. I wanted Jake to be happy. I wanted him to try harder.

"Jake, I—I'm sorry. I'd hoped that—I—"

"It's okay," he interrupted. "Look, I've been meaning to tell you. There's this woman who moved into my apartment building. I really like her."

I blinked. He what?

"I would have told you sooner, but I wasn't sure. It was only after being with Kolonda last night that I realized I feel differently about this other woman. Different as in really good. Her name's Courtney, and I'm pretty sure she likes me the same way." He grinned. "Don't look so shocked. I'm not totally inept, you know."

Oh, I knew. "That's great," I recovered enough to say. "I'm really glad."

"I want you to meet her. Not right away, but soon."

I knew what he meant. He wanted their relationship to be more solid before he introduced the ex-and-still-good friend to his new love interest.

"Okay," I said. "Good." I stepped away. "I have to go. They're waiting for me at the police station."

"Be safe." He backed up a step before turning on his heel and heading into his store.

"Come on." Cody appeared at my elbow, his voice like gravel. "Let's get out of here." I was glad to let him lead me outside.

Once in my car, I pushed thoughts of Jake aside and extended the sketchbook to Cody. "Look what Tawnia drew. I recognize Winston Drewmore, but I have no idea who the other guy is."

Cody was so still, I glanced over to make sure he was okay. "What?"

"I know the other man," he said. "You would, too, if you'd paid closer attention to what your detective's partner was working on this morning instead of flirting so much."

I scowled at him. "Spill it already."

"He's Frank O'Donald."

"Russo's enemy? The guy from New York that JoAnna Hamilton claims she doesn't know?"

He nodded. "She may not know him, but if Tawnia's drawing is correct, her young cousin certainly does. And it looks like O'Donald's in town."

Chapter 15

awnia's drawings were always correct. Well, at least those we'd figured out were coming from her unusual ability and not her regular drawing talent. She shared this gift with our biological grandmother, Cody's mother, who'd been forced into a sanitarium when she tried to warn the police about the "accidents" she drew. Cody had only been a boy. That she'd died in the sanitarium was one more thing for which he would never forgive himself.

I remembered Winston Drewmore's reluctance when Hamilton wanted to give us O'Donald's name. I'd thought at the time it was his fear of Russo tying his tongue, but now I wondered if he was involved in some other way.

At the precinct, as we waited outside an interrogation room, Shannon, Cody, and I discussed the possibilities. "You think Drewmore might have told O'Donald how to get into the lab?" Shannon asked.

I studied my sister's drawing. "I'm not sure, but apparently there's some connection. And like you said, it looks like he's not in New York at the moment."

"We have to remember that if Drewmore's involved, it basically means sabotaging his own company," Shannon said. "He is Hamilton's heir apparent." He thought a moment. "There is always the possibility that he decided to steal company secrets and go into business with O'Donald instead."

"You think he told O'Donald that Ralph Shatlock would be alone at the house that night?" My stomach twisted at the idea. I liked Winston and didn't want to believe he was capable of causing his relatives harm. He seemed to have a genuine concern for both Hamilton and her cousin, Maribel. "If it was him, why didn't they take Ralph Shatlock from the movie theater? That would have been better. No one besides Winston even knew Ralph went to a double feature every Friday."

"Maybe that was the point." Cody was slouched against the wall across from us. "The imprint on the filing cabinet told us they thought they'd find him there. But Drewmore said he was supposed to go to the meeting directly after the theater."

Shannon looked thoughtful. "You're saying that if Drewmore did tip O'Donald off, he purposefully sent him to the house when Shatlock *wasn't* there? That would mean he wanted the lab and the files destroyed, but didn't want to risk his cousin."

Cody shrugged. "Could be."

"Except Shatlock *was* there," I put in. "Just before the break-in. And possibly during it."

"Maybe whoever was in the hall while he opened the safe warned him, so he got out in time," Cody said.

"We have to prove first that it was O'Donald who orchestrated the break-in." Shannon glanced down the hall where Paige walked briskly in our direction. "We should be able to get him here soon, since he's apparently in town."

Paige reached us, immediately picking up on the new undercurrents. "What is it?"

I handed her the sketchbook open to the page with Winston Drewmore and Frank O'Donald. "Tawnia drew it."

Her eyes narrowed. "Very interesting. We'll have to ask them both about it. Obviously someone's not telling us everything. Mind if I keep this for a bit? I'd like to look at the other drawings to see if anything else matches up."

"Sure."

Later, though." Tucking the sketchbook under her arm, she jerked her head sideways at the interrogation room. "Right now, we need to chat with the head of Tarragon Inc. Shannon and I will go in, and afterward we'll see if we can't get something for you to read. I have the owners of Print Perfect waiting in another room, so we'll do the same with them." Her eyes slipped to my hands. "What's with the gloves?"

Shannon had asked me the same thing when I'd arrived, and I'd told him about my visit to Easton in a few short sentences, but explaining to Paige now would take too long. "Just taking a break from imprints."

She arched a brow but didn't reply, simply reaching up to pull back the blinds covering the observation window. "This is Zander Tarragon, CEO and primary shareholder of Tarragon Inc."

Cody kicked off the wall and came to stand behind me, staring into the room. "He can't see us, right?"

"That's right. One-way glass." Shannon's gaze went to me. "Until we know how and if these companies are involved, we don't want either of you to have direct contact with them. They might be dangerous."

Since someone had tried to wrap me in a rug and blow me

up, it was likely one or both of the parties already knew about me and my ability—unless Captain Piante was right about my involvement being accidental.

"Tarragon released two 3D printer models in Japan two years ago," Paige continued, "but had to recall one entirely, and the other has little practical use—despite the steep price tag of fifty thousand dollars. Still, their backing from several Japanese investors is solid, and their publicity claims they are close to releasing something that will help hospitals print living tissue, so that makes them a prime suspect for the break-in at Hamilton's lab."

"Doesn't it seem rather coincidental that two of Hamilton's scientists drown and then a year later Tarragon releases a 3D printer?" I asked.

Paige shook her head. "We can read coincidence into a lot of things, but the fact is that even if those men spilled everything they knew before drowning, it would take significantly more than a year to come out with something like that, especially since the lab break-in didn't result in anything."

"Well, the information they got out of the scientists might have been enough if Tarragon were already working on something similar," I said.

"True," Paige conceded. "And that reminds me. I got ahold of the investigating officer, and he said the teens accused of the break-in claim they were paid by a couple of guys who were with them at the time. When it all went bad, those men disappeared, leaving the kids to hold the bag."

"Did the officer believe them?" I asked.

"Yes. He also said he didn't believe the drowning deaths were an accident, though he had no conclusive proof otherwise. His biggest reason for believing there was foul play was that the Coast Guard received an anonymous tip that something was about to go wrong on the boat. Gave them their general location and everything. The Coast Guard tried to radio the boat to make sure everyone was okay, and when they didn't answer, they went to find them. The boat had already gone down. Sort of suspicious for it to happen so fast after the tip came in."

"Did they ever find the person who called?" Shannon and I asked together.

"No. I asked the officer to look through all the paperwork again to see if he'd missed anything, but he was certain there was nothing else." Paige reached for the door. "Well, here goes. Maybe we'll get a lucky break."

Shannon gave me an encouraging smile and followed her inside.

I shifted my gaze through the glass to the single occupant in the room, who sat in a chair, his fingers interlaced in front of him but not quite touching the table. He was a thin, compact man of indeterminate age, with short, straight black hair and dark eyes. He wore a black suit with white pinstripes and a white shirt underneath, even in this heat, but his smooth face and hands were tan as though he spent more time outdoors than in a boardroom. He was the perfect image of a Japanese business man, except in the fact that he was very definitely not Japanese.

Paige shook his hand and offered him a soft drink, which he refused, along with coffee and water. I knew she was primarily offering it to capture imprints, but the man wasn't biting.

"What do you know about Innovation Software and JoAnna Hamilton?" Paige asked when all the niceties were completed.

Tarragon dipped his head slightly. "They are my competition.

Well run. Good scientists. I respect them." Even his manners seemed politely Japanese.

"Well, someone broke into their lab last night. Destroyed everything. Their lead scientist is missing."

Tarragon looked properly dismayed. "That is unfortunate. I must call Ms. Hamilton and offer my condolences."

"So you know nothing about it?" Shannon asked.

Tarragon shook his head. "I assure you that we intend to beat Ms. Hamilton in this race, but not in such a manner." A smile tugged at the corner of his mouth, but in the next second it was gone and I wasn't sure if I had imagined it.

"What about three years ago? There are rumors that your company had something to do with the drowning deaths of her scientists."

Mr. Tarragon blinked at them and then said slowly, "I recall being questioned at the time, but I thought they concluded that the deaths were accidental." He shifted on his chair. "I was not aware that I am again a suspect in this matter. I think perhaps I should have my attorney present."

Shannon smiled. "That would be McGregor and Clancy, right? Yes, someone at your company referred them to us earlier, though your employee eventually relented and put us through to you. But by all means. Call them now. We can wait."

Mr. Tarragon pulled out his phone.

Paige rolled her eyes at us through the window, and I nodded sympathetically, though she couldn't see me.

"The guy's guilty of something," Cody said in my ear.

I didn't like Tarragon either.

"I think he knows about us, or at least you," Cody added. "See how he keeps his hands close to his body? Like he's trying not to touch anything."

I had to smile—Cody was even more suspicious than I was. I guess that happened when you lived a lifetime with our so-called gift. For an intense moment, I longed for the days when I used to expect the best from strangers. Maybe it was better that my ability didn't return.

In almost the same breath I thought of Winter and Summer and repented of the thought. I recalled moments with Shannon when he'd hugged me and his clothes had testified of how much he cared. I didn't want to let go of that.

I swallowed with difficulty and answered Cody. "Maybe. He could just be a germophobe."

Shannon and Paige emerged from the room, with Shannon motioning for an officer to keep an eye on Mr. Tarragon. "His attorney will be here soon, I think," he told the officer. "Send someone to let us know when he comes. We'll be down at interrogation two."

"Sorry about him asking for his attorney," I said to Shannon. "You did seem rather accusing, though."

"Did I?" He grinned. "Imagine that."

Paige laughed. "We *wanted* him to call the attorney. Shannon tried to talk with them this morning about Claire's husband and Tarragon, but their answering service wouldn't patch him through, even after he told them it was police business."

"Told me to call back next week," Shannon growled. "By then, they'd have a chance to sterilize their records. Now I'll catch them by surprise. If there's a connection to whatever Claire Philpot's husband is accused of doing and our case, we might catch a break." He started down the hall. "Come on. We probably have time to do this next interview before they get here to rescue their client."

The owners of Print Perfect were Arthur Mott and Harold Fisher, two nerdy college dropouts who between them had already guzzled half a dozen sodas. Both were thin and of average height and had brown hair in desperate need of a trim. They carried smart phones, which they constantly poked at as if their continued existence depended on their vigilance to the machines. Mott was rather large-headed and gaunt, his brown eyes small but intelligent. Fisher was severely slouch-shouldered and had thick-framed glasses that enlarged his blue eyes to the point of ridiculousness. His voice was an octave higher than his partner's and slightly nasal. I found it hard to take either of them seriously.

"Together they made over eighty million dollars during the first Internet boom," Paige said as we studied them behind the observation glass. "They even took it out before the crash. But they've used most of their funds on research. Our sources say that if they don't figure out something soon, they'll go bankrupt."

I wondered what made people with eighty million dollars lose it all to a new business. Was it the thrill of discovery? Greed?

Shannon and Paige went inside the room and repeated the same drill they'd carried out with Tarragon, but Mott and Fisher claimed not to know anything about the break-in or the old drownings.

"I would appreciate if you would pass Ms. Hamilton a message, though," Fisher said in his nasally voice. "I've been trying to contact her, but apparently she doesn't do email. Can you believe that?"

I did have a hard time imagining the cultured Hamilton sitting at a computer responding to email. Reading a printed one and ordering someone else to reply, yes, but going through spam and numerous emails didn't seem her style.

"And what is that?" Paige asked Fisher.

"We'd like to discuss a merger," Mott said. "We've designed several printers we think are unbeaten in quality. We could do a demonstration." A hint of desperation colored his words, and Shannon and Paige exchanged a pointed look.

"We'll give her the word," Shannon said, and Mott shoved a card at him.

Paige stepped toward the door. "If you don't mind waiting here a few minutes more. We might have more questions."

"Sure," Mott slumped in his chair and poked a few buttons on his phone.

Fisher smiled. "Yeah, we don't have plans."

I couldn't help but feel a little sorry for them. I wondered if they ever dated or if their phones were their significant others.

Paige and Shannon gingerly gathered up the soda cans, put them into a plastic garbage bag, and left the room.

"Well, what do you think?" Paige asked Shannon when the door shut behind them.

He shook his head. "Money is definitely a motive, and those guys have more brains in their little fingers than most men have in their entire heads. But they didn't destroy the lab themselves, and they'd need money to hire someone."

"They aren't totally destitute. Not yet." Paige relinquished the bag of soda cans to Cody, who'd started tugging on it.

He plunged his hand inside, his face a mask of concentration.

"Well?" Paige asked after a few moments.

Cody gave her a grin. "Fisher thinks you're totally hot. Wonders if he could ask you to go eat at his mother's for Sunday dinner. Apparently, that might get him lots of points with her."

Paige's lip curled. "Oh, save me from that."

"Good thing you've got a boyfriend," Shannon said with a smirk.

"Mott's worried that Hamilton might steal his ideas if she agrees to a merger," Cody added. "He's also worried you'll save his DNA for some nefarious purpose—which, if you think about it, he's kind of right about. Not his DNA exactly, but reading his imprints could be classified as a bit nefarious."

"So nothing to incriminate them?" Shannon asked.

Cody shook his head. "Maybe if I could grab one of their phones."

"They're nothing more than kids," Paige said.

"Genius kids," Shannon corrected. "And more than capable of committing and covering up a break-in. They were in business when the scientists' drowning took place. They could be responsible. Hiring young teens to take the fall for the break-in back then sounds about right up their alley."

My head was whirling again, not because I was dizzy, but because of all the what-ifs. "True, but I think we all agree that Tarragon is also capable of murder and the break-in."

Paige chewed on her lip. "Why didn't he touch anything? That's what bugs me."

"Me too." There was a tenseness around Shannon's eyes that told me he was worried. I knew exactly why. The interviews hadn't brought us closer to a solution, and with so many suspects, how could we possibly protect Hamilton's brother—provided we could find him?

"Tarragon's attorney should be here any minute," Paige said. "Maybe they'll shed some light on all this. We also need to talk to Winston Drewmore about his involvement with O'Donald. We're already waiting on a call from O'Donald himself. If we'd known he was in town, we might have been able to lean a bit harder on his answering service when we first talked to them."

"Any clue why O'Donald and Russo are enemies? I mean, are they simply business rivals, or is there something more?" In my mind I still pictured O'Donald as a strong, charismatic man like Nic Russo rather than the ordinary-looking man from Tawnia's picture. He was into organized crime, and therefore suspect, but anyone who opposed Russo couldn't be all bad. Maybe.

"We're still looking into that," Paige said. "There was a shooting incident at one of Russo's offices six years ago that O'Donald might have had something to do with, but neither side was forthcoming with information."

"Imagine that. Anyway, I have Winston's card." I fished in my bag for the one he'd given me at Hamilton's. "I'll call him."

Shannon scowled, showing clearly his hatred of situations he couldn't control, and I had to agree—nothing seemed to line up in this case. I gave him a smile. "Don't worry. I won't tell him anything—at least not until I get a full confession."

I was rewarded by a smile that left me tingling and wishing we were alone somewhere. I'd even eat that sticky pasta he was so fond of if we could put this day behind us.

"Let's look at that drawing again," Paige said, pulling the sketchbook from under her arm, but her perusal was interrupted by Shannon's new captain.

Piante was a burly, fifty-something man with thick black hair shaved to a quarter-inch all around his head. He stood a foot taller than most of his men, and today his customary dark dress pants were topped by a button-down shirt a strange shade of puke green. "Tarragon's attorney is here," he said, glancing through the observation window at the Print Perfect guys before refocusing on Shannon and Paige. "Oh, and guess what, In Loving Memory just filed a complaint about you two."

Shannon grinned. "I'd say we're getting closer then."

"Let's just hope those prints on the George Washington bust come back with a positive match." Piante nodded at me without exactly acknowledging my presence before striding down the hall in the direction of the bullpen. I knew I made him nervous—I made them all nervous—but he really liked Shannon and no one could deny that I helped put the bad guys behind bars.

"A complaint?" I asked.

Shannon laughed. "After you guys read the bust imprint, I called and let them know we were looking at murder charges. See if I could get them to make a move. Huang and his guys are keeping an eye on them for us." His eyes skimmed my gloves before coming to rest on my face. "Well, our boy geniuses can cool their heels here a bit longer while we talk to Tarragon's attorney."

"I can't wait." Paige's voice was nearly a sneer. She opened Tawnia's sketchbook and began to turn pages. "Maybe there's something here we can use against them."

As we closed in on the other interrogation room where we'd left Tarragon, I could see a well-groomed, blond-haired, dark-suited man in his mid-thirties moving toward the door with a uniformed escort. My nerves hummed tautly as I studied him—good-looking, immaculate, and probably sporting a Harvard law degree.

That Tarragon's attorneys were the same people Claire Philpot's husband used to work for might not be such a case-altering coincidence as I'd hoped. McGregor and Clancy were a prestigious firm, and it was only reasonable that someone as important and strongly backed as Tarragon would choose them for representation. Still, with all the other odd connections in this case, I hoped something more suspicious would emerge.

In front of me, Paige's step faltered abruptly as she uttered a tiny gasp. She turned on her heel. "Did your sister draw all of these this morning?"

I looked over the sketchbook. "I think so. At least those right before and after the one with Winston. Why?"

She pushed the book at me and the others crowded around to see what had disturbed her.

For a moment I feared she was looking at the drawing of Easton Godfrey, and that perhaps he had a rap sheet as long as my arm, but she wasn't looking at him or at the drawing of Winston and the mobster, but at a third picture Tawnia hadn't mentioned to me. I leaned closer, seeing a man with either a very trim beard or several weeks of neglected growth. He was dressed in jeans and a black T-shirt, topped by another shirt that was slightly parted by a breeze, and was climbing stairs in the front of a building I didn't recognize, one booted foot raised to take a step. His narrow, haggard face looked out at us, eyes intent and searching. Haunted.

"Tawnia's doing an ad for outdoor clothing. I—" I fell silent as a jolt of memory shot through me. The gray-patterned outer shirt . . . I'd seen that man the previous day, twice in fact—once at the estate sale and once outside my apartment, where he'd been only wearing the black T-shirt.

"He's been following me," I said at the same time Paige said, "I know him."

"He has?" Paige asked me.

"What?" Shannon looked at us both.

Cody shook his head. "I've never seen him."

"Well?" Shannon nodded at me to go first.

"He was in the attic at the estate sale, looking at the rug. And I thought I saw him outside my apartment last night when we found the door ajar." I shook my head. "I knew he looked familiar, but he was turned away from me. Now I'm almost certain it was the same man from the sale."

Our gaze shifted to Paige, whose face had grown pale. "I didn't see his face, but I remember the guy in the attic. I'd know him anywhere, though, even with the beard. Either he's Bridger Philpot or his twin."

"Claire's husband?" I said. "No way."

Three years he'd been dead of a heart attack. Three years his wife and two grown children had mourned him. I didn't know if Claire would ever stop mourning him.

"It can't be him," Paige continued. "I knew Bridger. He wouldn't do something like this. Not to Claire. He adored her."

Yet it might explain the money missing from his account, the transfers not even his wife could explain. And maybe the money his employers claimed was missing as well.

Shannon made a sympathetic noise in the back of his throat. "Maybe no one knew Bridger Philpot as well as they thought."

Chapter 16

"We need to find out more about Bridger's cases," Paige said. "No way can I tell Claire about this. She has so much faith in him."

Cody grunted. "Could be he has an explanation."

"Not for this." Paige's voice was clipped.

"Then maybe it ain't him," Cody said with a shrug. "I mean, he had a heart attack, didn't you say? That would be kind of hard to fake, since you need a doctor to sign the death certificate."

I turned the page in Tawnia's sketchbook, seeing with relief that there were no more surprises awaiting us.

"The Philpots are connected, Bridger especially. Or he was." Paige lifted her chin with determination. "If it is Bridger, I'm going to kill him myself." Her eyes met mine briefly, and I knew her well enough to understand why she was so shaken. If Claire and Bridger, who'd been so much in love and so right for each other, had such serious secrets, how could Paige possibly think to have a successful relationship with a man? She'd been burned before.

I put a hand on her arm. "Let's give Bridger the benefit of the doubt until we catch up to him and see what he has to say." The relationship my adoptive parents had shared was the major reason I dared to go ahead with Shannon. Well, that and because I believed deep down that Shannon would lay himself on a bed of hot tar and nails before he'd hurt me.

He really would.

My gaze flew to his—only to find him watching me. A connection opened up between us, a connection so deep and wide and meaningful that for a moment I couldn't breathe. Maybe this was the real reason I'd always avoided looking into his eyes when I was dating Jake. Maybe this promise had always been there staring back at me.

Shannon hesitated a moment, his mouth opening and then shutting again without utterance.

I smiled, dipping my head slightly, and he nodded. Later, we would talk. When had I started reading him so well? When had he become an extension of myself?

Cody and I hurried after Shannon to the observation window. "So," Cody grunted as Shannon and Paige disappeared into the room with the attorney, "what was that? I bet they felt that electricity clear in Florida."

"That was none of your business, old man. Now be quiet so I can listen."

Chuckling, he turned to face the glass window.

After a few niceties, everyone sat at the table and Shannon got down to business. "Your firm is suing Bridger Philpot's estate for sums embezzled from your company. How much is missing and how do you know Philpot took it?"

The attorney blinked, apparently not expecting that line of questioning. "Are you here to interrogate us or our client?"

"We believe this may be connected to our case," Shannon said. "Philpot's been dead three years and suddenly you decide to go after the funds? What gives?"

"Actually, the timing was not our choice. The funds Bridger took weren't from our company, but from one of our clients. We were about to confront Bridger when he died. We hoped to slowly reimburse the company ourselves by doing work without charge for them, but five million dollars is a rather hefty amount to work off. With the decline in the economy, we are now forced to seek reimbursement."

Five million dollars? Claire hadn't mentioned the amount her husband had been charged with taking, but this made her concern even more understandable.

"Ha," Cody snarled. "Those leeches charge like five hundred bucks an hour. That would add up in no time."

Though I might share the sentiment, I was glad we were only observing through the glass, so he wasn't heard. "You mean like the five hundred you told Hamilton I charge?" I couldn't resist saying.

He frowned. "It ain't the same thing. She can afford it."

So, apparently, could anyone who chose McGregor and Clancy as their attorneys.

Inside the room, Paige whistled. "Five million dollars. Who's the client?"

"I'm not at liberty to say." But the attorney's eyes drifted to Mr. Tarragon before he dragged them back to the detectives.

Next to me, Cody snorted. "Bet they love him during trials."

"So, he stole from you, Mr. Tarragon." Shannon's voice was bland, and I knew he was fishing for something more.

"No one said anything about Mr. Tarragon," the attorney

blurted, his Harvard aplomb deserting him. "If you have any more questions, I insist that you take them to our senior partner. He—"

Tarragon lifted a hand to silence him. "Yes, Bridger Philpot was my attorney, and he did steal from me."

"I'll need to see those records," Shannon said swiftly.

"Why?" asked the attorney, recovering his composure. To Tarragon, he added, "Zander, you are not required to show them anything."

Shannon studied the attorney. "Mr. Tarragon had to show you some proof about the missing funds, I assume, and since our department has been asked by Claire Philpot to look into the claims, you know as well as I do that any judge is going to order you to turn over the records. You can't sue someone without proof, so you might as well give us the information now. Save everyone time."

Mr. Tarragon stood up from the table. "You will not need the records because the case will be dropped." He stared hard at his attorney.

The younger man didn't back down. "If you're going to continue to require us to reimburse you, we need—"

"I will come to an understanding with your partners. I assure you, they will be pleased." Mr. Tarragon turned his gaze to Shannon and Paige. "Please tell Mrs. Philpot that the suit will be dropped and that I am sorry for her trouble. I liked her husband, and though he stole from me in the end, I did not relish the idea of seeing his widow punished. Now, if you have further questions, I would suggest asking them quickly. I have an appointment this afternoon that I cannot reschedule."

Paige jumped in with more questions, but when they seemed unlikely to shed more light on the case, I reverted to my own thoughts. Why had Tarragon made McGregor and Clancy drop the suit? He had to be hiding something because I couldn't believe he'd do it out of the goodness of his heart. The attorney had already made it clear they weren't willing to continue to work for free, so either Tarragon was hiding something big—perhaps the break-in at Hamilton's lab?—or money was no longer a concern. Maybe that meant he'd caught up with Ralph Shatlock and planned to use him to create 3D printers.

Or maybe he'd simply signed another investor.

A vision of Russo filled my mind. Could the mobster be playing both sides, determined to get his weapon-building machines at any price?

I sighed. My thoughts were going nowhere useful. Neither was the conversation with Tarragon. The more questions Paige asked, the more closemouthed Tarragon and his attorney became.

Five million dollars. Had Bridger Philpot really taken the money? That would have made it possible for him to disappear in style. Except all of the money in the world couldn't replace losing someone you loved. Maybe that's why Bridger looked so haunted.

If it was Bridger. I couldn't forget the supposed heart attack.

Easing away from the glass, I drew out my phone and made a call.

Winston Drewmore picked up on the second ring. "Hi, it's Autumn Rain," I said.

"Autumn, what a pleasure. I'm glad you called."

"Oh, have you heard from your cousin?"

"Ralph? No, unfortunately. But I was still hoping to hear from you." For a moment he sounded like an unsure teenager.

"I mean, I know you're going out with that cop, but there's no reason we can't be friends."

Okay, that wasn't so subtle. Besides Jake, I'd never known a guy without a girlfriend who truly wanted to be good friends with a girl, and in the end Jake had wanted more too.

"Look, I need to talk to you in person about your case." I had, after all, been hired to find his cousin, though we didn't really know if he was missing or hiding at this point. "Soon, if you can get away."

"I can leave now. I was just about to go out for a late lunch. Where do you want me to meet you?" His voice was all business now, which I told myself was a good thing.

I was about to ask him to come down to the station, but Shannon and Paige were still going strong with Tarragon, and I knew they'd have more questions as well for the boy geniuses from Print Perfect. O'Donald, too, if they could catch up to him. Maybe I could help them with this last bit of business. In fact, Winston would likely tell me more if I talked to him alone. Well, alone and with whoever Russo had assigned to follow me. And Cody, because I doubted I could get rid of him.

"Look, do you know where Smokey's is?" It'd been several hours since lunch, and if what Easton had said was true, I'd experienced a lot of imprints at his office, and I needed nourishment. In fact, I was beginning to feel downright starved. The more I ate, the sooner I might recover my talent.

Maybe.

"That's across from your shop, isn't it?"

He knew where I worked? For a moment the knowledge disturbed me until I remembered he and his cousin had tracked me down at my apartment. Of course they knew about Autumn's Antiques. The store wasn't a secret.

"Can you meet me there now?"

"How about in fifteen minutes?"

"Great." Fifteen minutes meant he wasn't at his cousin's in Lake Oswego. But was he still with O'Donald? It didn't make any difference to me. I doubted O'Donald was even involved. It was beginning to look more and more like Bridger Philpot, or his lookalike, had something to do with just about everything.

Even kidnapping me? The thought sent shudders through my body. I didn't even know the man, and the idea that he was stalking me seemed ludicrous, but there it was.

Poor Claire. If it was Philpot, how would she take learning her husband was a thief and a cheat, that he'd traded her and their family for five million dollars?

Then again, what was he doing back here now instead of sipping mai tais on a beach somewhere? It was a question I couldn't answer. Besides, I'd agreed with Paige to give him the benefit of the doubt. For now.

"Cody, look at this." I walked over to his side, pushing Tawnia's sketchbook under his nose. "Remember the imprint on the safe? Could Bridger be the man you saw in the hallway?"

Cody closed his eyes for a moment. "Can't say for sure. His shirt was black, but I couldn't see his face or the rest of him."

I'd bet a million people wore black every day in the United States. Of course not everyone was linked to Tarragon and my case. Or Hamilton's missing brother.

"He might have taken Ralph Shatlock," I said.

Cody rubbed his chin. "I didn't get the sense that Shatlock was being taken, but it could have happened that way."

"Look, I'm going to meet Winston at Smokey's. Tell Shannon, okay?"

"Tell him yourself. I'm going with you."

"I'll get more out of him alone."

"Maybe. But you might also get jumped again, and this time your boyfriend and that gun-happy partner of his won't be around to shoot at the bad guys, and then you'll go missing and your sister will never speak to me again, and I'll spend the rest of my short life searching for you and likely end up in some foreign jail. I'll die a lonely old man without ever holding my grandchild because she never had time to get used to me. Nope. I'm going."

Another of his ridiculous stories. *Stubborn old man,* I thought. At the same time I wondered if he was coming along because he felt he owed me, or because he'd really started to care. I was his daughter, true, but that didn't mean anything, not after the past we'd shared. Or hadn't shared.

"A foreign jail. Really?" I said. "That's the best you can come up with? What about skydiving in the Bermuda Triangle, swooping in just in time to save me from Davy Jones's locker?"

He only grunted, so I pulled out my phone again and texted Shannon, letting him know we were going to Smokey's and then back to my shop. It was best leaving him to his job anyway. He'd think better without me hanging around, and Cody and I were next to useless with Tarragon, since his fastidiousness kept him from leaving imprints. I'd make more progress if I pinpointed O'Donald's connection with Winston, even if it was to prove he wasn't involved in the break-in at the lab.

Outside the tall building that housed the Portland Police Bureau, I waved at Russo's men in their black sedan. They averted their gazes so quickly, I almost laughed.

My smile died when I spied a white van across the street half a block down. Tightness pulled in my chest. Hadn't I seen it before? Or at least one similar? Rectangular, without a lot of slopes. *Yesterday,* I thought. *When I was with Ace.* If there were two men waiting inside, it would be more than a coincidence. I'd have to go back inside and tell Shannon.

I climbed in the car and started the engine, but as we approached the white van, it became clear the cab was empty. *Just another white van,* I thought. The city was filled with them.

We hadn't gone a block when I stopped at a light and Cody thumbed at a café. "We should have met him there. It's closer, and I'm hungry."

"They don't have organic food. Besides, it's too close to the police station." It was probably a cop hangout, even on a Saturday.

"What's wrong with that?"

I spent enough time being stared at by officers, and it was worse now that rumors were beginning to leak about my relationship with Shannon. Though I didn't consult on all his cases, I had to wonder how long the captain would let us work together. "I'd rather eat organic."

"Ah."

Maybe I also wanted more space between me and the white van. I was getting paranoid. Ace had said he didn't know the people in the van outside my store yesterday, that they were likely waiting for someone. Maybe he'd been right.

As if my thoughts had conjured up the man, I spotted Ace's damaged BMW outside the café Cody had indicated. *Perhaps working his police contacts,* I thought, since he'd been at the station that morning. Was that him silhouetted in the window at a table with two others? Probably old partners from when he'd been on the force. Even as I caught that glimpse, two of the shadowed figures arose.

The traffic light turned green, and I pushed on the gas.

"Anyway, I need to check on Tawnia. If it's still busy, I'll have to stay at the shop. Destiny isn't going to be a perfect angel all day."

"No? I thought angel was her job description." His voice had gone all soft, and I knew he'd been smitten like the rest of us.

I pulled into an empty parking place outside my shop, glad to see that Tawnia's car was nowhere in sight. The fact that there were plenty of available spots told me customers had gone elsewhere, so Randa and Thera wouldn't need me right away. There was also no white van in sight, and the tightness in my chest vanished. We hurried across the street to Smokey's.

We'd already received our orders—turkey pot pie for me and beef stew for Cody—when Winston Drewmore arrived at the restaurant, which for some reason seemed larger to me today without Russo taking up space.

I could see Winston was a little surprised that we'd gone ahead without him, so after waving him over I said casually, "As you can see, we take food seriously around here. Probably because I never know when I'm going to be called in on a case."

"Ha," Cody said. "You've always been this way, from what I hear."

Winston looked at Cody and then at me. "Does, uh, your bodyguard always eat with you?"

Oh, that's right. Winston and JoAnna Hamilton believed Cody was my bodyguard. "Well, he's worked with me for so long," I hedged.

Winston waited and finally I met Cody's gaze. "I'm going over to the next table to discuss a few things with Winston." Good thing it was between rush times, or we'd be stuck at the same table, and Winston would never tell me what I wanted to know.

As I moved away, Cody nodded without appearing concerned, but the line between his eyes deepened. I wasn't worried. I could handle Winston.

A waitress I didn't know came to take Winton's order of a roast beef sandwich with fried zucchini instead of regular fries. Winston glanced over his shoulder at Cody before beginning. "Sorry about that little scene, but I wanted to get you alone to tell you that Ralph called me."

"He did?"

He nodded, his seriousness making him appear older than my first impression of him. "Just now when I was on my way over. Said he was with a friend." He frowned, marring the smoothness of his skin. "That's odd because Ralph doesn't have friends, not that I've ever seen. His life is his work. He never does anything or goes anywhere else—except the movies. Anyway, I told him about the break-in and asked about the computer drive with the backup program files he took from the safe. He said to meet him at the theater at five to get it. He has the files but says they aren't safe with him."

Five gave us an hour. Not much time to plan a strategy. "That's a relief. But why didn't you tell him to go to the police station? They could protect him."

"I did. He said the guy he's with told him it wasn't safe. That someone was watching." Winston's puzzlement shifted to a scowl, which was more attractive—more real—than his usual ready smile. "For all I know, those men from last night have him and are telling him what to say. You know, so that I'll go down there."

"Maybe, but why would they need you?" The way it came out wasn't exactly complimentary, and that Winston didn't take offense said a lot for him.

"Exactly. That's the only reason I haven't called that detective boyfriend of yours. Still, I need to tell someone, and since JoAnna hired you, I thought you could help me get Ralph and the backup drive somewhere safe."

"Where?" The only place secure was the police station.

"That's what I'm not sure about. My safe-deposit box would be best for the computer drive because it's so close and almost impossible to get into in a short period of time, but the bank is closed on Saturdays. The only other safe option is to take both Ralph and the drive to our building in Washington. The guards are always on duty there."

"Have you told Ms. Hamilton?"

He shook his head. "Not yet. She'll be relieved to know her brother is okay—and that he has the backup." He gave me a grin that was a ghost of his usual smile. "Guess if Ralph's okay, you're not really on the case anymore."

"That's okay. I'm glad he's safe. Did he say anything about the other backup? The rigged one he made for Russo?"

"Only that he believed it was safe, but it was better not to depend on it because it wasn't in his hands at the moment. Guess he stashed it somewhere. Probably to keep the two separate."

The waitress arrived with his sandwich, and as she served him, I scooped up a couple bites of pot pie. Now that it had cooled a bit, the taste was even better.

"Uh, Autumn," Winston said, as the waitress left. "I don't mean to be nosy, but what's with the gloves?"

"It's an imprint thing," I said, waving a hand as nonchalantly as I could. So what if I looked stupid wearing gloves in warm weather? It wasn't like he was telling me anything new.

He crunched his forehead and said, "Okaaay. Well, no

matter. Seems to be going on a lot. My cousin was wearing some like those today. Yesterday, too." His easy smile was back as he took a huge bite of one of his sandwich halves.

Ah, yes, his cousin. I remembered the dainty pair from Hamilton's house last night and how she'd slipped them into a drawer. That's what I must have remembered when Easton Godfrey mentioned gloves earlier today. I had wondered about them. JoAnna Hamilton didn't read imprints and she didn't seem the gardening type. Not even rich people like her wore dress gloves these days, though if I'd seen her cousin Maribel—Winston's grandmother—wearing them with her peach dress, I probably wouldn't have batted an eyelash.

"Must be kind of strange working with your grandmother's cousin," I said. "She seems like a nice woman—your grand-mother, that is. Kind."

He smiled. "She is. She raised me, and she was always there. Always. She's given me stability. It hasn't been easy for her on her own, but she'd do anything for me. Of course I always knew I'd eventually work for JoAnna."

"What about your own mother?" I wouldn't have asked the question if he hadn't opened the subject. I knew he was Maribel Hamilton's grandson, and thus a first cousin a couple times removed from JoAnna Hamilton, but that was the only thing he'd told us about his personal life.

He shrugged. "There isn't much to tell. My grandmother married right out of high school, and when her husband died, she pretty much focused on their daughter—my mother—but she ended up dying the year after I was born from the same genetic disease that took my grandfather. She wasn't even twenty."

A terrible story. "I'm sorry." I knew what it was to mourn the woman who'd given me birth, a woman I'd never known.

Again the shrug. "I've had it better than most orphans." He cracked a smile. "But for the record, I don't have the genetic disease."

I was glad for Maribel's sake. Losing a husband and a daughter was bad enough. "Your father?"

"Not in the picture." His smile vanished, so I guessed it was a sore spot with him. Maybe he'd been abandoned when his mother had been sick. Or perhaps the man had come looking for money after his son became successful with Hamilton's company. It wasn't my place to ask.

"Drewmore was my grandmother's married name," he added. "She reverted back to Hamilton when I was a teen, but I kept it."

"What about JoAnna? I supposed she sort of helped out." Though once I thought about it, I couldn't imagine the woman doing anything motherly.

"Oh, we didn't live together when I was young. Grandmother and I had a house in New York, and we saw JoAnna when we lived there, but my grandmother . . . well, when I was about ten she became a little disoriented."

Disoriented, yes, I could see that applying very aptly to Maribel Hamilton. I could also imagine her being loving and focused on raising a child.

"It was the city environment, I believe," Winston continued. "Eventually JoAnna bought the house in Lake Oswego, and Grandmother and I stayed there. It was a good life for a boy. Growing up on the lake, I mean. After that, it was college and the company. JoAnna and I'd take turns visiting Grandmother on the weekends when the business was in New York. We finally moved the entire company here to some family land across the Washington border. That's worked out a lot better for us. We didn't like leaving my grandmother alone with the housekeeper. So what about you? What's your story?"

Though he'd shared his background, I wasn't sure enough of his innocence to tell him how Tawnia and I had been separated by the doctor who delivered us, given to different adoptive families. How as an adult Tawnia had moved from state to state and job to job, feeling compelled, and how the collapse of the bridge that stole Winter's life had finally brought us together. People always thought that part amazing, but it was only a matter of time until fate allowed us to meet.

"Oh, there's nothing much more than what you already know," I told Winston. "Nothing exciting. Well, besides the imprints, that is. I started reading those when my dad died. Guess it was the trauma. It's kept me busy."

"I'll bet."

I let a few seconds of silence pass before I added, "I guess I should tell you why I called you here." I forked in another large bite of pot pie, hoping it wasn't my last.

His smile was infectious. "Not just because you wanted to see me, huh?" He shook his head. "Sorry, it's a joke. Bad timing for it, right? With my company teetering on the edge. So why *did* you call?" He glanced at his phone to check the time.

I knew he was worried about meeting Shatlock, and we still had to figure out how to do that safely. I wasn't going to let Winston show up alone at the meeting place.

I swallowed my food and reached down for my bag, removing Tawnia's pad and flipping it to the drawing of him and Frank O'Donald. "I need you to explain this."

He paled, the grin leaking from his face. Still, he braved it through. "What exactly are you asking?"

His response was more proof that he wasn't only a young,

pretty face. JoAnna Hamilton had groomed him well. Don't volunteer anything. Find out first what question is being asked. It hurt my heart a little seeing this side of him because I suspected he didn't come to it naturally, just as I hadn't always expected the worst from people.

This time I was glad to oblige his question, since I obviously wasn't getting information out of him the other way. I didn't even care if Shannon and Paige got mad. The drawing wasn't official evidence. My sister had provided it, and that made me responsible.

"I want to know what you were doing with Frank O'Donald this morning. If I recall correctly, you don't know him personally."

"I didn't say that." His eyes didn't quite meet mine. "I have met with Frank O'Donald several times, in fact. I've known him for months, but JoAnna doesn't know that. My business with Frank has nothing to do with any of this. He's not involved—at least not in the way you think."

"Oh?" I cast a regretful glance at my abandoned fork. We'd have to go soon, if we were going to meet Hamilton's brother. "And what do I think?"

"That I'm selling her out. The company."

"It did cross my mind."

"It's not like that. Frank and I are friends. Our relationship is strictly personal."

Could Winston be so blind?

"No," I said. "Men like Frank O'Donald don't have friends. To him, people are divided into three categories: enemies, people he uses, and family. Some are all three. But he doesn't have friends. You might think he does, but that would be a mistake. He's like Nicholas Russo. I don't know how O'Donald fits into this, but he is using you, probably to get control over your company."

"You're wrong. It's not like that." His blue eyes held a hint of pleading.

"Then what's it like, huh?" I pressed. "I'm listening. Do you attend the same country club? Do you play tennis together? Oh, wait, he's from New York. Maybe you attended charity benefits together before your company moved its headquarters here. Maybe he donates money to starving children in Africa— money he makes from dealing drugs at our children's schools."

Winston pushed back his plate, his food unfinished. "It's not something you'd understand."

"Why wouldn't I?" I leaned forward. Behind Winston, Cody had finished eating and was staring at us, his body alert.

"I know you're adopted," Winston said, "but you had two loving parents. You don't know what it's like to grow up not knowing."

I spread both gloved hands on the table. "Don't I? I met my birth father for the first time five months ago. In fact, I was investigating him in regards to a young girl's disappearance. Now what does not growing up with parents have to do with Frank O'Donald?"

"Because," he said with a sigh. "Frank O'Donald is my father."

Chapter 17

"*Y*our father?" I shook my head. "No. He's too old." Mid-sixties, I'd heard someone say. "You're what—twenty-seven?"

"Twenty-eight."

"So he'd have been nearing forty when you were born. Your mother was too young for a guy like that. Not even twenty you said."

He shrugged and didn't meet my eyes. "Nevertheless, he's my father. He didn't know, though. I wrote to him six months ago when I found my real birth certificate at the house. I contacted him. We had a blood test, and he is my father."

"So now he wants to be part of your life?" I meant it sarcastically, but because of my own experience with Cody, it came out as a real question.

"Yes, he does." A hint of a smile played on Winston's lips.

"Does your grandmother and Ms. Hamilton know about him?"

"You mean do they know he's my father? Yes. I told JoAnna just before we signed the contract with Russo, and then my grandmother later that same day. But I didn't tell either of them that I'd been to see him several times, or that he knows I'm his son."

I grabbed my fork and took two more bites of pie. Eating helped me think; things were becoming clearer already. "So this is why you two didn't want me reading the imprints on Russo's contract."

He nodded. "I'd left my briefcase after we signed, and when I went back to get it, I heard Russo saying something about you to one of his guys. They shut up quick when they saw me. Anyway, JoAnna and I did some asking around, and we followed you yesterday to see what you were like." He sighed. "She was really worried. If Russo knows I'm O'Donald's son, it might change everything."

"Why? You'd think he'd be happy to make financial gains through a competitor's son."

"You'd think." Winston stared down at his sandwich. "There seems to be some kind of feud between them, but I haven't been able to get any information about it."

"It might be connected with a shooting about six years ago. You hear anything about that?"

"No. Anyway, I thought JoAnna might withdraw from the contract altogether once I told her about you, but we really have no choice if we want to save the business."

Something wasn't adding up again. "What aren't you telling me?"

This time he met my gaze without wavering. "I've told you everything. I don't want JoAnna's business—our business—to fail, but I won't be denied a relationship with my father. I want to know him."

Pity swept through me. Couldn't he understand that

nothing good would come from being the son of a mobster? I only hoped the man already had an heir, or Winston might find himself forced into the business, where I doubted he'd last long—that is if Maribel and JoAnna had managed to instill any kind of morality during his formative years.

"After learning about the connection between you and O'Donald," I said slowly, "people might think it wasn't coincidence that someone broke into your lab when they did—exactly when your cousin wasn't supposed to be there. As though someone wanted the information stolen, and wanted to pretend to be going along with some master plan, but didn't want to risk Ralph's life."

Winston shook his head. "I see where you're going. Absolutely not. I might have mentioned the lab to Frank, but I didn't tell him to break in or give him any codes. Even if I didn't value my own career, I would never do that to JoAnna."

I wanted to believe him.

"I also don't think Frank would do anything like this to my family." Winston sighed. "Anyway, I should go now. I need to get the computer drive from Ralph, and I want to be there early to make sure I'm not followed. I think a van might be trailing me—maybe it's whoever broke in last night."

"What color?"

"White."

Apprehension shuddered up my spine. Yet if a white van was actually following me from time to time, it couldn't be the same one trailing him.

"I thought you could be my backup," Winston added into the silence. "Maybe call the police if anything looks odd."

"Russo's men are outside," I said. "They've been following me to make sure I stay in one piece to look at the contract."

His lips curled. "Then that won't work. Can't let Russo get ahold of the unprotected backup, even if he is my business partner."

"Wait, I think I have an idea. It would mean a little subterfuge and ditching our cars, but it should work. I mean, it has before."

He smiled. "Okay, I'm game." He glanced behind him at Cody. "What about him?"

I sighed. "Unfortunately, he's coming with us."

"That's not so bad. He can help keep watch. He's probably trained for things like this." Pulling a few bills from his pocket, he signaled the waitress for the check.

I didn't have the heart to tell him the only training Cody had was whatever he taught himself with target shooting on his hundred acres. And maybe his skill with a paintbrush, chisel, hammer, and knife—or whatever else he used to create his sculptures.

We filled Cody in as we went outside and crossed the street. "Shouldn't we tell the detectives?" he asked.

I nodded. "I'll text Shannon as soon as we get to the theater. We won't be in any danger before we get the hard drive."

"Where are we going now?" Cody asked as we reached the jazz shop next to Autumn's Antiques. "Back to your shop? I thought we had to hurry."

"No, we're going inside here. Just wait and you'll see why." I turned abruptly and led the way inside the jazz shop where Stu looked up smiling from his counter, his long hair covering his earphones.

"Just using your back entrance," I said, pointing to the back so he wouldn't have to remove his earphones.

He nodded and returned to reading the CD cover. His shop had a few browsers, but only one of them glanced our way.

"Now where's the theater?" I asked Winston as we emerged into the alleyway. "We'll need to call a taxi."

Winston frowned. "We don't have a lot of time."

"No worries. They'll be here in ten minutes."

We waited inside a baby clothing store, where Cody insisted on buying several outfits for Destiny. I had to laugh at the curiosity on Winston's face.

"I'll explain later," I whispered, and to Cody I added even more quietly, "Would you contain yourself? Since when does a bodyguard buy baby clothes on the job?"

"Oh, right. I forgot you told 'em that."

"Me?"

"Look, will it be okay if I have the clerk keep the clothes here? You can pick them up later. I might need my hands free."

"To do what? Carve a log statue?"

He scowled. "Be serious."

"Hey, you're the one picking out baby clothes."

Minutes later in the taxi, I started feeling nervous. Maybe because it was hot wearing shoes and gloves and being wedged in between the two men in the back seat. I lifted the material of my long skirt from my legs a few times to let in a bit of air. I was itching to take off the moccasins and gloves, to feel a connection with the earth again, but I was also afraid that I wouldn't feel anything. Better to wait until absolutely necessary. That's what Cody was here for.

A vibration by my feet had me scrounging for my purse. I checked the caller ID. Nicholas Russo. I wondered what he wanted. Well, I had a few questions for him of my own.

"Hello?"

"Aren't you worried about someone taking another shot at you?" he asked without preamble.

"I take it your men took a peek inside the jazz store."

"I need you alive to read that contract."

"I don't need to read it. I can tell you right now that Hamilton and Drewmore are on the up-and-up. They intend to keep their bargain with you. What I'm more interested in is Frank O'Donald. Why are you such enemies?"

The silence on the phone told me I'd guessed it in one. "How'd you know about him?" Russo said finally.

His question caught me by surprise. How we'd learned about O'Donald might bear some looking into. JoAnna Hamilton had told us, and if not for her, Winston wouldn't have said anything. It was almost as if she wanted the police to focus on O'Donald. Did she hope it would keep him from Winston?

For some reason my mind kept going back to the break-in that just *happened* to occur on the day that Ralph Shatlock was supposed to be away. Was Hamilton involved? Or maybe Shatlock himself? The door to the lab hadn't been forced, and that meant someone knew the code. Yet it didn't make sense for them to sabotage their own company, and why would Hamilton and Winston come to me for help if they'd been involved? Unless there was more I wasn't seeing.

"It doesn't matter how I know," I told Russo. "You should have been more forthcoming with the police. They know about the shooting six years ago. What happened? Is that what made you enemies?"

"I don't know what you're talking about." The mobster's voice was clipped. "And if you know what's good for you, you'll drop it."

"You won't tell me anything?"

More silence and then, "I still expect you to read that contract and tell me everything on it." The line went dead.

He knows JoAnna Hamilton is hiding something, I thought. *Or suspects.* I had to give the man credit. But I still didn't know how Winston's father figured into the case.

"We're almost there." Winston leaned forward and spoke to the cab driver. "Pull over here."

"You want me to wait?" The man was short and blond and young to be a cabby, I thought, and his oversized biceps told me where he spent most of his time.

Winston glanced at me as he replied, "Uh, yeah. Keep the meter running or whatever."

The man nodded.

We climbed out cautiously into the busy street, but no one appeared to notice us, and no suspicious cars or white vans lurked nearby. We crossed to the theater parking lot that was half full with matinee goers. I felt myself relax marginally. Not likely anything sinister could happen with all these witnesses about.

"Where will he be?" I asked Winston. I'd imagined Ralph Shatlock would be waiting for us outside, but I couldn't see anyone resembling him. I knew from the Internet that he was sixty-five, eleven years younger than his half sister. Like her, he had dark hair, the creeping gray obviously winning the battle, and he was also thin, but that was the only resemblance I'd noted in the pictures.

"Maybe inside."

I didn't want to text Shannon if Shatlock didn't show. We bypassed the ticket booth and went inside the lobby, where we casually got in line for popcorn. I scanned the area, hoping he'd appear soon. No way would I eat whatever processed junk they put on movie theater popcorn, though my sister had told me dozens of times that it was food fit for kings.

Winston's pants blurted out an obnoxious tune. "Sorry," he said, plunging his hand into the pocket of his dress pants. "It's the only way I can hear it in my desk at work." He drew a pattern on the screen, unlocking the phone. "Hello? Ralph, where are you? What? Okay."

He hung up, his brow tight. "He says he's waiting for us in the taxi. Saw us arrive, apparently."

Cody scowled. "Ain't even five yet."

"Well, come on." I led the way outside, feeling for my phone. If Shatlock really was here, I'd call Shannon and have him meet us wherever Winston planned to take the computer drive.

We hurried over to the taxi where Shatlock was indeed in the front seat with the driver. We climbed rapidly in the back, with me still scanning the area. Was that a white van up ahead? Yes. In fact, there were two now, but only one had that rectangular shape I dreaded.

"Ralph, why didn't you—" Winston's voice cut off as the older man turned toward us.

Shatlock was short and frail-looking, and freckles splattered over his rounded cheeks like flecks of mud. All the wrinkles in his face gathered around his eyes, half hidden by glasses. Half because one of the hinged stems of his eye glasses was missing, making them sit crookedly on his face. His nose was bloodied, and he had several scrapes on his cheeks and brow. His blue eyes had a wild, frightened look.

"I'm sorry," he said. One hand snaked up to push the broken glasses up over his eyes. His fingernails were torn and bloodied.

Our driver turned around to face us—not the blond,

muscled young man, but another blond man twice his age and half again his size, with a pockmarked face and a meanness in his eyes that made my stomach churn. In his hands he held a gun. With a silencer. At least a .45 by the size.

"I'm sorry," Shatlock said again. "They caught up to us."

Winston leaned forward. "Us? What about the hard drive?"

Shatlock's gaze turned to one of triumph. "I tried to give it to my friend, but there wasn't time. They almost got it." A tiny hysterical giggle burst through his speech. "I destroyed it." He lifted shaking hands to show us the broken nails.

"What friend?" I asked.

"Bridger. Don't know his last name. He was trying to help. He's been tracking these guys for years and found out what they were planning." Shatlock's face crumpled. "They shot him."

"Shut up!" the driver ordered. "Now, miss, hand me your bag, slow and careful."

Shatlock could only be talking about Bridger Philpot, which meant he was alive. But if what Shatlock said was true, he was working against these guys, not for them.

"Now!" the gun in the driver's hand waved at Shatlock. "Or I'll shoot him."

"Who are you?" I asked. "What did you do with our real driver?" One of him, four of us, Cody and I both with pistols. The odds were good in our favor, if we picked our moment. I glanced at Cody, saw him begin to lean forward so he'd have access to the concealed weapon in his waistband holster.

Though directly behind the driver, his movement didn't go undetected. With lightning speed, the gun shifted in my direction. Don't move!" He put a hand to what must be a communication device in his ear. "Better get over here and help. All's clear but they're getting antsy."

Ten seconds later, both doors on either side of us flew open and two dark-haired men appeared, one relieving Cody of his gun and the other patting down Winston.

I handed the driver my purse with a hard smile. "At least tell us who you're working for." Had Russo discovered what we were up to? I didn't recognize any of the men, but that wasn't saying much. Maybe Russo was more serious than I'd calculated about getting control of this technology. At the same time, I knew Tarragon or Print Perfect could be every bit as responsible.

"Move over," the man standing next to Cody said, gesturing with a gun. An old scar ran the length of his arm, looking jagged as it emerged from his snug yellow polo. "Looks like we're all about to get cozy." He pushed inside and pulled the car door shut, making the three of us in the back seat squish together until I was half on top of Winston.

The man who had patted down Winston, slammed the other back door and climbed in the front of the taxi beside Shatlock, his weapon still ready for business. The driver lowered his gun from my face and put the car in gear.

Relief poured through me now that I wasn't about to have my brains splattered all over the back seat. "So where is the taxi driver?" I asked for the second time. I'd dragged him into this, and I'd be responsible if anything happened to him. They couldn't have let him go, or he'd report to the police, so where was he?

No one answered. Next to me, Winston swallowed hard, emitting a faint, despondent sound. I spared him a glance, only to see that his face was as white as Cody's hair.

"I—I know you," he said, staring at the thug in front of him, the man who'd checked him for weapons. "You—you're

Frank's—" Winston stopped, apparently too stunned to complete his thought.

The man gave him a sneering grin. "That's right. All these months of pumping and you didn't tell him your uncle wasn't going to be around on Friday. Guess that shows you have some sense. No matter, at least we took care of the lab, and it looks like we got your uncle in the end without your help."

Cousin, I wanted to correct him. Ralph was Winston's cousin twice removed. Or something. But I didn't think anyone cared.

Winston blinked, looking like a confused little boy whose favorite dog had died. No, like a man who'd lost his father. Perhaps he had.

Reaching out, I took his hand. He clung to me so tightly my fingers began to ache.

What now? I asked myself.

I wished I'd made Cody stay at the station or given him the slip.

Had I left the GPS feature running on my phone? And if I had, would Shannon even think to look?

As we pulled into traffic, I saw something that gave me a tiny spurt of hope: an older black BMW with dings I recognized only too well.

Ace.

Chapter 18

A few minutes later, I became aware of a faint bumping sound coming from the trunk area. Erratic, but coming often enough that it didn't seem to be something inanimate. The taxi driver? Was he coming in and out of consciousness, trying to get free? I glanced at Cody and he nodded slightly, his eyes darting to the back of the seat to indicate where he thought the sound originated, but neither Winston nor the thug next to Cody seemed to notice the noise. I hoped the taxi driver would stay quiet; it might be his only chance at getting out of this unharmed.

To my surprise, the pockmarked thug didn't drive far, but pulled over in front of the rectangular white van. The other thug in the front seat turned to us. "We're moving to the van," he said. "These taxis have GPS devices, and we don't want uninvited guests at our party. No funny business now."

There wasn't a chance of that. We were marched singly to the van, each of us with a gun jabbed in our ribs. The people in the cars whizzing past didn't seem to notice, though with the car and the van blocking their view, I wasn't surprised. Ace's BMW was no longer in sight, but that didn't mean he wasn't nearby. Inside the van, it felt chokingly hot, and I hoped if the taxi driver was in the trunk of the taxi that he'd be able to get out before he baked to death in the heat.

Twenty-five minutes later we were driving through the countryside, southwest of downtown Portland, where houses were spaced miles apart. Nothing looked familiar, though I'd attended at least a few estate sales in the area. Finally, the van drove up to a mansion set far back on a large forested lot. Not behind a gated entrance, but far from the narrow main road and shielded by enough trees to be completely isolated.

I'd spent the last half of the drive thinking about Bridger Philpot. If he died yet again, what would happen to his wife? Ralph said he'd been helping, and I hoped that was true because at least he'd die a good guy, though Tarragon's missing money and Bridger's faked death didn't say much in his favor.

I wanted to ask Ralph all kinds of questions about Bridger, like how they met and where the supposedly dead attorney had been the past three years. I think I had some idea of how he'd supported himself, if Tarragon's claims were true.

But why did Bridger steal money from Tarragon when he was already wealthy in his own right? It didn't make sense, unless he'd done it knowing he was going to fake his death and didn't want to leave his family without funds.

My head ached trying to figure it all out, though not as much as before I'd put on my gloves. A good sign, I hoped.

We pulled to a stop. "Out," ordered the man in front of Winston. He had green eyes, I saw now, emphasized by his dark brows and lashes. Nice looking. Not at all like the dark-haired man squeezed in with us in the back, whose nose had apparently been broken and badly healed, or the blond driver whose face brought a moon crater to mind.

While not quite ugly, the square two-story house was nothing exceptional except for its large size, as if designed in the blandest of styles and with a minimum of color to perhaps attract a wider pool of buyers. Buyers in the multimillion dollar range.

We were hustled not into the mansion but down a flagstone pathway licked with moss, past a pool and a large flower garden, to another, smaller building. Perhaps the guesthouse. It sported the same blah design and coloring as the main house and was bigger than my apartment.

"Make yourselves comfortable," Green Eyes told us, opening the door.

Winston shook his head. "I want to talk to Frank."

"You'll do that soon, I'm sure."

"He can't keep us here!" Winston's voice rose.

"He can do anything he wants."

"Sit down," Cody growled, throwing himself on a brown leather sofa. "Stop making a fool of yourself."

Winston blinked, but his mouth clapped shut. He sat down stiffly on an easy chair. "Please tell Frank I want to see him."

The thug nodded and turned to his men. "Stay alert. Kill them if you have to."

I hoped that didn't mean all of us were expendable. How many sons did Frank O'Donald have anyway?

Green Eyes left and his men stood guard, one at the front door and the other at the far end of the room where it opened onto a hallway. I sat on the sofa next to Cody, kicking off my shoes and pulling my feet up under me, wrapped in my gray skirt in case there was an imprint on the sofa, though Cody was touching it with his bare hands and didn't seem distressed.

"Winston," I said quietly. "What do you know about Frank's family? Do you have half siblings?"

He stared at me blankly for a long moment before dredging up a reply. "One. You just met him. Name's Frank Junior. They call him Frankie Jay."

"Ah." Green Eyes was his half brother. No wonder he had an attitude. Must have been a surprise when Winston showed up after all these years of being Daddy's one and only.

"Who are you anyway?" Ralph Shatlock asked me from where he stood by the sofa. "How do you know Winston?"

I gave him a wry smile. "We were hired to find you, which, I might add, we have done. I'm Autumn Rain. I find people. I'm also a consultant for the Portland Police Bureau. Cody Beckett here is a colleague."

"Nice to meet you." Shatlock dipped his head, one hand massaging his chest as though it pained him. "Who exactly hired you?"

"Your sister. She was worried after the break-in."

Shatlock frowned. "I was going to call, but they had guys following us." He glanced at our guards. "We'd thought we'd finally ditched them."

"Mr. Shatlock," I said. "I need to know about your friend, Bridger. It's kind of important."

"Call me Ralph." He sat on the sofa armrest. "I only met Bridger a month ago. I don't even know his full name—he said it wasn't safe for me to know—but I trust him. He's been tracking some people who are responsible for killing my assistants three years ago." Ralph shook his head, and when his eyes met mine, they were reddened. "I was just working, you know?

Developing something new and exciting. I never thought anything I might discover could cause someone's death." He stared down at the floor and added more quietly, "I send their families money, but it's not enough. It's never enough to make up for those kids not having a dad."

"What more did Bridger tell you?" I wanted to know what had brought Bridger back to Portland. Was it that Shatlock had finally invented a 3D printer that was worth stealing?

"I don't know," Ralph said. "He's been keeping an eye on the guys who killed my scientists—for years, apparently, but now he finally thinks he has enough to prove the scientists were murdered. Maybe enough to put away the guy who did it."

"So he says," Winston came out of his self-pity long enough to say.

Ralph shrugged. The hand rubbing his chest had stopped, but he left his fist jammed against his breastbone. "I believe Bridger. They shot him just now when they grabbed me. I saw him fall."

Winston bristled. "So you think my father killed those men and wants to steal our property?"

"Your father? But who told you . . ." Ralph's brow furrowed, his eyes flying first to one guard and then the other. "Is that the Frank you meant in the car? Frank O'Donald? Does he know about you?"

Winston glared at him, his fingers digging into the padded armrests. "You knew? All this time? And you said nothing?"

Ralph looked away. "Wasn't my place to tell. Besides, with a man like O'Donald, you're better off not knowing."

I had to agree. If Winston hadn't contacted his birth father, we might not be in this mess.

"He's a bad man," Ralph added. "A very bad man. We're

all lucky to be alive right now. Your mother did the right thing not telling you."

"I knew you'd defend her. That's all you and everyone else ever does is tell me how lucky I am because of what she's doing for me. Maybe it might mean something if I believed it." Winston jumped to his feet and stalked over to the blond, pockmarked guard by the front door. "Tell my *father* I want to see him. Now."

Ralph moved from the armrest to the seat of the sofa, his hands falling to his lap. I could see they were shaking. I shot Cody a glance, confused. They talked about Winston's mother as if she were alive.

Cody's eyes went to the easy chair where Winston had been sitting. I knew he wondered if Winston had left an imprint on the armrests. I nodded slightly, my own fingers itching to read them.

In a smooth motion that belied his stiff leg, Cody stood, took several steps, and dropped into the easy chair, his hands on the armrests. His eyes glazed over before he pulled them back onto his lap. *JoAnna,* he mouthed at me.

No way. "Wait a minute," I said to Ralph, keeping my voice low. "Is JoAnna Hamilton Winston's mother? But she can't possibly—she would have been in her forties when he was born." Her *late* forties.

Ralph blinked. "Forty-eight to be exact." He shot a glance at Winston, who was still glaring at the guard by the door. "My sister thought she'd finally found real love. Never mind that Frank was almost ten years younger and a mobster to boot. Her biological clock was ticking, and that didn't help matters. She learned soon enough what kind of man he was. They were married less than three months, but even that wasn't real since he was still legally married to another woman. That's why she never told Frank about Winston. Or Winston about his father. Their marriage has been expunged from all the records."

He frowned and shook his head before adding, "But these things have a way of coming back. When we started this whole thing with Russo, I warned her not to deal with him. I worried that either he or Frank would find out about Winston. But JoAnna got wind that Tarragon had a new investor, and she figured Russo was our only chance to survive. Don't think too badly of her for it. She wants the company for Winston."

"What's between Russo and O'Donald anyway?" I asked.

Ralph opened his mouth to reply, but Winston's raised voice distracted him, and he glanced toward where his cousin—no, his nephew—stood before the guard.

"Did you hear me?" Winston was saying. "Do I have to repeat it a third time? You tell O'Donald that his *other* son wants to see him."

He tried to push his way past the guard, but the man waved him back with his gun.

"You gonna shoot me?" Winston taunted, sounding more frightened than bold.

The guard looked mean enough to do just that, so I jumped up from the sofa and hurried over, grabbing Winston's arm. "He'll come when he can, I'm sure. Just wait. Please, think of the rest of us."

Winston resisted for several tense seconds before wilting like a potted herb left too long in the heat. I brought him back to the sofa where he slumped, looking angry and confused.

I settled next to him, once more pulling my feet up under me. What had he told his father? His half brother hinted that they'd used him, but still it didn't seem likely Winston would tell them where his uncle did most of his work these days, or the code to the lab. Surely he wasn't that stupid.

Yet I knew how stupid trying to connect with a lost parent could make a person. I'd almost been shot several times trying to prove Cody innocent, though it turned out he wasn't exactly that.

"So you were going to tell us wh—" Cody broke off at hearing another commotion at the front door.

Green Eyes—Frankie Jay—entered, followed by a man I recognized from Tawnia's drawing. He was lean, slightly above average height, with gray hair and shoulders that tilted faintly forward like Winston's. He walked with a loose, liquid grace that couldn't be depicted by pencil, strangely reminding me of a dancer. He was good-looking in a pointed sort of way, like an animal with sharp teeth, and confidence exuded from him in waves. He wore an expensive tan suit and matching shoes, as if dressed for a concert or other performance. This was a strong, charismatic man who knew exactly what he wanted and where he was going—no matter who he had to step on to get there. He was sixty-seven, I knew, but like JoAnna Hamilton, he looked younger. They must have made an eye-catching couple thirty years ago. Still would, if they'd remained together, though it was obvious now, as it likely hadn't been then, that she was older.

Seeing Frank O'Donald, I understood why Winston believed O'Donald was different. In spite of the sharpness in his features, he didn't look like a mobster. Still, as much as Winston wanted to believe otherwise, O'Donald wasn't a typical father, not even to Frankie Jay, his other son, who he motioned away now with a flick of his wrist.

Winston bounced to his feet and met his father halfway

across the room. "Frank, what's going on? Why have you brought us here?"

Ralph leaned toward me. "This makes more sense now that I know O'Donald's involved," he whispered. "Bridger told me a company called Tarragon Inc. was behind the deaths three years ago, but we've pretty much decimated them as a competitor—especially with their latest recalls. Then we'd heard they had a new investor, and that's why we decided to approach Nicholas Russo—so we'd have the ability to keep our lead and beat them to the market." He scowled, his blue eyes wide and bright. "If O'Donald is somehow involved with Tarragon, there's no telling what O'Donald will do to get back at JoAnna now that he knows about Winston."

The connection explained the break-in at the secret lab and would also explain why Tarragon didn't care if he received further reimbursement from McGregor and Clancy to replace the money Bridger had supposedly stolen. In Frank O'Donald, his company had another backer, one more powerful than all his Japanese contacts. A lawsuit and an investigation, however, would not be to their advantage, if they had as much to hide as I suspected.

I unfolded my legs and stood, slipping my feet back into the moccasins, which had already rubbed the skin raw at the top of my right heel.

"I need an explanation," Winston insisted.

"Don't worry," Frank told him. "I'll fill you in on all the details later. At the moment, suffice to say that it's time you took your rightful place at my side. Your knowledge of nano-technology will come in handy as we partner with Tarragon to create something truly beneficial to the world."

"I won't steal from my mother." Winston's hands fisted at his sides.

O'Donald's eyes pinned him. "Steal?" His voice was deadly calm. "It seems JoAnna has been the one to steal from both of us. She has stolen years we can never replace. We have much to make up for, but together we'll make the best of it. You've given me a lot of useful information over these past months, however unintentionally, but as my oldest son, it's time you take on a larger role in my organization."

Winston was the oldest? My eyes rushed to Winston's half brother standing behind his father, his green eyes hard and merciless. Whereas Winston looked young and often uncertain and shy, this man was hardened, professional, and ruthless—exactly like his father. Every line in his body told me he wasn't happy to discover any brother, much less an older one.

"I didn't tell you anything!" But Winston's protest was unsure, as if he'd lost confidence in everything he'd ever known. He glanced at me, his eyes hollow, pleading. There was nothing I could say to help.

My stare returned to O'Donald, whose gaze snagged on my gloves. "You must be the woman Russo brought in to examine his contract. Winston told me about you this morning. I can only imagine JoAnna's reaction when she learned that her secret might be discovered." A hint of a smile came to the pointed face, but in the next instant, the smile slid away. "If Russo had found out about Winston before I knew to protect him, my son would likely be dead right now. There have been numerous attempts on Frankie Jay."

I knew Russo killed people. I knew he had businesses that were illegal and likely caused many to suffer, but sometimes it was hard to separate that knowledge from the man who had let his cousin leave the business, a man whose hopes for the future were focused on his new baby son.

"What did you do to Russo?" I spoke before I could stop myself. "Why would he hurt Winston just because he's your son?"

Again the flicker of a smile. "Because I killed his wife."

Stunned silence filled the room. In front of me, Winston stiffened.

"His first wife," O'Donald clarified. "Oh, it wasn't exactly planned. We were jockeying for a business deal, and the team I sent in wasn't careful. Of course, if you ask me officially, I will deny any connection. Besides, how could I know his pregnant wife would be there? In Russo's view, taking my son's life would make up for the death of his unborn child."

"The baby was a boy?" I asked.

O'Donald nodded. "Or so I heard. But as I said, I personally had nothing to do with it."

Yet he was responsible. I could see the triumph in the sharp blue eyes—eyes that despite the similar color looked nothing like Winston's.

You did it on purpose, I wanted to say, but I wasn't that stupid. If we were to get out of here at all, it would be only if O'Donald believed we weren't any kind of a threat.

"Look, Cody and I aren't a part of this." My nervousness showed in the spill of words. "We're hired help, is all. Please let us go. We won't say anything to Russo or to JoAnna Hamilton. This is between her and Winston. Even if we did say anything, who would believe us? We're nobody."

A tick in O'Donald's cheek signaled impatience. "We'll see. Perhaps you can go after all of this is played out."

Behind him Frankie Jay smirked, making me realize that if O'Donald had his way, none of us would ever live a normal life again—if we lived at all. Our survival hinged only on our usefulness.

For the moment, Winston was safe, and probably Ralph as well, since he was needed by Tarragon, especially now that they didn't have the computer drive. Perhaps even I could be useful to O'Donald. But unless we revealed his ability, Cody was expendable. And if we did reveal his secret, we would both be at risk, one of us redundant.

That meant we had one choice: to escape in any way we could.

Chapter 19

"It was you at the estate sale yesterday," I said to O'Donald. "You tried to have me taken." I should have kept my mouth shut, but I was furious at how this man played with other people's lives. I wanted everything to go back to the way it had been before my experience in the rug. If my ability hadn't vanished, I might have learned enough through imprints to not be standing here at all.

One side of O'Donald's mouth lifted in the slightest arrogant sneer. "I don't know what you're talking about. Before this morning, I didn't even know you existed." His eyes wandered over my red blouse and gray skirt. "Though I must say, I am pleased to make your acquaintance. I think we'll be great friends, you and I. You could go far in my employ." There was an added insinuation in his words that made me cringe.

"Wait a stinkin' minute," Cody thundered. "You keep your hands off her."

O'Donald's gaze skimmed over him with a cruel twist of his lips. Behind him Frankie Jay brought up his gun. Apparently Cody hadn't gotten the memo about his expendability.

I whirled and launched myself at Cody, hammering my fist at his chest. "I've had enough of you. Leave me alone, old man! You hear me? Always putting yourself into my business. You work for me, so sit down and shut your mouth."

I shoved him, willing him to stay quiet. Something in my eyes must have done the trick—or maybe he thought deep down I meant every word—because he stumbled back and fell into the easy chair.

O'Donald laughed. It was an easy, free sound that invited others to laugh with him. I hated him even more for that. An evil man should have an equally evil laugh. "I have a feeling this is going to be fun," he said.

He had no idea. Somehow I was going to make him pay for the words I'd had to say to Cody, but for the moment at least, I'd bought the old man more time.

O'Donald's attention shifted now to Ralph, who'd remained sitting on the sofa. "I heard there was a problem with your backup drive," he said. "You shouldn't have destroyed it."

Ralph gave him a nod. "I'm beginning to see that. Well, no matter. Give me someplace to work, and I'll figure it out."

"Good. Because there's no way Nicholas Russo is ever going to get his hands on this technology. You owe me, Ralph, and so does your sister." With a sharp, triumphant smile, O'Donald turned on his heel and sauntered toward the door. "Frankie Jay, have your men wait outside. Let's give our guests a little privacy. Please, all of you feel free to make yourselves at home. There is a fully stocked kitchen if you're hungry."

Fully stocked. I wondered who we were kicking out of their digs, though the place really didn't have a lived-in appearance.

"Come along, Winston," O'Donald added. "We have things to discuss."

Winston cast me a glance, but we all knew he didn't really have a choice. Besides, it would be better for him to learn as much as possible, so he could report back to us. Meanwhile, if we had an opportunity to escape, I couldn't really count on him to be much help, and that meant he was safer with his father. I nodded slightly.

The minute O'Donald and his crew strutted from the house, Ralph jumped to his feet, hands fisted at his sides. "He always was an idiot," he said in a dark mutter. "Like I could recreate years of research all on my own."

I blinked. "You had me sold. What are you going to do?"

"Stall until we're rescued. Tarragon and his people won't be so easy to fool, though. Even at our company's main lab with what information we have stored there, it'd take a year or more to get as close as I was before all this happened—and then only if I had enough help working around the clock." He heaved a sigh.

"What about the rigged backup you made for Russo?" I asked. "Where is that?"

Ralph rolled his eyes, not seeming surprised that we knew about the backup. "Like I would tell you. Besides, I don't exactly know where it is at the moment. Last I saw it was at the lab."

I glanced at the door, thinking belatedly that maybe we shouldn't be conversing so freely. "Wait. How do we know this place isn't bugged?"

Ralph shook his head. "There hasn't been time. Besides, O'Donald doesn't need to listen to us. He knows we'll give him whatever he wants in order to stay alive."

Okay, we'd go with that for the moment. "So back to the lab. Someone removed the backup you made for Russo?" I prompted.

He nodded. "Bridger called to warn me that O'Donald's men were planning something big. I knew it had to concern the lab, so I hurried home early from the theater. JoAnna had already left for her office, and she was expecting me at the meeting with Russo, but my rigged backup was gone. Still, I had a pretty good idea what had happened to it. I called Bridger because he was closer, and he checked it out for me while I deleted the backup in the lab. I mean, it's password protected, but you never know. By the time I'd finished, Bridger had arrived at the house. Said the rigged backup was secure and that we'd retrieve it later. We were removing the other backup from the safe when O'Donald's men arrived. We barely made it out of there without them seeing us. Luckily, I keep a rowboat out back."

Apparently, Bridger had been in deep and he'd paid for it, perhaps with his life. I felt an ache in my stomach that had nothing to do with our situation. Poor Claire. To lose him again like this wasn't going to be easy.

"You think you'll be able to find it?" I pressed.

Ralph grimaced. "Without Bridger, I can only hope. I'm not sure where he might have moved it."

"Will you two stop it with the backup already? We have to get out of here." This from Cody, who still sat where I'd pushed him.

I took a tentative step toward him. "Look, Cody, about what I said—"

He waved my words away. "I understand. I don't know why I let him get to me like that. I'm a stupid old man, that's for sure."

The pressure in my chest eased. "Let's just concentrate on how we're getting out of here."

"Not us," Cody said. "You. We'd only slow you down." He said the words reluctantly, but I was glad he'd come to that conclusion. I'd worked with Shannon and Paige long enough to know I could depend on them to pull their own, but protecting Cody and Ralph might get me killed—and them in the process.

"What are you thinking?" I asked.

Cody glanced at the front window. "Not sure. We should probably wait until dark, though."

"For what?" Ralph was rubbing his chest again. I wasn't sure, but I thought his breath might be coming a little too fast. He sat down abruptly on the sofa.

"Is something wrong?" I asked.

"Hey, that's a good idea," Cody said, eyeing Ralph. "You fake a heart attack like that Bridger guy did the first time around and create a distraction so Autumn can get away. And better you than me because I get the feeling O'Donald would think it a favor if I croaked."

"Uh, I don't think he's faking." I hurried over to the couch. "Ralph, talk to us."

Ralph took another labored breath. "They hit me earlier. I—I have a bit of a heart problem, and I've been without my medication today."

This didn't sound good. "Winston didn't tell me you had heart trouble."

"The kid doesn't know," Ralph panted. "JoAnna either, though she suspects, I think. Anyway, I'll be okay. I can go a couple days without medication." As if to deny the words, he slumped over on his side, his broken glasses askew. All the color was gone from his face, as though leached by some parasite, but he was still conscious.

With all the excitement today, it'd be a miracle if he *didn't* have a heart attack. "We'd better get them to tell O'Donald," I told Cody.

Cody shook his head. "He can't do anything. Unless he has a personal physician standing by. If he calls an ambulance, he gets in big trouble for abducting us."

"I'll be fine," Ralph protested. "I just need to rest."

I put my fingers against Ralph's throat. His heartbeat was faint and erratic. Something was wrong. Even if he wasn't dying right this minute, another day without his medication might kill him. At least O'Donald could do something about that.

I sprinted to the front door, yanking it opened. The brown-haired thug with the broken nose and arm scar stepped in my path and raised his gun. "It's Ralph," I said. "I think he's having a heart attack. He hasn't taken his medication today." Without waiting for a reply, I returned to the sofa where Ralph was leaning back against the cushions.

The thug came inside, talking on the phone. "Okay," he said. "I understand."

"We need an ambulance," I said. It was worth a shot.

The thug blinked at me and shook his head. "He ain't going nowhere." To Ralph, he added, "Old man, O'Donald says maybe you'd better remember where you put your other backup. He's sure you have one. Maybe if you tell us, he'll find you a doctor." With that, he stalked out the door, closing it firmly behind him.

Cody and I stared at each other. I had thought that if anything happened to Ralph, O'Donald's plans would be ruined, but suddenly I wasn't so sure. Ralph was the heart and soul and brains of JoAnna Hamilton's nanotech project, and with him out of the way, her company would probably collapse. Without JoAnna's company, Russo's claim to nanotechnology would never come to fruition, and with O'Donald's backing, Tarragon would eventually finish the race, with or without Ralph's help. Maybe they'd hire the scientists Ralph had been working with once Software Innovation went under. Worse, maybe they already knew where Ralph's backup had been stashed.

I bet O'Donald realized it would take Ralph years to recreate his own work without the help of his notes. Maybe a year was too long to keep a kidnapped victim hidden. If all this was true, O'Donald was assured of his revenge and the only reason any of us were still alive at the moment was to lull Winston into falling more easily into whatever life his father planned for him.

If I was right, that made Ralph expendable every bit as much as Cody—and he was looking worse by the minute.

"Cody, I need you to cause another distraction," I said. "Get him in here again. The other man, too, if you can. I'll find another way out and go for help."

"Don't worry. We'll make it good," Ralph said between gasps. He might be a peaceful scientist, but the glint in his eyes made me wonder what kind of double features he'd been watching at the theater.

I smiled. "Just don't put more stress on your heart."

"I tell you—I'm okay." But a note of something new had entered his voice: fear.

I started for the kitchen with the intent of finding a back door, but Cody's hand shot out and stopped me.

"Look," he said, "one more thing. O'Donald might be telling the truth about not being involved in the rug incident yesterday morning, but his two thugs reacted when you spoke of it. They know something. I'd bet on it. Frankie Jay too."

Either O'Donald was a good liar, or his men were hiding something from him. How likely was that? Unless Frankie Jay had ordered them to silence. Now there was a man who'd sell out his own father.

"I'll keep that in mind," I told Cody.

He took a step back. "Be safe."

I felt an urge to hug him just in case, but we hadn't reached that point in our relationship. Maybe we never would. Then again, he'd bought Destiny baby clothes. I nodded and turned away.

The kitchen was much larger than my own. One thing I'd give O'Donald is that he knew how to travel in style. I wondered what the kitchen in the main house looked like. I loved to cook, and I bet it had every amenity, as well as large windows to let in the light, which to me was every bit as important as the food.

My moccasins squeaked against the floor, and I wished I could discard them. But I couldn't afford to become dizzy as I had at taekwondo that morning. As I'd hoped, there was a door leading outside, and my hand closed around the knob as Cody began to shout.

"Help! Help! He's dying! Please help!" His voice was gruff and stressed, and I could only hope he wasn't telling the truth.

I tugged on the door.

Locked. With no way to open it from the inside.

They changed the knobs, I thought, seeing how the door-knob didn't line up with the indentation in the paint left by the previous one. They'd had time for some preparation, at least.

No solution except for the window over the sink, and all the while my precious seconds were ticking away. But the window was nailed shut. Ruined, actually. If the place was rented, they'd never get back their deposit. No time to search bedrooms for possible exits.

No further sounds came from the living room, and I hoped the guards had taken Ralph to the mansion to treat him. Wrapping my gloved hand in a dishtowel, I punched the window. The glass shattered, though the sound wasn't as loud as I expected. Much easier, it turned out, than breaking cement blocks during my martial arts class. Still using the towel, I hurriedly broke out the window edges, checked for guards outside, and slithered through, feet first. I cut the inside of my right arm on a piece of glass, but I was free.

A garden abutted the area behind the guesthouse, more forest than the carefully tended garden in front of the house, with a path that wandered like a vein around the shrubs and other greenery to places unknown. I sprinted down the path, squeezing into the brush as I heard someone round the side of the guesthouse—perhaps alerted by the breaking glass.

Holding my gloved hand over the cut on my arm, I peered through the shrubs at my pursuer—blond hair, face like a crater, shoulders double the size of mine. The only thing I might have on this guy was surprise and my black belt training, but he had ninety pounds on me so my chances of besting him weren't high. All he had to do was to avoid my blows long enough to land a lucky one of his own. The power behind one big arm would flatten me to the ground. Besides, he had a gun.

I pushed farther into the bushes that tugged on my blouse and skirt, like hands holding me back. Though the skirt was new and my favorite, I should have found some scissors to cut half of it away. I wouldn't be able to run or kick properly in it. Pulling it from a rosebush, I stumbled through the greenery and flowers until I fell out onto another path leading away from the house. Should I take it? Maybe it would lead to a road where I could flag down some help. But we seemed to be out in the countryside and I had no idea exactly where. I balanced the safety of leaving versus the chances of finding someplace to make a call on the premises. Of course, if they were renting the house, which I was sure was the case, they might not even have a landline.

"Did you find her?" I heard Crater Face shout. He sounded close, though I couldn't see him through the bushes.

Farther away, a deep voice answered. "She's not in the house."

"I heard a noise over here. He going to be okay?"

"Frankie Jay took him up to the main house. I think he's faking."

"He is old, so maybe he's not faking."

"One less problem if he croaks."

"Be better if we had the backup first. Maybe he told her where it is."

"Maybe not. Maybe she just took the opportunity to escape."

"Whatever. I'm going to enjoy teaching her a lesson."

I shivered, not liking the idea of Crater Face getting close enough to teach me anything.

"Wish we had more guys."

Crater Face snorted. "Won't need 'em. Go check the front. She might have snuck around there."

I longed for darkness, but it was still hours away. It seemed I had no choice but to angle away from the guesthouse. I moved slowly, carefully, but my skirt caught on a branch and snapped it.

Footsteps came fast in my direction.

Giving up all pretense of stealth, I ran, my heart vaulting into overtime. I wished for bare feet. I missed the connection with nature, the steadiness I felt when my feet could discover for themselves each high and low of the path instead of receiving information filtered through leather.

My skirt, though fairly wide, was hindering me, and I reached down, found a hole made by the rosebush, and ripped it at roughly knee length, tossing the material aside. I ran faster.

My heart had begun to steady when a figure loomed directly ahead of me. The blond's face was red with exertion, the pockmarks dripping with sweat. He gripped a pistol in one hand. I waited for him to call for backup, but apparently he wanted me all to himself.

I didn't want to know for what.

Pistol or no, I dropped into my fighting stance: fists up, head slightly tucked, feet apart but ready to pivot.

Crater Face laughed. "You think you can fight, huh? This is going to be fun." He put his gun back in his holster.

I knew size wasn't on my side, and while I didn't believe in coincidence, I did believe in luck and goodwill. You received back exactly what you sent out into the universe, and I'd been trying all my life to send out good.

I still wouldn't be able to beat him.

But I was going to try.

He leapt toward me.

Chapter 20

I sidestepped, bringing my hands up, joining them together, and slamming them down on the back of his neck as he lunged past me. I followed with a kick to the back of his knee that sent him down to the mossy cobblestone path.

He grunted but jumped back to his feet. Now he was angry, which might or might not play in my favor. He came at me again, punching hard. I yanked my head back, snapping my foot forward into his gut.

He cursed and swung again. I blocked with my left, and drew first blood with my right jab at his cheek. He stepped back, breathing heavy, his eyes calculating and intelligent. Not a good sign for me. This time he came at me more cautiously. A tentative right, easily blocked, followed by a left that would have knocked me out if I hadn't stepped partially out of the way, causing the blow to land off-center. Pain reverberated through my head.

I threw two punches and another kick, two of which landed

but didn't seem to faze him. He didn't kick back, something I could be grateful for, but he'd obviously had some boxing training. Or maybe he'd just beaten up a lot of guys.

"You might as well give up," he taunted. "I promise I won't hurt you anymore. You'll probably enjoy what I'm going to do to you next."

For an answer, I kicked his groin, landing to the side but causing enough pain to make him scream.

"You'll pay for that." He managed a blow to my shoulder and then to my gut. I took advantage of his extension by delivering a right jab to his face. His nose popped but it only made him laugh.

On and on we went, with his meat hooks slugging, and me jabbing or kicking, dodging or blocking. My cheek and lip were split. My ribs hurt, and I suspected one of my kidneys was damaged.

I wondered how long I could keep this up.

At least until I passed out, because once I stopped fighting I knew he'd kill me.

The next minute I was on the ground, my head whirling from a blow. He jumped after me, but in the second before his body covered mine, I rolled into a bush at the edge of the path. Something with thorns.

Crater Face crashed into the cobblestones, but his eyes radiated triumph. Coming to his knees, he grabbed my hair and began pulling me toward him.

"Stop right there! I'll shoot!"

My attacker froze, looking toward the voice. I took the opportunity to use my right hook, freeing myself from his grasp. I scuttled backwards a couple feet, my eyes finally going to the newcomer.

"Easton?" I said. Was I in some kind of shock? What was Dr. Godfrey doing here? While I was happy he'd interrupted, I couldn't think of a single reason for his appearance. Cody had warned me that Easton Godfrey would haunt me now that he knew of my ability, but here and now?

Easton ignored me. "Get away from her." His thick dark bangs had fallen down over his eyes, and the twisted side of his mouth when he grimaced made him look meaner, like a vigilante from some film. I might have been comforted, if not for the frightened expression in his eyes or the way his hand holding the gun shook.

Crater Face noticed as well. "You think you can shoot me, little man? What is that anyway? A pea-shooter? You'd have to hit me with a dozen rounds to stop me from making you very, very sorry."

I comforted myself with the fact that at least they weren't working together.

What I needed was a weapon myself. Maybe a rock? I looked around, but there was nothing in sight. Nothing but a small bird feeder near a little cast iron bench slightly off the path. I arose, every muscle in my body protesting the effort.

Still kneeling, Crater Face lifted one foot and planted it on the ground.

"Stop!" Easton said, sounding less sure now.

The bird feeder was cemented into the ground.

Crater Face sprang toward Easton, but I was ready with the bench. I swung hard, slamming it. Praying.

A sickening thud and Crater Face dropped.

Easton stared, his gun lowered. "Did you kill him?"

My stomach twisted. What if I had? I'd never killed anyone before.

"If I did, you should be glad," I retorted. "He was going to kill you." I leaned over to check, but Crater Face had a pulse—and much stronger than was probably safe for us. He wouldn't be out long.

"Do you have a phone?" I asked Easton. "And what are you doing here anyway?"

"Don't move!"

I blinked. "What?" He had the gun up again, this time trained on me.

"We're going to my lab for some tests. I promise I'll let you go after that."

"Are you insane? I was kidnapped by these people. They still have Cody and a man who's probably having a heart attack. We have to get help or they're both going to die."

"It's only a few tests." The gun didn't waver. "I'll let you go in a few days."

"Days?" He really was insane. "You'll go to jail for the sake of your research?"

He shrugged. "You might not press charges. Not after you see how important it is."

"Or more likely after you give me enough drugs to make me forget. Is that it? Is that what you did to Cody to make him hate you so much?"

A flush covered his face, but he didn't answer. "Come on. Let's go before he wakes up. I'm parked out that way. You go first." His hand wasn't shaking now; apparently he wasn't as scared of me as he had been the thug. Which made sense because I'd been really afraid of Crater Face myself.

I wasn't a bit afraid of Easton, though, gun or no gun. I would take it from him at the first opportunity, but for now I wanted to get as far away from Crater Face as possible. Besides, I was thoroughly lost, and even if I could find a phone to call Shannon, I couldn't tell him where I was.

I hurried down the path, my muscles still aching, though the pain was easing now in my face and kidney. Maybe I was only bruised.

"Look, we have to call the police and an ambulance," I said, pausing at a fork in the path. The forest had completely taken over now, with no flowers or manicured bushes, which must mean we'd left the private property.

"Go right," Easton said.

Fine, I'd go right. "So, how'd you find me anyway?"

"I followed you." He smirked when I glanced back at him. "I slipped a GPS into your purse at my lab, and I followed the signal. I saw you get in the van with those guys."

"You didn't call the police?" The doctor had to be absolutely nuts.

"I thought you knew them. You all seemed kind of cozy."

It was all I could do not to slap him. *Easy*, I told myself. I needed his car to get Cody and Ralph out of here.

A few minutes more and his cream-colored sedan was in sight through a break in the trees and bushes. Relief flooded me. I was directionally impaired, but a road and a car meant I could get to safety. Once I called the police.

I hurried until I was about ten feet from the car—and stopped.

"Keep going," he said.

I turned around. "No."

He scowled. "I'll shoot. Don't think that I won't."

"Look, I'll do your tests when all this is over because I want answers, but it will be on my terms. That is if I don't hand you over to the police." I strode toward him.

"Stop!" he demanded, retreating a few steps.

"No." Reaching out, I yanked the .22 from his grasp. "Now give me your phone."

He reached into his pocket and handed it over, looking miserable. I wished I had time to give him something to look really miserable over, but I had none to waste.

I dialed Shannon's number. No answer. I didn't know if he was busy or if he didn't pick up because he didn't recognize the number. I tried Paige next, but her phone went to voicemail, a sure sign she was using it.

"Get in. You drive," I said. On the way to wherever I decided to go, I'd call 911 and text Shannon. I couldn't risk going back in to help Cody and Ralph alone—not until I'd notified someone in authority.

"Someone's coming." Easton dived for the door of his car.

The road was narrow and close enough to O'Donald's house that I felt the same nervousness—until I saw the marked-up BMW.

Ace. Finally he'd used some of those detective skills he claimed to have. I didn't really like the man, but he was better than Easton for company. At least he'd never tried to abduct me.

He pulled over and rolled down the window, giving me his secretive grin. "I see you've been fighting again," he said lazily, as if we had all the time in the world. "Your face is kind of banged up. Tsk, tsk. Interesting what you've done to your skirt. I think the uneven hem suits you."

I didn't bother glancing down. "Took you long enough to get here. I was beginning to think you didn't see the men take us. I mean, you were there. You had to see something. Why were you at the theater anyway?"

Ace gave me his usual grin. "You're not the only one who works with cops."

"Where'd they put the taxi driver? I thought I'd heard him in the trunk of the taxi."

"He was. They'd knocked him out, but he's okay."

That was a relief.

"So," Ace drawled, "what's going on here? I mean besides O'Donald kidnapping you?" That he knew it was O'Donald said something more for his detective skills.

"I have to get Shannon here."

"Already called him when I saw where they'd brought you. He should be there soon. Maybe they're at the house already."

"What about an ambulance?" I asked. "Ralph's having a heart attack. He needs help the second Shannon cleans out O'Donald's men."

Ace reached in his pants pocket for his phone and his thin fingers flew over the surface. A second later, the phone vibrated with an incoming message. "Okay. Ambulance on the way."

I relaxed, though part of me rejected that the end should come so quickly and easily after all my bruises and scrapes. Well, it wasn't over exactly, not until Cody, Ralph, and Winston were safe. Even then we still needed to find Bridger—or his body, most likely.

Ace climbed from his car and jerked his head at Easton. "Who's he?"

I looked to see Easton patting himself down—probably in search of his car keys. "You don't want to know," I said. "Easton, come here."

Reluctantly, Easton sidled over, cowering like a dog before

a spiteful master. He nodded at Ace, who nodded back. "Look, I'm not a part of this," Easton said. "I just want to leave."

"You should have thought of that before," I retorted.

Easton scowled. "I wanted to do more tests before you get your ability back—and without Cody breathing down my neck. I've never had this opportunity before."

"Ability back?" Ace asked. Then he laughed. "So that's why you weren't touching things. Hah, maybe now I can solve a few cases for the police instead of you stealing my bread and butter out from under me."

I hadn't realized I'd been doing that, but I guess maybe I had. Some cases I only needed to read one object to point officers in the right direction. From there, the guilty usually trapped themselves.

Without warning, Easton grabbed his phone from my hand and darted across the street, vanishing into the woods.

"That was weird." I wasn't sure if I was more surprised that he'd chosen the phone instead of the pistol or that he'd acted at all.

Ace shrugged. "We don't need him." He glanced at the gun. "I see you've picked up a toy."

"Not mine. Easton's. Look, come back to the house with me. I have to check on Ralph."

Ace's eyes narrowed. "Don't you mean Cody, your father?"

Why would Ace be digging into my background? "Cody's not my father in any way except biologically. But yes, I do feel a responsibility toward him." I was lying, of course. There was more between us now. I couldn't forget that he'd dropped everything to come help me. I couldn't forget the baby clothes.

Ace frowned. "Okay, but we go in slow. If we don't have a good shot, we wait for backup."

"You said yourself Shannon was on his way."

"Are you sure we shouldn't wait for him?"

"I'm sure." I couldn't trust Cody's life to any possible delay. Even now Frankie Jay might be taking his anger out on him.

Ace's phone rang. He glanced at the screen before answering. "Ace here." He paused. "Yes. No worries. She's here with me. Yes, of course I'll take care of her." He hung up and grinned. "Your boyfriend's very possessive."

"That was Shannon? Why didn't you let me talk to him?"

"Oh, sorry. Didn't think about it." He shrugged and started forward. "Come on, get in the car. I think I saw a better way back down the street to enter the property. No one will even know we're there."

That was what he'd said the last time we'd worked together, right before he'd almost gotten us both killed. I should probably rethink going in with him, but my worry for Cody was building.

We drove up the road, the BMW inching along. "It's somewhere up here," Ace said. "There." He came to a stop, just as I heard a clunk coming from the direction of his trunk. Had the back tires rolled over something? I listened, but I didn't hear anything further.

I took the opportunity to check Easton's gun. Both the chamber and the magazine were empty. "It figures," I mumbled as I tossed the gun into Ace's dashboard. "What a loser."

"Hey, careful with my car." Ace turned off the engine and reached for the gun as I opened my door. He was welcome to the useless piece of junk.

We slipped through the woods, ears straining. Ace found a path through the forest that soon gave way to a garden that led to the guesthouse, but there was no movement around the building and the front door gaped open. I crouched behind a bush with Ace, wondering what to do next. The sinking feeling in my gut was now telling me Cody was in danger.

Wait, was that a connection I felt to Cody? Like the one I shared with my sister?

No, it couldn't be. I'd never felt that with Cody before, only my parents and Tawnia. But something was there. Something faint, tugging at my chest, like an invisible cord. I stared at the gloves. Could that mean my ability had returned?

Well, it didn't matter, not now. I needed to find Cody.

"Ace, I think . . ." I looked around, but Ace was gone.

I hadn't heard him cry out, so he must have gone on ahead and not realized that I hadn't followed. A brief movement from the side of the main house drew my attention. Had Ace found a way in? Keeping hunched, I ran that way. The garden was elaborately cultivated in back of the mansion, with fewer trees and several wide expanses of lawn. I hoped no one would look out a window and spy me slipping across the open places to the side of the mansion where a lilac bush promised concealment.

I almost tripped over the leg before I saw it. Worn jeans, caked with blood. The rest of the body hidden behind the greenery. Everything motionless. I crept forward cautiously.

Rounding the bush, I saw Bridger Philpot sprawled, eyes shut but his chest faintly moving. Gray patterned cloth that I recognized as the shirt he'd worn at the estate sale wrapped his upper leg and also wound around his middle. One of his eyes was swollen and black.

What on earth is he doing here? My only idea was that they'd brought him here like us, and he'd escaped, though how that was possible in his condition, I didn't know.

His eyes clicked opened, changing from resignation to hopefulness as he focused on my face. "Autumn Rain?"

I nodded. "Bridger Philpot?"

His turn to nod.

I knelt down by him, smelling coppery blood and unwashed male body. Up close, he looked every one of his fifty-odd years, except for the scruffy hair that was still mostly black. His face was haggard and his body thin to the point of emaciation.

"Ralph Shatlock told me you'd been shot," I said, "but how'd you get here?"

"We were outside the theater and saw Winston arrive," he said, his voice weak. "Ralph was heading inside with the hard drive while I kept watch. When they enticed the taxi driver away on some pretense and went after Ralph, I yelled a warning. They shot me. Had a silencer. No one even noticed." He barked a low laugh that sounded too moist to be healthy. "Ralph was banging that hard drive on the ground, breaking it open. That's what people stared at. Did he manage to destroy it?"

I nodded. "What happened after you were shot?"

"They put me in the taxi trunk. Probably thought I was dead. But they build 'em with releases now, and as soon as I came to, I got out. They'd even left the keys. I knew this is where they'd come, so I drove here to help Ralph."

Bridger drew himself up on an elbow, and gave me a thin grin. "Turns out, I'm not much help. I could only get this far."

"The police are on their way. Just sit tight."

Bridger fell back onto the grass, his eyes flickering shut, his mouth clenched in pain. "If I'd known then what I know now, I would have done things so much differently." His words ended in a half sob.

"I've met your wife." It was the only thing I could think to say to him that might help. "Several times in fact. She's a lovely woman."

His eyes closed. "She's the only reason I keep going, but I don't even know if she'll take me back after what I've done."

I didn't know enough of what he'd been through to answer that, though I suspected Claire would be willing to listen to his reasons. I put a hand on his shoulder. "Look, I'm going to try to find my friends, but I'll be back, okay? There's an ambulance on the way. You're going to be just fine."

His hand shot out to stop me, his eyes opening. "I want— if I don't make it, can you tell my wife I did it for us? To keep our family safe?"

"From O'Donald?"

Bridger shook his head. "Tarragon. He's working with O'Donald now, but he wasn't then." He shut his eyes momentarily with his pain.

"This has to do with Hamilton's scientists who died, doesn't it?" I glanced at the mansion, hoping any minute to hear Shannon or Paige. What was taking them so long?

"Tarragon was going to steal information from them and have me patent it to legitimize his claim. But I followed him to New York and confronted him. He threatened my family if I didn't go along."

It was a terrible moral dilemma, and I could tell he still agonized over his choices. "But you interfered anyway."

"The scientists still died." His voice sounded forlorn. "And Tarragon knew it was me who called the Coast Guard."

"That's when you came up with the idea of dying?"

He nodded. "I figured it wouldn't take more than six

months to get enough dirt to bury them, and I could come home." He swiped a thin hand across his face.

Except his planned six months had stretched to three long years. Would I have been willing to stay away that long to protect my family? *Yes,* I decided. You did what you had to do, and my experiences with Russo had taught me that men like him and Tarragon didn't flinch at taking revenge.

"How did O'Donald get involved?"

"He contacted Tarragon a few months ago, and I knew this was what I'd been waiting for. They were planning something, and I was going to nail them." His brow furrowed. "Oddly enough, I think their connection has something to do with Winston Drewmore, though I'm not sure what exactly. Maybe the kid sold out his cousin."

"Mother," I said. "JoAnna Hamilton is his mother, not his grandmother's cousin. O'Donald is his father."

Bridger's good eye blinked. "That explains why you're all still alive."

I hoped he was right and that everyone *was* still alive. "And that explains why you were at the estate sale yesterday."

"I was following Winston. I thought he'd be going to see O'Donald again. Didn't take me long to see that they were following you around." He gave a dry chuckle. "Made it easier for me, especially inside that house. I just went wherever you were, and I knew they'd show up. But I didn't learn anything."

"As far as I can tell, Winston knew nothing about his father's plans. He wants a relationship."

"Poor kid," Bridger muttered. "Look, tell my wife that I—"

"No. You tell her yourself."

He frowned, and I glared back at him. "You can go the

distance. I heard you have a new grandson. You'll want to meet him. You've come too far to give up now."

He nodded, two spots of red appearing on his pale cheeks. "Thanks for the pep talk." His voice was raw and full of pain but underlined with new determination.

Of course there was still the very real possibility that he wouldn't make it. The police hadn't arrived, and my anxiety for Cody was increasing by the moment. And what had happened to Ace? "Where is Ralph's other backup?" I asked Bridger.

He laughed, a weak pitiful thing, but still a laugh. "You don't know?"

"If Ralph doesn't know where you stashed it, how could I?"

"Well, he does know, even if he doesn't realize it. But I don't think I'm going to spill it now. Not until we're out of this place."

He had a point. What I didn't know I couldn't blab to O'Donald, not even to save Cody. Of course there was always the chance that the backup had been moved or discovered since Bridger put it away.

I couldn't delay any longer. "I have to go find my friends."

"Go ahead. I'm just going to lie here a moment and then I'll follow you, okay?"

"Okay." We both knew he was going nowhere anytime soon, and that if an ambulance didn't arrive in the next little while, I really would have to explain to his wife what little I knew about his intentions these past three years.

I looked at him and he returned my gaze steadily, an understanding between strangers, one we didn't need to voice.

"Luck," he called as I rose to my feet and headed to a tree that grew at the corner of the mansion, stretching upwards toward an upstairs window that faced the lilac bush. The tree wasn't close enough to get me in the window, but one of the long branches stretched sideways toward the back of the huge house, close to an upstairs balcony that ran along the entire back side. Maybe with enough luck I could reach it.

I was about to begin climbing when a gunshot reverberated through the air.

Chapter 21

Abandoning my tree plan, I ran across the grass and onto the patio behind the mansion, hurtling over a cast iron chair that was in my way. I finally reached the back door, pausing only briefly to yank it open. More shots rang out through the once quiet evening.

Belatedly, I wondered what I would do if a thug with a gun was on the other side of the door, but by then it was too late. I was moving on instinct to find Cody, following the very thin connection I knew I was probably imagining.

There was no thug. Only a deserted kitchen the size of a small restaurant and beyond that a doorway to an elaborate dining room where I finally found Cody crouching behind a long wooden table he'd turned over for protection. An inert Ralph lay to one side. Cody was shooting at Frankie Jay, who occasionally fired back from another doorway on the other side of the room. The thug with the broken nose lay sprawled on the floor between Frankie Jay and the table.

I pressed myself against the wall by the door, inching my way across the kitchen. I had no idea where Winston and

O'Donald were, but the click of the gun Cody must have borrowed from the fallen thug told me he was out of ammo.

Frankie Jay laughed. "Guess that's it, old man."

"Maybe, maybe not," Cody growled. "I could be saving one just for you."

I sprinted out another door leading from the kitchen. Down a hallway I plunged, searching for the other entrance to the dining room, the one that would put me behind Frankie Jay. My heart measured out the few seconds I knew remained to Cody before Frankie Jay took his revenge.

Where was Winston? What if he and Frank O'Donald had already left the house? Did Winston know his uncle was dying?

One thing at a time.

Down the hall, I could see half of Frankie Jay as he leaned into the dining room to taunt Cody, perhaps testing to see if he was bluffing about the one remaining bullet. What was Cody thinking? About his dark past, or the future he wouldn't get to share with Tawnia and me?

Frankie Jay entered the room, which left me free to race down the hallway and go in behind him. At the last moment, he must have heard me because he turned—right into my fist. Had I planned it for weeks, I couldn't have executed it better. His head whipped back, surprise etched on his face. I chopped at the hand with the gun, following with a jab to his stomach that made him curl, clutching his middle.

Obscenities fell from his mouth as he tried to bring up the hand that still clutched the gun.

Cody was already leaping over the table, dragging his bad leg behind him. He wrested the gun from Frankie Jay's hand and shoved it under his nose. "Mind your manners. You're in the presence of a lady."

When Frankie Jay let spew another slew of curses, Cody drew back his left hand and punched him hard in the face. Cody might not be a young man, but he was fit and his artist hands were strong. Frankie Jay collapsed, his words cutting off abruptly.

"Where's Winston?" I asked Cody.

Cody shook his head. "Haven't seen him. They brought us here and gave Ralph something, but after they realized you'd gotten away, it was pretty clear they were planning to cut their losses. So I took matters into my own hands. I heard someone leave a while ago, though, probably O'Donald. Look, let's use my laces and tie him up."

I wondered if there was any proof O'Donald had been here at all. Maybe after all he'd done, he'd walk away unscathed.

"The police should be here any minute." Kneeling, I untied the laces on Cody's tennis shoes. "Ace called them. He's here somewhere, by the way. Maybe he managed to find Winston." That is, if the PI hadn't deserted me at the first sign of trouble. Maybe he hadn't quit the police force after all. Maybe it had quit him.

I tied Frankie Jay's hands behind his back and leaned over him, slapping his face lightly to bring him around. "Where's your dad? Where's Winston?"

His reply was another stream of swear words that stopped when Cody took a step closer.

Deciding he wasn't going to tell me anything, I left Frankie Jay with Cody and went to check on Ralph, who seemed to be sleeping peacefully on the floor behind the table, his pulse strong. He should be okay until the ambulance arrived. Right now I was more worried about Bridger bleeding outside by the lilac bush.

"I'd better look for Winston," I said.

Cody scowled. "You should just stay here."

"Winston might be in trouble."

He nodded reluctantly. "I'll keep an eye on junior. I bet there's more stuff in the kitchen I can tie him with."

"Good idea." I paused at the door. "Oh, and Cody, that was pretty good table-jumping for a man with a hurt leg."

"Wasn't it, though?" He grinned modestly.

Relief spread through me. *He's okay. We're both okay.*

I searched the rest of the mansion, but besides two uniformed maids cringing in a bedroom closet with a gnarled man who I learned was the gardener, the place was empty. Wherever Frank O'Donald had gone, he'd taken Winston with him.

Still no sign of the police, and I was starting to grow angry—particularly at Shannon. Not because he was responsible, but because anger was better than worrying about Bridger bleeding to death and Ralph lapsing into a coma or dying. This house was a good thirty-minute drive from the station, but with sirens, they should have been here long ago. Something was wrong—and I was going to confront Ace once I found him. His incompetence was inexcusable.

I'd found no phones in the house, and the maids didn't have phones—apparently O'Donald didn't permit cell phones on the premise. Neither could I coax the frightened trio from the closet. Finally, I shut the door and let them stay.

Still no police.

I believed Shannon loved me, and that he would move heaven and earth to get to my side if he so much as suspected I was in danger. It didn't make sense that he wasn't here.

Unless he hadn't been called.

The thought struck me so hard I sat down at the top of the huge spiral staircase leading down to the entryway. Memories came all at once: Ace outside my store, him staring at the white van, his appearance at the theater, his bitterness toward Russo.

Ace could be working for O'Donald. With the thought came a sick feeling that churned acid in my stomach. I remembered the phone call he'd said was from Shannon. What was it he'd said exactly? "She's here with me. Yes, of course I'll take care of her."

Would Shannon really ask him to take care of me? No.

Fear crawled across my shoulders and tingled to the tips of my fingers. *I have to be wrong about this,* I thought. Ace had been connected with the police department for as long as I had known Shannon. The officers trusted him—how could I not?

Because it fit. With his connections, he'd have access to all the information I did, and more through O'Donald, who'd been pumping Winston for months. Ace had known where JoAnna Hamilton lived and about Russo being in town. That meant he'd been watching her or Russo, or both—and me once I'd joined the case. No wonder he'd been so intent on what I did or didn't touch. He'd probably watched to make sure I didn't find an imprint that betrayed his intentions. He also could have disabled the alarms at JoAnna's, seizing the opportunity to gain intel on our visit, adding it to information he might have already gathered while spying on them, perhaps for the past few months. He was trained to observe, and when Hamilton had taken us down to her lab yesterday, she'd been fast with the code, but not overly secretive. She was too arrogant to believe an enemy would come into the heart of her lair.

I didn't want to believe. Surely there was some other explanation. But I came up with nothing.

Somewhere in the house I heard a loud *clunk*. Was it a door?

That started me thinking about the thump I'd heard in the back of Ace's car. Bridger said he'd been in the taxi's trunk, and he hadn't mentioned sharing it with the driver, so where was that man now? Had Ace been the person who'd enticed the driver away from the taxi while we were inside the theater? If so, the driver might be the one making the noise inside Ace's trunk. Maybe he was tied up and couldn't use the interior release, if there even was one in the old car.

Of course the most important thought at the moment was what Ace had been doing all the time I'd been talking to Bridger and helping Cody. And searching the house.

Get moving, I told myself. I needed to act, to save Ralph and Bridger. To protect Cody. But my body refused to obey.

Steps below in the entryway alerted me to a presence. At last my muscles loosened, and I stood as Ace came into view, a small gun in his hand. Maybe Easton's, but if so, I doubted the magazine was empty now.

He lowered the gun when he saw me.

So that's how you're going to play it, I thought.

"Where have you been?" I hoped the impatience in my voice sounded natural.

"Trying to stop O'Donald. He took off with the kid and a big guy with scars all over his face. They roughed me up. I barely got away."

He didn't look roughed up. "No sign of the police?" I asked.

He shook his head.

I contemplated whether I should go down the stairs, or put more space between us by going up. Closer meant an opportunity to get the gun away from him, but farther away meant less likelihood of him shooting me before I was close enough to do any good. I'd never seen him carry a gun before, but he'd been a police officer, so he knew how to use one. And despite Crater Face's disdain, a .22 could do a lot of damage in the right hands.

I remembered the first time I'd seen Ace in Russo's office, grinning that secret smile at me. I'd been pretty sure I could take him in a fair fight. He was short and thin like me, and probably strong, but I'd practiced martial arts every day for almost a year since I'd begun lessons again.

Unfortunately, the gun tipped the balance in his favor.

"Call Shannon again," I said. "We've got to get Ralph to the hospital." I didn't mention Bridger. But maybe Ace had already stumbled over Bridger and had made sure he wouldn't be a problem.

Ace shook his head. "Can't. They got my phone."

His phone but not the gun? Yeah, right. If I hadn't already decided he was lying, I knew the truth now.

"Then I'll search for a phone upstairs." Making up my mind, I turned and fled. There had to be some way to contact the police before he got rid of me and then finished off the others, one by one.

Or maybe he'd already taken care of them. I pushed aside the thought. I'd been searching upstairs for a long time, but not that long. I hadn't heard any shots. Besides, I was sure I still felt a thin tie with Cody.

"Wait, Autumn!" Ace came after me.

I dived down the hall into a family room and out into another hallway. Ace's shouts grew faint behind me. I'd already searched everything upstairs, and I hadn't seen any sign of a phone. Where could one be? All our cell phones had been taken away and probably disabled or destroyed, but if I found the pieces, I might be able to make one work. Maybe they'd been careless and left our pistols somewhere as well. It was a thin hope, but one I'd gladly cling to until I worked out a better plan. Easton was probably long gone in that car of his, and I didn't hold much hope of him calling the police in to rescue me.

"Autumn?" Ace's voice, moving closer.

How to get downstairs past him?

"I guess this means you've figured it out," Ace called. "I actually didn't see O'Donald. What I've really been doing is making sure that odd friend of yours didn't call the police."

Odd friend? I had to consider that for a moment. Oh, he had to mean Easton.

"I realized he'd seen me talking to Frankie Jay outside the theater," Ace continued. "When he took off into the woods, I knew he'd recognized me and that I'd have to go back for him. But he's taken care of now, all wrapped up downstairs with your other friends. Unfortunately, I'm under orders to make sure none of you leave here alive."

He was too close. I slipped into a bedroom, remembering the long balcony that had stretched the entire length of the second floor. The tree, I thought. Maybe if I could get to the end of the balcony, I could find a way down.

"Oh, I'm not going to kill anyone myself," Ace said. "Except maybe you, since you keep messing up my cases. I'm going to leave the others to Frankie Jay. Might have already done the deed by the time I get back. He was pretty mad at being tied up. Now that he's free, he might be too angry to wait for us."

Oh, no, I thought. *Cody.*

"Or maybe I'll save you for Frankie Jay." Ace's voice was

louder now. "I'm nice that way, especially to him. Turns out he went to school with my cousin. We're good friends now."

I sprinted across the room and slipped under the flowing yellow curtains covering a glass door. The door slid open easily. Ace was still talking, but I couldn't make out what he was saying. I ran the length of the balcony until I got to the end where the tree limb poked out from the side of the house.

The limb was a lot farther away than I remember. Not two feet, but more like five. Of course, I'd never really checked out the distance because the shooting had begun.

I glanced behind me and saw Ace burst onto the balcony from one of the bedrooms, his smile looking macabre and sinister instead of secretive. "Nowhere to go, Autumn. But this makes the perfect place for an accident. Just like the ones that have been plaguing In Loving Memory clients."

That stopped me. "What?"

Ace laughed. "You didn't expect that, did you? Yeah, I know all about that investigation. In fact, when I heard you were helping with the case, I went to the owner, that skeletal guy, and let him know what you and Shannon were really up to pretending to shop at his estate sales. He even hired me to do something about it." He barked a laugh. "Not that I was really going to do anything, but it was easy money. What could he do when I failed to get you off the case, turn me in? But he did start bugging me for results—he's a bit gone in the head, you know, ever since his son died. It was beginning to be a problem, and since he'd already murdered at least half a dozen old people, I couldn't be sure he wouldn't go after me. Murder is kind of addicting, I hear, if you get away with it enough."

"He murdered the old people himself?" Ugh. I still remembered all too vividly the imprint on the rug.

"Right. And then I heard Winston tell JoAnna that Russo was bringing you in to read the contract, and that reminded me that Russo wasn't the only one who could benefit from your ability."

"You went to O'Donald!" The words felt ripped from my throat.

Ace grinned, leaning casually against the railing, fingering the gun in his hand. "The son, not the father. I offered my services. As I said, I already sort of knew Frankie Jay, and about their feud with Russo. Frankie Jay hired me on the spot. He was desperate to know his father's plans for his other whelp—can't say I blame him for that—so I told him you were just the person to find what he needed. That way he could do something before his entire inheritance went to a stranger. I thought it fitting to choose the estate sale for his guys to make a move. Kill two birds with one stone, so to speak—get the In Loving Memory guy off my case and help out Frankie Jay. I was only too glad to do him a favor, especially with this nanotechnology on the line. They're not really all that close to creating living organs, but the technology they do have will revolutionize several industries. There's so much money involved that not even I can comprehend it, and I'm good with numbers."

So Frankie Jay had been behind my attempted kidnapping. "If Frankie Jay wanted my help, why would he try to blow up the van?"

"Are you kidding? He couldn't have any of it getting back to O'Donald. These people are loyal to family, but they're not above teaching their kids a lesson. Frankie Jay was taking a big chance going behind his father's back like that, and he wasn't about to let you ruin that."

I was beginning to think they were all crazy.

Ace came at me fast then, feet pounding on the wood—and all the while sporting that horrendous grin. I slipped off my moccasins, leapt onto the balcony railing, and jumped.

I hit the tree hard, but my arms curled around the branch. A shot exploded behind me.

I was slipping. I scrabbled desperately, but I was still slipping. Just before my arms pulled free, I aimed my feet toward a lower branch, arching my body toward the trunk. I landed on the branch and was propelled forward, my cheek slamming into the bark of the trunk. I bit back a cry.

From my vantage point I glimpsed Bridger, lying motionless by the lilac bush. No new wound that I could see, so I figured Ace hadn't found him—yet.

Another bullet embedded in the tree close to me, but I was already scooting around the trunk. If I climbed down one more branch, I might be able to jump to the ground without a problem.

Except Ace was coming after me. I felt the impact as he hit the first branch. His next stop would be the branch I was on. If I went down, he'd have a clear shot. So I started climbing, following the branches around until the tree was between us.

There, he was following my path. I grabbed a higher branch and swung off it, targeting his chest with my feet. Breath whooshed from him, and for a moment I felt triumph.

Then his fingers wrapped around my ankles.

I kicked, but he held on. The gloves on my hands were tight enough that they helped me hold onto the branch as his weight pulled me down onto the rough bark. But I knew I couldn't hold on forever.

One of his hands came off my ankle. I worried for a minute

that he'd let go to shoot, but the gun was no longer in his hands. I raised my foot and kicked down. Hard. Then again. At last he let go, but my own fingers slipped seconds later. Down we plunged, falling through several leafy tree branches.

We landed on the bushes below, and before I had a chance to be grateful I hadn't been impaled on a sharp branch, he was on his feet and coming toward me. I rolled from the bush and jumped up, fists raised.

Perhaps I'd always known it would come down to this day, Ace and me slugging it out. If I hadn't already been beaten by Crater Face and fallen from a tree, I might have been more confident at the outcome.

Ace threw two punches and a kick. He knew how to hit, but the kick left him wide open. I sent a blow to his stomach, followed by an uppercut that tumbled him backwards. I bounced forward a couple steps. He staggered to his feet, and I knocked him down again.

He wasn't smiling now.

"If you've hurt Cody," I said. "You'll regret it. I promise you."

Ace jumped to his feet again, reaching for something. I heard the click of a knife.

What now? I'd come so far, and I was so close.

Ace laughed, waving the knife in my direction. Then his eyes went to something over my shoulder, his grin faltering.

I started struggling as arms closed around me from behind.

Chapter 22

"It's okay," a voice said in my ear. "I'll take it from here."

"Shannon!" Tears stung my eyes.

He was already moving, setting me to the side and lunging at Ace, fury etched on his face. My fear faded away as he grabbed Ace's knife hand and slammed it against his knee, sending the knife flying. He flung himself on Ace, knocking him to the ground. Shannon began punching repeatedly, his fists a blur, hitting into Ace so hard I was amazed that all his parts stayed connected.

Paige passed me hurriedly, pushing a cuffed Frankie Jay in front of her, a gun at his back. "Shannon!" she barked. "Stop!"

Shannon paused on top of Ace, his fist drawn back, the muscles in his arms flexing. He punched again. Ace sobbed.

Behind Paige, I saw Cody and Easton emerging from the house, their wrists tied together with rope. A long, blood-dripping cut ran the length of Cody's forehead and his face was bruised, but he smiled when he saw me, one hand lifting in a wave.

My knees felt weak. Ace had told the truth about letting Frankie Jay go, and Frankie Jay apparently had taken his anger out on Cody. But he was alive. If Shannon and Paige hadn't arrived in time, things could have been much, much worse.

Shannon's hands went around Ace's throat. "Give me one reason I shouldn't kill you," he growled.

Ace choked but didn't speak, as if understanding that anything he might say would push Shannon too far.

"Shannon!" Paige said again. "Get off him."

"I said give me a reason!" Shannon gritted. Ace's face had gone from white to red and was now turning blue.

Cody came toward us, his limp more pronounced than earlier. He cleared his throat noisily. "Hey, can I help do him in? And I bet Autumn would like to take a couple swipes." I was about to tell Cody to shut his trap when he winked at me.

"Yeah, save some for the rest of us," I told Shannon.

Paige put her hand on Shannon's shoulder. "I got him. Let. Go. Now."

Reluctantly, Shannon released Ace and stood, stepping toward me. Paige rolled Ace over and cuffed him, giving him a shake for good measure.

Shannon held me tightly for a long moment, enough that I didn't feel I'd come apart when at last he held me back to look into my face. His eyes drank me in, taking in my scrapes and bruises.

"How'd you find us?" I asked, hoping I didn't sound as awful as I felt.

Shannon took my hand, and when he answered his voice was tight and low. "I saw a number on my phone I didn't recognize. The same number had called Paige, but there was no answer when we called back. Just a voice mail box from some doctor. We looked him up and saw what he did and figured it might involve you. When you didn't pick up your phone, and we couldn't get a hit on its GPS, we did a triangulation and pinpointed the calls from the doctor's phone to this area. The site correlated with the GPS signal of a taxicab reported missing." He paused and then added, "I'm sorry it took so long to find you."

So was I. "O'Donald's gone. He's taken Winston."

His finger smoothed my cheek, and I marveled that such a simple touch could mean so much—could make me *feel* so much. And it had nothing to do with imprints.

"He's behind this, then," he said. To Paige, he added, "Better call it in."

She nodded. "I'll have them put out an APB."

I knew I'd have to explain everything, but first things first. "Bridger Philpot's over there behind the lilacs. He's the one who drove the taxicab here. He needs an ambulance. He's been trying to get evidence on Tarragon since he faked his death. He's been shot. He may not make it."

Paige paled. "I'd better call Claire."

After that everything seemed to happen at once. While Cody and I detailed our adventures, a half dozen officers arrived, followed closely by three ambulances. Ace and Frankie Jay were arrested, and the EMTs went to work on Ralph and Bridger, and also on the thug lying in the dining room. The thug was pronounced dead, and Ralph was whisked away in one of the ambulances, but Claire arrived before Bridger was stable enough to move. She ran to the gurney, sobbing, and pressed her cheek against his. Bridger curled a hand around her neck and hugged her as if he'd never let go.

"You're here," he murmured. "I'm sorry, honey. So sorry. I didn't realize I'd be away so long. I needed enough evidence to make sure Tarragon couldn't touch our family."

"You're alive! That's all that matters. You've come back to me." Claire continued to sob as she clung to his hand. I had no doubt about her feelings, and I didn't think he would either, once he'd recovered enough to understand. Maybe he'd done the right thing. Shannon could bawl him out later for not going to the police, but his actions might have been the only thing that saved his family. I only hoped we had enough evidence to convict everyone, or Claire's family might still be in danger.

Shannon made me sit on a patio chair and called an EMT over to check me out. As they bandaged my wounds, he paced nearby, his phone plastered to his ear. With poor grace, Cody endured administrations from another EMT for the cut on his forehead, which I suspected Frankie Jay had given him with the gun. If they hadn't already put Ace in a police car, I would have had another go at him for that.

Easton also lurked nearby, looking miraculously unscathed, and I glared at him. "I'm not going to tell the detectives what you did because you saved me back there with that big thug," I told him in an undertone, "but if you ever try to force me to do anything again, believe me, I'll have you in prison so fast that you won't know what happened."

"And I'll just kill you," Cody growled. "That's if there's anything left of you after her boyfriend gets through. He's that detective over there, if you haven't figured that out yet."

Easton paled and hunched his shoulders, cringing away from Cody. "I wasn't going to hurt her."

I didn't know if I believed that, but I did know I wasn't going to turn my back on him any time soon.

Shannon put his phone in his pocket and hurried over to me. At first I thought he'd overheard the conversation, but he didn't look twice at Easton. "They've found O'Donald. He's holed up in a hotel downtown, and we think he has Winston with him. We have some uniforms there now, but there's a complication. JoAnna Hamilton and her cousin, Maribel, just got there and went inside."

I came to my feet. "There's no telling what he'll do to them. He's not happy about JoAnna hiding Winston's identity all these years. We have to get there fast."

"I think you need an X-ray for your ribs," protested the EMT, a burly man with ebony skin that reminded me of Jake's sister, Randa. "One might be fractured."

It didn't hurt too much when I breathed, and I'd been able to survive my flight down the tree, so even if he was right, I wasn't going to let it hold me back now. "Later," I said. Besides, they couldn't really do anything for cracked ribs except wrap them, and I could do that for a lot less money at home. I also had herbs to help the bruising. Right now what I needed was to see O'Donald put away.

I looked at Shannon and he nodded. "Okay, you can come, but the next thug is mine." He said it jokingly, but his fury at Ace hadn't gone away, and he was looking for a fight. I'd feel the same if he'd been hurt. Still, I was glad he respected my need to see the case through.

"I'm going too." Cody popped to his feet.

"You can't," said the brown-haired EMT with a leg brace in his hand. "You have a broken leg, sir. I'm sure of it."

I stared at Cody. "A broken leg? That fall from the haystack broke your leg and you've been walking around on it all day?"

"Naw." He shook his head. "Frankie Jay had a little fun with me after Ace freed him. But I'm fine."

The EMT gave Shannon a pleading look.

"Take him to the hospital," Shannon said. To Cody, he added, "We'll come over right after we're finished and let you know what happened."

Cody scowled, but Shannon was already turning away.

"Please get it fixed," I told Cody. "It's all over now. We're not in danger anymore. Please."

"Okay, but Autumn," His hand darted to my shoulder, "When Ace showed up, I . . . well, I didn't know if you . . . oh, I just want to say that I'm glad you're okay."

"So am I." I meant I was glad that *he* was okay, but we really didn't need words. For the first time in my life, I stepped close and hugged him. He hugged me back, and when we pulled away, neither of us let our eyes meet. I hurried after Shannon. As I moved further away from Cody, the connection between us thinned, but I could still feel it.

I could really feel it.

Lifting one gloved hand, I swiped under my eye, hoping no one noticed.

Paige met us inside the house, carrying my bag. "Autumn, isn't this yours? We found it in a van."

"Yeah, thanks." I dug through the bag, and besides the missing gun and cell phone, nothing else had been disturbed. I even had "normal" over-the-counter painkillers inside because of the accident, and I downed two without water for the ache in my back where my left kidney usually minded its own business. That, I would have to get checked out.

"By the way," I remembered to tell Paige and Shannon. "It

was Frankie Jay's men who were behind that bit with the rug yesterday morning. Ace sicced them on me. He was following us. But he also said that one of the owners from In Loving Memory hired him to do something to throw us off the case."

"Which one?"

"The tall one whose father started the business. Nye, wasn't it? The guy who practically threw us out. I bet Ace will testify if it saves him from doing more time."

Shannon's nostrils flared. "Oh, he'll talk. I'll see to that." For a moment his voice was bleak, and I remembered the woman officer who'd left the force to work with Ace. Had her death really been an accident? We had to believe that it was, but we would never know for sure.

Paige opened the front door, ushering us through. "I called the precinct and told them to find Tarragon while we deal with O'Donald. With Bridger's testimony, and hopefully Frankie Jay's, we should have enough to book him for the murders of Hamilton's scientists at the very least."

The sidewalk felt warm on my bare feet, and I realized I hadn't retrieved the moccasins. Maybe later.

Shannon opened the passenger door of his white Mustang before hurrying around to the driver's side. Paige slipped into the back, allowing me the front, and I was glad to be near Shannon. Drinking in his presence calmed me.

"Poor Winston." I felt sorry for him—and for his mother; their nightmare wasn't yet over. Maybe it was just beginning. O'Donald had powerful attorneys who might be able to free him from any charges, and he wasn't likely to walk away from his firstborn. For all the terrible things I knew about organized crime, I'd learned they had a strong sense of family, and once a member, you either remained with them or you died. There seemed to be no in between. "I hope you're able to arrest O'Donald and make it stick. For Winston's sake."

Paige sighed. "And Bridger and Claire's. But even with all the evidence, that will be difficult since O'Donald wasn't there when we found you. But if Winston will testify, it could happen."

"If he's still alive." Shannon pulled onto the road and began picking up speed. All too suddenly, Ace's BMW was up ahead, and I remembered the taxi driver.

"Wait, pull over," I said. "I think there's a man in the trunk of that car."

Shannon swerved to the side while Paige stared at me curiously. "Uh, are you developing another gift you want to tell me about?"

"Good grief, no." I rolled my eyes. "Ace and I drove here from where Easton took me, and I thought I heard something in the back. No one found the taxicab driver, did they? No one mentioned if he was in the cab that Bridger drove here."

We had no keys, but Shannon forced his way inside the BMW and pulled a release lever near the driver's seat. Inside the trunk lay the blond driver, curled in a fetal position. Paige checked for a heartbeat.

"He's alive," she said, turning on her phone. "But we'll need an ambulance." She hesitated a few seconds before adding, "I'll wait here with him and catch up to you at the hotel. If you decide to go in with guns, please wait for me. I really need to shoot something."

"Me too." Shannon's voice was a growl. "Get evidence here as well. I want to make sure Ace pays for this."

This time Shannon drove even faster, placing a police light on top of the car and using his siren as we approached a more populated area. We arrived at the hotel in downtown Portland as my painkillers started working. Excellent timing.

The hotel wasn't cordoned off, but officers guarded the door, and civilians were slowly being ushered outside. I wondered if the gradual pace was to prevent O'Donald from suspecting anything if he should look out the window.

A tall young uniformed officer met us in the lobby, his black skin reflecting the fluorescent lights. "Dwight," Shannon said with a nod. "Everything still the same?"

Dwight nodded, his bright eyes calm and ready. "They're in room four thirty-six. Don't know we're here yet, though they've asked for room service and have to be wondering what's taking so long. The elevator's over here."

"A word, please," Nicholas Russo, dressed in a dark suit, stepped out from a group of civilians waiting their turn to leave the hotel. His shoulders looked wider than usual, his smile more charming. Not one dark hair was out of place.

"What are you doing here?" I snapped. I couldn't even turn around without falling across one more person I never wanted to see again.

He held a hand up, though to warn me off or to calm me, I wasn't sure. "I'm simply protecting my interests. I've been hearing a lot of things from my contacts. Is it true Winston Drewmore is O'Donald's son?"

News traveled fast. "Not if it means you're going to kill him," I retorted.

Russo laughed. "I don't kill people."

"I know what O'Donald did to your wife, but Winston's not a part of that. You have to understand."

The lines of Russo's face hardened. Why had I ever thought him compelling? "And you have to understand that O'Donald's son is alive and mine is dead."

"You have another son now."

His jaw worked. "O'Donald must pay. He knows the score."

"We don't have time for this." Shannon put his arm around me. "Russo, you foul up my operation here, and I will book you myself."

Russo didn't reply, but I felt his eyes gouging at my back as we walked to the elevator, guarded by more police officers who made sure no one went to the upper floor where O'Donald had taken Winston.

"That reminds me," Dwight said to Shannon. "The captain told me to tell you that Boyd Nye's prints were found on the Washington bust."

Shannon smiled grimly "Good. With the new testimony about him that we've uncovered, we'll be able to convict him for sure."

I thought of the gaunt owner of In Loving Memory and how his son had died so unexpectedly. I wondered if that was what had unhinged him. Maybe he'd decided life was too short to eke out a living struggling to make ends meet day after day. I almost felt sorry for him. At least he hadn't been behind me getting wrapped in that rug. No, that had been all Ace's doing—and Frankie Jay's.

The hallway outside room 436 felt crowded with a dozen officers in full assault gear and one hotel manager who looked calm despite the tension. An officer named Lloyd Warren came toward us, apparently in charge.

"We've blocked off the area and cleared out the entire floor.

Also the one above and below." Warren had dark hair and was bulky for an officer—a bulk that formed a solid wall of muscle. He'd only been in Portland less than six months, and I had the feeling he didn't like me much. "We have the key to get inside."

"I'll try to talk to them first." Shannon motioned to the hotel manager. "What's the number I'd dial from my phone?" Shannon punched in the numbers and the phone inside the room began ringing.

"This is detective Shannon Martin with the Portland police," he said as someone picked up. "Is this Frank O'Donald? No? Well, is O'Donald there?" He nodded to show us the answer was positive. "What about Winston Drewmore and the Hamiltons? Is everyone all right?"

Shannon covered the phone. "He didn't answer. He's talking to someone else. I'm not sure he'll—"

Two gunshots thundered through the quiet of the hallway, one after the other, a sharp staccato. *Boom, boom!*

"In! Now!" Shannon pulled his gun and motioned for Officer Warren to use the hotel master key. "Autumn, get back."

Please don't let it be Winston, I thought.

Several officers with shields leapt to the front as Warren flung open the door. Shannon followed them with his pistol and more officers poured in after with their rifles. Yet within a minute, I heard the all-clear and some of the officers began leaving.

I ventured inside and immediately wished I hadn't. Frank O'Donald sprawled in an easy chair, a bloody mess staining the front of his white dress shirt. A tiny pistol lay on the ground in front of him. JoAnna and Maribel Hamilton sat on a couch opposite the unmoving O'Donald, both staring at him with blank expressions. Winston stood near the couch, disbelief radiating from his eyes.

Today JoAnna wore another flowing dress, a coral one that cast an attractive color on her face. Her makeup was precise, her hair piled on her head. I wondered if she'd already been dressed up before she came, or if she'd taken more than usual care with her toiletry and clothing to impress her old flame. I wondered how it felt, now that age had crept up on her, to understand that she couldn't recapture those years or their passion. To know that O'Donald hated her for what she'd hidden from him.

Maribel wore a powder blue suit that did nothing for her figure, despite its obvious expense. Her hands were clad in dainty white gloves, and her hair was also swept up on her head, but unlike her cousin's, it was less carefully done, as though she'd hurried.

They weren't alone in the room. Crater Face lay on the floor in handcuffs, shock and surprise stamped on his pasty face. An officer poised over him, and other officers, their guns drawn, loomed over the old ladies.

"What happened here?" Shannon demanded. The way he spoke told me he'd already asked the question at least once before. He looked at Crater Face. "Did you kill your boss?"

Crater Face lifted his head, shaking it violently. "I was talking on the phone. I turned and"—he glared at Winston and the old ladies—"one of them. They musta done it." His neck strained as he looked again at O'Donald. "He can't be dead."

"Oh, he's dead all right." Shannon looked at Officer Warren. "Better have your men get this guy out of here. Be sure to get a full statement—including about what went on at that mansion."

Crater Face didn't notice me as officers hauled him to his

feet and marched him from the room. I felt a little deflated since there were a few choice things I wanted to say to him now that Shannon and a dozen officers had my back.

"So." Shannon turned to face the other three. "Sit down, Winston."

Winston obeyed woodenly, sinking to the end of the couch beside JoAnna, his eyes flicking briefly to me, but like the thug, he didn't register my presence.

"We know what happened at O'Donald's rental house," Shannon said. "What we don't know is what happened here. Is anyone going to fill me in?" No one answered, though Winston's gaze wandered first to his mother and then to Maribel, as though searching for an answer.

He must have pulled the trigger, I thought. But where had he gotten the gun? It wasn't my .380 or Cody's .45, but a small .22, a gun a casual user might own. A scientist, a school teacher, or a woman who wanted something small to fit in her purse. Easton Godfrey had carried a similar pistol, but the police had confiscated it from the mansion after Ace had been arrested.

"I suppose that's just as well." Shannon looked up at Officer Warren. "I want to question them individually. Keep them apart on the way to the station."

"There's no need." JoAnna Hamilton stood, her head lifted regally. "I did it. I shot him. He said he was going to kill Ralph, ruin my business, and take my—Winston." Even now she couldn't admit Winston was her son. So many years of pretending couldn't be undone in an instant.

"Oh?" Shannon said. "Or maybe you're protecting your *son*. Maybe Winston shot him."

JoAnna drew in a quick breath. "Certainly not. I brought

the gun. It's mine. You can check the registration." She spoke smoothly and met his eyes with no indication of falsehood.

She was lying. She might actually own the .22, but her weapon of choice would have been something bigger. A woman in a man's world, she was well accustomed to proving herself.

I approached Winston. "Did you do it? Because after what happened today, I think everyone would understand. He betrayed you."

"He didn't do it," JoAnna grated. "Winston, don't say another word. We want—all of us want—an attorney."

There it was. With that request, there was nothing more we could do, and if no proof could be found, we might never know the truth of what happened in this room.

Except, I could help. I'd known ever since I'd first felt that connection with Cody. The connection told me he was family, but it also told me my ability was kicking in again.

Maybe.

One by one, I pulled off the fingers of my gloves. Shannon watched me. "Are you sure?" he asked in a voice low enough that none of the other officers would hear.

I nodded. The worst that could happen was that I'd get dizzy again. But I'd had hours of rest from imprints, and maybe I could do this for JoAnna Hamilton, and for Winston too. They needed to face what had happened today and go on with their lives.

"We'll have to wait for fingerprinting then."

We didn't have long to wait because the forensic team had already arrived. Shannon had them dust the gun to find a place for me to touch. The textured grip was cleared and it was all I would need. I touched the plastic gingerly with a knuckle, unsure what to expect. Silence filled the room. I found it interesting that JoAnna Hamilton didn't seem worried.

The imprint, when it came, almost made me exclaim aloud, not because it was shocking, but because it materialized at all. It was like taking off a bandage from my eyes and finally being able to see.

Contentment and anticipation. Yes. This would be a nice little gun to have around. I would teach Winston to shoot the next time he came to visit from Oregon. "Wrap it up," I said. "I'll take it."

That was it. A fifteen-year-old imprint. Nothing more. No dizziness. I waited to see if anything else came, but the imprint only repeated.

I lifted my hand and looked at JoAnna. "You never taught Winston to use it, did you? Though that's what you bought it for."

She nodded, her lips tightly clenched.

"Well?" Shannon asked me.

I nodded. "I know who used this gun to kill Frank O'Donald."

Chapter 23

I knew who killed O'Donald not because of the imprint
but because of the lack of one. Neither Winston nor
the women were cold-blooded killers, and such a traumatic event would leave an imprint—one I was grateful not
to read. But that meant only one of them could have killed
O'Donald without leaving that imprint.

When Winston had commented earlier on my gloves, he'd
mentioned his cousin wearing them. At the time, I thought he'd
meant JoAnna, but he'd actually been talking about Maribel,
who I'd thought was his grandmother. A slip of the tongue.

She was wearing gloves again today.

Maribel folded her hands neatly in her lap. "I raised
Winston from a baby. He's *mine*. He was always mine. Not
JoAnna's." Her eyes wandered until they landed on me, looking
a little wild.

"Maribel, shut up," JoAnna said. "Don't say anything until
you talk to our attorney."

"I don't want an attorney." Maribel looked up at her cousin.
"I told you not to deal with Russo. I told you! I knew from the

beginning that Frank would be back and that Russo would find out our secret." She refocused on Shannon. "Russo was going to kill my boy—it was just a matter of time. Killing Frank O'Donald was the only way to protect Winston. As a mother, I did what had to be done."

"Maribel, no." Winston's agonized voice confirmed that Maribel was telling the truth. He'd stand by and let his mother take the blame without comment, but not the woman who'd loved and tended him all his life. "Please."

Maribel reached over the empty place where JoAnna had been sitting and patted his hand. "It's okay, dear. I wanted to do it for you. He's a terrible man, and he would have made you do terrible things."

The irony of her comment was not lost on me or Shannon, who shook his head. This was one of the times when his job became more than hard. When morality battled against justice instead of being on the same side.

Maribel looked at me next. "I was afraid you would learn about my plan, so after you came to visit, I put on gloves whenever I was in the house." She smiled pleasantly. "It worked, didn't it? You didn't find out, and of course, Frank didn't suspect me. He thought I was harmless. Everyone always does. But I would do anything to protect my baby, to give her a chance."

Her? Was Maribel mixing Winston up with the daughter she'd lost? Maybe that part of the story had been true. Regardless, she was crazy, or unbalanced at the very least.

"Come on," Shannon said gently, offering his hand to Maribel. "I'll help you downstairs where Officer Warren here will drive you to the station."

"What she needs is a doctor," JoAnna snapped.

"Can I go with her?" Winston jumped up from the couch.

Shannon nodded. "We have a psychologist. He'll talk to her there."

We made a sad little party moving to the elevator. JoAnna's face was tight and pale now, Winston had tears in his eyes, and the few officers who accompanied us were somber. Shannon frowned as he texted Paige. Only Maribel seemed unconcerned as she hummed a little tune I didn't recognize.

Russo was still in the lobby when we exited the elevator. Shannon tried to hurry Maribel past him, but she paused, lifting her face toward the man. "Frank's dead," she told him with a smile. "I got you your revenge. Now you won't have to take the blood of my son. Promise me you won't. I did you a favor, and now you owe me one. I want his life."

Russo contemplated her for the space of several heartbeats. "All right," he said finally. "I will consider O'Donald's debt paid." His gaze shifted to JoAnna. "Word from the hospital says your brother is in a coma. They're not sure if or when he'll awake. His backup programs remain lost, which means years of delay. Under terms of the contract, our association is hereby annulled. If the situation changes, feel free to contact me again for renegotiation." His gaze shifted to me. "It appears I won't be needing your services at this time, Miss Rain. Good evening." Pivoting on his heel, he turned, flanked by his bodyguards, their combined bulk becoming a receding wall in front of us.

At this time. Alarming words since it meant I'd probably hear from him again.

JoAnna's face had become pinched, but her only response was to her cousin. "Maribel, I need to go to the hospital to be with Ralph."

Maribel patted her hand. "Of course you do, dear. Don't worry about me. I have Winston."

Shannon and I watched them all drive away. He put an arm around me. "I think we'd better go to the hospital ourselves. I'm sure you want to know how Cody is."

What he meant was that he wanted me to get checked out by a doctor, but the growing pain in my kidney meant I wasn't going to disappoint him. I hoped it was only bruised and that a couple doses of dandelion root would put me back to rights.

"Aren't we going to wait for Paige?" I said as we climbed in the car.

"No. I texted her, and she says since everything is settled here, she's going to the station to book Tarragon. She would like us to check on Ralph while we're at the hospital. Apparently, Russo's information is correct. He still hasn't come to."

"Probably whatever O'Donald gave him. Did they test his blood?"

"They're doing that now."

Poor JoAnna. Despite her austere demeanor, at some point I'd stopped thinking of her as "Hamilton." She'd lost so much: her brother was in a coma, her cousin was going to prison or a mental hospital, and her relationship with her son might never be the same. Her business had been set back years and would perhaps fail if the rigged backup couldn't be retrieved and decoded. Some might say it was punishment for the way she'd lived her life, for the many people she'd lied to and stepped on, but that didn't mean I didn't feel sorry for her. People did change. Cody had.

"If only JoAnna had her brother's backups," Shannon said, his mind running a similar path. "She'd be a lot better off. She could release the model like they'd planned."

I nodded. "I wonder what the version they were going to release is like. The machine they showed me was pretty incredible. I almost didn't believe it when I saw it had printed my—"

And just like that I knew where the backup disk was. "Shannon, we have to make a detour to my apartment."

"But you need to—"

"Please. Remember last night when my door was open? Well, I thought I saw Bridger outside, but he never explained why he was there—he couldn't have been following Winston then. If I'm right about why he was there, we may have something to give to JoAnna and Winston after all." I mentally kicked myself for not figuring it out earlier.

"Okay." His phone rang, and he pulled it out and glanced at the caller ID. "It's your sister."

"Better answer, or she'll just keep calling."

"Hi, Tawnia," he said without taking his eyes from the road. "Sure. Here she is." He passed the phone to me.

"Autumn!" came my sister's voice, high and worried. "Are you okay?"

"I'm fine. But Cody hurt his leg again."

"I know. I'm leaving the hospital with him now. They put his leg in a cast. Apparently it's pretty bad. What did you guys do? He won't tell me anything except that you're okay. You really have to be careful about getting him into these things. He's not a young man anymore." Her voice faded as she talked to someone I couldn't hear. "Yes, you're going home with me. I won't take no for an answer." Then her voice was back to normal. "Autumn, you promise you're okay?"

"I'm fine. Well, besides a few bruises." I winked at Shannon. "A scratch, really."

He laughed. That was our code for a more serious injury.

"What about imprints?"

"It's coming back," I said, not masking the happiness in my voice. I was actually wearing the gloves again, though, to give myself more time to heal. In retrospect, trying to read an imprint containing an intent to murder might not have been the best idea this soon. I'd been lucky.

"I'm glad."

"Thanks." I'd like to think I would never again complain about my ability, but I knew there would probably come a time. Human nature and all that.

"Well, just so you know," Tawnia said, "I'm taking Cody home—whether he likes it or not." Her voice faded again on the last phrase. "He had some crazy idea of driving back to Hayesville tonight."

I laughed, glad my sister had taken charge of the old man. I wondered if he'd tell her about the baby clothes, or if she'd have to track him down to say thanks after she finally received them.

"Hey, I gotta go," I said, as Shannon drew up to my apartment building.

The stop took only minutes, with Shannon insisting on going inside by himself, gun drawn just in case. I was content to let him play the hero. I grinned when I saw that along with what I'd asked for, he was also bringing me a pair of socks.

"You never know what kind of imprints might be on the floor at a hospital," he said.

We made it to the hospital without incident. It almost felt strange without a van or Russo's men following our trail. An ER doctor diagnosed me with a slight rib fracture and a bruised kidney. Nothing that wouldn't heal in a couple weeks, though apparently it was going to keep hurting for a good while.

"Kind of like those bruises on your face," the doctor added. "When they're completely gone, you can assume most of the kidney bruise will be healed as well." If he thought it odd that I was wearing gloves and socks without shoes, he didn't comment.

After a nurse wrapped my ribs and gave me another painkiller, we went to check on Ralph but ran into Claire Philpot and Jazzy Storm on the way. Claire's face was glowing and she looked ready to fly. "He's out of surgery. He's going to make it!" she told us. "Thank you so much, Autumn."

I hadn't done anything, though I suppose if I hadn't gotten mixed up in the whole mess, neither Shannon nor I would have been at O'Donald's rental house to save him. "I'm happy for you."

"It's like a movie," Jazzy exclaimed, twirling a stubby lock of her blue hair. "That Tarragon guy asked him to file a patent for some real high-tech printer, and he got suspicious because they didn't have anything ready. So he investigated his own clients. Even sent a PI to Japan."

"That was the ticket he bought," Claire picked up the narration. "Apparently Tarragon was going to use Bridger to legitimize their claims for the nanotechnology they planned to steal. When Bridger confronted him, Tarragon threatened our family, and when Bridger tried to save those scientists, Tarragon's men destroyed the entire boat. The money missing from our accounts—that was so he could live until he could prove their guilt."

"Well, he socked it to Tarragon before he disappeared," Jazzy put in, her eyes alive with excitement. "He hired some kids to set off the alarm at that software company so Tarragon couldn't break in like he'd planned. Then he took tons of their money and gave it to a relief fund in Japan. Can you believe that?"

So that's where the stolen money came in. It all made sense now.

Claire put a calming hand on Jazzy's shoulder, though she looked less likely than the girl to keep her feet on solid ground. "Bridger wanted to make sure Tarragon wouldn't try to do it all again once he was out of the picture. But five million to a guy like that . . . It didn't keep him down for long." She shook her head. "Anyway, I tried to be angry that Bridger didn't let me know he was alive, at least in secret, but I'm too happy to have him back."

"I think he did the right thing," Jazzy said, lifting her chin defensively, her eyes locking onto Claire's. "I mean, they killed the scientists! And they almost killed Bridger and that other scientist today. They're nothing but cold-blooded murderers. If you'd known, you would never have stayed away from Bridger. You'd have gone straight to the police, and that creep Tarragon would have been out for revenge. He'd have probably sent a hit man or something. I wouldn't want anything to happen to you, Claire. Or your kids. Your husband definitely did the right thing."

"Maybe." Claire leaned into the girl. They looked so incongruous—the teen with the blue hair and the professional attorney—but it was obvious they'd found what they needed in each other.

"We'd better get back to him," Claire said after a few seconds of silence. "I was just talking to the kids. Come and see us when you can, Autumn. I'm sure Bridger has more to add to his story."

After three years away, I didn't doubt it. "I will," I said.

We watched Claire float down the hall. "It's a good thing we got there in time," Shannon said, his hand slipping into mine.

"I know. To lose him again like that—" I let out a rush of breath. "Come on. Let's go find JoAnna."

JoAnna Hamilton was standing in the waiting room talking with none other than Arthur Mott and Harold Fisher, the two nerdy owners of Print Perfect. Both had a soda can in one hand and their smart phones in the other.

"Guess someone told them she was here," Shannon whispered. "I think they have a business proposition for her."

"Now hardly seems the time."

He shrugged. "They're young." As if that excused everything.

JoAnna looked up as we crossed the room. Showing a surprising sensitivity, the Print Perfect guys nodded at us and stepped back a few feet, giving us a modicum of privacy.

"How's he doing?" I asked JoAnna.

The hint of a smile reached her lips. "His heart suffered some damage from the attack, but he's going to be okay. Eventually. It appears Frank's men gave him a sedative, which wasn't the best thing for a heart condition. Fortunately, it did calm his anxiety, which might have saved his life." She paused before adding to me, "Thank you for finding him. For saving him. An officer who was here earlier told me what you did."

"All part of the job," I said.

She reached in her purse and handed me a check for two thousand dollars. "It's probably not enough, given your hourly rate, but it's something. I want you to know that if I somehow manage to save my business, I'll see that you get some stock."

"I can't take this. Use it for your business." I tried to give back the check, but she shook her head.

"Please. I can still well afford that amount."

I guess her level of poor was nowhere near mine, which I

should have realized, considering the size of her house. "Okay. Thank you." It would pay for my medical expenses, at least, if Shannon couldn't get the police department to spring for them.

"Look, there is good news," I said. "I have something for you." I pulled the music box from my bag.

When she saw it, her control crumpled, and she had to hold her hand over her mouth several long seconds until she regained her composure. "It's all gone. It'll take years, even with Ralph, to get back where we were. We'll be too late. Everything I've built for my son is lost."

"No." I shook my head, lowering my voice so that only she and Shannon could hear. "Not with this."

She stared at me, understanding slowly penetrating her face. "You mean . . .?"

I nodded. "This isn't my music box. It's the copy. There's no music assembly. Remember? Your brother didn't have time to recreate that. The funny thing is, this music assembly case isn't empty. Ralph stored something in it." I gave her an apologetic grin. "I think I would have figured it out sooner if I'd told Ralph I was the one you'd had him copy the original box for. He figured out that you'd given me the wrong one by mistake, but when we met, he didn't know who I was, so he didn't ask about it. He sent his friend Bridger Philpot to get the box and hide it elsewhere, but Bridger broke into my apartment and didn't find it. He waited for me to come home, saw me carrying it, and must have decided it was safer to leave with me." Or maybe Shannon's presence had scared him off. It really didn't matter now. "It's been at my apartment all this time."

JoAnna hugged the little box to her chest, tears in her eyes. "Thank you so much. You don't know what you've done for me."

I smiled. "Just don't open it before Ralph's better okay? I hear it needs a special touch."

Not even that dimmed her happiness.

Shannon and I had turned to leave when I remembered the rocker. "JoAnna," I said, hesitating. Something had been bothering me, and this might be my only chance to learn the truth. "The child's rocking chair at that estate sale. With all the beautiful antiques you own, why did you choose it?" Something of so little comparative value, I meant.

She smiled. "Because it reminds me of a rocking chair at the private clinic where I gave birth to Winston." She hesitated a few seconds before adding in a softer voice, "I knew I wouldn't be able to tell him I was his mother until he was much older, that Maribel would be raising him. That was okay—it was what I needed to do to protect him. But for that short time, it was just us. The best two weeks of my life."

"I'm glad." I'd never tell her about the negative imprint, not that I would ever see her again. Maybe her good memories would be enough to eventually cover it and bring her family joy.

As we left, JoAnna turned back to her young companions, both of whom instantly looked away from their phones. "Okay, gentlemen, I have decided to accept your proposal. Let's do this job together. But remember that I will retain control of the company—and its investments."

Outside, dusk had fallen, and the world was still. "I think this is my favorite time of day," Shannon said as we climbed into the Mustang. "When all the work is finished but it's not too late to find something else to do."

"Me too." As long as that something had to do with him.

Before long I realized he wasn't heading to my apartment. "Where are we going?"

"You'll see."

His statement brought a flurry of interest that quickly turned to disappointment when he pulled into a parking space across the street from the police station. "Guess you need to check on things, huh?"

He pulled out his phone and studied his messages. "Let's see. Boyd Nye was arrested for the In Loving Memory murders, Frankie Jay and Tarragon were also booked for murder, kidnapping, and assault. Maribel Hamilton is being held as well, and Ace will be charged with a bunch of crimes too long to list. The prosecutor is sure he'll serve time, which, considering the years he spent as a police officer, will not be pleasant. I think that about covers all our most pressing cases."

"Then what are we doing here?" I let a little irritation slip into my voice. I was entitled, after all I'd been through. I wanted a lot of food and to snuggle with my boyfriend while we watched a movie or something. A boring movie with no guns or action or loud noises.

"You can't guess?"

"No." I studied the building, but nothing came to me.

"This was where we began our first case almost exactly a year ago. Do you remember?"

I remembered well—the case with the missing little girl. Shannon hadn't known what to do with me and my so-called gift when he'd shown up at my antiques shop at the request of the child's father. He'd acted like he wanted to throw me in jail instead of working with me.

"You dropped everything and came here with me, barefooted despite the fact that it was cold enough for a jacket. You came even when crossing the bridge still made you panic. You faced me with fire in your eyes and told me exactly what you thought of me."

"Well, you did try to pay me not to find anything," I reminded him. I'd tossed his hundred-dollar bill out of the window.

"I thought you were a scammer. Then you touched the girl's bike and I was sure of it—until your description pinpointed the suspect."

Too late, I wanted to say, but I didn't because I knew I'd saved at least one other girl that day, and prevented the sick creep from taking others.

Shannon took my hands, slowly pulling off one glove and then the other—his touch an intimate caress. "I'd never been so attracted to a woman. Never." His thumb skidded across my bare skin, sending delicious tingles along the surface. "That was hard to deal with because even after that day, I didn't want to believe."

"Poor baby."

In a swift motion, his hand tightened on mine and pulled me closer. His eyes—those incredible eyes that I'd spent all too much time avoiding in the past year—stared into mine and the feeling I'd experienced earlier inside the police station came back in a rush.

Everything between us this past year boiled down to this moment.

"I wanted to do this right," Shannon said softly, a hitch in his voice. "I had a dinner all planned." He grinned. "No, not pasta, I promise. It was going to be at my house. Candlelight on the patio, the whole works. But today didn't go at all as I planned, and then I realized that tomorrow might not either.

Or the next day. We never know what the future might hold, when one of us might get into just a bit more trouble than we expect." He paused, shaking his head at my frown. "I'm not asking you to change. I know I overreact sometimes, but I care about you too much to demand a limit, and I know you feel the same about my choices. You're doing what you love, and I'm doing what I love, and we've been fortunate to do a lot of it together."

Yes, Shannon wouldn't be Shannon without his drive and dedication—or even without his suspicious nature that had kept us apart so long. Maybe in the future, we'd both have to reexamine our life goals, but for the time being we needed to use our gifts to help others, even if it was sometimes dangerous.

"We have to seize our opportunities." His face was closer now—so close that he was breathing my air. I expected him to kiss me—I *needed* him to kiss me, but he didn't close the gap separating us.

He took another breath and plunged on. "The fact is that I'm crazy in love with you, Autumn Rain, and I want you to marry me. So will you? Marry me, that is." He released one hand and dug into his pocket, slipping a ring onto my finger. "I've been carrying this around for months now. It's a copy of that antique ring you liked."

The simple band was set with small stones of two alternating colors. I'd lost the bid for the antique version at an auction clear back in December when it went beyond my budget, and I still regretted not winning it.

"Not an exact copy, and the stones represent us instead of whoever owned that one."

A ring he couldn't return if I said no.

But Shannon was the blood that pumped in my veins, the

reason I continued doing what I loved even when it was hard, the man who had such a hold on my heart that I wasn't sure how I'd ever been happy before he came into my life.

"Yes," I said, my voice low and hoarse. "Yes, I'll marry you, Shannon Martin."

He kissed me then, pulling me tight and angling his lips over mine. The world stopped as it always did when it was just the two of us. I moved closer, my bare hand brushing the steering wheel. Emotions flared in a brief imprint: fear that I wouldn't accept his proposal. Love so large it couldn't be contained.

I experienced a surge of glee. My gift was back and Shannon was mine.

The vibrating of Shannon's phone penetrated our emotions. With a growl, he answered. "Martin here." He listened for a moment and then said, "Autumn's with me now. You want us to do what?"

He covered the phone. "Work," he explained. "A homicide. Paige says there's evidence she thinks you should look at."

Before I could agree, he spoke into the phone. "Sorry. Autumn needs to rest, and I'm officially off duty. Tell them not to call me at least until Monday—I'll be celebrating my engagement. Yes, you heard me. But you go ahead without us. Take Warren with you." He turned off the phone and grinned like someone who'd won a million dollars.

Every part of me felt vibrant and alive. He was right. For once, work could wait. This weekend was for us.

But on Monday, I'd do my thing again and solve another case.

TEYLA BRANTON has worked in publishing for over twenty years. She loves writing women's fiction and traveling, and she hopes to write and travel a lot more. As a mother of seven, it's not easy to find time to write, but the semi-ordered chaos gives her a constant source of writing material. She's been known to wear pajamas all day when working on a deadline, and is often distracted enough to burn dinner. (Okay, pretty much 90% of the time.) A sign on her office door reads: Danger. Enter at Your Own Risk. Writer at Work.

Under the name Teyla Branton, she writes urban fantasy, paranormal romance, and science fiction. She also writes romance, romantic suspense, and women's fiction under the name Rachel Branton. For more information or to sign up to hear about new releases, please visit www.TeylaBranton.com.